PRAISE FOR THE FB

DOUBLE CROSS

"DiAnn Mills always gives us a good thriller, filled with inspirational thoughts, and *Double Cross* is another great one!"
FRESHFICTION.COM

"Tension explodes at every corner within these pages. . . . Mills's writing is transparently crisp, backed up with solid research, filled with believable characters and sparks of romantic chemistry."
NOVELCROSSING.COM

"For the romantic suspense fan, there is plenty of action and twists present. For the inspirational reader, the faith elements fit nicely into the context of the story. . . . The romance is tenderly beautiful, and the ending bittersweet."
ROMANTIC TIMES

FIREWALL

"Mills takes readers on an explosive ride. . . . A story as romantic as it is exciting, *Firewall* will appeal to fans of Dee Henderson's romantic suspense stories."
BOOKLIST

"With an intricate plot involving domestic terrorism that could have been ripped from the headlines, Mills's romantic thriller makes for compelling reading."
LIBRARY JOURNAL

"A fast-moving, intricately plotted thriller."
PUBLISHERS WEEKLY

"Mills once again demonstrates her spectacular writing skills in her latest action-packed work. . . . The story moves at a fast pace that will keep readers riveted until the climactic end."
ROMANTIC TIMES

DEADLOCK

DEADLOCK

FBI: HOUSTON

DiANN MILLS

Tyndale House Publishers, Inc.
Carol Stream, Illinois

Visit Tyndale online at www.tyndale.com.

Visit DiAnn Mills at www.diannmills.com.

TYNDALE and Tyndale's quill logo are registered trademarks of Tyndale House Publishers, Inc.

Deadlock

Designed by Nicole Grimes

Edited by Erin E. Smith

Published in association with the literary agency of Books & Such Literary Agency,
52 Mission Circle, Suite 122, PMB 170, Santa Rosa, CA 95409.

Scripture quotations are taken from the Revised Standard Version of the Bible, copyright
© 1952 [2nd edition, 1971] by the Division of Christian Education of the National Council
of the Churches of Christ in the United States of America. Used by permission. All rights
reserved.

Deadlock is a work of fiction. Where real people, events, establishments, organizations, or
locales appear, they are used fictitiously. All other elements of the novel are drawn from the
author's imagination.

Library of Congress Cataloging-in-Publication Data

Mills, DiAnn.
   Deadlock / DiAnn Mills.
      pages ; cm. — (FBI: Houston ; 3)
     ISBN 978-1-4143-8995-0 (softcover)
  1. United States. Federal Bureau of Investigation—Officials and employees—Fiction.
2. Serial murder investigation—Texas—Houston—Fiction.   3. Government investigators—
Fiction.   I. Title.
   PS3613.I567D43 2015
   813'.6—dc23   2015017847

Printed in the United States of America

21	20	19	18	17	16	15
7	6	5	4	3	2	1

To Stephanie Broene and Erin Smith, Tyndale House editors.

Thank you for all your support and encouragement.

Our brainstorming sessions are amazing!

ACKNOWLEDGMENTS

I want to thank the following people for helping me with *Deadlock*. You are amazing!

Special Agent Shauna Dunlap, media coordinator, FBI Houston Division—You are the best! Thank you for your friendship and for answering my endless questions.

Pat Durham—Your experiences with a parrot helped Jasper come alive. Thank you for the fun!

Lynette Eason—Not everyone can have a fabulous brainstorming partner who shares the same birthday. We're dynamite together.

Beau Egert—Thanks for your perspective on my plots.

Julie Garmon—I so appreciate your time and critiques. My stories would lack so much depth without you.

Guy Gourley, MA, LPC, NCC—Your insight into the mind helped me make this book real and powerful.

Dr. Richard Mabry—I'd be lost without your expertise about the human body and what it can handle!

Dean Mills—My sweet husband! You have more patience and love than any man on earth. Thanks for your encouragement and support.

Tom Morrisey—Every time I think I have a handle on weapons and how they work, you show me I have so much to learn. Thanks for always helping me out.

Lynellen Perry—Congratulations for winning the contest: name my character. You chose Elizabeth Maddrey, your dear friend.

Scott Silverii, PhD, Chief of Police, Thibodaux, Louisiana—Thanks for showing me how a small woman could maneuver her way out of danger.

CHAPTER 1

HOUSTON, TEXAS
NOVEMBER
7:15 A.M. MONDAY

FBI Special Agent Bethany Sanchez swung open the door of her truck with the same jitters she had her first day at Quantico. On this gray morning, she was beginning a violent crime assignment and would meet her new partner, Special Agent Thatcher Graves, the man who'd sent her brother to jail.

Bethany caught her breath and took in the unfamiliar surroundings. The residential area was flooded with Houston police officers and unmarked cars, part of a task force between HPD and the FBI. Alicia Javon had been murdered here late yesterday afternoon, leaving behind a husband and two daughters.

The homes rose like monuments in this older, exclusive neighborhood, a mirror of refinement and dollar signs. The Javons' two-story brick with classic black shutters was no exception. Not a dog or cat in sight. In her parents' neighborhood, dogs ran loose and usually in packs, whether the four-legged or two-legged type. Here, a pair of squirrels scampered up an oak. The bushes and hedges received regular manicures. Freshly mowed yard. The three-car garage was the size of her apartment.

Contrast the tranquility with a woman who'd been shot, and it was Bethany's job to help bring down the killer.

1

She arched her shoulders and walked to the front door, wishing her first day in violent crime could have been less stressful. She'd been up most of the night giving herself a pep talk about working with Thatcher Graves despite their history. A little confidence on her end would boost her ego. She looked like a professional. Wore a black pantsuit and a white blouse. Hair secured at the nape. No rings. No bracelets. Just tiny gold balls in her earlobes, a small gold cross necklace, and a keen sense of determination that had never failed her.

After greeting two police officers and displaying her credentials, she entered the home, and another officer directed her toward a hum of activity to the right. She passed through a living area, where an upright bass, grand piano, and harp filled a third of the space. Beyond there she'd find Special Agent Thatcher Graves.

Her gaze pulled ahead. She wanted the partnership to work so badly that her blood pressure flared at the thought of it. She moved through the room to the kitchen. Thatcher bent behind the crime scene tape, where the body had been found. He glanced up, his earth-colored eyes stormy.

She extended her hand and hoped he didn't observe the trembling. "Good morning, I'm Bethany Sanchez."

He stood and towered over her, but most men did over her small frame. "My new partner. The gal from the civil rights division who solved a cold hate crime in the Hispanic community. And was influential in bringing peace to an Asian business district where a prostitution ring worked the streets. Welcome to violent crime." He gripped her hand, not too firm and not an ounce of wimp. "We've met before."

She offered a slight smile while her stomach rolled. "Yes, we have."

"I think it was the Labor Day picnic. Certainly not what the victim had here."

Had he forgotten *Papá*'s threat at the courthouse, or did he expect her to elaborate? "I understand there's a link between this murder and a previous one, and that's why the FBI's been called in."

"Right. Three weeks ago, Ruth Caswell, an elderly woman in the River Oaks area, was murdered. She was under hospice care but otherwise lived alone. Shot with a 9mm to the forehead, hollow-point bullet, and the killer left a plastic scorpion on her body. At that time, HPD requested our help, due to the unusual circumstances. Alicia Javon's murder appears to be identical, but it'll take weeks before we learn if the two women were killed with the same weapon."

"Didn't realize the lab was so far behind. Fingerprints?"

"Too soon to have the report. We'll see about the DNA."

"Anything to go on?"

"Looks like a serial killing."

"But the husband is a viable suspect. Looks to me like a domestic squabble that went bad."

He lifted a brow. "I've been at this longer than you have. The family will arrive in the next thirty minutes for an interview. They spent the night at a hotel."

"Can't blame them." She glanced around the kitchen. A stockpot rested on the stove, a box of pasta beside it. A dinner that never happened. "I wouldn't want to stay here either. What else do you have?"

He grabbed a large Starbucks cup from the kitchen counter and toasted her. The man wore a muscular build like an Italian suit. "You fit your MO."

She lifted a brow. "What do you mean?"

"No-nonsense. Gets the job done. Analytical. Outstanding record—"

"Whoa. You're armed, and all I have is office chatter and media headlines."

He sipped the coffee. "I'm sure it's all true."

Egotistical, but with a sense of humor. She stared into his chiseled face. "I hope not or I'm doomed."

"Doubt it, General Sanchez. Your reputation is outstanding."

She drew in a breath. The ring of his tone pierced her like a dull knife.

"Guess I won't call you a general again." The muscles in his jaw tightened. "Okay, back to the case. The killer is most likely a psychopath."

"We need more information to make that determination, a suspect whose behavior we can psychologically examine to determine if he's hearing voices and the like."

"Not every psychopath is a killer, but serial killers are psychopaths."

She'd mull his explanation when she had time to think about it. "Has the blood spatter been analyzed?"

"Yes. Nothing additional for us to follow up on there. I've been here since five thirty poring over the reports, trying to find a motive for both murders. We have two victims killed with the same type of weapon and identical scorpions left on each body. I sent a copy of the reports to you about an hour ago."

"Hold on a moment while I retrieve them." She eased her shoulder bag to the floor and snatched her phone, berating herself for not checking it sooner. She scrolled through the various reports. There it was. "Go ahead. I'm ready."

"Alicia Javon was a forty-five-year-old wife and mother. She held a vice president position at Danford Accounting. Two daughters are enrolled at Rice University majoring in music. Her husband is currently unemployed and on disability due to a spinal injury sustained in an auto accident. He told the police his wife's Bible and several pieces of her jewelry are missing. All heirlooms from her family. HPD noted a sizable inheritance from her family's estate."

Bethany read the list of diamonds, rubies, and sapphires stolen. Motive? "The husband claims the jewelry is insured. Has HPD checked the pawnshops?"

"Yes, and they will continue," Thatcher said. "No signs of forced entry."

"She may have known her killer or opened the door without

a visual check. Where was her husband? Do her daughters live at home?"

"The girls were out with their father. Walked in and discovered the body," he said. "It's in the report. I labeled it Scorpion."

Ouch. Could this get much worse?

"Hey, I'm messing with you. Don't worry about it."

She smiled but didn't feel it. "I noted Mrs. Javon's arm was in a cast. Worth looking into."

"I agree. Have a few thoughts about the injury."

"Theory or fact?" Immediately she regretted her question. Arguing fact and logic solved nothing. "That was inappropriate. I know you operate on instinct, and you're quite successful."

"But you have no respect for my methods, right?"

She reddened. "I'd like to think our partnership could work well organically."

He took another sip of coffee. "Well said. We could fail or become a dynamic team. When we're finished here, let's head back to the office and discuss the case."

A police officer stepped into the kitchen. "The family has arrived."

"They're early." Thatcher glanced out the kitchen window to a patio and pool area, his face stoic. "Tell them Special Agent Sanchez and I will talk to them in a few minutes. We're stepping outside for privacy."

CHAPTER 2

Bethany swallowed her incompetency and followed Thatcher outside. She'd been in such a nervous tizzy this morning that she hadn't checked her phone. Now she had to waste time reviewing what he'd already learned about Alicia Javon's murder.

Great way to begin a homicide investigation.

Thatcher stopped on the opposite side of the pool, and she quickly scrolled to his latest findings.

"Take your time," he said.

She nodded, not looking to see whether he was being kind or condescending. She finished reading and had put her phone away when both cells notified them of an update. They read the new information.

Paul Javon's background added a spin to the case. "This is priceless," she said. "An ambulance was called to the Javon home three times for Alicia and transported her to the medical center. She was treated for injuries, once for a mild concussion and another time to remove a contact after a cabinet door hit her in the eye. She said they were accidents."

"Her husband claimed her cast was the result of a fall down the stairs. Only a bully abuses a woman."

"Can't explain it away either." Bethany studied the house, a deep-redbrick color, as though fired in the kilns of time.

"Right there with you," he said. "If he mistreated his wife, then he might be strong-arming the daughters too."

"I've seen enough abuse of women and kids to last a lifetime. Just let me see one bruise, and I'll be tempted to cuff him." She studied the waterfall flowing into the pool. No doubt ice-cold. "From experience, it will be difficult to get solid answers from the daughters. Blood runs thicker than murder charges. And bruises and broken arms." She sensed his gaze on her. Was he wondering how she felt about Lucas? Of course he recognized her—why not?

"Would you start the interview, play the caring female role?" he said. "A nod will signal for me to take over."

"Is the nod a guideline for any interview?"

"Sure. Relax, you'll be fine. This isn't a competition." He gestured toward the door.

Later she'd dissect his words, but right now her brain needed to form questions and absorb facts.

Paul Javon met them in the living room wearing a grievous smile. Tall, blond hair, built like an athlete. Good-looking, if a gal went for the pretty-boy type. She'd expected him to be more immobile with his disability.

"You must be the FBI agents." His words choked out.

Thatcher and Bethany introduced themselves and displayed their IDs.

"I hope you can find my wife's killer," Javon said. "Most people think tragedies strike other families, not your own. Seems like a nightmare with no end."

"We're sorry for your loss," Thatcher said, his tone genuine.

Bethany walked to the harp. She had no musical ability, except to adjust the volume on her car radio or sound system at home. "I understand your daughters are quite musical."

"Yes. Alicia was too. . . . Both girls are in college on music scholarships. We're . . . I mean, I'm so envious of their talent." He joined Bethany. "I have videos of the three playing right here."

He glanced around. "The Christmas video is my favorite. The room decorated in red and gold."

"I can see you're proud of them."

He nodded and dabbed beneath his eye. "All the girls and I have left are memories. I feel Alicia in every room. Hear her sweet voice. Smell her perfume." He touched the harp. "The animal who did this has to pay." He picked up a family photo on the fireplace mantel. "This was taken last summer. See how beautiful . . . my Alicia. I have to keep remembering her this way, not how we found her."

"I understand," Bethany said, wishing she had a crystal ball to see inside Javon's words. "Have you recalled anything that can help us find your wife's killer?"

"I want to cooperate in every way. Please, sit down." He gestured to a pair of pale-green, cushioned chairs. His shoulders slumped. Grief or drama? "I apologize for my emotions. This is raw. Hard. This time yesterday, she was alive." He swiped at his eyes. "I'll let my daughters know you're here. They went upstairs to grab a few things."

He already had enough strikes against him with Alicia's medical history. *Slow down, Bethany.* A judge and jury determined the innocence or guilt of a man. Her job was to help Thatcher and the FBI bring in whoever had motive and evidence stacked against him. She adjusted her condemnation and fixed her best compassionate smile.

"We're here," a female voice said.

Two young women entered the room. Shannon was twenty-one and Carly nineteen. Both resembled their mother with thick auburn hair and brown eyes. One of the girls limped. Bethany mentally noted to find out if the condition stemmed from a physical defect, an accident, or if her father had substituted one of his daughters for Alicia.

"I'm Special Agent Graves and this is Special Agent Sanchez," Thatcher said. "You have our sympathies in the loss of your mother, and we value your time today. Our questions may duplicate what has already been asked by HPD, but repetition sometimes jars the memory. We know this is difficult, but it's necessary to find the source of your tragedy. We'll make our visit as brief as possible."

The young women flanked their father on a sofa. Shannon leaned into him, but Carly hugged the opposite end. Javon placed a massive arm around Shannon's shoulders. "We discussed your interview, and we're ready for whatever it takes to stop the killer."

He reached out for Carly. "Honey, come closer. These agents are here to help." He pulled her to him and kissed her cheek. She frowned.

Repulsed? Bethany kept her smile intact. "We're looking for any details," she said. "The smallest incident may open doors for us to make an arrest."

"We're a close family." Javon glanced at his daughters. "Have you thought of anything to help the agents?"

Had Javon's daughters seen him hit their mother? Carly's arctic eyes and a slight recoil from her father indicated disgust.

Thatcher nodded for Bethany to continue the interview. Paul Javon was way too congenial—*charming* described him best. He reminded her of her brother, Lucas, when he was around their family, causing Bethany's patience level to rise near tilt.

"Our report says HPD imaged your wife's computer. Did that include all of the electronics in your home?" she said.

"Just my wife's," Paul said. "We have three other computers and three iPads, so looking at their content makes sense."

Bethany jotted down his comments.

"Mom used my laptop a few times." The first words Carly had offered. "I can insert a flash drive to copy the contents."

"That's not necessary." Her father patted her knee. "The FBI has professional tech people to handle it."

"It would be my way of helping." Carly's words were emotionless.

"No. I have this covered." His fingers dug into her knee.

"How long will this interview take?" Shannon said. "I don't mean to be rude, but I have an hour before a class. Then we have

Mom's memorial service to plan." She gasped as though reality had punched her in the gut.

"You don't need to attend school today." Her father reached for her hand, and she closed her eyes. "Let your sister and I help you through this."

"I really don't know how I can help," Shannon said. "I want to wake up and find Mom's at work and everything's fine."

"Can you tell us about your mother?" Bethany sensed the young woman was sincerely distressed.

A tear trickled over Shannon's cheek. "She took care of us. Made sure we were always okay. When we had late study nights, she stayed up with us, sometimes cooking and making coffee and other times quizzing us." She talked on about her mother's fine qualities. No signs of deceit were evident. "Carly, Mom, and I loved to play music together."

"Thank you." Bethany poured compassion into her words. She turned to the younger woman. "What about you, Carly?"

She folded trembling hands. "Mom was active in church, and I admired that about her. Although I didn't jump on board the religious train, I understood her commitment. I volunteered with her at a homeless shelter for women. She worked with them to better themselves, and I played with the kids." Carly spoke in a monotone as though guarding every word.

"Agent Thatcher, what questions do you have?"

"Do either of you know of anyone who disliked your mom?"

"No, sir." The two voices sounded like a choir.

"Are you acquainted with Ruth Caswell?"

The two responded negatively, along with their father. "She's the other woman who was recently murdered?" Javon said.

"Yes, sir. Any disagreements with a neighbor, friend, or coworker?"

"None." Shannon drew in a ragged breath. "I can't believe she's gone . . . and how she died."

Carly slipped out of her father's hold. "I have nothing to help you. I wish I did. No strangers. No arguments. No mention of anything out of the ordinary." Her right foot wiggled. "If I think of something, I could contact you."

Thatcher and Bethany handed each of the family members their business cards.

"We might need to talk to you again," Thatcher said. "Thanks so much for your help. We're finished except for a few questions for your father."

"Daddy, are you okay?" Shannon said.

He smiled. "Of course, baby. You go ahead and make sure you have what you need from upstairs. Carly, you've been exposed to enough. I'll continue in private with the agents."

The gentle, caring father. If not for Alicia's unexplained injuries, Bethany might have swallowed his words. No point in his daughters hearing their conversation. The girls exited the room, leaving Thatcher and Bethany alone with Paul Javon. She nodded at Thatcher to take over.

"Would you like a cup of coffee or iced tea?" Javon said.

"We're fine," Thatcher said. "Would you tell us about your relationship with Alicia?"

He rubbed his face. "We had a rock-solid marriage."

"So good that she had multiple trips to the hospital?"

Thatcher's question met dead silence for a long moment.

"We worked out our differences in counseling."

"Guess you did."

"Ask our pastor. He'll testify to the fact. He helped us through a rough period. We . . . we had a trip planned to Rome. Just the two of us, a second honeymoon." His gaze darted about the room, then back to Thatcher. "I'll contact Pastor Lee right now. Have him make a copy of our sessions. Sir, I loved my wife with all my heart."

"All right. Would you have your pastor e-mail the records to the address on my card?"

"Yes, of course. Would you like for me to call him now?"

"Later's fine. The police report says you found Alicia's body in the kitchen."

"The girls and I had gone to a concert at Rice University. I pulled the car into the garage, and Carly found her first. When she screamed, Shannon and I hurried inside. It was a horrible, bloody scene."

"What'd you do then?"

"Checked for a pulse while Shannon phoned 911. I then had my girls wait on the driveway in case the killer was still inside. And they didn't need to view their mother."

His words matched the police report.

"Mr. Javon, did you touch your wife other than to check her pulse or in any way damage or remove evidence?" Thatcher said.

Javon struggled to speak. "I'm sorry. No, nothing."

More confirmation from HPD's findings.

"How did you feel about Alicia supporting you?"

Bethany positioned her pen to write Javon's response. Thatcher's theory about a serial killer just crashed with Javon's answers.

Javon stiffened. "I'm disabled and suffer from chronic fatigue."

"You didn't answer my questions."

"I admit it was tough. After the first of the year, I planned to open a consulting business at home for new start-up businesses. Just a few hours a day. Alicia supported the idea." Javon tugged on his ear.

"How did she break her arm?"

"She fell down the stairs. It's in the medical report."

"Were you present when it happened?"

"I was. She slipped. Alicia wore flip-flops around the house."

Bethany zeroed in on the guy. Did Thatcher think he was innocent? That losing his job and having his wife support him had caused their problems? Depression could have altered his reactions to things that were said and done. Anger issues. Abuse unchecked only got worse.

"But you hurt her in the past." Thatcher peered emotionlessly into Javon's face. "Sent her to the hospital a few times."

"I have problems—"

"Let's hear them."

"Agent Graves, I'm feeling bad enough about all this without being accused of murder. She—"

"Neither of us have accused you of murder. I'm simply asking you about your relationship with your wife."

Javon drew in a breath. Was it for show? "I believe my wife was the target of a crazed killer, a serial killer." Tears dripped down his face. "The scorpion on her body proves it, like the other murdered woman. Alicia was my whole world. You can go through everything I own. Cell phone records. Credit card bills. Bank accounts. Take it all. I had nothing to do with my wife's murder. I loved her."

Bethany had heard her brother declare his innocence with the same feigned emotions. She didn't believe his lies, and she wasn't falling for this one.

"Mr. Javon," she said, "your concern for your wife is commendable. Our reports indicate Alicia recently inherited over eight million dollars from her deceased parents. You could buy a lot of punching bags for that."

CHAPTER 3

Thatcher gestured for Bethany to enter the interview room ahead of him. The petite young Hispanic woman before him had a bull-dog reputation when it came to nailing a civil rights crime. A champion for the mistreated. She'd arranged for victims to have counseling over and above her job, and he admired her altruism. But she also had a nickname of ice queen.

From her lack of eye contact, she was far too anxious. Could be she didn't make the grade for violent crime, and the civil rights division was the best for the bureau and her. Violent crime required a balance of sensitivity to victims and their families with an investigator mind-set. As much as he'd like the partnership to work, he had doubts. They must have complete trust in each other, and that took time—a disaster if unsuccessful.

They processed cases differently, and she apparently had no respect for his methods.

Lack of respect could make you angry.

Lack of trust could get you killed.

Last year while working a case, he'd nearly gotten killed by allowing arrogance to rule his actions. He thought he had the perfect plan to end a crime spree and skipped a few protocol steps. An HPD officer saw a killer aiming at him and brought him down. But if Thatcher had trusted the officer instead of playing bad-boy

15

agent, the incident never would have happened. That man had become his closest friend.

Bethany eased onto a chair. She had a can of Diet Dr Pepper in one hand and a legal pad in the other. He sat across from her with another cup of coffee and the murder victims' files.

He opened both case files and spread them over the table. "I work fast when I'm on a case. We have two murders, and we'll be flip-flopping interviews and angles continuously. Will this be a problem?"

"What if it's not a serial killer on the loose? Then we're wasting valuable time. Look at how he abused his wife. I believe the evidence points to Paul Javon being responsible for his wife's murder."

His patience had grown paper-thin. "Who's the senior agent?"

She sighed. "Point taken."

"Thank you. We're partners, not enemies. What else can you bring to the table?"

"I use a spreadsheet and various graphs to keep facts straight."

"All right. We copy each other on every e-mail, and every interview is together. If one of us receives information, the other gets it ASAP. Ready to get a few things documented?" When she nodded, he smiled, more for her benefit than his. "Here's what we have—the police investigative reports, crime scene info and photos, autopsy reports and those photos, security cam information for Ruth Caswell, which the killer disabled, and background information on both victims. Compare every piece of data I give you."

She drew a line down the middle of her legal pad. "Go for it."

For the first time he noticed her huge brown eyes. "White females. Neither sexually assaulted. Ruth Caswell, age eighty-six, was killed at approximately 5:15 p.m. on October 12," he said. "Alicia Javon, age forty-five, killed between 4:30 and 6 p.m. on November 5. Four weeks apart. Different days of the week. Both women were shot execution style, 9mm to the forehead with a hollow-point bullet. Forced entry through a window for Caswell. No signs of forced entry for Javon. Their clothing was intact.

Brown plastic scorpions, a variety sold at Walmart and Toys"R"Us, found on the victims' chests, tails pointed toward the forehead. Fingerprints on scorpions, negative. DNA on Caswell, negative. Waiting on DNA report from Javon scorpion and other collected samples. Both women robbed. Neither woman appeared to be acquainted with the other." He stood and paced the floor. "None of the stolen items have been recovered. Since the personal property was insured and registered with identifying numbers, tracking them will be easier. Few leads on the Caswell murder, and—"

"The best lead on Alicia Javon seems to have an alibi. Javon could have easily found out the kind of plastic scorpion used in Caswell's murder."

Thatcher sensed heat rising in his face. Her conclusions were that of a rookie. "How many murders have you solved?"

"I'm just saying Javon had more to gain with Alicia out of the way." She sighed again as though waiting for him to object. "The ballistics report will prove if the same gun was used, eventually determining which one of us is right."

"Right or wrong about our suspicions isn't what solving a murder is all about." He peered into her face, wishing his old partner sat across from him. "Two people are dead, and it's our job to find out who killed them and make an arrest. Clear?"

She blinked. "Yes, and I agree. Phone records?"

"Caswell's landline cleared, but the woman was dying and her calls were from family, friends, hospice, etc. So far Javon's landline and cell phones check out. Computer imaging takes a few days. But initially, we've found nothing to flag."

Bethany glanced up. "Where was the hospice nurse when Ruth Caswell was killed?"

"Her name is Mae Kenters, and she claims not to have heard or seen anyone. She stepped out of Caswell's room for her scheduled cup of coffee and break. Gone about fifteen minutes before returning to find the woman dead." He handed Bethany the file. "We pulled a boot print, military grade, size 8½, near a window

where the killer gained entrance to Caswell's second-floor bedroom. The debris from the shoe matched the newly spread mulch
below. HPD interviewed the landscaping company and conducted
follow-ups on employees. One man wore the same shoe size, but
he checked out."

"Did both women use the same doctor, medical clinic, or
hospital?"

"All different providers."

"Are you terming Ruth Caswell's investigation cold?" she said.

A defeatist attitude was not in his gene pool. "I've solved
every murder case I've worked on. No plans to admit failure now.
Indications are theft ranks as motive. But that doesn't hold water.
Why steal valuables and murder a dying old woman? Why enter
through her bedroom window when the house is huge? So the
killer cased the house, disarmed the security system, and was aware
when the nurse typically took her break? Makes me question if
the killer worked alone. Several antique guns were stolen from an
adjacent bedroom, but nothing's been reported from gun collec-
tors and pawnshops. Not theft, murder."

"All in about ten minutes? Has a background been done on
Mae Kenters?" she said.

"We have HPD's report. No priors on her." He considered the
circumstances surrounding Ruth Caswell. "Make a note for us
to bring Mae Kenters in today for another interview, sometime
this afternoon. Her HPD statement is in the file with my phone
follow-up. Very nervous woman. Add to the note for me to call
Ruth Caswell's son. He might have information regarding Alicia
or other Javon family members. Also, his mother's religious preference since Alicia's Bible was stolen."

"Sure." She looked at the list. "What else do you have?"

"That's it until various reports are completed. Do you see
anything?"

She studied her list. "Makes sense to talk to neighbors of both
victims. See if they saw anything usual. Examine those findings."

"Landscape company. Housekeeping services. Remodeling. Home repairs. Food deliveries, including fast food that could supply the Javons and hospice nurses. All services that had access to the homes for a three-month period."

"Whoa, slow down."

"Quantico doesn't teach shorthand anymore?" He snapped his fingers. "Life insurance companies and the current sales rep assigned to both women. Blood type."

She pressed her lips together. "You're far out there, a waste in—"

"Bend your rules, Bethany. You might be surprised what you find."

She fumed, but he ignored it. "What about traffic cam footage near the Caswell home for the past three months," she said. "The Javons have an alarm system, but not cameras. Traffic cams might help there too."

"Good call. We're looking for a single unique trait. At this point, it looks like our killer chose a targeted stranger. But the relationship will be defined as we move through the evidence." He eased onto the chair, adrenaline and caffeine coursing through his veins. "Your thoughts?"

She folded her arms on the table. "Less than one percent of the murders committed in our country are conducted by serial killers, and I know the definition per the FBI. But Javon could have hired a killer for the eight million."

He wanted a partner, not memorized protocol. "Then why didn't he set up an accident or an overdose of pills to get her out of the way?"

She held up a finger. "We need proof. He's definitely a piece of work—a coward and a bully. Unregenerate in my opinion. Do you believe his show of grief?"

"No."

"The victims' ages don't fall among the high percentage of murdered victims."

"They're still dead."

She startled. "True. I'm merely thinking aloud with the information we have. Paul Javon has motive and a background of violence."

"Could be no motive at all. The killer can, so he does. It could be more than one driving force. Or Javon wanted control of the inheritance. I don't rule out anything, especially a serial killing."

"What about Alicia Javon's missing Bible?"

"Hard to say. She could have audibly prayed before being shot, and the killer reacted. Or it could be an indication of something else. Add these to the list—past addresses, elementary, middle, and high schools. College. Employment history. Any infractions? Daily habits. Political views. Community affairs."

"We don't have time for thin theories—" She reddened. "I'm sorry. No excuse for my rudeness, except I'm a superachiever on steroids. I'm used to comparing facts and going forward with what can be proven."

Maybe this partnership wouldn't work. "The human mind doesn't necessarily work on facts."

"What are we looking for to narrow in on the killer or killers?"

"First of all, you're doing great. The psychology of any killer is always a huge factor, because usually the psychological gratification is what spurs him on. In this case, we're working through two murders that have a few characteristics indicating a serial killing, and that requires a complex homicide investigation on many levels. I was assigned to my first murder case about eight years ago. Only two years out of Quantico, and I was scared stupid. My partner had been in violent crime for a dozen years, and he guided me through the investigation."

"So we examine the two murders as though they were individual killings and find the common trait that connects the two? If there is one."

"Yep. We have people to interview today and a report to compile at the close and information to send to behavioral analysts at Quantico."

Her cell phone buzzed with a text. She glanced at it, frowned, and dropped it back into her purse.

Thatcher checked the time. "Are you ready to visit Alicia Javon's pastor?"

"First? What about those closest to her? The first forty-eight hours is the most crucial time in an investigation. Look at how the younger daughter reacted to her father. She's our best interviewee."

Taking a gulp of coffee, he allowed silence to prove his point. "Do you honestly think Carly Javon will point a finger at her dad with her mother's body barely cold? She knows he has an alibi. Give her a few hours or a couple of days to think this through—and plan her mother's funeral."

He once again doubted the flexibility of the woman before him. "Pastors are also counselors, and counselors often hear what's going on in a person's life. Alicia could have confided in someone she trusted about a stalking, a quarrel, an association with Ruth Caswell, or—"

"Nothing."

He lifted his coffee cup. "We'll find out, now, won't we?"

"Thatcher, I think we could complement each other and use every angle to end this crime and others." She shrugged. "But we'll have to work at it."

"When my old partner took a transfer, I was bummed. We thought alike, and we were always on the same wavelength. But I've been thinking about you and me, instinct versus logic. We could be a force to be reckoned with, if we don't kill each other first."

CHAPTER 4

While Bethany waited for Thatcher to join her in the FBI lower hallway, she lifted the Diet Dr Pepper to her lips, like the classic commercial—10, 2, 4, and anytime in between when she needed a burst of energy. Liquid courage trickled down her throat. She'd made a fool of herself. By noon she might be back in the civil rights division. Still, she believed pressing Paul Javon and his younger daughter would provide faster results than interviewing their pastor. A whole list took precedence over speaking to the pastor, one being to transcribe the notes she'd just taken into a spreadsheet. At least in the car, she could concentrate on FBI and HPD reports on her phone.

She reached for her phone to read the text from *Mamá*, sent when she and Thatcher were discussing the case.

Lucas released from jail. Says he needs money.

Let her brother get a job and earn a living honestly instead of armed robbery, which only got him eleven months. *Mamá* and *Papá* would hand over whatever he needed. She glanced at the text's recipients. It went to her sisters too. No surprise. Baby brother's actions were always justified. She closed her eyes while guilt assaulted her for not responding. Then she texted her mother.

I know a contractor who needs workers

Lucas is fragile & can't take a job right now. How much will you give?

None

I'm really sad & disappointed

Exasperation caused her to drop her cell back into her purse. She'd concentrate on her new assignment and pray Lucas had learned something in jail besides new ways to con everyone in his universe.

✳   ✳   ✳

10:56 A.M. MONDAY

While Thatcher and Bethany walked to his Mustang in the FBI parking lot, he phoned Nick Caswell, Ruth's son and only living heir.

"Dr. Caswell, I have a few questions for you," Thatcher said. "Do you know Alicia Javon, or had your mother ever mentioned her?"

"I don't recall the name, but I'll look into it and ask my wife. Why do you ask?"

"Alicia Javon was murdered yesterday, and there are some similarities between her case and your mother's. At this point we're compiling history on both women for the past six months. If you can get your hands on a list of all those who had contact with your mother, including services at her home, that will expedite the investigation. I'll send a follow-up e-mail later on today with specifics."

"Whatever it takes. Shouldn't be too tedious since I managed her affairs for the past year."

"Thanks. Was your mother religious?"

"Depends on the season of the year. I'd say more generous than religious."

Thatcher thanked him and set the phone aside. "Nick's an orthopedic surgeon, a good man." He pointed to his car. "There's my ride." She hadn't said a word, and from the look on her face, her mood could be served with shaved ice.

Once he pulled onto 290, he chose to try breaking her chill. "How about an interrogation?"

She swung his way. "With the pastor?"

"No, us." He chuckled. "Hours and days of work are ahead of us. We need to know each other on a personal level."

"I really wonder if a Q & A is necessary."

Why was this woman so private? Unless his reputation with women had her cautious. "If we're in a shoot-out, I want to know my back's covered."

"Makes sense. What's your plan?"

"You've proved yourself an outstanding agent in the civil rights division. Why transfer to violent crime?"

She blinked. "The challenge."

"Really?"

"I'm not a stranger to violent crime."

"I see where you were raised. Any killings affect you personally?"

"All of them."

"How?" Textbook answers didn't let him inside the real agent, the one who was influenced by life's curveballs to work a murder.

She moistened her lips. "Where I grew up, a boy's arrest is his initiation into manhood, and blood in the streets is a fact of life."

Tough girl. "Revenge or justice?"

She lifted her gaze. "Justice."

"What's your favorite candy?"

"What?"

"Humor me for a moment."

"None."

"Do you have a dog?"

"No."

"Why a Ford pickup?"

"I'm short. Helps me see better."

"Siblings?"

"Three sisters and one brother. I'm next to the youngest. I threw in the extra for more points."

He laughed. She could lighten up. "Your name isn't Spanish."

"My parents wanted the best of both worlds for their kids."

"Hobbies?"

"The FBI."

"Why the FBI?"

"Why not?"

"This isn't a test. Our quirky traits make us unique."

She remained stiff. "You're asking weird questions. Am I winning or losing?"

"This isn't a game. From your answers, I can't bribe you with candy to enter my notes into the computer. I can't show up at your door to walk your dog so you'll bring me coffee in the mornings. We both drive Fords. You have a large family, and you hate to lose. Diet Dr Pepper is your beverage of choice, although I think it tastes like bad medicine. You're performance-oriented, and your reasons for choosing a career in the FBI and specifically violent crime are private."

Her eyes flashed. "In other words, a certain amount of familiarity between us is necessary. I'm not used to a partner being privy to my personal life."

"You weren't investigating a murder. My weakness could be your strength and the other way around."

"You might be right."

Getting her to loosen up was like shooting blanks at a moving target. "For the record—red licorice, no dog, drive a Mustang, only kid, enjoy country-western music, and my dad offered me ten grand if I joined the FBI." He grinned. "I like sports, and it's how you play the game."

"I play to win."

"Figured so."

CHAPTER 5

After battling Houston traffic from the FBI office to University Boulevard, Thatcher stood with Bethany in the office reception area of Alicia Javon's church with Pastor Lee. Dark caverns shadowed beneath the aging man's eyes. He represented truth, but he seemed hesitant to meet with the two agents. Perhaps the idea of a murdered church member scraped raw against a message of love and forgiveness. His shoulders held the weight of too many people expecting too much from one man.

"Would you rather come to our office?" Thatcher said.

Pastor Lee sighed. "We can talk now for a few minutes."

Once seated in the pastor's office, Thatcher sensed the man's barrier in his reluctance to make eye contact. Walls were built to protect, not hide, and he saw fear and exhaustion in the pastor's demeanor. Thatcher understood the horror of spilled blood when life flowed to nonexistence. He experienced the inevitable finality every time an innocent person walked into death's trap. Right now, he needed to soothe Pastor Lee's nervousness. They were on his side.

"Pastor, our job is to find out who killed Alicia Javon," he said.

Red rimmed his eyes. "The family and my members are suffering. Paul suggested a memorial service right away since Alicia wished to be cremated, and we have no idea when you people will release her body." He paused. "Can't you let us go on with our lives?"

Thatcher leaned toward him. "We don't ignore a murder. The person responsible for Mrs. Javon's death has possibly killed another woman and is free to kill again. Is that what you want? What if the killer is a member of your church? Even someone you respect?"

Pastor Lee's drawn features paled. "The thought makes me ill. I'm sorry about my lack of cooperation. I'll help you." He closed the door to his office. "Are you recording this conversation?"

"Can we?"

"I prefer not."

Thatcher could have persuaded him without using shock tactics, but he was in what-works mode, and that meant dealing with Pastor Lee's difficult emotions. "We appreciate your time in this tragedy."

"Alicia's family is in bad shape. I was at their hotel until two this morning."

"That's why we've got to work together to find the killer. Special Agent Sanchez and I are committed to ending the murders."

The man glanced at Bethany. His features hardened. Did he have a problem with a female agent? Or a Hispanic? His church was upper-crust white bread. . . .

"We understand how you'd like to put this behind you," Bethany said. "The sooner this case is solved, the easier everyone will rest. Special Agent Graves will ask the questions, and I'll write your responses." She pulled a notepad from her purse and opened it to a clean page. The woman with huge dark eyes and inches-long lashes wore professionalism in one package, and she must have seen the revulsion for something in Pastor Lee.

"I want this nightmare ended," the pastor said. "With closure, the Javons can grieve without fear."

"Have they shared their apprehension with HPD?" Thatcher said.

"Yes, of course. I think that's natural when a loved one is murdered. However, none of the other family members have been threatened. Neither was Alicia. They were an excellent Christian family."

There were holes in the story. Every family had its share of dysfunction, and the Javons were at the top of the list. "We're ready to get started." Thatcher nodded at Bethany, and she clicked her pen.

"Pastor Lee, we're looking for a connection between Alicia and another recently murdered woman. Do you know Ruth Caswell?"

"Other than hearing her name as a victim, no."

"Did Mrs. Javon ever confide in you about concern for her life?"

"Never." He folded his hands into a tight fist.

"Anyone who might be upset with her? A situation at her place of employment, here at church, or in the community?"

"Not to my knowledge."

"Was she active in your church? Did she hold a leadership position?"

"She led a Tuesday night Bible study at a women's shelter." The lines in Pastor Lee's face softened. "I've been told the women loved her."

"The facility could be housing the killer's family or girlfriend," Thatcher said. "What is the name of the facility?"

"Noah's Loft. It's located in the northeast part of town," Pastor Lee said. "Her group wasn't just a Bible study, but an outreach built on enriching the lives of each resident through faith. She supported them in every way possible. Even helped them write résumés so they could find jobs."

"What about her husband?"

"Paul is a good man. A deacon."

"I see Paul Javon is unemployed. Did they have any problems, marital or otherwise?"

Pastor Lee swiped at his nose. Did he have any knowledge of Paul Javon's earlier interview? "Not any more than anyone else."

A lie. Body stiffened.

"Normal couple. Volunteered in the church. Beautiful and talented daughters."

"I don't think you're being honest about the Javons' relationship." Thatcher believed it was time to pull off the gloves. "If you are aware of anything about the case, now is the time to step forward." Why would a man of God hold back anything that would help solve a murder?

"What I have is trivial."

"We'll decide the value."

Pastor Lee stared at his desk. "The Javons were having marital difficulties. I counseled them. The last time they were in my office, I saw complete reconciliation." He toyed with a pen on his desk. "I shouldn't be telling you this—their confidentiality is at stake. They're upstanding members."

"The law says when a crime has been committed, confidentiality no longer applies. You wouldn't want to be held liable in Alicia's death."

His nostrils flared. "You're making insinuations with no validation."

Thatcher nodded for Bethany to take over.

"Pastor Lee, Alicia couldn't defend herself from her attacker because her arm was in a cast. Her husband admitted to anger issues," she said, her voice soft with a hint of her Hispanic roots. "What made you think the situation was improving?"

Pastor Lee waited before answering, no doubt to ease the red flaming his face. "They were in my office a week ago. They planned a trip together. They—"

"What are you not telling us?" she said.

Pastor Lee's shoulders rose. "I've told you everything. Paul and Alicia worked out their minor differences. If you don't mind, agents, I have a memorial service to prepare for the Javon family." He pushed back from his desk and walked to the door.

"What kind of marital difficulties?" Bethany obviously wouldn't let this go easily. Persistence. Thatcher valued tenacity.

His eyes narrowed. "I'm not at liberty to discuss it."

"Special Agent Graves explained the repercussions of withholding evidence in a murder case. You claim their problems were settled." Her calm manner spread through the office. "Do you know the death stats on family violence? Over 200,000 domestic violence incidents were reported in Texas last year, and over 84 percent of abuse victims are women."

Pastor Lee opened the door. "If you're implying what I think you are, you're making a ridiculous accusation. A man who fasts forty days for his marriage is a righteous man. Agents, have a blessed day."

While Thatcher and Bethany walked to his car, he processed the pastor's words. "He's keeping information from us."

"Counseling confidentiality is one thing, and I respect him for his boundaries. But his avoidance of responding to questions tells me the Javons' relationship had hit bottom."

"Intuition or fact?"

"I do have my feelings side and no room for those who protect the guilty."

She had the SS syndrome, sweet sarcasm. So far Bethany Sanchez communicated like an FBI robot. Not a good set of traits when he relied on her to watch his back. "We'll follow up on this interview. See if the good pastor will open up a little more."

"Might take another body to convince him," she said. "We should have stayed right there in his office and asked him to pray about his decision to protect a murder suspect."

Thatcher swung her a grin. "I'm all over it."

She returned a smile. "Where to now?"

"Alicia's employment."

She started, no doubt disagreeing with their next move.

"You have reservations?" he said.

She shook her head. "It's my first day. But if we talk to Pastor Lee again, I want at him."

"Are we changing roles, partner?"

"Probably not. Did you note he referred to the Javons in the present tense, while Alicia's husband referred to her in the past?"

"Now that you mention it, the present tense seems to indicate Pastor Lee has no doubts about the couple having a solid marriage, which we know isn't true."

"Maybe he doesn't know the whole truth. A man who abuses his wife, then fasts for his marriage is not about to admit he's at fault."

On this one, she had a good point.

Once on the road in Thatcher's silver Mustang, they swung onto 610 north toward the Galleria area, where Danford Accounting represented many of the wealthy citizens of Houston. Up ahead, an overturned truck sent four lanes down to two, and traffic slowed to a crawl in the far right lanes. Add a blinding downpour to the mix. Not exactly what Thatcher needed today with a list of interviews glaring at him. Emergency vehicles and police cars swarmed the area.

"We could walk faster than this," Thatcher said. "What I wouldn't give for a siren."

"You could always work for HPD."

Thatcher had that one coming. "Ah, no thanks. I wouldn't be able to keep the uniform clean."

Bethany chuckled. "From what I've heard, you'd bankrupt the department in replacing them. Unless you worked undercover."

"I'll stick with the FBI. Hey, you did well back there, and I don't blow smoke."

"Thanks. Pastor—" A text came through on her phone.

"For us?"

"I wish." She stared out the window. "I apologize for the two personal interruptions today."

"No problem."

She kept her attention on the highway.

Something had Bethany unnerved, and his sources said she was always in control.

CHAPTER 6

Bethany and Thatcher rode the elevator to the fourth floor of Danford Accounting, where Alicia Javon had held a VP position. Bethany watched the numbers rise and considered her last text.

U will pay 4 this.

Her lunatic brother still blamed her for his recent jail stay.

Pastor Lee had revealed enough to send her into analysis mode. He'd been agitated. When someone concealed the truth, it had to be pried out. The man wore stress like a turtle's shell, and it would take a hard crack for him to open up. Wasn't God supposed to handle convictions? He certainly bore down on her faults. She'd experienced ugly secrets, deeds covered up that made a person edgy. Pastor Lee needed a reason to tell all, including the consequences of harboring evidence. She wanted to talk to the pastor again today. But Thatcher had another agenda.

Jealousy and greed were prime motivators for murder. The answers could be at Danford Accounting.

"You're quiet," Thatcher said, his gaze fixed on the elevator door.

"Thinking."

He nodded as though he understood. "It's only your first day."

"Yes, sir."

"Oh, I like the sound of those two words. Can I hear them again?"

"Not today."

He chuckled. "We all have a learning curve. Same plan as at the church office?"

"Sure." The interview with Felix Danford seemed like another chance for her to gain credibility. She gauged her racing pulse. "Before we leave here today, we need a list of employees for background checks. Right down to the janitor."

"Okay—"

"Don't ever call me general."

"Hey, loosen up, which is what I started to say before you interrupted."

How many times had she heard those words? "I'll work on my attitude. Perfectionism is a nasty implant. Guess what you heard about me is true." She tried desperately to relax.

"Get through our first day, and tomorrow will be much easier."

"Thanks. I'm really a super gal. Fun-loving." She wished it were true.

"I'll reserve my thoughts until I see you party."

Bethany knew for certain she respected Thatcher as an agent, but not his methods of investigation. She had to climb down from her edgy attitude. Get answers to stop the killer or killers and move on to the next case.

Why hadn't Thatcher mentioned the awkward situation with her brother? Before the day was over, she'd have to bring it up. Get the bad salsa out into the open and deal with it.

Once they stepped off the elevator, the agents displayed their badges to a leggy receptionist who gestured them to a waiting area. She returned to her desk, no doubt to find someone who could get rid of them. Fat chance.

Danford Accounting handled the finances for several real estate companies in Houston and around Texas. They had recently added a division for legal firms. The contemporary, plush furnishings displayed their wealth in striking chrome, black, white, and red—the colors of power and passion.

"Alicia Javon made well over six figures." Bethany sank into a white leather chair. "I did some research while you were driving. She supported several charities, including her husband's ventures. He closed a software business over three years ago."

"That had to put a dent in their income. I'd like to know more about Alicia's personality. Power driven? Control freak? Hard to live with? Could be her death was caused by her husband's discontent or a work-related vendetta."

The runway receptionist walked toward them. She flipped a lock of long blonde hair behind her ear, most likely for Thatcher's benefit.

He smiled at Bethany. "Let's see if anyone had cause to murder Alicia Javon."

※ ※ ※

1:25 P.M. MONDAY

Thatcher sensed the hostility from Felix Danford, the president of Danford Accounting, the moment he and Bethany introduced themselves. A quick glance from her told him she felt like roadkill too. Danford motioned for them to sit several feet away, where a matching pair of white leather sofas faced each other. A wall of windows behind the massive chrome desk was blinding.

"You're joining us?" Thatcher's question bordered on irritation. "We hadn't planned to conduct an interview in the next room. Why not have a seat over here?"

Danford's gaze tossed a dagger, but he complied by sitting on a sofa across from them. "What can I do to help solve Alicia's murder?" He crossed his legs, a leisurely picture of a silver-haired CEO dressed in a black Italian suit, when moments before he appeared uncooperative.

Unaddressed emotions could level a man, even a CEO.

"Can I get you two anything? Coffee? Water?" When they declined, he drew in a breath. "I'm assuming you have the police report and the imaging from her computer."

"We do." Thatcher picked up on a twist of arrogance. "Have you remembered a conversation or seeing anything that could help us since you spoke to HPD?"

"Alicia ranked as the epitome of leadership. Her work ethic was impeccable." His impassive features on an unlined face threw Thatcher until he remembered Danford's age. Botox made it hard to read a person. "She stayed late and arrived early. Projects completed ahead of schedule. Excellent rapport with clients and staff. Didn't get involved in office politics or gossip. Never heard her lose her temper or condescend to an employee."

Had he rehearsed those choppy lines? "How long had Mrs. Javon been in her current position?"

"Eight years. Top of the line. I'd need to resign for Alicia to have risen any higher in the company." He smiled, revealing sandblasted-white teeth. "As you can see, no one here would have wanted her hurt."

"She was murdered," Bethany said. "Big stretch from hurt."

Danford glanced away. "I was being discreet."

"Discreet is for polite society," she said. "Murder is never polite."

Danford wasn't married. Was he an ambitious executive who wanted Alicia out of the way? Or did he fear she wanted too much control? "Special Agent Sanchez and I need to talk to your employees. We also will need to look at the victim's projects."

A muscle twitched near Danford's mouth. "We're on deadline with several of them, most of which were on her computer. But I don't want to stand in the way of an investigation. One member of her staff is on vacation. That leaves two others. You should be finished within the hour."

Thatcher despised someone telling him how to run an interview. "A thorough investigation means we talk to all employees. Agent Sanchez and I work efficiently together."

Danford hesitated.

"Is there a problem?"

"The staff is apprehensive about the murder, as though one of them could be next. I'm merely being protective." He glanced at Bethany. *"Discreet."*

"Do you think the killer is among your employees?"

Danford pulled a cell phone from his jacket pocket. "I'm contacting my attorney. I've nothing to hide, but if you're going to disrupt my employees, I need legal guidance. Would you mind stepping outside while I make the call?"

"Doesn't matter what your attorney advises," Thatcher said. "We intend to talk to every person who works here. Perhaps you prefer we issue a subpoena for your employees. And I'll personally make sure we have a search warrant to access all your files."

"Wait a minute," Danford said. "I agree—whoever did this to Alicia has to be brought to justice. But I pay my attorney for his counsel. I cannot answer any more questions or subject my employees to interviews until I speak to my attorney."

"Agent Sanchez, we're finished here for now."

Bethany and Thatcher walked to the door. "We'll be in touch," Thatcher said.

"When you have a signed, legal search warrant to come barging in here again, we'll talk."

CHAPTER 7

On the way to Thatcher's car, Bethany explored what they'd learned about Alicia Javon. The Javons' marital relationship had disaster written all over it, then add to that Danford's responses to their questions . . . Did Alicia's ambition pose a threat to the business? Was he protecting his rights or hiding something?

Her stomach rumbled. "Sorry."

"We missed lunch," he said. "What works for you?"

If she didn't eat soon, she'd be in bad shape. Thank you, diabetes. "What about a burger? Anything fast."

"You're on. We could do Taco Bell."

"Thatcher, I don't eat jalapeños and nachos at every meal."

He cringed. "Didn't mean to sound like I was profiling you. Are you going to nominate me for sensitivity training classes?"

She might appreciate this guy yet. "A new class starts every month." She opened the door to his Mustang and slid onto the tan leather seat. "Have you had an Hispanic partner before?"

"No. A woman once, but she transferred to New York."

"I'll give you cultural training instead. How's that?"

"You're one up on me," he said. "I'm thinking through what we've learned. Other than father and husband of the year, what else struck you about Javon?"

"Control. He pulled Carly next to him when she anchored herself on the opposite end of the sofa."

"Could he be telling the truth? He'd abused Alicia, got help, then his wife's murdered?"

"Hard to think sweet things about a wife beater." She knew far too many women who'd been hurt by an overpowering man. "The verdict's out on Danford."

"He's hiding something."

She wanted to say there wasn't proof, but chose otherwise. Thatcher was merely following normal procedures for a man of his caliber.

"I can read your thoughts, and you want to know the why of my observation," he said.

"I do."

"He can hide his feelings with Botox but not the grip of his hands at the mention of her name."

"I didn't see it."

"A point for us to follow up on."

She'd have to do a better job reading body language.

He pulled into McDonald's. "This work to refuel?"

"Perfect. I need to tell you something, get it out in the open. I never met Alicia Javon, but I heard outstanding things about her from the director at Noah's Loft. Elizabeth and I are close friends. She persuaded me to volunteer, and my first session is this Saturday. It's a coincidence, I know. But I'll see if any of the women were better acquainted with our victim."

"Good. See what you can learn. Discreetly of course."

She drew in another breath. "Thatcher, during lunch, can I ask a few more questions?"

"About the case?"

"Not exactly."

"Right. More insight into our partnership."

While munching on fries and chicken nuggets, Bethany studied Thatcher. This partnership meant learning from each other, and her reluctance to respond appropriately to Thatcher's questions delayed any progress. If SSA Preston learned how she communicated with Thatcher this morning, he might reassign her to civil rights.

He dipped his fries in ranch dressing and emptied more on his jalapeño burger. Must be his version of Tex-Mex. From what she'd seen since 7:15, he handled himself well as an agent, even if she hadn't. Good-looking too.

"Your turn to fire questions," he said with a gulp of Coke.

"Worst mistake you ever made in your career—and it can't be me."

He laughed. "Believing another agent wouldn't be on the take, and he was."

"Where is he now?"

"Prison."

Made sense. "Best day of your life?"

"Two weeks ago."

When he didn't elaborate, she continued. "Favorite vacation place."

"Wyoming. There's a dude ranch near wild mustangs."

"Thus your car?"

"Closest I'll come to owning the real thing."

"What matters to you most?"

He dipped three fries into ranch dressing and popped them into his mouth. "Being an agent who doesn't fold."

She hadn't expected that. "Describe what 'not folding' means to you."

"Are you sure you want to hear this?" She nodded, and he took a long drink before continuing. "In working violent crime, I witness a lot of negative emotions. In order to separate myself from a life of cynicism, I find it important to evaluate my own less-than-positive emotions, search for the root cause, and deal with it."

"As in ignore or deny?"

"Nope. Acknowledge them."

Should she dig deeper into his beliefs? "How do you specifically approach negative emotions?"

"The battle is won first in the mind. If I'm afraid of the killer, think he's smarter than me, or am concerned he's a better shot, I'm a dead man."

"*Buen punto.* I'll work on mastering my psychological skills."

"As long as applying those skills comes first in your mind." He glanced away, then back to her. "My commitment to the bureau says I need to replace fear with courage, and anger with commitment."

"What kind of commitment?"

"To help new agents in violent crime overcome textbook answers."

She bit her tongue to keep from leveling him with a comment. Instead she raised her hand for a high five.

"I want to prove we can work well together," he said. "I requested you when I learned about your interest in violent crime."

Her eyes widened. "We're like oil and water."

"Or salt and pepper. Entirely different but together unbeatable. Your record is impressive."

Truth about her FBI involvement slammed against her heart. She could be a little transparent. "The reason I joined the FBI is when I was twelve, I saw my best friend gunned down on the sidewalk in front of her house. She got in the way of a drive-by and bled out before an ambulance arrived. I decided then to spend my life in some type of law enforcement. Research led me to the FBI."

"From the civil rights division to violent crime," he said quietly.

"Protecting the innocent from selfish individuals, like far too many in my neighborhood."

"Thanks."

She brightened for a moment. "Didn't hurt at all." But the driving question still persisted. "Thatcher, why haven't you said a word about my brother?"

He stopped with his sandwich in midair. "Your brother?"

"Lucas Sanchez."

He set his nearly eaten burger on its wrapper. "He's your brother?"

She should have kept her mouth shut. Too late now. "Yes, and I was with my family outside the courthouse when my father threatened to break your legs."

He shook his head. "I don't remember seeing you. Honestly, I made no name association with your brother. Is that why you act like I haven't showered in a week?"

She took a sip of her Diet Dr Pepper. "I'm usually standoffish and all business. But I do want to apologize for my father's threats. He could have been arrested." She set her drink on the table. "Of course, it wouldn't be the first time a Sanchez's temper landed him in jail."

He waved her away. "He was upset. My testimony obviously sealed your brother's conviction."

She hesitated. "I support my family, not necessarily their opinions."

A trace of compassion crossed his face, but he had no idea how difficult her family could be when it came to Lucas. "How is he doing?"

"Released today after another eleven-month stint." She didn't expect any signs of rehabilitation until he initiated a change.

"Does your family know we're partners?"

"No. My career isn't a family topic."

"I'm sorry."

That hit her pride. "I don't need your pity. I make my own decisions."

He scooped up the rest of his burger.

Stupid pride. "Forget it. My brother's a sore subject. More like festering."

"No problem."

"Now you know about my supportive family. What about your parents?"

"Mom lives in Tulsa. Dad passed a year ago." He lifted a brow. "Dad's a sore subject. Maybe after six months or so, we can dive into my dysfunctional upbringing."

How long would it take for her to really know and understand Thatcher? She longed for a partner who predicted her actions and reactions just like she'd do his. Even a friend. Though he referred to their partnership as salt and pepper, she had no intentions of kowtowing to his way of working a case.

CHAPTER 8

Thatcher pressed Send on an e-mail to Nick Caswell requesting in detail the information discussed earlier. He copied Bethany and leaned back for some think time. The Caswell case kept turning up cold, but deepening the investigation and comparing the findings with Alicia Javon's case sparked hope. Had to keep digging.

Thatcher noted Mae Kenters's arrival thirty minutes before the scheduled hour. She was a pleasant, robust woman who swallowed with every word. Her apparent nervousness didn't mean she harbored information about a crime. Many people were uneasy in an FBI interview, as though simply being in the building meant they were accused of a crime. But instinct wouldn't let him close the file on her. He'd asked Bethany to lead out, sensing Mae would appreciate a female agent.

Bethany smiled. "I commend your hospice work. Certainly not a career where I'd excel."

"Thank you. I gain a lot of self-satisfaction in ministering to the suffering and their families. It's what God has purposed me to do."

Bethany patted a file. "Ms. Kenters, we have HPD records here of your statement regarding Ruth Caswell's death. I'm going to read it aloud. At this point, we aren't going over your testimony unless you've remembered a detail."

Ms. Kenters listened through the reading. "No, ma'am. Nothing's changed." Her hazel eyes clouded.

"Were you close to Mrs. Caswell?"

"Oh yes. We're more than nurses for our hospice patients. We're counselors and friends."

"What kind of things did you do for her other than nursing?"

"I read Scripture and sang hymns."

Bethany sighed. "I hope I have someone like you when I pass."

Something unrecognizable flickered in her eyes. Thatcher made a mental note.

"Had Mrs. Caswell mentioned being upset with anyone?" Bethany said.

"No. She was a sweet lady who lived her beliefs until she no longer breathed."

"Was your break always at the same time?"

"Pretty much. With her medication, she normally slept, and I took advantage of the time to brew a cup of tea."

"Did anyone else know your schedule?"

"No. I always had my cell phone with me, and it monitored Ruth's vitals."

"What about sound?"

"Just the vitals."

"So you didn't hear anything?"

Ms. Kenters pressed her lips together before speaking. "I've gone over this before with HPD, and I have nothing to offer."

Bethany tilted her head. "I've found posing questions in different ways and at different times often shakes a memory."

"Not for me. I'm straightforward. Remember everything."

"I have only a few more. Have you ever volunteered at Noah's Loft?"

"What is it?"

"A women's shelter."

"No, ma'am. I'm pretty busy without adding more work."

"Are you involved in any volunteer work?"

"I help out in the nursery at church."

Bethany smiled. "I do too. The toddlers."

"I care for the newborns." Ms. Kenters relaxed. "Not much different between them and many of my hospice patients. Both need care either coming into this world or leaving."

Bethany should have brought up babies sooner. Good job.

"I have a photo I'd like for you to see." Bethany opened the file and displayed Alicia's pic. "Do you recognize this woman?"

The woman stared at it with a blank expression. "I'm sorry. I wish I could help you."

"Special Agent Graves and I appreciate your willingness to assist us." Bethany replaced the photo. "Ms. Kenters, are you afraid for your life?"

Bethany had picked up on her fear too.

The woman blanched. "Should I be?"

"The killer could think you saw him crawl through the window."

"But I didn't." Ms. Kenters touched her throat. "I had a nightmare. Must be what you sense from me."

"May I suggest counseling to help you through the tragedy? I recommend not going out at night alone. In the meantime, I'll make sure the media is informed you have no idea what the killer looked like."

Bethany's strategy hit the excellent mark.

"Thank you," the woman whispered.

"Thanks for the clarification and your time today. An agent will escort you to a waiting area. I'll join you momentarily."

After the woman left, Thatcher slid into the same chair Mae Kenters had occupied. "You were outstanding."

"But?"

He smiled. "My gut tells me she knows more than what she's saying."

"I work on facts, and her responses line up with previous interviews."

Thatcher studied her. Bethany thought they were finished with Mae Kenters. But the woman showed fear in every movement.

CHAPTER 9

Bethany drove the few minutes home from the FBI building to her apartment. When she was assigned to the Houston office, she chose housing close by. Made sense. Still did. No reason to live close to her family with the hurricane-like problems between them. Reuniting with *Mamá* and *Papá* meant supporting Lucas and worshiping God in their church. *Papá* believed his denomination held the keys to heaven, and the rest of the family sided with him. She was estranged, shunned, and saw no hope of reconciliation. Truth was the only superglue that could mend the cracks in her family. Why did she keep thinking about it? She was such a type A personality even her blood type was A+. A fixer. A crusader. Perfectionist.

After a hectic day of studying reports, conducting and arranging interviews, creating a spreadsheet and graphs, combing through paperwork, and examining HPD write-ups on the victims, her head spun with the cacophony of data. No wonder. Although if today was an indication of how she and Thatcher complemented each other, she'd be back in civil rights before eight in the morning. Seemed like she stubbornly insisted on her own way too much of the time. If given the opportunity to prove herself, she'd apply herself.

Thatcher Graves—not at all what she'd expected and not at

all like the rumors. She'd heard the worst about him and had her shield ready for the overconfident womanizer. Today's Q & A revealed a couple of commonalities. Her brother was off-limits for discussion, and so was Thatcher's dad. The questions they'd tossed at each other had helped relieve some of her tension. Tomorrow they planned to give it another whirl during lunch. As long as they were still partners then.

The moment she stepped inside her apartment, her parrot greeted her. "You're lookin' good, girl."

"Thank you, Jasper." By habit, she looked for the piece of paper on the floor indicating if someone had been inside her apartment. Intact. She walked to his cage, opened it, and he perched on her hand. "Did you miss me?"

He leaned his head against her cheek. "Like a toothache."

She laughed. "Anything else?"

"Hide the gun. Hide the gun."

"Okay, Jasper."

"Call the cops."

"Are you hungry?"

"Order pizza."

"Not tonight." She kicked off her so-called comfy shoes and dropped her purse on the table. Jasper had been a part of her life for the past eight years—her sidekick, who could be sassy. And incredibly quick in picking up phrases. "I'm changing clothes."

"Can I watch?" His previous owner must have taught him that line.

"Not nice, Jasper."

"Sorry. Jasper's sweet."

"Yes," she said. "Jasper's sweet."

He rode on her shoulder to her bedroom, where she set him on her dresser. She unbuttoned her jacket and pulled out the pins holding her hair in place. The moment she released them, the throbbing around her scalp diminished. Couldn't wear the thick mess back too often.

She drew in the fragrance of lavender and vanilla, fresh and feminine. Her two-bedroom apartment was her sanctuary, soft colors of pale green and peach throughout. Every piece of furniture was white, pure and clean like she wanted her life. Accessories dipped into her love for distressed metals, mostly black with dried flowers.

The door to her closet wasn't completely closed. Odd, but she'd been scattered this morning. She slipped into sweatpants and a T-shirt while her stomach protested its empty condition.

Mamá had met her at the park yesterday and sent home frijoles and chiles rellenos. *Mamá* wanted her reconciled to the family, but Bethany refused to sacrifice her principles. A quick trip to the microwave and into her tummy. Of course *Papá* had no idea the two had met or he'd have been furious. He claimed his God blessed the meal, not Bethany's, as though she contaminated his food.

In the kitchen, she scraped *Mamá's* gift onto a favorite yellow, red, and green plate, covered it with wax paper, and stood on tiptoe to slip it into the microwave. While it warmed, she fed Jasper a tortilla smothered in peanut butter, his favorite, and allowed him to perch on her shoulder for a while longer.

Other things besides Jasper held priority this evening, beginning with the two murders and the killer's or—as she believed—killers' motive. Her mind raced with Thatcher's request to the FIG regarding a psychological profile with what they knew about the crimes. Perhaps an update? At the moment she saw no link between the two. Thatcher's reasoning of both women being murdered by a serial killer frustrated her.

I'm so predictable. First day on the job, and I want to make an arrest.

The microwave signaled her food was warm. She lifted it onto the counter. The smell of beans, peppers, and beef ushered her home. In the morning on the way to work, after *Papá* left for the shop and Lucas would still be asleep, she'd call *Mamá*. Maybe they could talk—really talk—about her brother.

After she'd eaten, she called Elizabeth, her friend and director of Noah's Loft, and confirmed Saturday's first volunteer assignment. Actually she wanted to ensure her friend would be there.

"Yes, you're on the schedule for one o'clock." Elizabeth's voice rang soft yet clear. "And we can really use you. How did your new assignment go today?"

"Crazy. Hectic. My head's spinning."

"Is your new partner young, old, married, single?" Elizabeth, the eternal romantic.

"Extremely good-looking if I could get past his personality. I made a huge mistake early on. But I plan to do better tomorrow."

"Rather you work violent crime than me. Seriously, Bethany? I'll take my residents and their problems any day over your job."

"Are you short on volunteers now with Alicia Javon's death?"

"You have no idea. I miss her already. She volunteered three days a week, and the women and kids loved her. We all did."

"I'm working her case."

"Do you think one of the residents might know something?" Elizabeth's voice grew cold.

"She could have mentioned a fear or a stalking."

"I shudder at the thought. Please don't tell me you want to use my precious ladies on your first day of volunteering."

"I care about oppressed women," Bethany said. "You haven't told them about my agent status, right?"

"Not a word. I promised you I'd keep your job a secret." Elizabeth's tone grew chillier.

"I don't want to jeopardize my relationship with those women or the investigation."

"Do you think that's fair when they've gone through so much?"

Bethany's stomach churned at the idea of upsetting her friend, but a murder needed to be solved. Actually two. "I'm not there to make arrests."

"But you want to question them about Alicia."

Bethany didn't want to argue with her. Elizabeth protected

the women and children at Noah's Loft like a mother hen. "You respect what she did for the residents, but you don't want her murder solved?"

"It's complicated."

"You love the residents and you want to keep them safe from those who've mistreated them, just as I do. You spend hours preparing them to enter society as strong and independent women. But when a killer steps in with his agenda, you hesitate?"

"That makes me sound horrible. No one here would hurt her."

Bethany wished she had the words to relay her passion for ending the killings. "Talking to them allows me to make sure Noah's Loft is free of predators. I'll ask if any of them want to share about Alicia. You and I could do this together."

After several seconds, Elizabeth sighed. "All right. I want Alicia's killer found too."

Bethany ended the call and stared at her cell phone. Had she just imposed on her good friend, the one who listened when her family treated her like three-day-old fish, the one who accepted her odd ways and left-brained thinking? She texted Elizabeth.

I care about u, dear friend. Sorry about pushing my agenda

Bethany placed her dishes in the dishwasher. Her phone alerted her to a text.

No problem. I understand. C U Saturday.

Yes! Thnx. U know me better than anyone.

I'm ur friend. And I want Alicia's murder solved.

I'm doing all I can 2 find him.

No need 2 prove anything 2 me. I know ur faith and ur heart 4 God.

Bethany's heart was heavy for far too many things. She quickly slipped into workout gear. Running six miles on the treadmill to alleviate some of the stress made sense, but sweating didn't alter the reality of wanting to help solve a murder while getting used to a partner who swore his gut told him more than his brains.

CHAPTER 10

Thatcher lowered his garage door and cut the engine to his car. What a day. A heavy workout had only succeeded in making him more tired. Leaning back against the headrest, he closed his eyes to focus on a total reliance on God to overcome the machinery of work tension.

Two murders. Two bodies with no obvious link. Yet something tied the victims together tight enough to get them killed. He mulled over the stolen items—antique guns, a Bible, and heirloom jewelry. What did they have in common? Unless the killer had connections, he'd have to hold on to the goods until the smoke cleared. Religious agenda might help the psychological profile.

Mae Kenters, caring hospice nurse, was concealing information. He wanted to explore her actions on the security camera footage. Nick Caswell said tonight he'd never believe Mae had anything to do with his mother's death.

Time and evidence would reveal the truth.

He wanted a ballistics report now, except he'd never get the lab to expedite the findings, not without solid proof to back up his serial killer theory. And he didn't want another body. Once Thatcher had eaten, he'd wrestle with it more.

He opened the car door and dug for his house key. So much to do in so little time. But that seemed to be the cliché for every violent crime case. He rode the elevator to his loft condo, then entered and breathed in the comforts of home. He'd chosen an open floor plan, no confining rooms for him. Since moving to the Hyde Park area of the Inner Loop, he'd enjoyed everything from the beautiful scenery to running along the bayou. But tonight, home failed to raise his spirits.

He turned the oven on broil and pulled out a pan and four pieces of last night's pepperoni pizza. The business of getting to know Bethany Sanchez . . . No-nonsense and drop-dead gorgeous. How could a woman have such huge brown eyes? He hoped her performance-oriented perfectionism didn't get them killed. Actually, they were survival skills from dealing with her family. To think her brother was Lucas Sanchez. Every law enforcement official in the city knew his name, and most had a few expletives to go with it.

After today, he questioned his instincts that a woman with her skills could term their partnership invincible. Despite the hunger gnawing at his belly and the dull ache at the base of his skull, he chuckled. Bethany obviously didn't know her father had also threatened to slice him into little pieces for arresting and testifying against his son.

With the cheese sizzling on his pizza, he scooped up a hot piece and ate while standing at the counter. He focused on Alicia Javon. Felix Danford demanded a search warrant upon the advice of his attorney. Thatcher understood the reasoning behind the legal procedure. Or was there a hidden agenda? Neither of the interviews with Danford or the Javon family rang true. Body language spoke louder than words, and none of them were telling the truth. Was Alicia really a beloved wife, mother, and competent woman in the business world, or was there something else?

Paul Javon didn't deny physically abusing his wife. But he also visibly regretted his actions and grieved her loss. Why did Alicia endure the beatings and continue to support him? Because of their daughters? But they were older, and why would they insist their mother stay in an unsafe environment? The younger, Carly, shied away from her father's touch. Thatcher made a note to request she come to the FBI office for further questioning, an interview Bethany wanted earlier in the day.

Could Alicia's religion have played into her choice to stick it out? Had she or her worthless husband initiated the counseling? Definitely a question for Pastor Lee. Glancing at the time, Thatcher dug into his pocket for the pastor's mobile number. Thirty seconds later he put his phone away. Pastor Lee hadn't appreciated the inquiry, but he did state Paul initiated the marriage counseling.

A file came through from Pastor Lee with notes about the Javons' sessions. Not much there. A few confusing sentences as if words had been deleted. But one thing surfaced—Paul requested his wife end all volunteer work so they could spend more time together. He felt she neglected him. She agreed. In fact, Alicia consented and took the blame for every issue. So this justified the ongoing abuse? According to the pastor's notes, Paul looked like a dutiful husband who had lost his job and needed his wife's support. What a bunch of garbage.

Was Alicia's volunteer work an opportunity to show her faith or escape her husband? The hefty inheritance from her parents' estate looked like a killer's motive. Although first conclusions in a case usually brought a timely arrest, something about Paul Javon as Scorpion didn't make sense, which confirmed a serial killer on the loose. Why end the life of Ruth Caswell, an old woman who had only days left on this earth?

Thatcher pushed the questions aside until tomorrow. A good night's sleep would help him find the connectors.

He picked up his phone to call Mom. The conversation with Bethany had reminded him of how much he valued his relationship with his only living family member. The dividing line with his dad had never been bridged, but Thatcher could make it up to his mother.

He pressed in her number. "This is your favorite son."

She giggled, a sweet sound he'd always treasured. "I only have one."

"And it's me."

"Good to hear your voice. How's your new partner?"

"She has potential."

"My evasive son. Do you have plans this weekend?"

Which meant, would he be flying to Tulsa? "On a big case, Mom. But soon."

They chatted for a few minutes, then said good night. He wanted to tell her about a decision he'd made, but it didn't happen. Too many times his choices upset her, and he had a feeling this one would send her over the top.

CHAPTER 11

Bethany phoned Thatcher to let him know she planned to stop by Noah's Loft before coming into the office.

"I want a few words with the director. It may be after eight thirty before I get there, depending on the traffic."

"How often do you plan to volunteer?"

"Two Saturdays a month for only a few hours. No one but the director is aware of my FBI affiliation. I'm hoping someone will have information about the Javon murder. The idea of waiting until Saturday to talk to the residents and staff gives the killer an opportunity to cover his tracks or strike again. I'll call when I'm on my way to the office. Any updates other than last night's conversation with Pastor Lee?"

"Just hunches, but we can discuss them later."

Hunches weren't facts and were worthless in a court of law, and they led to mistakes. Concluding the call, Bethany deliberated her own conclusions about yesterday's interviews. The partnership with Thatcher could be termed as in the dating stage, and she had to prove herself. But she refused to hold back on her own principles. After feeding Jasper, she stepped into her closet for a box of clothing articles to deliver this morning. No surprise she'd found clothes she'd never worn, products of a habit she detested. A few sweaters still had tags. At least someone would put these to good use.

Images of Alicia Javon and Ruth Caswell crept into her mind. Why did the innocent always suffer the most?

Once in her truck with a few minutes to spare, she pressed in *Mamá*'s cell phone number.

"What do you want, Bethany? You shouldn't call me," her mother said in Spanish.

"I wanted to see if you're okay. I'm on my way to see Elizabeth and—"

"You mean you're checking on Lucas."

She closed her eyes. "I suppose so."

"He'll be fine once he's rested and has good food in him. Jail hurts his heart."

You mean his pride. "What are his plans?"

"Why do you care?"

"Because he's my brother."

"I hear you have a new position at the FBI, and you're working with Thatcher Graves?"

"How did you find out?" And so soon?

"One of *Papá*'s friends is a police officer, and he told *Papá*. Said you two were working a woman's murder. Bethany, Agent Graves sent Lucas to jail the first time."

"Thatcher was only doing his job. He—"

"He hurt your brother. Can't you refuse to work with him?"

"What would you have me do, *Mamá*?"

She sighed. "Nothing. We're getting Lucas set up in his own apartment."

"So he has a job?"

"When he's healthy and mentally ready."

She clenched her jaw. "*Mamá*, you can't support him forever. Does he want to go back to school?"

"Enough. My precious son needs to heal. This second time in jail was very difficult, thanks to you."

"Would you have him call me?"

"So you can belittle him? Find an excuse to arrest him again?

Don't call until you're ready to be a member of this family. *Papá's* orders." Her mother said good-bye.

How would she get Lucas's number? The text she'd gotten from him earlier came from a blocked number. She called his old number but no one answered. Neither was there a voice mail box.

She turned on an FM station to classical music, soothing her mind as she drove to see Elizabeth. No surprise Lucas had persuaded their parents of his need to be taken care of. Nothing ever changed there.

A short while later, she pulled into the driveway of the unmarked facility known as Noah's Loft, a twelve-thousand-square-foot Tudor-style home that had been converted into a women's shelter. From the street, nothing indicated the circumstances of those who lived inside. An iron gate across the driveway could be interpreted as a way to keep a dog or a child from roaming instead of a means of protecting the residents. But it could be scaled.

The way her mind slid into possible crime scenarios, she could only imagine what an irate man could do if he learned his significant other or children had taken refuge within those walls. Many of the women and children had been physically abused. Two of her own cases in civil rights had once found refuge here. They'd gone on to secure a new life since then. At Noah's Loft they could restore their dignity and self-confidence. The children were homeschooled by volunteers to keep them safe. She'd seen the bloodcurdling results of domestic violence in her old neighborhood. A huge reason why she gave of her time and money for what too many ignored.

Approximately forty women and children lived here. Their identities were confidential, and they could stay as long as they desired. A board of directors supervised Elizabeth's goals of providing health care, GED studies, résumé assistance, homemaking skills, child care essentials, and assistance in finding vocational training so the women could become independent.

Bethany searched both sides of the street for vehicles with

passengers before lifting the box of nearly new clothes from her mocha-steel Ford Ranger. A resident met her at the door and stated Elizabeth was in her office.

A few moments later, Elizabeth and Bethany met in a small, cluttered room stacked high with donations not yet disbursed among the residents. Bethany added hers to the pile. She picked up a coloring book and a plastic bag of broken crayons from a chair, then stacked them onto the puzzles.

"I apologize for the mess." Elizabeth cringed. "But you already know it comes with the job."

"No need to apologize. Reminds me of being at my parents' with all my nieces and nephews—before I was eliminated from the family roster."

"Their loss." Her light-brown hair hung in waves past her shoulders.

"Lucas is out of jail. And my family learned about my transfer to violent crime and my new partner's name." Bethany stopped herself. "Know what? That's the last time you'll hear me whining about the mess. Time I got over it." She drew in a breath. "Hope you don't mind my stopping by this morning. Feel badly about how I pushed you last night."

"I was at fault too. Tired and on overload. I really see how a killer on the prowl could endanger the residents no matter how tight the security." Sadness swept over her face. "Alicia did a fabulous job with all of them. Usually it's our women and children who are in danger, not a volunteer. Especially not one as gracious and loving as Alicia. Who would want her dead?" She lifted a tissue from a box on her desk.

"Is there anything I can do?"

"I think encouraging the others to talk is a good idea. A memorial service is wise for closure." Elizabeth dabbed her nose. She didn't mention Bethany wanting to shake out any clues, and Bethany didn't bring it up. "I have a few things she left here, personal effects." She pointed to a box in the corner. "Her daughter Carly plans to pick them up this afternoon."

"My partner and I interviewed the family. They appear to be working through the grieving process."

"Alicia never mentioned her husband, but she talked about the girls. They're all musically inclined. Sometimes she sang to the children, and we all listened."

Bethany nodded. "I met her daughters. Beautiful."

When her pale-blue eyes pooled, Elizabeth grasped another tissue. "I'll snap out of this. Thought I'd gotten past the shock. I've arranged for our ladies' minister to do a few counseling sessions, except she's tied up for the next month. Fortunately a volunteer has stepped into her role. She's coming by five days a week."

"Wonderful."

"She's here now with several of the residents upstairs. Would you like to meet her?"

"Of course." These women needed continuous support, and a new face could help them through the process. "But first, I have a quick question—well, two. Do the names Mae Kenters or Ruth Caswell mean anything to you?"

"No, other than the Caswell woman's recent murder."

"Okay. Thanks. I'm ready to meet your new volunteer."

Elizabeth led Bethany up a flight of creaky stairs to a huge open space where a noisy group of women and children were gathered. The tattered blue sofa needed replacing. Her church supported Noah's Loft, and she'd make them aware of the need. Or she'd make the purchase herself.

"There she is," Elizabeth whispered and pointed. "Working a floor puzzle with the children."

A woman in her late thirties, wearing huge pink glasses, smiled, and Elizabeth beckoned her. "Dorian, do you have a minute? I'd like for you to meet someone."

Green eyes under a mop of short blonde hair met Bethany, and the slender figure popped up like one of the kids. She stepped over toys and arms and legs with an extended hand.

"This is Bethany Sanchez," Elizabeth said to the woman. "Bethany, I'd like you to meet Dorian Crawford."

"What a pleasure." Dorian pumped her hand. "Glad you're here. Are you staying? Goodness, you're pretty." The woman talked faster than an auctioneer.

"Thanks. I don't want to keep you. So glad you've stepped in for Alicia."

Dorian beamed. "I could never take her place, but I can do my part. We're all learning together."

"Miss Dorian," a small African American boy said. "Can we play Twister again?"

"Sure. In a few minutes. When we're done, we'll throw a few balls in the backyard. See if you can improve your batting average."

Bethany appreciated the woman's interest. Enthusiasm was the secret to staying young, and Dorian obviously had the energy to make a difference in the residents' lives.

One of the staff members from downstairs called to Elizabeth, and she excused herself.

"Alicia was quite involved with the residents here," Bethany said.

Dorian nodded like a bobblehead doll. "One of her specialties was helping them with English and grammar for their résumés. I'm not qualified. Barely made it through high school—too many years ago." Long bangs hung into her eyes. "But you'd be perfect. You look highly educated. We could use a person of your caliber. Do you have a day job?"

How quickly could Bethany excuse herself? "My job keeps me busy, unless I used my volunteer time twice a month."

"Can't you do any better?"

Bethany inwardly sighed. "One hour a week, on Saturday afternoons."

"Wonderful." Dorian clapped her hands as though she were ten.

"Understand my job could pull me away at a moment's notice."

She glared. "I'll see if I can find someone for those times. You know this is about commitment. I'd like your cell phone number."

"Elizabeth has it."

"Well, I'll be here in case you call in with other plans." She whirled around and descended the steps.

Bethany watched Dorian leave. Good thing she'd left before Bethany unleashed a lecture on manners. The possibility of the woman having a form of Asperger's or Tourette's stomped across her mind. Elizabeth must be really desperate for volunteers. Then again, what had Bethany gotten herself into? Okay . . . she could spend one hour a week to help women better themselves. Refusing had *selfish* written all over it, but Dorian needed to curb her outbursts. If it occurred again, Bethany would whip out a few guidelines.

She made her way to a group of women and chatted with them and the children. After an appropriate time she raised the question: "Were you friends with Alicia Javon?"

A woman tilted her head. "Because of her tutoring, my son and I will be moving from here to an apartment tomorrow."

"She taught me how to read English," another woman said.

A staff member mounted the stairway. "Miss Bethany, we have a problem. Your rear tire's flat."

Bethany phoned AAA while descending the stairs and making her way out to her truck. The rear sank to the pavement on the right side. Under her windshield wiper, a piece of paper was wrapped around a rusty nail and held together by a rubber band.

Reaching inside her purse, she pulled out a pair of latex gloves to explore whatever someone had left. Frustration hovered like a dark cloud.

You have no idea what I can do.

Mamá must have told Lucas where she was going. When would he stop his game?

CHAPTER 12

Thatcher listened to Bethany's explanation of why she was late returning from Noah's Loft. Flat tire. She stood in the doorway of his cubicle, ramrod straight with frown lines across her forehead. What had originally looked like a surefire way for her to gain insight into Alicia Javon's death now had a hitch.

"But if you can put up with the new volunteer, you have an opportunity to get closer to the women." He wouldn't have gotten involved volunteering in the first place. He did enough of that in college and grad school, but she must find it rewarding. "I don't recommend pulling your Glock on her. Might ruin your image."

Bethany grinned. "I'll do my best."

"Should we conduct a background on any of the residents?"

"Not at this point," she said. "Only Elizabeth is aware of my FBI status."

"You're going undercover?"

"Don't think so. But I'll find answers if any of the residents have insight into Alicia."

"Glad to see you made it today."

"You had doubts?"

"We both have, but we're overcomers."

She leaned against the side of his cubicle and tilted her head. "Thanks. I needed a little reinforcement."

"Keep frowning, and it'll stick."

"I'll think happy thoughts."

Oh, the sarcasm. "We have a busy day lined up. My preference for getting information is through people. Stats and online research are solid, but people can rarely disguise their true feelings."

She glanced away. "Have you profiled me?"

"I did."

She reddened. "I'm sure you saw that I'm a solid performer."

That was the Bethany Sanchez he expected. "Always." He laughed but she didn't respond. "On with the case. Let's check out Paul Javon's alibi. Won't take long to run by Rice University."

She jotted it down. "Thank you. I think it will change your perspective about who killed Alicia. What else?"

"Yesterday you wanted to talk to Carly Javon further, so let's bring her in for an interview."

"She doesn't think much of her dad, and I'd like to hear her explanation."

He pressed in Carly Javon's cell number and pushed Speaker. A gallon of coffee was fueling his reasoning, but this family had more than its share of secrets. He raked his fingers through his hair. Most families had closet stuff. His included. When the girl answered, he introduced himself.

"Why are you calling me?" Carly clipped each word.

"Your mother's unsolved murder is part of an FBI investigation." When she didn't respond, he continued, "We need to ask you a few more questions, preferably at our office."

"What kind of questions?"

"Your father is a person of interest."

"Why aren't you talking to him?"

"He'll be coming later."

She released an expletive he no longer used. "My mother's memorial service is at two this afternoon."

"You're not surprised by my call, Carly. Special Agent Sanchez and I read your body language. You didn't want a thing to do with your father yesterday."

"Right," she whispered. "I expected you to contact me."

"Do you or Shannon have reason to be afraid?" Her silence told him all he wanted to know. "Do you want us to pick you up?"

"I can be there around ten thirty," Carly said. "The office on 290? Big green building?"

"Yes. You can bring your sister, especially if she's concerned about her safety."

"Shannon spent the night with a friend. She and Dad get along okay. It's me who has the big mouth and refuses to take his orders."

Thatcher confirmed the time again, then noted the interview on his phone's calendar. He was quickly beginning to value Bethany's perception, although she'd not refer to it as intuition. "How are you?" He pointed to his chair. "This is not the hot seat, but a clear-the-air seat."

"Is this a part of my training?"

"Didn't you read the manual?"

"Yes, but this part must have slipped my mind." She eased onto the chair. "Now what?" She felt under the seat. "No gum here or wires to record my responses."

He chuckled. "Okay, your eyes tell me little sleep. If it's personal, none of my business, except you have to be alert for the job. If you spent the night beating yourself up over yesterday, then we need to talk."

"Not personal. I studied the behavioral habits of serial killers, in case you're right."

"Tell me what you've learned. My guess is you memorized all the reports."

She massaged her neck muscles. "From the top ten characteristics of serial killers, which you already know, I'm aware of what to look for when we conduct interviews."

He nodded. "And?"

"Social outcasts. Highly intelligent. Lousy home life. Substance abuse. The same list could be applied to any criminal." Her eyes clouded for a moment. "I studied a serial murder report on a symposium done in August and September of 2005. Were you there?"

"No, but my partner was. Bethany, I'm glad you're diligent, but you also need your rest."

"I will . . . tonight."

"Great. Why didn't you tell me you had diabetes?"

She blew out frustration. "It's controlled with diet, and I plan to have snacks with me all the time. Looks like my trust level with you has hit bottom."

"We can only move up."

CHAPTER 13

Thatcher and Bethany sat across from Carly Javon at a table in an FBI interview room. He handed the young woman a bottle of water. Her tangled, auburn hair indicated more of a crisis than the absence of a hairbrush. When Thatcher had met her at the Javon home, he'd noted an attractive young woman who sharply resembled her mother. She also had a pronounced limp. His suspicions about the family grew. Yesterday she endured tough questions, but her appearance wasn't unkempt. What had happened?

Carly uncapped the bottle of water with shaky fingers and took a drink. "Thanks. It's good and cold. This is being recorded, right?"

"Yes." He allowed his eyes to speak caring into his words. "You have a limp."

"Temporary." She replaced the cap, avoiding him. "I fell down the stairs."

"Like your mother?"

She picked at chipped, deep-purple nail polish. "We're both clumsy."

"Did you both fall the same way?"

She snapped to attention. "Are the injuries relevant to finding her killer?" Her trembling lips betrayed fragile emotions.

"Depends if your mother's broken arm was the result of a push."

71

"It's not important."

"Were you pushed?" Thatcher said gently. "Agent Sanchez and I think you were hurt like your mother was." He nodded at Bethany to continue the interview. This needed a woman's touch, and she had the expertise from her years of working civil rights.

"Carly, most people have families who love and support each other," she said. "Then there are nightmare families. We don't want to tell anyone about the dysfunction. Sometimes we ignore it. Will it to go away. It's not an argument or a difference of opinion, but an evil grip."

Thatcher heard sincerity in his partner's words, and Lucas Sanchez's name bannered across his mind.

"Is your home a nightmare?" Bethany said. "You're not alone. I'm right there with you, and I'm a good listener."

Carly slipped a tangled strand of hair behind her ear. No eye contact.

Bethany leaned in. "We can't help you or solve your mother's murder unless you're honest with us."

She lifted a tear-glazed face. "I understand. That's why I'm here, to do whatever I can to find my mother's killer. It's just hard."

"The truth frees us from pain."

"I hope so. Dad thinks Mom's been lumped into a serial killer's pile, and no one cares."

"We do. Lots of people do, and we're not stopping until the killer is found. Right now, Agent Graves has more questions."

How could he get Carly to admit her father had caused her injury? Would she press charges against him? "Were you out late last night?"

She shook her head. "I know what you're thinking. I look awful, but I haven't been partying. I spent the night with my aunt. Too tired this morning to shower, fix myself up. Then there's the memorial. Guess I'll fix myself up for the service, for Mom."

Depression? "I thought your family was staying at a hotel?"

"Too close for me." She focused on the water bottle. "Even when Dad's in a good mood, I can't stand being around him."

"Why?"

"We've never gotten along. It's worse since Mom's gone."

"Are you saying since she died, he's taking out his anger on you?"

"Yes," she said. "I act more like Mom. Must be a reminder."

"Did your father have anything to do with the death of your mother?"

"He might have." She breathed in deeply. "But I can't figure out how."

"What makes you think so?"

"He has a horrible temper. After he lost his job, he exploded over the smallest things. It got worse the longer he was unemployed." She took another sip of water. "He can act like the best dad and husband in the world. You saw how he offered information, cried, behaved like he really cared. The weird thing is he can snap into rage at a moment's notice."

"In what way?"

"In the beginning, he just yelled. Then he started shoving Mom around. Then used his fists." Her face hardened. "Mom always forgave him and could calm him down even when he was hitting her. If he was mad at me, she stood between us." A painful memory seemed to hold her captive. "I never understood why she took it. She could have kicked him out. I'd have helped her."

"I'm sorry." And he meant it. "Did your dad push your mother down the stairs?"

She nodded. "Mom never wore flip-flops. What a lie."

"And you?"

Carly shifted in her seat. "I forgot you were recording this."

"No one's going to hurt you. Take another drink of water." When she did, he continued. "I know these questions are difficult, but we have to get to the bottom of what happened to your mother. Did your dad cause your accident?"

"Yes," she whispered.

"What else can you tell us?"

Carly glanced at Bethany.

"Go ahead. It's safe here."

"Dad's controlling. He checked the car mileage when Mom went to work, the grocery store, church, to volunteer, or whatever. If it was a tiny bit over what he expected, he went ballistic."

"Did your mother complain, argue with him?"

"Sometimes. Another thing—Mom caught him having an affair. Not sure how she found out." Carly toyed with the bottle cap. "They had terrible arguments."

"Did she threaten divorce?"

"Yes. He beat her until she passed out, and he had to take her to the ER." Carly's features were like stone. "Why did she let him do that to her?"

"Maybe she hoped he'd get better," Bethany said. "They were in counseling. Did you see any improvement?"

"No. Made it worse. Guess he could play the good guy for only so long." She bit her lip hard.

"Does your dad own a gun?"

"I don't think so." She took another sip of water. "Something's not right. He demanded we go with him to the concert, and then Mom's murdered."

"He forced you and Shannon to go with him?"

"He threatened to hurt Mom."

Thatcher admired the young woman's struggle to be strong. "Her death is not your fault."

Her shoulders slumped. "My aunt and uncle said the same thing, but I can't get past it."

Thatcher had investigated too many family relationships that erupted into violence. "What size shoe does your dad wear?"

Carly gave him a quizzical stare. "Thirteen."

That diminished the likelihood of Paul Javon's being on the

Caswell premises when Ruth was killed. The shoe imprint there indicated an eight and a half.

"Do you suspect the woman your dad's been seeing?" Bethany said.

Her face was a swirl of fiery emotions. "I hate the thought of Dad planning Mom's death. But I suspect him and his girlfriend." For a moment it looked like she'd weep, but she regained her composure. "I don't know her name or what she looks like."

He'd let Bethany continue. Carly appeared more comfortable with her.

"Another question—did your dad leave during the concert performance?"

She glanced away. "I don't think so, but I was sitting beside Shannon, not him."

"Did your mother talk to you or Shannon about the girlfriend?"

"I'm not sure Shannon knows. I overhead Mom and Dad arguing."

"Would the woman's information be on your mother's phone? Maybe a photo?" Bethany said.

"Remember, Dad said her cell was lost. Thought the killer took it."

Thatcher recalled that the call logs of Alicia's and Paul's phone numbers indicated nothing out of the ordinary. He motioned to Bethany for him to pose a question. "Do you believe your father may have a burner phone?"

"Possibly. Maybe I can find it."

"Not a wise move," he said. "Don't go there."

"I have to."

He nodded at Bethany rather than argue and upset Carly.

"You aren't equipped to solve your mother's murder," Bethany said. "You're of no help to her or your family if you're hurt."

She offered a faint smile. "I'm moving out this afternoon. He knows about it, just not when, and he's not happy. Told me I had to pack and move when he could supervise what I took. Also told me I had to give him my key."

Naturally. Her father realized Carly had the guts to tell the truth about their family issues. And now he wouldn't have someone to take out his frustration on.

"Are you moving into an apartment?" Bethany's voice trailed soft, caring.

"No, with my aunt and uncle."

"Promise us you'll be careful."

"I will, and I made a copy of the house key. Left it at my aunt's house. He might change the locks though."

"Carly, that's dangerous. I strongly advise you to let us handle the investigation."

"I don't care. I heard him threaten Mom too many times. He knows how she died." Her eyes darkened. "Mom left her inheritance to Shannon and me, and he's trying to fight it. We're supposed to pay for our living expenses and reimburse him for what Mom spent on our education and our cars. He won't get a penny from me."

Bethany shook her head. "Would he come after you at your aunt and uncle's home?"

"My uncle would shoot him. He has a gun."

Sounded like spontaneous combustion.

"Could we have their names and contact information?"

Carly pulled a piece of paper from her purse. "Already have it for you. If something happens to me or Shannon, you'll arrest Dad, right?"

"He'll be here later this afternoon for further questioning. I don't think he'd come after either of you when he knows we suspect him of having information about your mother's death."

Carly wrapped her fingers around the water bottle. "I've seen him angry. I know what he's capable of doing."

"If we gave you the date of Ruth Caswell's death, could you confirm your father's whereabouts?" Thatcher valued Bethany's investigative skills, and he'd agreed to scoping out the concert area of Rice University, but these cases had serial killer stamped all over them.

"I can try." Carly pulled up her phone's calendar while Bethany provided the date and time. A few seconds later, she lifted her gaze. "He was at home when Mrs. Caswell was killed. I remember because he had bronchitis and kept us awake with his coughing. Does that mean he's no longer a suspect in connection with Mom?"

Thatcher continued before Bethany discounted his theory. "Does the name Mae Kenters mean anything to you?"

"No, sir."

"Agent Sanchez and I, along with the entire FBI, aren't resting until we find answers."

"I figured you'd not walk away. You come across as a bad—well, you know what I mean, but you're the kind of guy who'll find out what happened to Mom." She swept a look at them. "Both of you."

"Thanks," he said. "I'm concerned about your plans today. Is your uncle helping you move?"

"Yes, sir. Dad and Shannon are going to dinner tonight. He'll be furious I packed up while he was gone, but I'm not stupid. I'd like to search my mom's room."

Thatcher believed her father had the temper to do serious damage. "You're not a trained investigator."

She lifted her chin. "Won't do any good to try to stop me."

Talking down her stubbornness was like punching a brick wall. At least she had her aunt and uncle's help in making the transition. "What about Shannon's safety?"

"She's afraid of Dad. Will do whatever he asks."

"If anything goes wrong, call us or 911. Just move your personal belongings and stay clear." He stared into her eyes. Frightened and alone, no matter how brave she tried to be.

"Yes, sir."

Bethany and Thatcher thanked Carly for her assistance and escorted her from the building. They watched her drive away from the visitor parking area.

"Paul Javon was involved in his wife's death," Bethany said. "No doubt in my mind. I'm filing for a search warrant in case he decides his cooperation with us is over."

✳ ✳ ✳

11:50 A.M. TUESDAY

Bethany hurried with Thatcher to the Rice University security office. Her heart thudded at the prospect of arresting Javon for his wife's murder. Had he excused himself in the middle of the concert? She hoped so, and soon they'd have access to the university's security cameras.

"You really think this is going to seal it for Javon?" Thatcher said, opening the door to the main office.

"I do. He has all the characteristics and motive of a wife killer. Trust me on this—any coincidence to Ruth Caswell's murder is contrived."

The two viewed the camera footage on the university's system. The three Javons entered the concert building one hour before the murder and left together after the concert was over.

"Can we see the fire exit?" she said. But it revealed nothing. "The restrooms?"

"Bethany, it's not possible." Thatcher pointed to the screen. "He couldn't have left the hall without this camera catching him."

Thatcher was right, and she'd wasted his time. Shaking her head, she stepped away from the computer. She'd been so sure Javon had killed Alicia. "This proves he was here," she said. "But I'm not convinced that he didn't hire someone to kill her, like his girlfriend."

CHAPTER 14

1:15 P.M. TUESDAY

Bethany reviewed the status on the search warrant for Danford Accounting. The judge hadn't ruled on it, the process of a slow system. She and Thatcher had gotten takeout for lunch in order to discuss interviews. They'd subpoenaed Mae Kenters's cell phone records and pored over security camera footage from Ruth Caswell's and traffic cams near the Javons' home.

"I think we should attend Alicia's memorial service," Thatcher said.

Disbelief rattled her nerves. "Are you kidding? I don't think the killer will get a case of the guilts and confess."

"Depends on the motive. I'd like to see who's at the service."

"By making a grand entrance?"

"Not exactly."

Realization hit her and she slid him a sideways glance. "Are you suggesting we do the incognito thing and observe who enters the church?"

"I am."

"Your gut instinct says we'll see someone unusual?"

"You got it."

"I so disagree. We could work more efficiently by laying out both deaths, working with Quantico on analytics. Examining the current evidence. The security cam footage review is tedious work."

79

"Didn't you say we could work organically?"

The man would drive her crazy. "In the sense of working together, not chasing a rabbit trail. Except . . . the killer could be at the church to toss off suspicion. Like whoever Javon hired to kill his wife."

"This will give us a list of who attends Alicia's compared to Ruth Caswell's funeral. Might lead us in the right direction."

So they were back to his serial killer theory. "I have no faith in your speculation, but you're on."

Forty minutes later, they parked his Mustang far enough from the church so as not to attract attention. Thatcher used his binoculars and snapped photos with his phone while she jotted down his comments—mostly nonessential to the case.

"This feels like a rejected script from an *NCIS* episode." He snapped another pic.

"Which one?"

"Oh, you watch it."

"For laughs. Why are so few people here? I expected the church to be packed since the Javons are Houstonians."

"Paul has limited it to invited guests only. I see a man checking IDs at the door. Wanna bet our names aren't on the list?" Thatcher said.

"I only bet on sure things," she said a little more sharply than she intended. "But it does look unlikely."

"I'll let you ask him this afternoon. Might make our interview a little lively."

Pastor Lee stepped outside the front of the church and shook hands with Felix Danford. Thatcher indicated she record the exchange.

"I'm curious why Danford's on the elite list," Thatcher said.

"Because Javon's afraid of what he might say."

"Another question for the afternoon."

The photos would have to be run through the FIG before anything substantial resulted from comparing both services. And

Javon probably wouldn't tell them a thing because he had too much to lose.

"A day and a half into the job and neither of us are bleeding." He swung a smile her way.

No wonder he had a reputation with the ladies. Definitely off-limits between FBI guidelines and her stipulation of not getting involved with a gamer.

The only things they had in common were sending Lucas to jail and a commitment to bring in killers.

* * *

5:45 P.M. TUESDAY

Bethany stood outside an interview room with Thatcher and observed Paul Javon. With Carly's revelation about him having an affair, Bethany wanted a confession to all his underhanded activities. Drama led the way with his dabbing beneath his eyes, burying his face in his hands, and glancing around the small room.

"He's ensuring we catch his grief on camera," Thatcher said. "But I don't buy it."

"I'm relying on his temper to take precedence in the interview. Alicia's memorial service lasted all of thirty minutes. Incredibly sad for a woman who'd been well loved."

"Maybe his display is for a postponed dinner with Shannon. Why don't you lead out? He obviously prefers bullying women, and I'd like to see him lose control."

The two entered the interview room. Javon stared up with red-rimmed eyes, wearing sorrow like a medal of honor. He indicated he and Shannon had a dinner date later. Didn't want to leave his daughter alone. No mention of Carly.

"How can I help you?" Javon said, his words syrupy. "I admit the past few days have been a nightmare. Media want interviews, and I'm not up to it, especially when I have nothing new to say about HPD's and the FBI's ineptitude at finding my wife's killer. Is this necessary within a couple hours of Alicia's memorial?"

Bethany pushed sympathy into her tone. "We want this solved quickly. I imagine Carly and Shannon are comforting each other, and we'll do our best to expedite our questioning." She placed his file before her. "A few things have come to our attention."

"Yes, ma'am." He folded his hands on the table.

"Per your words to Pastor Lee, anger issues have stalked you, but you found counseling, dealt with it, and took positive steps to save your marriage."

"Correct."

"I'm sure, in the midst of this tragedy, those issues have resurfaced. How are you handling the anger?"

He inhaled deeply. Her benefit or his? "By talking to Pastor Lee and being honest about my feelings to my daughters."

"Could you explain how Carly received her leg injury?"

A muscle twitched beneath his eye. "She slipped on a wet spot in the kitchen. Why?"

Bethany stared into his face, stilling every emotion. "She told us she'd fallen down the stairs."

Javon saddened his expression. "With all the turmoil, I'd forgotten."

"We want to ensure she's not being abused."

His eyes flashed. "I'd never hurt my daughters."

"Where did beating your wife fall within your specs for abuse?"

He stiffened. "I may need to seek an attorney if this inappropriate questioning continues."

She'd succeeded in making him angrier. "We wouldn't want to interfere with your citizen's rights." She paused and hoped he was worried about what she'd ask next. "Why were those attending the service today limited to invited guests?"

"You people find out everything."

She plastered another smile. "We do."

"The girls and I decided the best way to move on with our lives was to have a short, intimate memorial. When we're able to cremate her, we'll do something else."

"Did Pastor Lee suggest this?"

"My idea."

"Your idea . . . and your daughters agreed."

"Exactly."

"Do you own a gun?"

He smiled. "Yes, a .22."

"The FBI team failed to find it during their search."

"It's in a repair shop. I'll give you the phone number."

"Thank you. Mr. Javon, how long have you been having an affair?"

He narrowed his brows. "What a ridiculous accusation."

"Is it? We'd like her name, please." She positioned her pen over a legal pad.

"Who concocted such a tale?"

"A reliable source. Special Agent Graves and I would like the woman's name."

He slammed his hand down on the table. "There is no other woman."

"Is this a formal denial?"

"Most assuredly. I demand to know the source of your lies."

She picked up his file and leafed through it. "Alicia wouldn't be the first wife murdered for another woman. In fact, with Shannon and Carly inheriting the eight million dollars, I'm concerned about their safety."

"I'm their father. It's my duty to protect them. You have a poisoned mind." He rose from the chair.

"Sit down." Bethany dumped force into her words. "Special Agent Graves, do you have questions for Mr. Javon?"

Thatcher reached out to shake his hand. "I apologize for not sympathizing with your loss earlier. Sometimes Special Agent Sanchez jumps ahead in stressful situations."

He sneered. "I noticed. Do you have a complaint department?"

Thatched nodded. "I'll send you the information via e-mail. Do you have any idea who would implicate you in this tragedy?"

"I don't. But trust me, when I find out, they will regret their actions."

"Sounds like you've been set up. All leads are helpful in solving your wife's murder."

"I'll handle the confrontation." He tossed a chilling glare at Bethany. "My way."

"By withholding information, we can arrest you for obstruction of justice in a murder investigation."

He glanced away, then back to her, his eyes hard as stone. "I have no idea who'd suspect me of having a relationship with anyone other than my wife. I meant I'd ask around. Of course I'd give you any names."

Bethany waved her hand. "Taking matters into your own hands could get you arrested."

He laughed and arched his back. "Did the bureau need to fill a quota when they hired you? Or did you sleep your way into your role?"

At last, Javon's colors had shown through.

"For your information," Thatcher said, "the FBI recruits the highly intelligent and skilled into our ranks. Special Agent Sanchez is not the one under scrutiny."

She shoved aside Javon's filthy accusation. "Mr. Javon, your affair is why you were brought back in for questioning."

CHAPTER 15

Bethany parked her truck in the covered parking area and locked it before heading to her apartment. A bit of a chill met her in the shadows, matching her mood. Her head whirled with the past two days. How would the investigation continue without evidence to arrest Paul Javon? Curiosity about the attendance for the Javon and Caswell services played havoc with her mind. Thatcher had been right—a connection would go a long way in solving the murders. At least then they'd have concrete information to explore.

She opened her apartment door.

Fury burned to her toes.

Her sofa, barely six months old, was slashed. A broken lamp. An overturned chair and small table.

"Jasper! Where are you?"

Her pet flew from her bedroom, down the hall, and to her shoulder. He trembled and nuzzled against her head.

"It's okay, fella. I'm here." She pulled the Glock from her purse with one hand and pressed in 911 with the other. Protocol stated she should back out and wait for HPD, but she ignored the rules, a rarity, and cleared every room. Nothing missing, only a mess to clean up. She reported the burglary to the FBI and texted Thatcher. Not sure why the latter, except to keep him informed.

Want me 2 come by?

Kind remark. Rather surprising. No thanx. I'm ok.

Past experience with Lucas indicated the intruder might be her brother. Especially with the flat tire and note from this morning. But she had no proof.

Two hours later, after completing the police officer's questioning and searching through dumped drawers and closet items, she discovered her grandmother's brooch was missing. The piece of jewelry had little monetary value, and only one person would have reason to take it. Only one person would break in and leave valuables behind and take something sentimental. Lucas.

She took Jasper with her and drove to her parents' home. The parrot still perched on her shoulder and would not be persuaded to take refuge in his cage. No longer did her pulse race wildly or her face grow hot. She didn't care about the reception she'd receive or the shouting match. She had her father's temper, and it was about to be unleashed.

As she parked at the curb in front of the Sanchez home, a twinge of "don't do this" nudged at her conscience. She shoved the warning aside. Prayers knocked at her heart, but she refused them.

She could more easily forgive a stranger than a family member who had nothing better to do than destroy property and steal while frightening a helpless bird.

The moment she approached the porch with Jasper, Lucas opened the door and closed it behind him without snapping on the outside light. He must have been expecting her. How long had it been since she'd seen him? The flick of a lighter illuminated his hardened features as he fired up a cigarette.

"What brings you here, Sis?" He drew in the nicotine. "Didn't the parents tell you to stay away?"

"I want to talk to you." She kept her voice even.

"Has Jasper become a guard bird?"

"Maybe. Let's take a walk." She started to add a bit of sarcasm about his healing from jail, but thought otherwise.

"What if I don't want to?"

"I'm not giving you a choice. We can have the conversation right here, and those inside can hear, or privately. You choose."

"For a minute, I thought you might pull your gun on me."

"Don't tempt me."

He shook his head. "Whatever you have to say can be said in earshot of *Papá* and *Mamá*. They know all you've done. Even working with Thatcher Graves."

"Did you follow me this morning and slash the tire on my truck?"

He chuckled. "Nope, but I wish I'd thought of it."

"Did you break into my apartment?"

He swore. *"¿Estás loca?"*

"No. Did you break into my apartment?"

"I've been right here catching up on sleep or at the shop all day."

"Was *Mamá* with you?"

"None of your business. I'm not a criminal."

"Prove it."

The door opened and *Papá* stepped in front of Lucas. "Leave. You're not welcome here ever."

Regret washed over her. What had she been thinking to interrupt her parents' evening? "All right."

"Is that all you have to say this time of night?" *Papá's* voice rose.

"I apologize for the late hour, but I needed to talk to Lucas."

"Now you have."

"May I ask where he was today?"

"None of your business unless you have a warrant. *Lárgate.*"

She'd leave his house because she'd been disrespectful, letting her rage rule her good sense. *"Perdóname."*

"¿Perdonarte? Imposible," Papá said. "You've done too much to destroy the family."

She left, her face once more in flames. This wouldn't end well, not with Lucas's history of violence and her family's history of coddling him.

CHAPTER 16

Thatcher drove with Bethany to Danford Accounting to thoroughly investigate the company and Alicia's coworkers. Fortunately, the judge had been in a good mood and signed their subpoenas and search warrants for Felix Danford and Paul Javon without a hitch. Murder had a way of pushing things.

Another pair of agents had been assigned to search Paul Javon's home. Not much Thatcher and Bethany could do, considering they'd interviewed him twice and were at a stalemate until he confessed to an affair.

Bethany sat on the passenger side, quiet, with her attention seemingly on the road. He'd made a commitment to get to know her better, find out more about what made her tick. She needed to talk about last night's break-in. Just because an agent underwent training didn't mean the violation of private property was any less taxing on the psyche.

Until they understood each other, the trust factor wasn't there.

"Are you okay?" he said. "Any word on your burglary?"

"I'm fine."

"Want to talk?"

"No." She rubbed the back of her neck. "Didn't get much sleep last night with all the activity. That's all."

"I'm a good listener, and whatever you say stays with me. Do you have an idea who broke into your place?"

"Of course not," she snapped.

"I have a feeling you do."

"Shelve it."

"Old boyfriend?"

"Enough, Thatcher. It's none of your business."

Her phone notified her of a text, and she took a look. Tense.

"Something for us?"

"No." She sighed. "Family stuff. Lucas is yanking my chain."

"Bethany, I don't ask to pry. I ask because I care about my partner."

She tossed him a pale glance and he grasped a snippet of her internal MO. Wasn't there anyone in her life to nurture her? Care?

She leaned her head against the door. "Okay, I'll do my best. Lucas isn't pleased with me. After your testimony sent my brother to jail, I did the same thing. Only my role got him eleven more months."

Whoa. Bethany had sent her brother to jail?

"Don't look so shocked, Thatcher. I walked into my sister's house, and Lucas was holding a gun to my brother-in-law's head. I made an arrest. He resisted and I took him down." She straightened. "My brother-in-law backed me up. Our testimony convicted him."

"I'd seen he'd been incarcerated for armed robbery. Never had a clue you were involved. Of course I didn't look either. On the night I arrested him, I was at a club on the northeast side of town looking for a murder suspect when he pulled a knife on a man. Killed him and claimed self-defense. Only got nine months."

"Sounds like Lucas."

"Is your family concerned he might retaliate against you or your brother-in-law?"

"Not hardly. I'm the black sheep. *Papá*'s banned me from the house. The ironic part is my sister was furious with me. Said the problem was a family matter. She hasn't spoken to me since, and she requested the church annul her marriage. Her ex-husband moved to Denver. Good thing. Lucas would have come after him."

Her family was old-school, and he knew plenty of Hispanic families who didn't operate that way. No wonder she'd shown a bond with Carly. "I'm sorry."

"I don't need your pity. And I'm not getting all defensive since I offered the reason for my preoccupation. The situation's on my mind. No big thing. Conversation ended about Lucas. Shouldn't have brought it up."

It *was* a big thing. Two days with Bethany and already he'd put together more of what had driven her to the FBI. She'd seen a friend die, and her family had ostracized her. Word from those who'd worked with her said she never talked about personal matters. Lucas must be a real piece of work, and her family must toss the guilt card on a regular basis.

As he'd concluded, the family hadn't won any awards.

And Bethany viewed her work as fulfilling deep emotional needs that she should be receiving from family.

She took a breath. "Are you taking the lead on Felix Danford's interview? In my mood, I might rip his head off."

He chuckled to break the tension. "Sure. I considered phoning him, but a face-to-face allows us to read his body language, even with Botox. I'd bet lunch he omitted a few things the other day."

"If you need a little help intimidating him, I'm your gal."

"Remind me never to make you mad." How could one olive-skinned beauty scare him to his toes?

Seated in Danford's office with the door closed, Thatcher smiled into the face of the firm's CEO. "Mr. Danford, we have additional questions for you. Special Agent Sanchez and I will not take much of your time, especially since agents are here imaging your files and conducting interviews with employees."

Danford folded his arms across his chest. "I thought you and I were finished. I have deadlines."

"They can wait," Thatcher said. "We have an unsolved murder, and a few matters have come to our attention."

He glared. "I don't have time to play games."

"And I forgot my chess set. I think you knew about Alicia's spousal abuse," he said. "So what was our initial interview about?"

He tapped his fingers on the desk. "She was a good friend, a loyal employee—"

"Cut the feel-good line. Were you in love with her?"

Danford placed both hands on his desk. "How dare you."

"Simply answer the question."

He stared at Thatcher. Deliberating his response? "Alicia had a husband." Danford fired his words like an automatic rifle.

"But you wanted more, right? I bet her injuries made you furious. Angry enough to kill."

Danford continued to glare. "Look. I cared for Alicia, and I think she felt the same about me. The relationship never got far enough for either of us to act. She wouldn't allow it."

"Are you in a relationship with anyone else?"

"No. I waited for Alicia." His face softened. "An incredible woman. Never understood her loyalty to God when her Bible says she could have left him. I urged her to kick the jerk out. Many times."

"Why didn't she?"

"Wanted to stick it out until her oldest daughter graduated from college. Not sure why the younger didn't play into the picture."

"What else?"

Danford refolded his arms. "I talked to her at length about the situation because . . . I loved her, and I was afraid he'd kill her. I didn't understand why she let him hurt her." He whirled his chair away from Thatcher and Bethany. "Give me a moment here."

"It's all right, Mr. Danford. We want the truth. We're not here to judge how you felt about Alicia."

He faced them again. "He called me with an invitation to her funeral. I went because she'd have wanted me there, and I had a few things to unload on him afterward."

"Like what?"

"His abuse and how I'd do everything within my power to have him arrested."

"What was his response?"

"Two words—'no evidence.'"

Spoken by a man who had a violent temper. "Can you give us anything else?"

"Alicia said he could be charming. So over-the-top that he made her crazy. The good moments were outstanding, but the bad ones were a nightmare. At times the relationship seemed like love, and other times she feared for herself and her daughters. When she finally made a decision to leave him, she ended up with a bullet in her head."

He believed Danford. No reason to lie. "What else?"

"He was having an affair. She discovered it by accident. Ammunition for divorce. I gave her my attorney's name, and she started the paperwork."

More confirmation from Carly's interview. "Did she confront him?"

"Yes, about the affair and her intentions to file for divorce. He broke her arm and knocked around the youngest daughter."

"So you cared about her but did nothing while he physically abused her."

His eyes hardened. "She asked me to stay out of it, said she was afraid he'd come after me. As if I couldn't handle myself against the coward. Friday afternoon before her death, she met with the attorney and a protective order was in the works. She believed that with a divorce, she and the girls would be free from him and we could make plans for the future."

"Did she mention her sizable inheritance?"

"I don't know a thing about her finances. Money wasn't an issue with us."

"Where were you when she was killed?"

"Meeting with clients in Dallas. I can back up my where-abouts." He leaned over his desk. "Look, Agent Graves, if I'd schemed to kill a member of the Javon family, it would have been her no-good husband. I'd have blown him to bits a long time ago with no remorse. So if he shows up dead, then you and I can have a little talk. I might even confess." He reached for a sticky note and scribbled something. "Here's my attorney's number. He can confirm my Dallas business trip."

"Fair enough. You've been a tremendous help. Have you given us everything this time?"

"In the beginning I thought her husband killed her, but the media claims a serial killer committed the crime. Alicia told me Javon threatened to kill her and their daughters if she left him."

More ammunition to arrest Paul Javon, but at this point Danford's word against his wouldn't stand in court, especially when Javon wasn't at home during his wife's murder. Later Thatcher would check to see if a restraining order had been filed and check out Danford's alibi. "I'm sorry about Alicia's death. Sounds like you two planned a good life together."

"All destroyed. Alicia wouldn't break her wedding vows. She needed someone to talk to, and I was safe. We talked at work only. No phone calls, texts, or e-mails. Nothing linking our friendship. In fact she'd leave her phone in her office during meetings in case he planted a bug."

"Had you met her husband before the funeral?"

"Social functions only. Possessive in every sense of the word. Wouldn't let her out of his sight. She told me he checked the mileage every evening when she returned from work to make sure she wasn't cheating on him." He slapped the top of his desk. "I'm telling you, the jerk was behind her murder."

CHAPTER 17

Thatcher's mind spun with Danford's confession as he drove the short distance from the Galleria to the FBI office. He doubted Alicia had told anyone about the attraction, but had anyone else at the office picked up on it?

Traffic brought them to a halt, frustrating when he had a job to do. "Can't believe this. Bumper-to-bumper and no reason why."

Bethany reached for her phone. "I'll check to see if there's been an accident. Could—"

Something sailed by Thatcher's face, splintering the driver's side window and sounding like someone had thrown gravel. A bullet! A sound he'd recognize anywhere.

He whipped his car onto the shoulder and out of the way of oncoming vehicles. Ducking, he drew his firearm while snapping his attention to Bethany, who sat stunned.

"Get down!"

When she didn't move, he pushed her face into her lap. He bent below the steering wheel.

"What's wrong with you?" He caught himself before destroying any confidence she might have. "Focus. The shot came from my side." He released her.

"I froze," she said through a ragged breath. "I wasn't prepared for this. Thinking about the case and—"

"An agent is always prepared." He exhaled to control his anger while waiting for another bullet to whiz by. He studied her. No blood. A hole on the passenger's side window indicated the bullet's exit. Shattered glass that looked like rock salt covered her lap and arm. She trembled. "Are you okay?"

"Yes." Her firm response didn't match her white knuckles, telling him she was berating herself.

A car horn blared behind him, and he resumed his driving position to pull as far right as possible. How could they return fire in creeping traffic?

Bethany rose, peering in every direction with her weapon in hand. "I'm sorry. Haven't been involved in a firefight for a long time."

"Get your training pants on." He bit back another remark while zeroing in on other vehicles. This wouldn't work between them when he couldn't trust her. He opened the door and stepped out to ensure no one else had been targeted. "Your performance is that of a rookie."

"It won't happen again," she said.

"Are you sure you're ready for this?"

She looked all around them, the shattered glass still on her lap. "Don't close the book on me, okay?" Her cell chirped with a text as she stepped out of the car and continued to scan the traffic to their left. "Do you see anyone?"

"Not a thing suspicious. The left lane has sped ahead. We'll take a look at the traffic cams once we're back at the office."

Her cell sounded the text reminder.

"Is that important?"

She grabbed her phone. "Lucas is at it again."

"What did he say?"

"That he's not finished with me. 'Don't sleep.'"

A chill snaked its way up his spine. "Are you sure the sender is your brother?"

"Oh yeah. He's done this kind of thing for years. I've got it handled."

Thatcher doubted Lucas could be controlled by anything but

a locked cell. "Radio in the shooting and arrange for the FBI to pick up my Mustang and deliver a loaner car."

A delay they didn't need.

✳ ✳ ✳

12:03 P.M. WEDNESDAY

Bethany sensed Thatcher standing in the door of her cubicle, and willing him away wouldn't cause him to leave.

"Do you need something?" she said, shoving an experienced agent tone into her words.

"Checking on you." He handed her a Diet Dr Pepper. "Did you eat?"

She frowned.

"Just asking."

"Not yet."

"I was hard on you."

Actually, he wasn't hard enough. "I could have gotten us or innocent people killed."

"You can't undo life. We move on and learn from our mistakes. I've jumped into things that should have gotten me killed. Adrenaline is my high, and I thrive on it."

When he smiled, her pulse sped and she caught her own emotions. "Appreciate your grace. Can't believe the traffic cams didn't provide any more of a lead than a string of vehicles hurtling down the interstate."

"We were followed and targeted. Scorpion is nervous."

After her blunder, she refused to argue with him. "What about your car?"

"Initially, all they have is a couple of bullet holes. Lab's checking it out. What's Lucas drive?"

"Chromed-out Harley. I looked after the shooting but didn't see him." She shook her head. "He's a bully. No way would he risk his freedom for revenge, especially by firing at federal agents. I have to think this through."

"Okay."

"The woman who schedules appointments at *Papá*'s shop is a friend. I'll text her." And she did.

"We have updates, thanks to the other agents on the cases," he said. "Traffic cameras in and around the two murders cleared. The landscaping company Ruth Caswell used has not done business for the Javons or Danford Accounting. Neither did the victims use the same housekeeping services. Backgrounds are in the works for employees who cleaned both homes. Nick Caswell affirmed no repairs of any type had been completed to his mother's home in over a year, and Mae Kenters always brought her own food. Blood types, insurance companies, and health provider reports are incomplete."

Bethany's head spun, and her stomach sounded like a cannon. "Can we grab lunch?"

"For one small person, you have the loudest growl."

"My stomach, right?" Irritation crept in with her hunger issues. "Let me fill you in, Thatcher. I'm also a victim of a disease called hangry."

"What's that?"

"I get angry when I don't eat."

"Sure you don't want to drive over to see Paul Javon?"

She raised a finger. "Good call. I'd like to have his girlfriend's name."

They choose a deli near the office. As she eased into his car, her stomach protested again. How embarrassing.

"I pulled out my stash of snacks from the Mustang." He flipped up the console between them. "Here's dried fruit and nuts, peanut butter crackers, and PowerBars."

No one had ever looked out for her like this, and gratitude rolled through her. "I thought you were transferring personal things into a plastic bag when we got the loaner. You got these for me?"

"Yes. Don't want my partner going into diabetic shock."

Thatcher believed she couldn't do her job because of health issues. "I'm fine."

"How about 'thank you'?"

"I'm sorry. Yes, thank you for your thoughtfulness."

At the deli, they ordered at the counter and found a corner booth near a side exit. Her controllable-without-meds diabetes would never come between her and her job.

"You have the shakes," he said.

"Not for long." A text from her friend confirmed Lucas had been at the shop with *Papá* since nine thirty. "Glad I made sure he wasn't up to no good."

"Me too. Neither of us are on his friend list."

"We have something in common." She stared into his dark-brown eyes, nearly hypnotized by their depths. *Stop it, girl!* "Did you believe Danford?" she said.

"Innocent of anything except being in love with Alicia. Not a hint of anything to discredit him."

She unwrapped her utensils from a thick paper napkin. "How did you know he was in love with Alicia?"

"His eyes softened when he spoke her name."

She hadn't seen it. "And what if he'd denied his attraction?"

"Are you going to buck my every move?"

"Is that what I'm doing?"

"You tell me."

His face tightened, and she regretted her lack of restraint. Disrespecting her father last night, messing up the earlier shooting, and now insulting her partner. *Please, God, help me. Is the constant juggle of this investigation and my family's issues setting me up for a fall?* She liked Thatcher. He treated her respectfully even when she deserved a shutdown, and he was entitled to the same from her. "Thatcher, I apologize. I'm being an oversensitive, irritating woman. No excuse."

"I'd rather have a spunky partner. Tell me, what would you have done before asking Danford about his relationship with Alicia?"

She took a deep breath. "I'd have checked security cameras in the building, pulled phone records, and had a few facts before I posed it. Carly mentioned Javon's girlfriend, but with Danford you had nothing but your gut."

He smiled with no condemnation. "Maybe you're just hangry."

She shrugged. "How long did it take you to learn the job?"

"Still learning."

A server set their food before them—for Bethany, a wild salmon salad, and for Thatcher, a roasted turkey breast club. She said a quick, silent prayer, then dug into her meal. After a few bites, she scrolled through messages. "Danford's alibi in Dallas checked out." She glanced into Thatcher's face. "And Alicia did file a restraining order, but it wasn't served."

"I'm suggesting surveillance on Javon." He took a bite of his sandwich. "His girlfriend might be persuaded to talk, once we locate her."

Their cells buzzed with a message, and she checked hers first. "The comparison of those who attended Alicia's memorial and Ruth's funeral are in, and we have no similarities."

"I still want to run the photos against facial recognition. Long shot, but who knows?"

She studied him, a man who believed their partnership had the potential to be unstoppable. Would they ever see eye-to-eye on a case, or would their methods delay solving two murders?

"Your eyes glaze over when you concentrate," he said.

"Always thinking. I hope Carly Javon moved in with her aunt and uncle."

"Call her."

She pressed in the young woman's cell number and waited. The call went to voice mail. "Hey, Carly, this is Special Agent Bethany Sanchez. Checking in to make sure you're okay." After requesting the young woman return her call, she pulled up her contact information and phoned the landline Carly had given for her aunt and uncle, Anita and Ken Cooke. A woman answered.

Bethany confirmed the woman was Anita Cooke and introduced herself. "I'm looking for Carly Javon. She gave me your
number if I couldn't reach her directly."

"Is this the agent she's been speaking with?"

"Yes, ma'am. Is she available?"

"Yes, of course. I needed to make sure her dad wasn't up to one
of his tricks again. The man needs to be locked up permanently.
Let me get her for you."

A few moments later Carly responded.

"So glad you made the move."

"Thanks. I found something you might be able to use. I'm now
sure my mother's death was no surprise to my dad."

An alarm triggered for the young woman's safety. "What have
you learned?"

"I'd rather discuss it with you in person."

"Okay," Bethany said slowly. "Did you put yourself in danger?"

"Depends on how you look at it."

"How soon are you available?"

"I can be there at three thirty."

"Good." She'd seen the results of family disputes in the streets
and the repercussions of violated civil rights. Maybe she hadn't
heard God correctly when she prayed about the change in divisions.
"Carly, I have no idea what you've been doing, but I'm concerned."

"What would you do if your mother had been murdered?"

CHAPTER 18

Bethany and Thatcher observed Carly Javon through one-way glass. She sat alone in an interview room. An ugly bruise on the left side of her face shone through a generous layer of makeup. Her hair was combed, and she wore jeans and a Rice University T-shirt.

Bethany hated this for Carly—the scars might never heal. "Looking at her makes me want to cuff her dad personally."

"What if her injuries have nothing to do with Alicia's murder?"

"It would at least get the jerk off the streets."

"Are you going to persuade Carly to press charges against dear old Dad?" Thatcher said.

"Her mother wouldn't have filed charges, but she's spunky."

Bethany opened the door to the interview room. "Carly, what's the story on your face?"

"The truth or a lame excuse?" She stared wide-eyed.

Bethany liked her. Now to see if she had the courage to nail her dad. "What do you think?"

"He didn't like the idea of me living with my aunt and uncle. Or taking my violin."

"Did you let yourself back into the house?"

"I did, and he surprised me. Not pretty." Carly clenched her jaw.

"How about allowing us to arrest him?" She eased onto a chair across from the girl. Thatcher joined them.

"Where do I sign? I came to you instead of the police because I trust you."

"Begin with what happened."

"He accused me of lying to you about his and Mom's relationship. He threatened my aunt and uncle. He also told me I was just like my mother and deserved whatever happened to me."

The coward needed to be stopped. "Was Shannon there?"

"She had a class."

"So you're ready to fight back?"

"I want him found guilty for his hand in killing my mother. Agent Sanchez, I'm convinced he knows how my mother died."

"Why?"

"I should have told you this sooner. Sorry. Mom confided in me about leaving him. I wanted to find out what he'd been doing online, so I searched through his deleted e-mails. If he'd been smart, he'd have permanently gotten rid of them. Anyway, four days before Mom was killed, he sent an inquiry to their attorney requesting a change in their wills, specifically that Mom didn't name Carly and me as beneficiaries, just him. He also wanted to know if the trust fund had him listed in the event Shannon and I were no longer alive." She drew in a sob. "I didn't see where the attorney responded."

No indication of those deleted e-mails had been reported by the investigators. Had they been permanently erased after Carly had seen them? "Was it the same computer we imaged?" Thatcher said.

"No. He has a laptop. He had plenty of time to hide or destroy evidence."

Bethany took the young woman's hand. "We realize how difficult this is for you."

Carly nodded. "If he's not stopped, he'll hurt my aunt and uncle. Maybe kill them too." She reached inside her purse and pulled out a tissue. "You called at the right time. I'm angry and I ache all over. Ready to do whatever it takes to have him arrested for murder, beginning with what he did to me last night."

"Excellent decision. What about your sister?" Bethany said.

"I think she's okay." A sad smile with a cracked and bleeding lip. "Shannon is so afraid of Dad that she'd never say a thing against him. But I have my priorities, and it's not bowing to him. None of this will stop me from getting my education. Mom set up a trust fund for me and Shannon a few years ago so we can finish and go on to grad school. Actually there's enough for doctorate work too. I could live on my own, but my aunt is Mom's sister, and I care about her."

"Does your aunt or uncle have any information about your mother's death? Do we need to question them?"

Carly shook her head. "My mother didn't want to involve them. They've always come to me with worry about Mom."

"Do you think your father was serious about changing and just couldn't?"

She snorted. "No. I think it was a front, the good guy role. The other woman probably has a lot to do with it. I mean, he had what he wanted—Mom supporting him and the girlfriend. When I was back home last night, I tried to find his girlfriend's name and Mom's cell phone. I don't believe for a minute it was stolen. But Dad keeps his bedroom door locked. Got caught before I could break in."

Bethany captured Thatcher's attention for him to take over. "We have a search warrant for your parents' home," he said. "Although your father gave us permission without one. You're a brave girl to come here twice to help. Can you tell me if any home repairs were done in the last few months?"

"No."

"Pizza deliveries?"

"Sure. Always used the same restaurant because they had coupons." When he handed her a pad of paper, she wrote the company and phone number.

"Have you learned anything new about Mom's murder?"

"We're making progress."

Bethany wished he'd agree with her about Paul Javon's guilt.

"You've helped us so much today," Thatcher said. "And you're filing charges before you leave, right?"

"Yes, sir."

"Your mom would be proud of you."

"I hope so. At least while he's in jail, he won't be hurting anyone."

Bethany refused to discount a threat to the Javon girls. "Have you talked Shannon into moving out?"

"She doesn't think Dad will hit her. I told her I used to feel the same way until he bloodied my nose. But I'm not giving up. She has a boyfriend, and he knows about the problems at home."

Could be another violent crime. "Promise me and Agent Graves you'll not go back into your dad's house for any reason. It's much too dangerous."

"Even when he's in jail? Doesn't matter. I have to learn the truth."

"There's nowhere you could look for anything the FBI hasn't already detailed," Bethany said.

Carly smiled. "Probably not."

CHAPTER 19

Bethany shut down her computer, ready to end the day. Slow progress with the case, but Paul Javon had been arrested on aggravated domestic assault charges and would see a judge in the morning. Carly consulted her uncle's attorney for legal counsel and gave him Pastor Lee's name. Paul Javon could be convicted for continuous violence against the family, which meant a heavy fine or two to ten years in prison.

She saw Thatcher leaning against the doorway of her cubicle. How could one man look so good?

"Want to grab something to eat?" he said.

They could discuss the case. Not a bad idea. "Can I run home and change clothes first?"

"Sorry. I'm on a time crunch."

He must have a date. "We can make it another time. Breakfast? On me?"

He raked his fingers through his hair. What was his problem? The cases? Had SSA Preston given her the ax? Did Thatcher need to talk?

"Know what? We can go now. In fact, I'm ready."

"Bethany, I have a gig. That's the reason I can't go later."

"What kind of a . . . gig?"

107

"Not many people know this, but I'm part of a band. When I can, I join them."

She hadn't seen that coming. "What do you play?"

"Guitar."

"What kind of music?"

"Country-western."

"My fav. Count me in." She grabbed her purse from her desk drawer. "I have jeans and boots in my truck. Leftovers from a western-day event at church. Won't take but a minute to change."

"Sure, but you don't have to do this. You'll be alone while I warm up with the rest of the guys and while we're playing sets until midnight."

"I can handle it." Watching Thatcher onstage with a guitar would be priceless. She'd be sure to snap a few pics. "I'll get into character."

"Hat too?"

"I draw the line there." She laughed. "I can hardly wait."

"Right. Hope you aren't disappointed."

At a local restaurant, they ordered chicken-fried steak, mashed potatoes, and rolls, with a salad to balance it out. Thatcher let her know the evening could change on a dime. "Although there are lots of agents on this case, we could get a call."

Time to focus on the murders. "Wish we were making more headway."

"Three days into it, we have an abuser in jail."

But not the killer. "Maybe a few days and assault charges will loosen his tongue."

"I doubt it."

At seven thirty, they pulled into the parking lot of a huge country-western club in west Houston. It often hosted big names from Nashville. Impressive.

Three men unloaded equipment from a van parked in front of the rustic entrance. "The rest of the guys are here," Thatcher said. "Ever been to this club?"

"No. Do you play here often?"

"Depends on how you look at it. My schedule means I might have to replace myself at the last minute. But I have someone who can fill in." He released his seat belt. "This is a great stress reliever. I want you to keep what happens tonight to yourself. Only two other agents and SSA Preston know about my hobby."

"Okay. If I want to blackmail you, this would be it?"

"Right." He feigned irritation, but his lips curved into a smile.

"I wanted to take pics, but I'll restrain myself. Who are the agents?"

"Grayson Hall and Laurel Evertson. We graduated from Quantico together. Also, Daniel Hilton, Laurel's fiancé." They exited his car, and he grabbed his guitar from the trunk. Two of the band members waved. "I've never brought a girl to a gig."

Bethany laughed. The confident agent who flirted with the ladies seemed uncomfortable. "Why did you invite me?"

Thatcher stared at her. "I honestly don't know. Maybe it's a way for you to get to know me better. I'm a risk taker."

"Not so sure I'm ready to unleash much more of my inner personal life." He already knew about her dad and brother. The rest was boring.

Inside the dimly lit club, a jukebox played the latest Keith Urban. Alcohol assaulted her nose, and she ordered a Diet Dr Pepper. She eased into a seat near the dance floor and watched Thatcher and the three guys set up equipment and warm up. He introduced her as a friend. Curiosity coursed through her about his guitar-playing expertise.

By eight thirty, the club was filled. Weird. Most places didn't pack a crowd until ten or ten thirty. Two cowboy types approached her for the extra seat, but she told them it was saved for one of the band members.

The band picked up their instruments. Thatcher took center stage. She started. Was he the lead singer? Thatcher Graves a singing cowboy? She drew in a breath. What if he was terrible? What would she say?

At the strum of his guitar, a blonde with more curves than Bethany would ever own made her way to Thatcher. She said something and he snickered. A moment later he shook his head. Maybe some of the office chatter was true.

Thatcher played a few chords. "Thank you for joining us tonight." He strummed the opening bars of a tune, and the crowd applauded. "So is this what you want to hear?"

When he broke into a song, Bethany shivered to her toes. Never had she imagined the clear, low tones coming from him. She didn't recognize the song, but with the chorus of "When all my dreams come true, they'll all be about you," the crowd roared, and so did she. His voice gave her goose bumps.

She listened and kept smiling. Couldn't help herself. Had he sung professionally?

After the first twenty-minute set, he joined her with a glass of water.

"Okay, you blew me away," she said. "You might have missed your calling."

He took a long drink of water, and she saw him from a different angle. Definitely a unique persona from Special Agent Thatcher Graves. This was a carefree nature she'd seen only glimpses of in the few short days they'd worked together.

"At one time, I recorded on a label in Nashville. Helped me through college. I wanted to continue with the music while practicing psychology, but my dad didn't approve of either career choice. He was right. The FBI is where I belong."

Another small hint of the real Thatcher Graves. "So when you can't make a gig, which one of the guys fills in?"

"Female singer. No competition."

"You're really good. I'm glad I came."

"Just keep it to yourself."

"I will. Ever work undercover with the band?"

He grinned. "Maybe. But not tonight."

The blonde from earlier moved closer and finagled her way onto his lap. She wrapped her arms around his neck. "Thatcher, I'm hurt. You haven't called me in weeks." She kissed him, but he turned away.

"I've been busy. Can't you see I'm with someone?"

Bethany avoided the scene and watched a waitress deliver a pitcher of beer and glasses to a table beside them. The shadow of an Hispanic man in the far corner captured her attention. For a moment she thought it was Lucas. . . . Should she excuse herself for the ladies' room? Check out the man at the far table?

The man stood, much too heavy for her brother. *Get a grip.* Lucas had better things to do than stalk his sister.

The blonde laughed. "Since when did you go for a Mexican?" she said. "She must be really good."

He scooted her off his lap and onto her feet. "Insulting my date doesn't make you look good."

The blonde swore and walked off.

"Sorry," he whispered. "She just confirmed all the gossip you've heard. The new Thatcher hasn't surfaced enough yet."

"Who is the new Thatcher?"

"I'm trying to show it."

By twelve thirty, they were driving back into town. Exhaustion pelted her body, and she'd be tired in the morning. Yet tonight had been worth it, and she was filled with admiration for Thatcher's talent. Women were all over him tonight, but he didn't seem interested. Maybe one day she'd ask to tag along again.

"I have the country-western band going. So what's something unusual about you?" he said.

"Nothing you could blackmail me about." Actually there was plenty about her brother and family she wouldn't want told. "I have an African gray parrot. His name's Jasper, and he has a huge vocabulary."

"Does he sing?"

"Sometimes. He does a mean head bob to salsa."

Her phone buzzed with a text, and she took a quick look.

Bethany, u keep bad company. Guess u will live & die with Graves.

CHAPTER 20

Thatcher invited Bethany for coffee at Starbucks near the FBI office. They both ordered breakfast sandwiches and black coffee. Two things in common this morning, except he added a scone.

"Are you sleeping any better?" He blew into the hot coffee. Usually he requested an ice cube to cool it. This morning his mind spun in too many directions.

"Sort of."

Which explained why he received texts all hours of the night. "So you think we should concentrate on Alicia's death."

"The Caswell murder keeps turning up cold. Nothing from Mae Kenters or the traffic cam footage gave us a lead."

"I don't give up, remember? I believe the murders are a serial killing."

"Gut instinct doesn't stand up in court. Paul Javon has motive oozing out his pores. Ruth Caswell hadn't been beaten. In fact, she didn't have a bruise on her."

"Aren't we feisty this morning?"

Her face softened. "I only meant we needed evidence. Can you tell me more about your reasoning?"

"The same method of execution and the two plastic scorpions link the cases. Alicia's broken arm was prior to her murder." Thatcher sipped his coffee. "The majority of serial killers pick

113

their victims at random. They kill because they can. The psychological gratification is their key. Most serial killers satisfy the blood demon, pacifying their craving for a while, and then lay low for months. Not in our cases. Have you analyzed it all?"

"Just shoving information into my head's data bank."

He nodded. "Anything kicking around in your head?"

"I'm thinking . . . constantly. Everything about Javon points to him shoving Alicia out of the way and devising a plan to eliminate his daughters for the eight mil. If I could only find proof."

"I want to bring in Shannon. She's the aloof one. Carly seems to protect her, and I'd like to know why."

"Danford said Alicia originally wasn't going to leave Paul until Shannon graduated from college."

He typed into his phone. "I'll arrange it when we get to the office."

She nibbled on her sandwich. "Why is it you know more about me than I do you?"

"I assumed the office gossip filled you in."

Her dimples masked the tough-girl agent. "I haven't seen that side."

He chuckled, realizing his reputation would haunt him forever. A report came in on both phones. "We have camera footage at Ruth Caswell's prior to Mae Kenters leaving the room for her break."

"Inside and outside the home?"

"Right. I'll want to zoom in on this at the office."

They finished their breakfast and were walking to the parking lot when another text alerted Bethany, and she snatched it. She paled and glanced around them.

"What's wrong?"

"Odd text."

"It obviously shook you up. A blocked number again?"

"Yes. Was Lucas at Starbucks? I always make sure to notice who's inside a place when I enter, but I didn't see him."

"What did he say?"

She handed him the phone. Drank 2 red-l b4 u arrived. Always 1 step ahead of u. Watch 4 me when you least expect it.

"Lucas wasn't in the coffee shop. And it really bothers me the sender knows every step you take."

She shook her head. "Wouldn't be the first time he kept tabs on me. He's been at this since I was a freshman in high school. Don't waste your time on my brother. We have more important things to do."

Thatcher's protective nature urged him to say more, but she'd take offense. Didn't stop the apprehension.

CHAPTER 21

At the office, Bethany noted Shannon Javon had a 4:15 interview today. The young woman could very well lawyer up. Odd, her father's lawyer phoned earlier stating his client had volunteered to take a polygraph. Fat good that did when it wasn't admissible in court.

Paul Javon had jail duty until Monday. When the judge heard "person of interest" regarding the serial murder case, he added mandatory anger management classes along with ninety-six hours of community service. Javon pleaded innocent to domestic abuse charges, but Carly's battered body and testimony proved otherwise. Shannon refused to affirm her sister's allegations against their father. But maybe she'd have time to think about it before their afternoon interview.

The security camera footage at Ruth Caswell's home prior to the crime failed to implicate Mae Kenters. Another dead end. Another point for the cold-case side.

Her computer alerted her to an e-mail from *Mamá*. Never uplifting news.

I'm too upset to call, so I'm sending an e-mail. If your brother comes to your apartment, don't let him in. He's gone off the deep end. Around nine this morning, he came back from a motorcycle ride. Stone drunk and high. Said he needed money. When we explained we didn't have cash at the house because of giving him money the day before, he said bad things and punched a hole in the living room wall. I don't know where we went wrong with him.

Your *papá* went to the bank to draw out a few thousand dollars. He says the more we give Lucas, the more he'll see how much we love him and change. Sorry to bother you. I only meant to warn you.

Don't let your *papá* know about this. I'm deleting it from my Sent file like you showed me.

Instead of responding to her mother's e-mail, she pressed in her parents' landline number and hoped *Papá* wasn't around to answer. Her brother had played the role of a bully his whole life. Why couldn't her parents see that?

Her mother answered.

"*Mamá*, are you okay?"

"I think so. Your *papá's* in the garage banging on something. Isn't going to work until after lunch. He called Lucas and left a voice message telling him the money was here." She sniffed, and Bethany envisioned her sitting alone in the kitchen.

Papá only worked in the garage when he was upset. *Mamá* cleaned house. Her brother broke the law. Bethany went shopping.

"Are you afraid?"

"Of my own son? Never. He's so hurt and troubled. Jail did that to him."

"He was this way before jail."

"He has nothing but his motorcycle. Life's been so unfair to him."

Bethany swallowed her frustration. "It's his fault he has no money or a job. You've helped him so many times he feels entitled. I bet he's never thanked you or *Papá*."

"I shouldn't be talking to you. Just be safe."

"I'm not letting him inside my apartment, and I can take care of myself."

"You call us to come get him. No point in involving the police." *Mamá* gasped. "You wouldn't shoot your own brother!"

A dull ache mounted in Bethany's skull. "At least in jail he wasn't drinking or fighting."

"I should hang up before your *papá* comes in."

"Right. For a moment I forgot I've been excommunicated from the church and my family." Bethany stopped herself before saying more. "I'm sorry. I'm being disrespectful. I love you, and I appreciate your letting me know about Lucas. Does he have the same cell number?"

"Don't call him. It would only upset him more." Her mother hung up without a good-bye or indicating Lucas had a different number.

An hour later, Bethany picked up her cell phone for the third time. Should she call Lucas or leave the situation alone? He'd hammered their relationship perhaps beyond repair. Her twenty-seven-year-old brother had a track record of poor choices, abandoned children, and multiple incarcerations. Bethany sighed. He was the son *Papá* had always wanted and could do no wrong. He—

Stop going over the situation. The past didn't have to dictate the future. Either she was committed to Lucas's betterment or not. Just not in the same way as her family.

She stared at her phone. Elizabeth had repeatedly told her she'd never be the one to help Lucas see the light. He held too much malevolence against her. The only prayer she could muster was "Help." Could he strike back any worse than he already had? His texts were annoying, but stealing *Abuela*'s brooch was low.

When no message came from heaven, she pressed in his old number.

He answered on the third ring. "Why are you bothering me?" He compared her to something too vile for her to think about.

"I wanted to see how you're doing."

"What do you think? Finally got out of jail, where they treated me worse than a dog. Does that answer your question?"

Jail wasn't designed to be a five-star resort. "Are you at the shop?"

"None of your business. Look, I have stuff to do. Don't call me anymore. You destroyed my life, remember? The rest of my family cares. They'll give me whatever I want. You have no part in my life."

"Because I want to help you stay out of jail?" Her heart sank to her toes.

"Aren't you the righteous one? This is your fault. The only reason you're not in my shoes is because you have your fancy FBI job. You never had to scrape for a living. You're nothing but a nosy—"

"Hey, enough."

He swore. "I see your type on every street corner. Sleep around with any man who'll help you get to the top."

The typical irrational Lucas response to anyone who tried to reason with him. But his lies hurt, and she refused to get into more of a verbal battle.

"No answer, huh?" he smirked.

"Lucas, stop the texts, and I want *Abuela*'s brooch returned."

"No one gives me orders. Since you're such a good FBI agent, work on your and Special Agent Graves's obituaries. He has the same nowhere future."

Her stomach lurched. "Are you threatening FBI agents? It's a federal offense."

"So have me arrested. Won't be the first time." He hung up.

✳ ✳ ✳

4:20 P.M. THURSDAY

Bethany escorted Shannon Javon from the reception area to an interview room where Thatcher waited. Not one word from the young woman until she was seated.

"This is ridiculous," Shannon said. "I'm only doing this for Carly."

This was the docile sister? Or was it a tough-girl act? "How is she?" Bethany poured sweetness into every word.

"AWOL. She belongs at home."

"Why?"

"Dad wants her there when he returns."

"So he can knock her around, or has he started on you?"

"He loves us, and with Mom gone, we need to be united as a family. The lies you people feed her have to be stopped." Shannon's fingernails were bitten to the quick.

"What lies?"

"The ones Carly keeps telling about our parents' relationship. She told the judge that Dad had contacted his attorney about their wills, requesting Carly and I be removed from Mom's inheritance. She even said Dad wanted to know if our trust funds reverted to him in the event of our deaths." She sobbed. "You influenced Carly to make our dad look evil."

"Shannon, we had nothing to do with your sister's testimony. Remember she took an oath to tell the truth. We have the court report. Special Agent Graves, would you like to read Paul Javon's response to Carly's claims?"

Thatcher nodded. "Your father admitted to the accusation. You were there." He picked up the court's proceedings. "He said Alicia had consulted an attorney about a divorce and he wanted to make sure she wouldn't leave him penniless with his disability. In addition, your father said Alicia was turning you and Carly against him. Is that true?"

Shannon's shoulders lifted and fell. "She wasn't turning us against Dad. Please tell me why I'm here. The nightmare doesn't stop."

Sympathy washed over Bethany. She recognized a weak young woman. "Are you holding back any information about your mother's killer?"

"No, ma'am."

"What about the name of your father's girlfriend?"

Shannon blanched. "I'll tell you the same thing I told the judge—I never heard Dad mention another woman."

"Did he have unexplained time away from home?"

"I don't know."

"Did your father abuse your mother?"

Shannon squeezed her fingers into her palms. "I refuse to answer such a question. You have Carly's statement. No matter how I respond, I hurt a family member."

"Do you believe your father had your mother murdered?"

Tears filled her eyes. "Are you insane?"

Bethany bored the young woman's face with a firm gaze. "Yes or no."

"My father is all I have left. Conversation ended."

CHAPTER 22

Thatcher closed his garage door. The rental was so small his hair brushed against the roof. Shattered windows in his Mustang, still in the FBI shop, ground at his nerves. Remembering his new partner's initial reaction to the shooting made him question what would happen the next time. Not an *if* but a *when*. This had nothing to do with requalifying with their firearms on a regular basis, but everything to do with a clear head. He walked to the elevator and finally into his home. As soon as his keys landed on the kitchen table, his cell phone rang—SSA Alan Preston. Not good.

"Yes, sir."

"Scorpion's daring us to find him." Preston's flat tone indicated the killer had struck again.

"Another victim?"

"Right. Got a call from HPD. This time a homeless man by the name of Ansel Spree, found with a bullet hole to the forehead and a plastic scorpion on his chest. The scorpion is identical to the other two, as though the killer bought a pack of them. HPD is sweeping the crime scene and agents are en route."

Could the killer have gotten sloppy this time? "When did it happen?"

"Estimation is between nine and eleven. I'm sending you the report now. I need you and Agent Sanchez on the scene ASAP."

Thatcher jotted a few notes about the victim and the address where he'd been found. "Have you contacted Bethany?"

"Not yet."

"Sir, I'll call her and explain the situation. She left about thirty minutes ago."

"Find a link. Both of you in my office at eight in the morning with evidence, not a deer-in-the-headlights look."

Maybe they'd have this figured out by then. "Yes, sir." When they finished, he phoned Bethany.

She answered on the first ring. "Is this another copycat like Alicia Javon?" she said after he gave her the update.

"Seriously? Get rid of that theory. Scorpion must have a list. Just wish we had his parameters. I'm sending you the initial report. The victim was found off Elgin in the Third Ward."

"Text me the address, and I'll meet you there."

Thatcher met her at the crime scene amid flashing red lights and two unmarked cars that he recognized as agents' vehicles. Bethany stepped from her truck, dressed in jeans, boots, and a black leather jacket, with her hair swept back in a ponytail. Undeniably attractive.

"I read the report on the way here," she said.

"While driving?"

"Good call, but I read at lights. When I have a chance, I'll see if Ansel's connected to Ruth Caswell."

What a stubborn woman. Protocol all the way.

They walked to the police officer posted by the crime scene barrier and displayed their badges. The dead man lay on his back to the right of the sidewalk, his position similar to the other two deaths.

Thatcher bent and she knelt beside him. The victim had been shot in the forehead with a hollow-tip bullet like the others. African American. Dirty and tattered. On the man's bloodstained chest sat a small brown plastic scorpion. A senseless killing.

Thatcher visibly examined the body and area of the crime scene. "We have a homeless man by the name of Ansel Spree. No family. HPD arrested him for robbing a dry cleaner's four years ago. He did two years. Unemployed. ID was on him. And a watch. Obviously theft wasn't a motive." He and Bethany moved away from the body. "Has to be someone who cares he's gone."

"He's a man who was murdered, and we care."

He valued the compassion in her tone. "Bethany, this case is taking a wider spectrum. Ansel Spree adds a dimension we've obviously overlooked with the other two."

"We can add his stats to the spreadsheet and graphs. Behavioral analytics is on it, but their report takes time."

Outside the tape, people gawked at the crime. Here in the Third Ward, too many residents didn't need an excuse to kill, and most often the killer stood in the crowd. Victims in the neighborhood wore the wrong colors, tats, tennis shoes, or filled a killer's quota. But Ansel Spree's death fell under another category—a serial killing.

"I'm going to mingle with the crowd," he said. "Might be an honest citizen among them, or one who could be bought."

"Your faith in humanity is inspiring." She stopped typing into her phone. "Be careful. Those aren't choir boys and girls. They . . . I'm not telling you anything new."

"I'll be back in a few."

"Wait while I type the findings and snap a few pics."

"Cops are everywhere," he said, irritation with her methods of investigation wearing through him.

"Go ahead, but you aren't the right color. Neither am I."

She'd made a good assessment, but his theory on facing fear kept him on the job. He knew how to handle himself. "Someone saw or heard something."

"Right." She aimed her phone over the body and moved around the victim, snapping more photos at various angles—some over the body and some from the sidewalk level. Although HPD had their photographer, Bethany was thorough. Not much got past her, which was why he respected her attention to detail.

He worked his way outside the crime tape to the onlookers.

Eighty percent of them carried guns and knives, and those were the women and children, but he wasn't there to pat anyone down.

A teen, probably around fifteen, stood alone in the shadows observing the scene.

Thatcher moved beside him. "Did you see that guy get shot?"

The kid swore. "Got in the way of a bullet."

"Hear the gun?"

He sneered and pointed to earbuds wrapped around his neck.

"When did you see the body?"

He shrugged and stuck the earbuds into place.

"Where do you stay?" Thatcher said.

"None of your business." He muttered a phrase Thatcher couldn't make out.

Three older teens stepped beside him. Great, Thatcher had approached the 103 Boys—100 percent Third Ward African American gang. They flashed their sign, and the younger teen told Thatcher what he could do.

"I'm looking for information on this murder."

"We don't know."

Another teen joined them, numbering five now in the group.

"Have you seen the dead man before?"

The younger teen pointed to the crime scene. "None of you belong here."

Thatcher sensed someone beside him, and he swung to Bethany.

"Hey, babe. Aren't we finished here? I came along for the ride, but I have plans." She snuggled in close to him.

"Better listen to your woman," the same teen said.

"He always does." She kissed his cheek and wrapped her arm around his waist. "Come on. Finish with this mess and let's go where it's quiet." When she tugged on him, he nodded at the teen and thanked him for his time.

Back at the crime scene, she released him. "Are you three-quarters stupid? They could have cut you down and left you to bleed out. And the cops wouldn't have known you were dead."

"I was just getting acquainted."

She jabbed a finger into his chest. "Don't forget where I grew up."

"You might be right . . . this time." Not a smart move. One of his weaknesses was to go where the adrenaline flowed.

She clenched her fists. "Next time I might not be around to save your rear. Hate to see you covered in blood."

He chuckled. "Yes, partner."

"I'd heard you managed a few out-there, dumb moves while on a case. This just proves it." She stopped herself. "Guess we're even in the stupid moves arena."

He'd acted on impulse and deserved the wrath of Bethany. Yet even her anger caused his admiration for her to grow. Where would these feelings take him? Eventual trust or something he wasn't ready to label?

CHAPTER 23

Bethany and Thatcher drank bad-tasting coffee at the FBI office. The vending machine was empty of Diet Dr Pepper, or she'd be filling up on it. She'd swung her chair into his cubicle. Both were too wired to consider going back to bed. They'd devoured a pizza . . . and since they couldn't agree on toppings, her half was spicy sausage and cheese, and his half was Canadian bacon and mushroom.

Thatcher started to take a sip of coffee, then set the cup down. "Since Monday, we've investigated three deaths by a serial killer. In case you haven't noticed, our best suspect's in jail with an alibi. Is the motivation money, power, or revenge?"

"A solid profile would be good, but I know there isn't one. We take what we know and do comparisons." She turned to her legal pad, recalling a report conducted by the National Center for the Analysis of Violent Crime. "The NCAVC is on this, but it's our job as investigators to feed them information."

"Bethany, slow down the analytics for a moment. HPD and the FBI are working every angle on these killings, and daily briefings are there for everyone's benefit. Our killer doesn't have to be a child-abused, chemically imbalanced loner who's looking for blood. He fits into society and may have a family and friends. The community consider themselves lucky to have him a part of great things. It goes deeper than a spreadsheet."

"I've studied the reports." Annoyance clicked at her nerves. "We haven't done the comparisons with similar crimes around the country that are unsolved."

"Our killer could decide today he's done with his game. With the lack of evidence to tie the crimes together, it could very well happen. Motivation that results in bizarre behavior."

"Okay, I get it. I want evidence and you want to understand why he acts."

"Wrong. We need to bring Scorpion down. In most homicides, the victims have a relationship to the offender." He sighed. "I'm frustrated."

"Me too."

"The boot print I found tonight matches up with the other one. We're looking at a small man, possible Asian or Hispanic or a teen." He snapped his fingers. "Maybe we're looking in the wrong place."

"Thatcher, you're punchy. Not making much sense."

"Hear me out. We have a wealthy older woman, a middle-aged professional, and a homeless man. Different cultures who were targeted by one killer, a scorpion. He planned their murders, which means it's what they represent that got them killed. We need to widen our investigation beyond the past few months, dig into our victims' backgrounds and those close to them. Find out who was imprisoned with Ansel Spree. How long had he been homeless? Where did Alicia work before Danford? What did Ruth Caswell do when she was healthy? Every list has potential. We search for the one common factor that got them all killed the same way."

She stared into his face, admiring his commitment. "We've taken a magnifying glass to reports, looking for something that either we're blind to or it isn't there." She folded the legal pad to a clean page. "Earlier you sent a request to expedite the ballistics report. We've confirmed the victims were not gun owners, except for Paul Javon's .22, which we've verified was in a repair shop. So you give me what you need for the FIG, and I'll record it."

"With a little grace, we could have something substantial in a few hours."

He said grace, not luck. She was too wound up to analyze it.

For the next two hours, the line to the FIG burned hot with requests.

"Houston has the only killer who uses a scorpion signature." Bethany leaned her head back and closed her eyes while a dull pain beat against her temples. "Maybe we should look at the habits of a scorpion." She caught herself. "I'm beginning to sound like you."

"That's not a bad thing. Our killer might have taken the persona of a predator. Those findings could be instrumental in identifying our killer."

"As in studying their habits?" She'd lost it for sure, but she had to do something or fall asleep. She stood and googled the creature on his computer and read a few paragraphs. "I'll share this with you in a second—just let me wrap my brain around the information first."

"We kids with no siblings have problems with patience, especially when you're using my computer."

"Get over it, Thatcher." She smirked. "Okay, scorpions have been around for thousands of years and are virtually indestructible, as in survivors. In our case, we have a predator."

"A given. What else?"

"About fifteen hundred species, and twenty-five of them have venom strong enough to kill a person." She took a sip of coffee—bad stuff, tasted like dirt.

He chuckled.

"What's so funny?"

"Watching you in action. Your processing is fascinating."

She ignored him. "We already know where your gut-instinct methods can take you."

"Ouch. Thanks for saving my hide. The kiss was good too."

"Very funny. We have three murders and an upset SSA." She continued to read. "Scorpions are nocturnal. Interesting info.

Listen to this—they basically eat insects, the kind humans don't value. The larger ones eat smaller scorpions."

"Scorpion views his victims as useless, dispensable. Obvious in our case."

"They have poor eyesight. Some species have the ability to slow down their metabolism if they can't find anything to eat."

He stretched neck muscles. "Sounds like the perfect time to disable them."

She'd want to think about this one. "Not really. They can snap to the hunt if lunch walks by. Here's an unusual fact. Stick a scorpion under an ultraviolet light, and it's fluorescent."

"Anything else?" he said.

She blinked, her eyes stinging as though sand had taken residence. "They need loose soil to exist." She read further. "Freeze one overnight and watch it thaw and come to life the next day. And they're difficult to control with insecticides. Now I'm curious about the types in Texas."

He jotted a few notes. "Am I rubbing off on you? This is sort of out there in the investigation."

"Theoretically, no. Do you want to hear about the Texas varieties?"

He laughed. "Go ahead."

"Not much info here. The striped bark scorpion is the most common and lives in the hill country. Their venom isn't strong enough to kill unless the person has an allergic reaction or goes into anaphylactic shock." She held her Styrofoam cup and stared across the cubicle into the hallway while her mind searched for meaning. "We're working on pure exhaustion here, but you're taking notes. What do you have?"

He picked up his pad of paper. "Our species has no problem eliminating his victims. I don't think bad eyesight applies." He tapped his finger on the desktop.

"What are you thinking?"

"I'm looking at the ability to slow his metabolism. For all

practical purposes, the scorpion looks lazy, but he's using a self-preservation method that works. Could say he has a good cover. No one suspects him as long as he stays hidden."

"That's true of most serial killers. Thatcher, have we lost it?" She glanced at the traits. "The one thing scorpions do for us is eat insects we deem useless or a nuisance. Including their own."

"Back to a profile—the victims don't have to fit into anything logical as long as it makes sense to Scorpion. In his world, our three victims have no value to him alive."

"We have a little time before our meeting with SSA Preston. Should we go home and shower so something besides our investigation doesn't stink?" she said.

"Good idea. Meet here at seven thirty?"

"Yes, and pray for a solid theory."

Her cell buzzed with a text. She knew the sender before looking. Spree could have been u or Graves.

✳ ✳ ✳

7:25 A.M. FRIDAY

Thatcher longed to blow the cobwebs out of his brain and shine light into the corners of the city to find Scorpion. Media demanded answers about the murders, accusing the FBI and HPD of not doing their jobs.

As he'd often contemplated during the past months, where did God fit in the evil of this world? Why didn't He stop the useless victimizing? The answers were there, and someday he'd find them. For now he asked for wisdom and guidance.

Bethany stood in the doorway of his cubicle and handed him a Starbucks. "Black like the dead of night," she said, echoing a remark he'd made in the wee hours of the morning.

"Thanks. Are you wide-awake?"

The circles under her pretty eyes answered for her. "Do you want the good news first or the bad news?"

A groan spread through him. "No more deaths, right?"

"No."

"Then bring on the good." He took the coffee. "Thanks. I know what it is—you put a tracer on your brother's texts."

She glanced down, not like Bethany. "Thatcher, when this is over, I'll handle the business with Lucas. Until then, I'll tolerate his trash."

"Are you afraid of him?"

Her impersonal expression told him exactly what he wanted to know. How would Bethany feel if she knew how well he read her?

"He's all mouth," she said.

"Not from his criminal history. Be careful and contact me immediately if trouble escalates."

Her eyes softened the way they had when he showed her the snacks in his loaner car. "I'll behave. I passed SSA Preston in the hall. He doesn't want a briefing this morning, but he requested a detailed report of last night, which we have. Oh, he knew we pulled an all-nighter."

"The bad news?"

She held up her phone. "Someone forwarded me a note posted on the *Chronicle*'s website. No sender. The title is 'Who's Minding Houston's FBI?'

"A serial murderer walks the streets of our city claiming three known victims. Every citizen is afraid and should be. Neither HPD nor the FBI have an arrest or a single clue. I don't blame our men in blue. They do their best while the FBI has two of the most inept agents on the case. Special Agent Thatcher Graves has worked violent crime long enough to have ended these killings on day one. Special Agent Bethany Sanchez is a reject from the civil rights division. Guess they had to put her somewhere. What a pathetic excuse representing Houston's elite bureau."

She looked up as though to gauge his reaction.

"Finish it."

She resumed reading.

"Our tax dollars pay for this? I have a few more conclusions about these incompetent agents. In point, who is responsible for the lack of law enforcement? Another note on Agent Graves—he's trigger-happy. Take a look at the bodies in his rearview mirror. He's a legal gunman, and Sanchez got her training on the northeast side of town. Wouldn't want either of them watching my back. Has anyone done the math? As in 'on the take'? Graves and Sanchez deserve whatever happens to them while a serial killer preys on the innocent of our city. Houston's FBI SSA Preston needs a replacement. He might be their poster child for supervision, but he has the intelligence of a gorilla. My advice? If you're in need of help, don't contact the FBI. Buy a gun. When are the citizens of our city going to take a stand and take back our city?"

"Good morning, Houston," Thatcher said.

"*Imbécil.*"

"Something stronger than *moron* just crossed my mind."

"Mine too, but I try not to use the language. Who else got this fabrication other than the media?"

"The whole world. I'll put a tracer on it."

CHAPTER 24

Bethany and Thatcher entered the upscale dry cleaner's near the Galleria, the one Ansel Spree had robbed. The business had a plush lounge area in warm brown tones, complete with a coffee bar, bottled water, and fresh fruit. Those who frequented the establishment had the income to pay a substantial price for services and in turn expect preferential treatment. Bethany desperately wanted to give SSA Preston and the community something solid from this interview. She despised the editorial letter casting doubt on the FBI's reputation.

Jafar Siddiqui, a gray-haired man of Middle Eastern descent, greeted them as the owner of the dry cleaner's.

Thatcher introduced himself and Bethany, and the two displayed their badges. "We'd like to ask you a few questions about Ansel Spree," he said.

Siddiqui stiffened. "He robbed me a few years ago and went to prison."

"Are you aware he's dead, a probable victim of a serial killer?"

"Yes, sir." He rubbed his forehead. "What does his death have to do with me?"

Thatcher showed him the photos of Ruth Caswell and Alicia Javon. "Are either of these women familiar?"

The man examined both pics, then asked their names and

typed them into his computer. "I don't recognize them, and neither woman is in our client history." He swallowed hard. "No one deserves to die at the hands of a killer."

"We agree, sir." Thatcher dropped his phone into his jacket pocket. "Can you tell us what transpired at the time of the robbery?"

Alarm flashed across his face. "It's all in the court records."

Bethany recalled Thatcher's theory on body language. The man was either nervous or hiding something.

"If you don't mind, we'd like to hear it from you," Thatcher said.

"Is there a problem? I'm a law-abiding man. Pay my taxes. And this Scorpion . . . will he come after my family?"

Bethany complimented the decor in an effort to calm the man. Did he think he was a suspect in the murder case? "This is not about you, sir. We're seeking additional information about Ansel Spree. We have no family for him. Perhaps something you remember will help our investigation."

He relaxed. "I'm sorry. I've been reading about the killings, and I'll do whatever I can to help. My memory isn't as accurate as when the robbery occurred."

Bethany smiled and caught Thatcher's nod to continue the questioning. "We understand. According to your testimony, approximately four years ago Ansel Spree robbed you at gunpoint. The unusual aspect is you stated Mr. Spree apologized for the crime."

"A peculiar thing," Siddiqui said. "While he waved a gun in my face, he told me he didn't want to take my money, but he had no choice."

"Did you ask why?" she said.

"No. My wife and granddaughter were with me, and I was concerned for them. Afraid for myself too. I believe the court report said Mr. Spree wished there'd been another way."

"Is there anything else you can tell us?" she said.

He slowly shook his head. "Mr. Spree came to see me about

two months ago. Apologized and claimed he'd never break the law again. Brought my wife flowers. Very interesting. Never heard from him again until I read about his murder this morning."

Bethany pulled out her business card. "If anything else comes to mind, would you please contact our office?"

The man's fingers trembled as he reached for the card.

Bethany met his gaze. "What are you not telling us? We want to help."

He gripped the counter. "Mr. Spree said something else when he apologized and brought the flowers." He stared at the counter, then regained eye contact. "I should have asked him what he meant. Maybe I could have prevented his death."

"What did he say?"

"He wanted to make up for the wrongs before he was killed. He said he'd rather die than rob anyone else."

Bethany didn't believe Spree's remark was flippant. "Thank you," she said. "We appreciate your time."

"Do you think my family needs to take precautions?"

Thatcher stepped forward. "Sir, we see no reason for you and your family to be afraid. Thank you for your assistance."

Once in Thatcher's loaner car, Bethany studied the dry cleaner's storefront. "If Spree knew he was about to be killed, did the other victims?"

"I was thinking the same thing." Thatcher started the engine. "I want a background on Jafar Siddiqui."

"Why? He repeated exactly what was in the original report. It's not necessary."

"Maybe in your opinion."

She bit back a retort. "What are you thinking?"

"How many violent crimes have you solved?"

She'd angered him again. "None, and I'm sorry." She pulled out her phone and typed in the request.

Thatcher drove toward the office. Fifteen minutes later, the FIG responded to both phones.

"This is rich," she said. "The week after Ansel Spree was sentenced for the robbery, Jafar Siddiqui was investigated for money laundering in connection with a terrorist group in Pakistan. He was later cleared for lack of evidence."

"What about his family? Shouldn't take long to have the FIG get back with us. Would you send them the request?"

"This has nothing to do with the Caswell or Javon cases," she said.

"Maybe."

She obeyed but failed to understand his reasoning. By the time they reached the office parking lot, they had the report on Siddiqui's family. His brother had fled the country when Jafar fell under investigation. The case had been reopened.

"Ansel might have stumbled onto more than a few dollars out of Siddiqui's money drawer," Thatcher said. "I'm staying on this."

"There's no remote connection between a Pakistani terrorist group and Scorpion."

"In your opinion."

She chose to say nothing.

CHAPTER 25

Thatcher had the virus called ineffectual. Talking heads were all over the media with their profile of Scorpion, but these so-called professionals were nothing more than reporters attempting to gain recognition. The editorial letter from earlier went viral, like someone had opened a scab on every FBI agent in the city.

Law enforcement sought a small man. He could have faced a stigma because of his size and not feel like a real man. By breaking the rules of society, killing could offer him a sense of power and control.

Thatcher's stomach had rumbled since midmorning, and ignoring it didn't make the pangs disappear. Bethany had to be hungry too and just as exhausted. He found her at the squad board, arms crossed over her tiny frame as she studied the victims' faces.

"I owe you an apology."

She avoided him. "Accepted. I can be difficult at times too."

He smiled. "Have you solved it?"

"I wish." She turned and gave him a smile. "Thinking about scorpion characteristics. Again."

Were those lashes for real? "And you've determined we're crazy?"

"Not exactly, even though it's not my normal method of analyzing an investigation. But a serial killer works his own psychosis. Not ready to write it into a report for SSA Preston."

"Are you as hungry as I am?" he said.

"Yeah. I did a PowerBar at ten thirty, but it's worn off."

"How about Mexican food?"

"I'm not in the mood to cook." Her finger traced Alicia Javon's face as though the answer lay in the touch. "But I'm open."

"What about Pappasito's?"

"Perfect. Love their food."

They left in Thatcher's car for the restaurant and within five minutes were pulling into the parking lot. He rubbed his eyes. "I could sleep for hours."

"Me too. Let's hope the food does the trick, and we don't fall asleep at our desks."

"After lunch, I want to talk to the medical examiners who performed the autopsies on each victim."

She grimaced. "That might have been a better stop this morning."

"And here I thought you'd want to see their tools."

"Not my idea of a post-lunch field trip." She sighed. "What do you do when you hit bottom?"

"I meet with my bud Daniel, the guy who's now engaged to Special Agent Laurel Evertson. We get together most Saturday mornings for breakfast. I unload then. What about you? Are you close to your mom?"

"Depends on the time of day. She believes in being submissive, so when she does contact me, it's usually about Dad's agenda and not pleasant. The director of Noah's Loft, Elizabeth Maddrey, is my good friend, so we talk a lot. Do you see your mother often?"

"No, but I call her once a week. She's lonely."

"I can see you're being supportive. You've been great with Carly."

He opened the car door. As they walked toward the restaurant, Bethany's cell rang.

Her face paled, and she covered the phone. "Go on in and get us a table. I'll be right there." She returned to lean against the car while he walked inside the restaurant. He hoped her news wasn't bad. A prayer swept through him. What he hadn't told Bethany about the Saturday morning meetings with Daniel was that they spent the time exploring the Bible.

He and Daniel Hilton had discussed law enforcement and the issue of why God failed to intervene and stop the bad guys—many times. More and more of what Thatcher once thought was confusing and didn't make sense now had clarity through the lens of the Bible, the one book he'd sworn he would never read. Three weeks ago, he'd prayed with Daniel to ask the Lord into his life. But he hadn't told anyone yet. Thatcher needed to digest his decision because for the first time, his out-of-the-box method of living had God in charge. Combine his old self with a love of psychology, and he could fill a volume with questions. But understanding would come. He had to acquire the trait of patience.

He was seated near the window where he could see Bethany, although her face was turned away from him. She dropped her phone into her purse and kicked the tire. He chuckled. Oh, she could be formidable. Heading his way, she swiped beneath her eye.

A dark-green Volkswagen sped straight toward her.

He pounded on the glass, frantically begging her to hear his warning. A young man rushed from between parked cars and dragged her to safety as the Volkswagen zoomed by.

Thatcher blew out his relief and hurried outside the restaurant to join them. The man was young, muscular, which accounted for his fast reflexes.

Thatcher reached out to shake the young man's hand. "Thanks for saving my friend's life."

"Glad to help."

"Oh yes, thank you." Bethany shook her head. "I wasn't paying attention."

The young man tugged on his baseball cap. "Are you okay?"

She nodded. "Working on lack of food and sleep makes one stupid."

"That was too close," Thatcher said. "But I got the license plate number. Did you see the driver?"

"No, I'm sorry," the young man said. "The driver probably has a record and no insurance."

"I saw nothing but a blur of green heading straight for me," Bethany said.

The young man took a step back. "Take care."

"Wait a minute," Bethany said. "What's your name?"

"Zack Adams."

"Can I do anything for you?"

"No. I was supposed to meet someone here, but they forgot."

"I see. Are you a student?" She pointed to his U of H T-shirt.

He beamed. "Junior at the University of Houston."

"In case HPD needs a witness to what happened, can I have your cell number?" she said.

As Zack rattled off his cell number, gut reaction kicked in, and Thatcher lifted his phone to snap the young man's pic. But Zack whipped his attention to the street before disappearing through a mass of vehicles.

Inside the restaurant, Bethany and Thatcher's table had been taken, and they were reseated away from the window. Bethany stared at her hands, a sign of inner turmoil, as he'd noted on other occasions. The phone call or the near hit? "What are you thinking?"

"The call was my brother, and when I refused to give him money, he exploded."

"You have enough on him for an arrest."

"Not yet. The case comes first."

"You have nothing to prove to me." His gaze lingered on her face.

She moistened her lips. "Thanks. My mind is on what just happened."

Thatcher didn't believe her for a second.

She pulled her cell from her purse and pressed in a number. A moment later she set the phone on the table. "Zack Adams's phone number is bogus. He was standing outside a Camry when we pulled up. If I'd been paying attention to my surroundings, I wouldn't have nearly been run over."

Thatcher waved his hand in front of her face. "Back up. What are you saying?"

She picked up her phone and typed. "I want to know if the FIG has anything on him, and who owns the runaway Volkswagen."

He gave her the license plate number. She was hungry and tired, running on fumes. But it appeared her actions backed up his suspicions.

"Would you forward me Zack's pic? I'm sending another inquiry."

Midway through Thatcher's pulled pork enchiladas and Bethany's beef fajitas, both phones alerted them to a message.

Thatcher grabbed his first. "The Volkswagen's license plates belong to a car reported stolen a month ago. There's no Zack Adams at the University of Houston. Neither is he enrolled in any of the Houston area colleges. The cell number he gave you doesn't appear in any college or university directory. No facial recognition with the baseball cap, and he turned just before I took it. Doesn't exist, which means no record either. Pull out your notepad. Let's figure out what just happened."

She took another bite of her fajitas and pushed the pad and paper toward him. "You write, and I'll talk."

He nodded. "Fire away."

"Poor choice of words, partner, but here goes. As I said earlier, Lucas called. He requested we talk privately, and I thought he was about to admit his poor choices. Dumb me. Once the phone clicks in my ear, I set out to join you, and a stolen car nearly hits me. I'm saved by a stranger who lies about his identity and doesn't want me calling him."

Thatcher carefully formed his words. "Here's what I think. Your brother followed us from the office. He set you up for a hit-and-run, and you're looking for a way to excuse him."

Her eyes blazed. "That's ridiculous. A stunt like this would land his rear back in jail, most likely prison."

He wanted to shake her. "You're doing the same thing as your family. 'Poor Lucas. It's pure coincidence his actions seem to parallel a potential hit-and-run.'"

She rubbed her forehead. "After this case is closed, I'll do something."

"Be an idiot if you want, but I'm not looking forward to writing 'I told you so' on your tombstone."

She tossed her napkin on the table. "Our case is not about Lucas." Her eyes shot arrows at him while fury sped through his veins. Tears welled in her eyes, and she stared down at her half-eaten food. "My family is no concern to you. I'm an agent, and my personal life isn't up for discussion."

"Family problems are the worst. I'd rather face a dozen bad guys unarmed. You're right—the case isn't about Lucas, but he's interfering with a good agent's investigation."

Confusion and reality met him as Bethany looked up. "Let's find Scorpion. Then I'll deal with Lucas."

What spoke the loudest to him was what she didn't say. Her response about handling Lucas later was fast becoming a worn excuse.

CHAPTER 26

Bethany stood in her cubicle and rubbed the chill bumps on her arm. In the past few days, Lucas had broken into her home and threatened her and Thatcher. Granted, he tried the death tactics whenever he was angry with anyone, but who was she fooling?

She fought the doubts and warring emotions that bombarded her mind about Lucas. Today's near hit-and-run reeked of a setup, just like Thatcher said. Her stomach twisted, not from lunch but from incidents destined to slow her timing. Thatcher, with his psychology background, had insight into criminal minds. Whereas she carried too much family guilt. Her brother had committed the worst of crimes, and nothing about him spoke of rehabilitation. But she didn't have time for any of this. Lucas Sanchez needed to be behind bars to protect those around him.

She was a fool to believe the driver of the stolen Volkswagen wasn't paying attention and panicked when she stepped into its path. Or that Zack Adams saved her from getting hurt and didn't want to get involved. If she weren't so exhausted, she'd have come to the same conclusion at lunch. And Thatcher wouldn't have had to swat her with his version of the truth.

Lucas's motivation had always been whatever pleased him at the moment.

Tonight she'd sleep. Her logic always worked better after a good night's rest. But her mind refused to stop spinning. The meeting with the medical examiner gave them a clinical report and little else. She'd spend the weekend analyzing the investigative reports.

A text seized her attention, but it wasn't from anyone she recognized. Lucas again? *Oh, God, I can't take much more.*

This is Dorian from Noah's Loft. Need help bailing a friend out of jail.

Bethany regretted the day Elizabeth introduced her to the woman. What nerve. What guts. Where did she get her cell number? Surely not Elizabeth.

Bethany typed in her response. I don't bail anyone out of jail. Why?

Shouldn't have gotten arrested. Where did u get my number?

None of ur business. R u going 2 help a good cause?

No. Call someone else.

Some do-gooder u r. All mouth no feet.

Bethany shouldn't have responded at all, but this crazy woman volunteered with those who expected healthy staff members. Why did Dorian think Bethany would hand over bail money? She set her phone aside, but another text sounded.

I no the right people.

Right people 4 what?

Kind that break windows & arms. No matter ur FBI.

How did you learn my job?

TV news

Bethany contacted the FIG for a trace. Moments later she learned the messages came from a burner phone.

Elizabeth needed to be informed about Dorian's inappropriate messages. Bethany pressed in her friend's number.

"Hi, Bethany, how's your day?"

"Right in line with what I do."

"I'm sorry."

"Elizabeth, I just received a text from Dorian Crawford."

"Our volunteer?"

"The same." Bethany read aloud the dialogue exchange.

"What was she thinking? I admit she's impulsive, and I've had to rein her in a few times this week. But I really doubt she's the one who texted you." Elizabeth blew out her anger, a trait Bethany rarely saw. "I should have better checked her references, but when Alicia was killed, I needed someone ASAP."

"It's not too late to check them."

"I will. By any chance, did you give her your phone number?" Elizabeth said. "Because my office and file drawers are always locked. No one has volunteer numbers but me."

"Absolutely not. I was about to ask if she had access to your files."

"No way," Elizabeth said. "This is crazy."

"I'll find out where she got my contact info." Bethany glanced at her watch. She had a few things to do before heading home. "Do you store info in the Cloud?"

"If you mean computer and iPhone, then yes."

"Dorian could have accessed my number that way."

"Trust me, she's not bright enough to figure out technology. Or I'd be worried about what else she could stumble onto. But I am talking to her about this as soon as I'm finished with a new resident."

"Elizabeth, I'll do it tomorrow. No point in dragging you into this. Maybe she found my number and my FBI status from somewhere else. I could have dropped a business card. This is my problem with Dorian, and I'll set her straight. All I ask is that you check her references."

✳ ✳ ✳

5:13 P.M. FRIDAY

Thatcher's sweaty palms made him feel like a teenager. If he didn't catch Bethany before she left for the weekend, he'd lose his nerve. He'd approached a lot of women in his day, mostly for selfish reasons, but Bethany had his senses on overload. Strange and unnerving. They were take-charge people, power-packed and determined to get the job done. Yet something about her drove him to distraction, as though he wanted more than a partner. So why did the thought of spending time with her outside work scare him?

He texted her, the coward's way of communication. Dinner plans 4 Sat?

No. Do u have a gig?

:) no. Talk scorpion case

K

Pick u up at 6:30? I no where u live.

Scary. Where r we going?

He hadn't thought that far. *Think, Thatcher.* What a rookie. Wanna go 2 Brio @ Memorial?

K

Taking a deep breath, he rested the back of his neck in his hands. Warning signs exploded, the kind he chose to ignore. Agents with emotional connections to each other added up to agents making stupid decisions.

Who was he kidding? Bethany probably had a boyfriend or had the sense to term her partner as off-limits.

How long had they known each other? And why had he invited her to dinner?

CHAPTER 27

Bethany parked at the curb of Noah's Loft with a twinge of regret. She should be working on the Scorpion case, but that meant letting Elizabeth and the residents down. Last night, she'd fallen into bed before eight and slept solid until the alarm went off at seven.

She gave herself a mental shake to concentrate on her double duty this morning: helping the residents work through the grieving process of losing Alicia and focusing on any of them who might have information about the murder.

Time to get her agent pants on.

She rang the doorbell and the cook greeted her in the hall. Sweet lady with a heart for those in need. The scent of coffee and a mix of apples and cinnamon wafted through the air. "Do I smell apple crisp with fresh coffee?"

"It'll be ready soon. I made a separate pan sweetened with Splenda. Elizabeth told us you're diabetic."

"How thoughtful." Bethany gave her a hug. "Are you doing okay?"

"As best as I can." The woman sucked in a breath. Alicia's death had these precious women incredibly distraught.

Bethany knocked and entered Elizabeth's office. "What's the plan?" She slipped onto a chair across from the desk.

"I've invited the residents into the meeting room for an informal

151

memorial ceremony, and I'll encourage them to share about Alicia."
Elizabeth frowned. "You look tired. Is this new position more work
than you bargained for?"

"Rough case, but I'm managing."

"Don't be afraid to admit you can't handle the stress."

"When have I ever given up?" Bethany laughed and it felt good.

"How about a few guys who tried to date you?"

"I was bored. Do you want to have dinner Sunday night?"

"Love it."

Bethany folded her hands. "Elizabeth, have you run a background on Dorian?"

"Not yet. There hasn't been a spare moment. By the way, she
moved in last night, so now she'll be helping full-time. Honestly, I
think she's simply lonely and needs a purpose. Let me know what
happens after your talk with her." Elizabeth worked 24-7 with
the residents. Married to her job instead of a loving husband. She
stood and picked up her worn Bible.

"New jeans?" Bethany said.

"If you call Goodwill new, then I'm all over it."

They laughed. "Our size?"

"Any doubts?" The tiny lines around her eyes deepened. "We
need to celebrate Alicia's life, but this will be hard."

Bethany wrapped her arm around Elizabeth's waist. "If it's not
hard, it's not worth it. Without tears, there's no healing."

Her eyes pooled. "Love you, my friend."

They walked up the stairs to the meeting room, where the
women and a few children were seated in chairs or on the floor.
Dorian Crawford, the last person Bethany wanted to see, rushed
to her side.

"Bethany, you're here. Wonderful. I'm so excited. Are we working on résumés afterward?" She pushed her pink-framed glasses
onto her nose.

Never had she heard one scrawny woman talk so fast. "Not
today. The memorial service takes precedence."

"Alicia would have done it all."

"I'm not Alicia. Perhaps you should find someone else to lead out in this."

Dorian touched her arm, and Bethany pulled back. "Oh, I'm sorry. You know me. Crazy Dorian. Guess you don't like anyone in your personal space."

Talk about over-the-top. "When the service is over, we need to talk."

"Now's fine."

"I prefer later."

Dorian lifted her chin. "I may be busy when you have the time."

Instantly Elizabeth stood by Bethany's side. "Let's get started," she said. "Dorian, I'd like for you to keep the children occupied. If they get restless, please take them outside."

"I want to speak to Bethany privately now," Dorian said.

"After the service." Elizabeth pointed to a group of children, and Bethany watched Dorian slump toward them.

Bethany craved a few feel-good moments before confronting the woman about the text to bail her friend out of jail.

Elizabeth spoke to the residents about Alicia Javon's volunteering, her incredible giving, and how much everyone at Noah's Loft missed her. For the next forty-five minutes, the residents gave testimonies of how Alicia had blessed their lives. She'd brought new clothes for the women and children, along with books, toys, and games. Two of the women no longer lived at the shelter but were supporting themselves and grateful for Alicia's tutoring and support.

Dorian stood, her eyes wild.

Elizabeth stopped speaking. "Is there a problem?"

"Yes. Can't you see? I forgot my vitamins." She whirled around and raced to the door, knocking over empty chairs.

Once the confusion settled, Elizabeth continued. "I have a six-week Bible study to help us through this difficult time. Attached to the study is a list of affirmations. I encourage you to read these every day. Next Saturday we'll begin our first study. Bethany and I will be facilitating it. If you'd like to speak privately to either of us about your experience with Alicia or if you have a prayer request, we'll remain here for the next few minutes." Elizabeth gestured behind her, where two sets of chairs were positioned. "We have apple crisp in the dining room, and I invite you and your children to enjoy it. Fresh coffee and hot chocolate are available too."

Dorian slipped back into place with the children as though she hadn't disrupted the group with her vitamin outburst.

Bethany wished Noah's Loft wasn't so desperate for help.

When the number of ladies in the room dwindled, Bethany walked to the back, where Dorian waited. She danced on her toes and glanced around the room. How could the woman interrupt a solemn occasion and not utter an apology?

Dorian approached her. "Today was great. Some of the women were laughing and others were crying. Even the kids, but I doubt if they have any clue what a murder looks like. Wow, what a way to have closure with Alicia's murder. Do you suppose the killer is one of the residents? Wouldn't that be a killer?"

Bethany flinched at the choice of words. "What I want to discuss is critical. You texted me, and your message was highly—"

"What are you talking about? I didn't text you. How could I without your number?"

"Please, do not interrupt me until I'm finished."

Dorian planted her hands on her hips like a pouting toddler.

"Yesterday afternoon you texted me." Bethany showed Dorian the saved messages.

Dorian read the messages, all the while shaking her head. "I swear to you, this is not me. I have no clue who hates me enough to send such an awful message. I don't have any friends in jail anyway." She glanced up. "Why a Galaxy instead of a cooler iPhone?"

Frustration rose from the bottom of Bethany's feet. If Dorian had Asperger's or Tourette's or ADD, then she needed help. "Stay on task. If you aren't the sender, who is?"

Dorian pulled an iPhone from her jeans pocket. "I'm innocent of your nasty accusations. Look at my cell. It's an iPhone 6. See, it has the latest features, not like yours."

Bethany wanted to grab her shoulders and rattle her teeth. "Dorian, if you ever send me a text again, you'll regret it. The fact that you obtained my phone number without permission is enough for me to ensure your volunteer work is ended."

"I'm innocent!" Her voice trilled throughout the room. "You hate me. You're jealous the residents like me so much. I bet you sent the text to yourself to make me look bad."

Bethany took Dorian's phone and checked the number and texts. Nothing indicated she'd been the sender. "Is this your only phone?"

"Why would I have two phones?" She held up her hands as though Bethany was pointing a gun at her, which wasn't far from the truth. Dorian raised her shoulders. "You really are a sick woman to make accusations like this. Someone ought to tie you to a psychiatrist's chair. I promise you, Elizabeth will ensure you no longer work with these women."

Bethany was in no mood for a verbal battle. She had too much to do working a tough case to busy herself with a crazy woman who had the attention span of a goldfish. She walked away. Dorian wasn't worth the bother.

Do your job, Bethany.

Do your job.

CHAPTER 28

At precisely 6:24, Thatcher received permission to enter Bethany's gated community. A chill came with the evening and the scent of a few fallen leaves from the oak trees outside her apartment building. He'd chosen a sweater and jeans for a casual get-to-know-each-other-better evening. He rang the doorbell and rubbed his hands on his jeans. His reaction was embarrassing.

She opened the door wearing jeans, a deep-red sweater, and a smile that deepened her dimples. He reminded himself this was his partner, who had no clue he was attracted to her.

"You look great," she said. "We must have gotten the same clothes memo."

"You look better than I do."

She laughed. "Thanks. I won't analyze that if you won't probe me with way-out questions."

"You haven't told me the best day of your life."

"Oh, someday. Come on in. I want you to meet Jasper."

"I'd almost forgotten about him." He stepped inside, and she gestured toward a huge cage in the corner of the living room. A gray parrot twisted his head.

She reached inside the cage, and he climbed onto her hand. "Jasper, I want you to meet somebody."

"Lookin' good, girl."

157

Thatcher joined her. "I'm a guy, Jasper."

"Be nice, Jasper," she said. "He's a guest."

"What's up, taco?" Jasper said.

Thatcher chuckled. "Never a dull moment here." He stuck his finger toward the bird.

"Watch it—he bites," she said. "And he's the jealous type." Her brown eyes sparkled. "We've been amigos for eight years."

"How old is he?"

"Thirty, and he'll live to fifty or more years old."

Thatcher started. "Didn't know that. Where did you find him?"

"At a parrot sanctuary. He just looked lost."

Jasper whistled the *Hawaii Five-O* theme.

"Okay, clown." She placed him inside his cage and grabbed a blanket.

"Please, not this," Jasper said.

"Sorry, buddy. We're leaving. I'm starved."

"I'll take care of her," Thatcher said. "Bye, Jasper. Nice meeting you."

"Bye, gringo."

Bethany wagged her finger at the bird. "Behave yourself while I'm gone."

Outside, Thatcher debated opening the car door for her. When they ate out during the week, they were partners. But his mama had raised him right, so he opened her door.

"Aren't you the gentleman?"

"I might not have enough money to pay for dinner, so I'm laying the groundwork."

She smiled, revealing those incredible dimples, and he questioned his sanity. They drove to Brio talking about Jasper, their day's work on the case, and their favorite country-western singers.

Once seated at the restaurant, and after their beverages had been delivered along with a basket of warm Italian bread, he relaxed. Bethany was his partner, a friend. They chose their food and decided to add a side of risotto with chicken and sweet potatoes.

He dug deep for guts. "I have motive for dinner tonight."

Her eyes widened. "Do I need my weapon?"

"You might. This is tough but needs to be said. You were great in opening up and telling me about your family. I'm a private person, but it's time I reciprocate and crack my exterior."

"I'm listening, and I don't judge. Most of the time."

Bluntness was one of those traits he admired about her. "Remember on Monday I told you the best day of my life was a few weeks ago?"

"Yes."

"And remember I said I meet with Laurel Evertson's fiancé on Saturday mornings?" When she nodded, he continued. "Happens to be the same guy who saved my life. He's no longer with HPD but in law school. Those meetings have been a Bible study, and a few weeks ago, I took the plunge and became a Christian."

"Wonderful. Why were you hesitant to tell me?"

He chuckled. "My bad-boy reputation. I want to show my faith, not spout it."

"Makes sense." She took a sip of her standard drink, Diet Dr Pepper. "I'll keep your decision to myself, and I respect your feeling comfortable with me to talk about it."

Now he felt foolish. "Okay, phase two."

"The case?"

He narrowed his gaze. "Yes, the case. I was hard on you about Lucas."

She held up her hand. "Those were things I must face. Unfortunately a lot of truth."

"I'm not apologizing, just wish I'd been a little easier on you."

She stared at her drink, then back to him. "Don't hold back on me. Because I'll never do it to you."

"Fair enough. Do you have any idea how tough it was to speak openly about my faith?" he said.

"I really understand. Oh, the stories I've heard about you." She sobered. "None of which I've seen. So . . . what church are you attending?"

"None yet. Thought about it but didn't know where to start."

"You could try mine. It's nondenominational, contemporary music. Incredible preaching."

"Okay. I have nothing to compare it to. Maybe tomorrow?"

"Sure." She wrote down an address. "Here, if you decide to join me. Nine thirty."

He slipped it into his wallet.

"You know why my family and I are at odds," she said. "What about yours?"

Okay, Thatcher, you're on. "Dad and I never got along. I was into music, had my own band. Add drinking and girls. Dad thought I should be in law enforcement before I broke the law and wouldn't qualify. I was interested in psychology. Still am. Did my grad work and entered practice. Enjoyed it, but I didn't want to spend the rest of my life seeing patients. Dad offered ten grand if I applied to the FBI." He shrugged. "Hard to turn it down."

"You're a great agent."

No condescension in her tone or eyes, and it warmed him. "Thanks. I despised my dad's nagging, hated him for it. But he saw in me what I didn't. Short story, he died of a stroke before we made amends."

"I'm sorry."

"Me too. Life seldom fits together the way we predict. I'd like to think he died knowing I loved him."

"I bet he was extremely proud of you."

"Possibly. Enough talk about me. We're investigating a case."

She reached for her glass. "The memorial service touched all of us. I saw Alicia's file. Nothing there but the basics. Pastor Lee wrote a glowing recommendation letter about her and Paul's work in the church. Thought I'd gag. What about your day?"

"Met with Daniel this morning. Worked out hard. And read everything documented on the Scorpion cases—multiple times. Made notes for us to follow up on." The server delivered their food. "Great, now we can eat."

She wiggled her shoulders, something he hadn't seen. "This is amazing, and I'm starved. Can I ask more questions between bites?"

"Of course. We're here to work, right?"

From the look on her face, her feelings for him were headed in the same direction as his.

Ten minutes into dinner, her cell alerted her to a text. She paled.

Dread punched him in the gut. "Lucas?"

She nodded. "'I have u on my schedule.'"

"This is no way to live," he said.

"Tonight, this very minute? I'd rather be on the front lines fighting to stay alive than allowing him to think he's frightened me," she said. "Soon."

CHAPTER 29

Bethany cut the price tag from a knee-length brown-and-orange jacket and tossed the tag into the trash. The colors blended perfectly with a tan sweater and slacks set for church this morning. She'd purchased it last season along with boots and a chunky necklace to match and forgotten they were in the back of her closet. One of her many vices. She picked up a pen beside a calendar on her nightstand. Day twenty-seven without going shopping. Somewhere there was an anonymous group for addicted shoppers. She also needed a twelve-step program to help her deal with a brother who was a criminal.

Her thoughts turned to last night's dinner . . . more on Thatcher than the case. The man gave *un hombre guapo* new definition. But referring to Thatcher as one good-looking hombre didn't change the FBI's recommended conduct policy, and she was definitely a rules girl.

When her phone rang, she expected the caller to be Thatcher declining church. In fact, it would be better if he'd changed his mind. Spending every day with him created havoc with more than his method of solving cases. But the number wasn't familiar and she answered.

"Agent Sanchez, this is Anita Cooke. We haven't heard from Carly. She was supposed to be home by four yesterday afternoon, and we've heard nothing. This isn't like her to worry us. There's more." Her voice broke. "I suspected Paul might have arranged to pay his bail, so a moment ago I called his cell phone. He answered. I panicked, just thinking of what he could do to her."

An image of Carly's battered body landed in her mind. "Did you talk to him?"

"Yes. He said he didn't keep track of her. When I asked if she'd been there, he hung up. He can get so angry."

"I'll see what I can do. What's the license plate of her car?"

While she pressed in the information on her phone, dread crept through her. Had Carly risked her life to find her mother's killer? Bethany should have been more insistent she stay away from her father's house. She focused on what little she knew about the young woman. "Where was she going?"

"She told me she had something to do at her father's house while he was in jail. I wanted her to wait for her uncle, but she wanted to handle the situation herself."

Carly hadn't tossed aside the private investigator role. "I'm assuming you've tried calling her."

"Yes, and texted her too."

"What about Shannon or Carly's friends?"

"They haven't heard from her either. Carly's such a good girl, and she gave me the numbers of several friends in case I couldn't reach her." She drew in a breath. "My husband wants to confront Paul."

"Mrs. Cooke, that's not a good idea. I suggest you wait there for my call or Carly's return."

"All right. I'm really frightened."

Bethany needed a clear head, and responsibility for Carly's welfare scratched at her conscience. While dressing, she called Thatcher and quickly explained Anita Cooke's call along with confirmation of Paul Javon's release from jail.

"I'll meet you at Javon's house," he said.

She snatched her keys. "I'm leaving now. Doubt if we make church on time."

At the Javon home, the drapes were open in the living room to reveal the harp and grand piano. Thatcher pulled in right behind her at the curb and exited. They walked up the sidewalk together, and he rang the doorbell three times.

"Do you suppose he saw us?" she said. "Or isn't at home?"

"We don't have a warrant. No legal reason to be here." Thatcher pressed the doorbell one more time. "We're wasting our time."

Her cell rang, and this time she recognized Anita Cooke's number. "Carly called us from a friend's house. She's pretty shaken. Her dad came home with a woman and caught her going through her mother's closet."

Bethany seized Thatcher's attention. "Is she all right?"

"We're going to pick her up now and take her to the ER. She thinks he broke her fingers."

"Which hospital?"

"Houston Methodist at the Medical Center."

"We're on our way." Bethany relayed the conversation to Thatcher. "If she can identify Javon's girlfriend, she could be in more danger than broken fingers and a battered body."

At the hospital's ER, Carly sat with a couple whom she introduced as Anita and Ken Cooke. Anita resembled her sister and nieces. Ken Cooke, a heavily bearded man, reminded Bethany of a rabbi. Make that an Old Testament prophet who spit brimstone and fire.

"I want Paul Javon behind bars for good," Ken said.

"We'll do our best to help you," Thatcher said. "Your niece is a brave girl."

Bethany glanced at Carly's right hand. Even under an ice pack, the swelling was evident. A fresh bruise beside her mouth indicated more mistreatment.

"Thanks for coming." Tears splattered Carly's face, the lines deepening in obvious pain. "I'm not as smart as I thought." She grimaced. "Wouldn't be surprised if my wrist is broken too."

"Any idea how long before you'll be treated?" Bethany said.

Carly gave a grim smile. "Two people are ahead of me."

Bethany eased into a seat beside the young woman. "Can you explain what happened?"

She took a breath and stared at her injured hand. "Never had a clue Dad would pay bail. But I should have figured it out. He'd changed the locks on the door, except the garage side door. I let myself in and picked the lock on their bedroom. I searched everywhere for Mom's phone—under the bed, between the mattress and box springs, in Mom's things, their closets. When I heard Dad coming up the stairs and a woman call his name and laugh, I panicked and tripped over a drawer. He walked in and went crazy." She leaned her head on Anita's shoulder. "I didn't have any place to run. I was trapped. He stood in the doorway and ranted. Wanted to know how I'd gotten inside the house. He went through my purse and found my key. Took all my cash."

"How did you get hurt?"

Carly was a kid wanting to right a wrong. "He accused me of framing him for Mom's murder. With each word he moved closer. He grabbed my fingers and bent them and my wrist back. I heard them pop and screamed. He must have been afraid of the neighbors because he let go." She took a deep breath. "I ran from the room. Never saw the woman."

Anita patted her shoulder.

"I'm so sorry. I failed, and now he'll come after Shannon."

Bethany's temper escalated. How could a man treat his own daughter like an animal? "Are you willing to press charges again?"

"Whatever it takes. He's a jerk, and I hate him."

Bethany refused to give the lecture on how those we love could also make us hate. She focused on Anita and Ken. "You'll make sure she files charges?"

"Already called the police and our lawyer. Paul murdered Alicia, and he nearly killed Carly."

"Sir," Thatcher said, "I understand—"

"Don't placate me."

"Paul Javon is a dangerous man, and he'll soon be under the

care of Harris County again. This time he won't be released so easily." Thatcher turned to Carly. "Promise me, Special Agent Sanchez, and your aunt and uncle that you will leave the investigation to trained people."

"Amen," Ken said.

"I promise," she whispered. "I'm worried about Shannon. She spent the afternoon with a friend, so I think she's okay."

Ken pulled his phone from his pants pocket. "I'm calling her now. The three of us together can persuade her to stay clear of your dad until he's arrested."

"Carly Javon," a nurse called.

Bethany gave her business card to Ken and watched the three disappear into the treatment area.

"Do you think she's told us everything?" Thatcher said.

"I have no reason to believe otherwise."

Thatcher stared at the doors leading to the ER. "Carly loved her mother, which means more heart than brains. She's a fighter. But she might not be as lucky the next time."

* * *

7:30 P.M. SUNDAY

Bethany had been looking forward all day to her dinner date with Elizabeth. They talked for hours, until their yawns signified a need for sleep. They were kindred hearts, even if they were from different cultures—Bethany's Hispanic heritage contrasting with her friend's milky-white features.

Bethany attempted to ignore the stress raging through her and concentrate on her friend, except her attention and thoughts about the murders always surfaced.

"You're all absorbed in the Scorpion case, aren't you?" Elizabeth said.

"Does it show? I'm sorry."

"I knew it was either the case or a man, and knowing you, it was work."

Bethany's pulse raced, and she hoped she wasn't developing feelings for off-limits Thatcher. Half the time, she didn't even like him. "I simply want the killer stopped. Feels like he's playing a game. Working hate crimes was easier, and someone would always talk. But that's not necessarily true in violent crime when a killer lives to strike again." She lifted her chin. "No more shoptalk. What have you been up to?"

Elizabeth had expressed a longing for family, and she'd met a nice guy about two months ago. A slow blush touched her cheeks. "Still seeing the same guy."

"I need details. Background? Any priors?" Bethany said with a laugh.

"He's a history teacher and basketball coach at a private Christian high school." Elizabeth's eyes held a soft, dreamy look. "Has a three-year-old little boy and is raising him alone. We've had good times together."

"Are you happy?"

Her eyes danced. "Very. But we'll see. Both of us are praying about our relationship."

"Wonderful. The thought of a relationship terrifies me."

"I think God instructs us to follow Him, afraid or not."

"Which is why I'm single and working violent crime."

Elizabeth touched her arm. "If you're waiting for problems in your family to fade away, I doubt it will happen."

CHAPTER 30

Bethany tossed back the sheet, unable to sleep or relax. Blundering and the weight of the unsolved murders weighed on her. Only one thing to do: outline what the investigation had found and try to make sense of it. Three murders and no connections. Paul Javon couldn't have committed the third murder because he was in jail. It was still possible he hired someone to kill his wife and make it look like a copycat. Was she right with her theory, and Thatcher spot-on that Scorpion had killed Ruth Caswell and Ansel Spree? Where were the answers?

Snapping on a light, she read through the various reports on her computer. Once she focused on what the FBI had learned about the killings, she pulled up a blank document and typed the creeping progress.

1. Paul Javon is in jail for the second time on assault charges. He pleaded innocent again to domestic abuse, but Carly's battered body, broken wrist and fingers, along with her testimony, indicate otherwise. Shannon refuses to affirm her sister's allegations against their father.
2. Felix Danford looks innocent of any wrongdoing.

Bethany hadn't absolved him completely, but his alibi had been confirmed by more than one person.

3. The FBI's informants claim the 103 Boys didn't attempt a copycat and murder Ansel Spree. The gang wouldn't lower themselves or give someone else credit for their work. Neither did they see it happen.
4. We are looking for a small man, and psychological traits play into his ego. So far, only one of the service personnel who might have been near Ruth's or Alicia's homes fits this description, and he isn't the killer.
5. The crime scene was swept each time for prints, but nothing was found.
6. The victims were shot point-blank, execution-style with the same type of bullet. But they still didn't have the ballistics report.
7. Ruth Caswell's killer stole traceable items. Pawnshops in the city are on alert.
8. Do the real killer or killers compare themselves to the often-deadly scorpion?

What had she missed?

She shivered . . . and reread the eight items. Progress and patience. The latter had always been her downfall.

※　※　※

7:30 A.M. MONDAY

Thatcher stared into the huge brown eyes of his partner, who looked like she needed another eight hours of sleep instead of drinking coffee at Starbucks. "What's on your mind this morning?"

"Last night Elizabeth gave me the name of the free medical clinic where she sends the residents. Small chance, but I wanted to see if Ansel Spree ever used it or if they knew Ruth Caswell."

"We don't turn it off, do we?"

"Apparently not. Thatcher, I feel so unqualified with this case. I want our partnership to work, but I'm losing faith in me offering anything substantial."

"Bethany, think like Scorpion. Understanding others gives us an edge to predict thoughts and behavior. We have to get inside his head, feel his highs and lows. Learn what excites him. Discourages him. But more importantly feel his pain. We're compiling information moment by moment. Will he continue to kill or flee? To him, his thoughts are justification for killing innocent people."

"I'll keep at it. I'm too stubborn to admit defeat. By the way, you handled Carly and the Cookes like silk."

"Thanks," he said. "Paul Javon's issues might lead us to Alicia's killer, but her death is the real thing. She was targeted by Scorpion."

"I'm not conceding yet. More to uncover. With the rush on the lab, the ballistics report will push us ahead, and we should have it tomorrow. Then we can discuss a copycat. Am I an asset or a pain?"

He laughed. "Trust me, you're doing a fine job. I value the way you evaluate evidence." Yet, his heart thumped a little harder when he saw her. How long could he hide his attraction?

"Appreciate the pep talk. I did a little digging in the early hours of the morning, and I found more information about Alicia and Paul Javon." She hesitated, as though thinking through what she'd learned.

He glanced up, his attention focused on her.

"Alicia was engaged before Paul. Six months after she married Paul, her ex-fiancé was jogging at night and killed by a hit-and-run. Still a cold case. HPD questioned Javon when an anonymous caller indicated Paul threatened to kill her ex. No alibi, but no evidence either."

He peered into her face, where a frown slowly formed. "This is a good thing. That's our job. What do you propose we do with this information?"

"Leverage. Twenty-four years ago, forensics weren't what they are today. Reopening a cold case might upset Paul enough to give us the name of his girlfriend. If he refuses, then his hands are dirty, and we're looking at a copycat."

"Good call, partner. I'm ready to talk to him."

She reached for her purse with one hand and her coffee with another. "I'm ready. Want to take my truck and pick up your car later?"

"As much as I despise my rental, I'll drive."

"What is it with you and always having to be behind the wheel?"

He grinned. "Power and control."

"Thought so. And the loaner has my snacks."

At the city jail, Thatcher waited for Paul Javon to respond to what Bethany had learned about the twenty-four-year-old unsolved murder. "Looks to me like we have enough evidence to reopen the cold case."

"I shouldn't have seen you without my attorney," Javon said. "The whole thing was a ridiculous accusation."

Thatcher stared into the man's face, using silence to add pressure. "You're right, Paul. The prosecutor will bring up the old case. Your attorney will ask to have it stricken, but what would look good is your cooperation. Give us your girlfriend's name and contact information, and I'll personally ensure it's in your record." He pushed a pad and pen in his direction. "It's a way to show your daughters a new beginning."

"All right. I'll give it to you. Haven't talked to her since my arrest." He printed the name Lisa Camry and a phone number.

"What was your last conversation about?"

"Old subject. She's pregnant. Money would make it go away, but she refuses an abortion." He ran his hand over his face. "Prior to Alicia's death, she showed me the medical report. I was furious and wanted proof it was my child."

"Were you able to confirm the paternity?"

His eyes narrowed. "No. I needed time to think about it."

"Where does she live?"

He shook his head.

"Won't or can't?"

"She lives with her invalid mother on the west side of town. We couldn't meet there, so we met at different hotels."

"Which ones?"

"That . . . that won't help you. I always took care of the room, and she entered through the back."

Thatcher pointed to the notepad. "I want a list of those hotels, the dates and times."

He closed his eyes. "She's too gentle and kind to hurt Alicia."

"Have you hit her too?"

"My anger issues never surfaced with her."

Thatcher stared into his face. The man was a bully and a coward. If he hadn't abused his girlfriend, it was because their relationship hadn't angered him yet. "Really? One more death on your hands goes against your conscience?"

CHAPTER 31

Outside the city jail, Bethany breathed in the satisfaction of a lead. Thatcher walked briskly, and she hurried to keep up, short legs working overtime. He said nothing, telling her his mind toyed with Paul Javon's moral code. Hopefully the judge would insist upon a psychiatric exam and get the man in counseling and on meds.

Medical professionals and prescriptions did no good for her brother. Lucas seemingly found no reason to change, except to get worse. No texts from Lucas since Saturday night. Maybe he'd weighed what revenge and threatening FBI agents would cost. Nice thought. One more incident, and the hour after Scorpion's arrest, she'd file charges against him.

"I want to talk to our friend at the dry cleaner's," Thatcher said, interrupting her musings.

"Why?"

"I want to talk about his brother, ensure there's nothing that could lead us to Scorpion."

"A new development?"

"No. Just giving him a little time to think about what he told us."

No point in arguing with Thatcher.

The moment the two entered the dry cleaner's, Siddiqui stepped from behind the counter, definitely shaken. "Let's talk in my office. I know why you're here."

Seated in a small room with the door closed, Thatcher opened the conversation. "Sir, you said you knew why we returned."

Siddiqui buried his face in his hands. "My brother."

"What can you tell us?"

"He's broken the law and left the country. My family has been disgraced."

"You were cleared previously."

Siddiqui nodded. "I'll always be on some list."

"I'm sorry," Bethany said, and she meant it. Past cases in the civil rights division where prejudice became the norm.

"Was your brother here on Friday when we conducted the interview?"

Siddiqui paled. "No. Agents, I'm trying to build my family's respect again. And I know nothing about Mr. Spree's murder. I wanted to help you."

"You did," Thatcher said. "His statement indicates he was aware of danger unless he cooperated with someone, most likely the killer. You provided important information, and I'll make sure your cooperation is written into your file."

Once in the car, Bethany worked through her irritation at Thatcher and pity for Siddiqui. Yes, she was right he had no part in killing Spree, but to hear his desire for respect made her sympathetic to his predicament.

"I hope he's able to bring honor to his family," she said.

"Our job isn't always catching the bad guys. Sometimes it's reassuring the good ones."

✳ ✳ ✳

11:03 A.M. MONDAY

Thatcher pulled into the subdivision on the west side of town, where Paul Javon claimed Lisa Camry lived with her mother. Small tract homes built in the sixties. Junk cars. Weeds.

"I bet Alicia's inheritance looked very good to a woman living here," Thatcher said.

"Not all the homes are deteriorating. But I agree. You should see the contrast in my parents' neighborhood. The well-kept homes look like roses among thorns."

She had another sensitive side.

They parked in the driveway of a small home, minus the neighborhood's abundance of yard decor. A lazy cat stretched out on the front porch. Freshly painted exterior. "Let's see what we find out about Lisa Camry."

"And hope she's home and didn't leave town since your call."

"Or waiting with a loaded gun?" He smiled and captured one of hers. Good.

A tall young woman opened the door, wearing a shaky smile and a wedding ring. Auburn hair and green eyes, with a striking resemblance to Alicia. After Thatcher and Bethany displayed their IDs, Lisa Camry ushered them into a small but neat living area and gestured for them to sit.

"As I explained on the phone, we have questions about Paul Javon," Thatcher said.

She nodded, her body stiff. "I figured as much." Her gaze focused beyond them, looking but not seeing. "How can I help you?"

"Are you having an affair with Paul Javon?"

She crossed her arms over her chest. "I'm a married woman."

"I assume that's a yes."

"My husband drives a truck. I get lonely. I met Paul at a club and we hit it off."

"Is your husband aware of your affair?"

"I'd never hurt him like that."

Thatcher lifted a brow. "How long have you been seeing Paul Javon?"

"About eight months."

"What were your plans?"

"I have no clue about his. Mine were to play it out until one of us got tired of the game." She shook her head. "Never dreamed he'd be a person of interest in a murder or beat up his wife and daughter." She paused. "I follow the news. . . . Anyway, I didn't tell him about my husband, but he told me his wife no longer cared for him."

"Has he ever hit you?"

Her green eyes slid him disbelief. "This lady packs, and I'd blow his head off if he even tried."

Maybe Paul needed a woman like Lisa to keep him in line. Time for Bethany to pose the sensitive questions. Thatcher turned to his partner—who also packed.

"Lisa, how often is your husband on the road?" Bethany said.

"Five days a week."

"I bet he's exhausted when he's home."

Lisa nodded sadly. "Not much difference than when he's gone. I do love him, but I have needs."

"Are you pregnant?"

"How did you know?"

"Paul told us earlier today. Is it his baby?"

"No. I thought he'd pay me off." She shrugged. "He always had lots of money and drove a BMW. I really want to get out of this neighborhood."

"What kind of gun do you own?"

"A .22."

"Any other guns in the house?"

"My husband's rifles." She touched her mouth. "I know nothing about Alicia Javon's death."

"I'm not making an accusation." Bethany's words were soft, soothing. "We have a murder to investigate. Actually, we have three."

"I know—a serial killer called Scorpion."

"Did Paul ever indicate he wanted his wife dead?"

"No. He rarely talked about her except to complain about her being gone so much. We had absent spouses in common, even if he didn't know about mine."

"Did he murder his wife?"

"No, I said."

"What about you? Did you kill Alicia Javon?"

She shivered. "No! I never saw her, and I was with my husband the day she was killed. I can prove it."

Bethany leaned closer to her. "We'll need to know where you and your husband were during that time."

"Whatever you need. I can't let my husband find out about this. He's excited about the baby . . . and I am too."

The poor guy who was married to Lisa. How long before either of them realized a child didn't keep a family together? Only trust could do that. Since the last few weeks and his decision to follow Christ, Thatcher believed God had to be the number one priority.

CHAPTER 32

Bethany digested the morning's findings. Working on a sleep deficit hammered at her body, but at least she'd taken time for lunch.

She was alerted to a message. She'd gotten to the point of dreading to see what came in next because it seemed each new development brought discouragement. Media was still running wild with the derogatory letter about the FBI's inability to bring in a killer.

The ballistics report. SSA Preston must have pulled strings to expedite it.

She soaked up the information. The same gun was used in all three murders.

She'd been wrong, so very wrong. Paul Javon was innocent of Alicia's murder—though guilty of abuse, which could have led to her death. She'd accused an innocent man, and the regret assaulting her twisted like a sharp knife.

A serial killer walked the streets of Houston claiming victims. What was the motive? She typed in a request to the FIG to see if the same gun had been used in any previous crimes.

Closing her eyes, she recalled the many times she'd argued with Thatcher about Alicia Javon's murder being done by a copycat. She owed him a huge apology.

She typed a text to him. Can we talk now? Ballistics report.

On my way.

She took a long drink of her Diet Dr Pepper and set it beside her computer. Thatcher stood in the doorway of her cubicle.

"Flash?" She forced a smile, referring to him as the DC Comic hero.

"I wish. Was on my way when you texted."

She drew in a breath. "I apologize. This seals a serial killer for all three murders."

He shook his head. "I could have been the one wrong, and this isn't over yet. Without your insistence, Carly would not have had the guts to stand up to her dad. You rock, partner. You're my girl." His face reddened, and he turned away.

She felt the implication in a place where she'd sworn never to go. Not with Thatcher Graves, the player or the agent.

Her phone buzzed a notification from the FIG, ending the awkward moment. She read the update. "Thatcher, listen to this. Two months before Ruth Caswell's death, another man was found dead by the landlord of his apartment building. Shot in the forehead by the same gun used to kill our Scorpion victims." Panic raced through her veins. "This poor man was murdered too. HPD labeled it cold, no suspects, no motives, and no leads. I hate this for all the families who are waiting on us to end the killings."

"Bethany, we're human. We're doing our best to find Scorpion. What was the victim's name?"

"Eldon Hoveland."

"Let's spend some time reviewing the police reports and interviews. Does the FIG indicate a scorpion found on the body?"

"No, but that might be in his file." She turned to her computer and typed in the request. A moment later she looked at him. "No scorpion found on Hoveland's body."

"I think we should explore this. I'll get a chair and join you."

"Sure," she said, her focus on the computer screen.

Thatcher returned with a chair. "I pulled up the reports on my phone."

"Good." She gave him her attention. "This could be the connection to make an arrest."

He nodded. "Read what you have and I'll follow along."

"Eldon Hoveland was found dead by the landlord of his apartment. He was in his late sixties. Cleaned office buildings and lived alone. Never been arrested. His daughter said nothing was missing from his apartment. The poor man probably didn't have anything worth taking. No forced entry either."

"The killer's gun but without the plastic scorpion," Thatcher said. "Maybe the plastic variety was an add-on after the Caswell murder, or the Hoveland murder had a different motive."

"I checked to see if Hoveland cleaned Danford's building for a connection with Alicia Javon, but nothing there." She blinked with the additional information. "According to his daughter, he was homeless for a while."

"What are the odds Hoveland and Spree knew each other?"

"Houston's a huge city, but maybe they met at a soup kitchen or under a bridge." She attempted to see the likelihood of the two men being acquainted, but her mind kept shutting down the possibility.

Thatcher scrolled through his phone. "I don't see any names that match up with Scorpion's victims."

She swallowed hard. "According to the report, the daughter's name is Annette Willis. Let's talk to her. What if the other murders link directly to him?"

"She could fill in a few missing pieces."

She stood before he had a chance to change his mind. "You drive."

Within the hour, Bethany and Thatcher sat at Annette's kitchen table.

"Dad had been estranged from the family for about five years. Then he found religion and everything turned around for him. He found a job and an apartment. Active in church. This was unfair, a death sentence for a changed man."

"How was your relationship with him?" Bethany said.

"While he was homeless, we often didn't hear from him. Later he told me he slept under bridges, on benches, and even a few times at the Lighthouse. He sank his soul into alcohol."

Bethany had seen too many times where addictions took once-good people. "What brought on the problem?"

"Mom died unexpectedly of a heart attack, and he drank his grief. When he recovered, he was the father I remembered."

"So the whole family accepted him back?"

Annette frowned. "Not exactly. My husband left during the time Dad was drinking heavily."

"The problem with your dad also led to marital disillusionment?"

Sadness swept over the woman's face. "My husband couldn't forgive some of the things Dad had done."

Bethany took Annette's hand when she saw the woman's pain. "Would you share with us what happened?"

"I suppose." She breathed in deeply. "Dad's drinking made him mean, violent at times. He showed up drunk at my husband's office during a critical meeting, destroyed valuables, and Lester lost his job."

"I'm sorry." Bethany glanced at her notes. They had the husband's name to run a background.

"So am I. He now lives in Austin. New job. A new, much-younger wife. A new baby."

Thatcher would refer to her ex-husband as having motive. Bethany jotted down the man's contact information.

"Can you give us the names of your dad's friends?"

"He came here alone and seldom talked about others. Dad was more interested in me and the kids. I only wish our family hadn't suffered so."

"Do you know of anyone who'd want to hurt your father?"

She dabbed at a tear. "No. He became such a sweet man. It's not right he died alone. I hope he didn't suffer."

"One of our victims had her Bible stolen. I'm assuming your father had a Bible too."

Annette nodded. "It was on the kitchen table. Untouched."

Bethany handed her a card. "If you remember a detail, please give me a call. Thank you for your time, and we're sorry for your loss."

"I keep thinking I'll climb out of this well of grief. But it hasn't happened."

Driving back to the office, Bethany fought against a shadow of darkness that stalked her. She tried to shake off a sense of her uselessness mixed with no idea where to investigate next. Prayer hit her radar, yet she sank further.

"You were good with Annette," Thatcher said. "Appreciate the request for her ex-husband's work and home contact information."

She offered a smile of thanks. Although any agent could have conducted the interview.

"What's got you down?"

"Doesn't matter, really."

"Doc Graves will be the judge of that."

He paid attention to her moods and her health—small things, and yet it made her feel taken care of. If only she didn't have to be so tough to survive. "My inability to help end this case."

"God's a good beginning."

"Easy for you?"

"Are you kidding? I'm an agent. I thrive on power and control."

She blew out her understanding. "When you first told me about your faith, I wanted to say it wasn't part of the office gossip. So thanks."

"For what?"

"Telling me how God entered your life. And making sure my head is on the case and not on junk. I've never told you my best day or favorite vacation or any of those things. Someday . . . I promise." She wanted to know him better. . . . The scent of him stirred a need she dreamed about and ran from at the same time.

Bethany, stop this ridiculous attraction before you ruin your career. Change the subject now.

"When are you going to tell me more about you?" she said.

"Soon. We men have a tough time expressing our emotions." He turned her way. "I read the textbook and even got a couple of degrees. Tell you what—one day soon I'll give you more of my boring life story. We both can have our own share time."

Before she could respond to his preschool comment, a text came in on her phone. The message made her ill.

"Tell me that's not your brother harassing you again."

She laid the phone on her lap. "Okay, I won't."

"Bethany?"

She chuckled to make light of Lucas's text. "He's making fun of our case."

"What did he say?"

"It's not important."

He swung toward her. "You're beating yourself up again about something you have no control over. What did he say?"

"All right. 'Only special Scorpions have enough poison 2 kill a person.' He must have researched the same site we did." She saw the sender was typing. "Here comes another one."

U r not smart enough 2 find the real killer.

CHAPTER 33

Bethany scrolled through the latest news, analyzing information for a lead to Scorpion and waiting for an update about Lester Willis. The Dallas office had scheduled an interview with him late this afternoon, but he looked clean. Probably another dead end, not that she wanted Annette's ex-husband to be a part of Scorpion. But an arrest would give her a perk. Then again, geographically speaking, the deaths were in Houston, not Dallas.

SSA Preston's eight-fifteen briefing had lasted long enough for him to order agents to triple their work effort and make an arrest. Bethany's sponge-like personality soaked up the urgency.

A blurb caught her attention. The director of a women's shelter on the northeast side of Houston had been attacked and hospitalized. Listed in critical condition.

Bethany's pulse raced as she pressed in Elizabeth's cell phone. It went directly to voice mail. She left a callback message and pressed in the number for Noah's Loft. No answer.

Turning to her computer, she typed in a request for details of the attack. The information scrolled across her screen—Elizabeth Maddrey had been found in her office with a head injury at approximately 5 a.m. A volunteer called 911.

The residents loved Elizabeth, although the men in most of those women's lives despised her. Bethany offered a prayer while phoning Memorial Hermann Northeast Hospital near the shelter.

Her dear friend remained in critical condition. Still unconscious. No visitors except for immediate family, who were with her now. Bethany talked to Mrs. Maddrey, who said it was useless for her to come until much later. Elizabeth's mother could be rather odd, at times rude. But Bethany would honor her wishes.

Elizabeth was the kindest, most generous person on the planet. Someone had better handcuff Bethany if she found out who'd hurt her. She texted Thatcher while grabbing her purse and keys.

Elizabeth in hospital. Serious. Attacked @ shelter. Going to Noah's Loft first. Will call.

She didn't wait for an answer. The Scorpion case could wait awhile. Hadn't Thatcher reminded her several times how many agents were working the case?

At Noah's Loft, three police cars blocked the driveway. Bethany exited and displayed her ID to a middle-aged officer. "Elizabeth Maddrey is a close friend."

He raised a brow. "Has the FBI been called in on this?"

"No, sir. Like I said, she's a friend. I'm asking for a concession here."

"I see. You're wanting to know about the assault?"

"Yes, sir."

"Ms. Maddrey was found unconscious in her office with a severe blow to the head. Looks like a blunt instrument."

"From behind? Her office was kept locked and is too small for someone to catch her by surprise."

"Yes. We've swept the area and checked for prints and DNA. No motive at this point."

"Who found her?"

He checked his notes. "A volunteer, the cook."

"I'm familiar with the woman."

"No sign of forced entry. Indications are one of the women housed here attacked her."

Bethany determined to learn the truth. "Have the residents been interviewed?"

"We have two officers inside finishing up. Taken us several hours. Nothing concrete yet."

She wished for once a crime could be solved immediately. "Did anyone see or hear anything?"

"They aren't talking. Probably afraid, but I'd think they'd want to cooperate. The cook who found her has been very helpful. I understand she's a pastor's wife."

"Right. Can I talk to her?"

"Sure. I'll walk you around to the backyard. Officers have used a picnic table back there to talk to the women."

Seated on a bench, the cook dabbed at her eyes, and Bethany took her hand. "I'm so sorry about this."

"Are you helping the police?"

Bethany nodded. She'd learn about her ID soon enough. "What happened this morning?"

"I heard Elizabeth arrive about four fifteen this morning. The night before she'd asked me to help with breakfast, so I was already here. A little before five, I walked to her office because we were short on milk. The door was closed. When I knocked, she didn't answer, so I called her name a few times. Finally I opened the door. There she lay, sprawled on the floor over toys." She drew in a ragged breath. "I used the phone on her desk to call 911. I gave the ER people her vitals, then waited until the ambulance and police arrived."

"Were any others working?"

"No. The ambulance woke several of them. Bethany, you're a good friend to help find out who did this."

"Thanks. Honestly, I'm FBI, and I will get to the bottom of who did this to Elizabeth."

"I had no idea. I'm glad you're here."

Bethany escorted the cook though the back door to the shelter. The officer who'd met with her originally was speaking to

Dorian and a female officer. He gestured for Bethany to remain where she stood. While she waited, she observed the goings-on around her, listening to conversations and studying body language. A few women were in tears. Others appeared numb.

The officer joined her. "The woman over there is our first suspect. Her name is Dorian Crawford. She's served time for armed robbery and prostitution. I wanted to find out what she was doing when Ms. Maddrey was attacked. She claims to know nothing and agreed to let us go through her room."

Dorian laughed at the female officer as though this were a party. She waved at Bethany. The peculiar woman had secured Bethany's identity, which could easily be found, and she'd exhibited mentally unstable behavior.

"She might open up to you," the male officer said.

"I'll see what I can learn." She approached Dorian. "We need to talk outside."

"I hope this won't take too long. Activities must go on. And the kids need games and toys." Her words raced like the Indy 500. "These women adore me. They're helpless, you know. I already told the officers what happened." She touched her heart. "Has the kitchen staff started lunch? I need to check. And we still need milk."

"Food prep can wait. Today can be a peanut butter and jelly day."

Dorian gasped. "Oh no. Elizabeth would never permit it. What if a resident had a nut allergy?"

Bethany took on her agent persona. "Dorian, it can wait." She made a mental note to conduct her own background. The women at the shelter often had shady pasts, but it didn't set them up for condemnation. Bethany and Dorian stepped into cooler temps and seated themselves on opposite sides of the picnic table.

"I'm telling all the residents you're FBI," she said.

"Be my guest." Bethany made no effort to shove kindness into her question.

"None of the women here will talk to you. You're a spy."

"A spy for what? Elizabeth is one of my dearest friends. She and I share the same concerns for the women and children here." She pointed to her cell phone. "I'd like to record our conversation."

"No way, Ms. FBI. If you're going to record me, I insist upon a lawyer. You must think because I volunteer here I'm stupid." Hostility seemed to seep from the pores of her skin. "Why didn't you tell the others about your FBI work?"

"Because I wanted to volunteer and help the residents, not have them think I'm on an investigation."

Dorian giggled. "But now you are."

An airhead or brilliant? "Why did you refer to me as a spy?"

Dorian glared. "Why are you firing questions at me like I'm a suspect?"

"Are you?"

Dorian pounded her fist against the picnic table. "What's that supposed to mean? Upset me, and I'll destroy your reputation. Media love a victim."

"Go for it." Bethany had no desire to get into a debate.

Dorian pursed her lips like a pouting two-year-old. "Since the first time I met you, you've been obnoxious."

"Some people bring out the best in me." Bethany reached deep for professionalism. "Who else knows where you volunteer?"

"No one but my former landlord. I don't have family." She sniffed. "These women and children are all I have. I live for them. You won't find a thing linking me to this morning's crime."

Smart woman or a lack of social skills? Dorian's facial muscles were relaxed. Her arms were folded in front of her, but not gripped. A smile intact without a hint of malevolence in her eyes.

The woman rose from the bench. "I believe we're done here. You have nothing to incriminate me that would stand in a court of law. From your history, Special Agent Bethany Sanchez, you don't fight well. What you did to your own brother puts you at the bottom of the food chain. I suggest you watch your back."

CHAPTER 34

Bethany curbed her tongue and watched Dorian stomp back to the shelter. A possible bipolar condition joined the list of mental issues going on with the woman. How had she learned about Lucas?

At the door, Dorian turned and covered her mouth. "I don't know what's wrong with me. Please forgive me, Bethany. I'm so sorry."

Whoa. She wanted to see the background on this woman now.

Dorian hurried back to her, tears streaming down her face. "I know you mean well, and you care about all of us here."

Bethany plastered on a smile. "It's all right, Dorian. I'm questioning you because the officer thought you might be able to help find out who attacked Elizabeth. Sit down, and we can chat."

She obliged, and Bethany searched her mind for the right words to approach her about Lucas. "Do you know my brother?"

She shook her head. "I heard on the news you sent him to prison for a family dispute."

Bethany knew for a fact the information had not been picked up by the media. "Where did you hear this?"

She shrugged. "I don't remember. Maybe if you tell me his name, I could help you."

Bethany offered a smile. Later she'd search through media records to see if she'd missed something about her testimony against Lucas. "It doesn't matter."

"You mean you sent your own brother to prison?"

"Let's focus on Elizabeth. Can you help us find out who attacked her?"

Dorian glanced around, blinking. "It's all a part of a scheme."

"What kind of scheme?"

"I can't say."

Bethany stifled her frustration. Remaining calm was at the top of her priorities. "Do you know why Elizabeth was attacked?"

Dorian's eyes glazed in an imbalanced stare. Thatcher should be here. "Because of the evil."

"What evil? Elizabeth is a wonderful person."

She glanced away, her lips quivering.

"What would it take for you to tell me what's going on?"

"Nothing and everything. I'm afraid the evil has killed my oldest son."

"You said you have no family."

"I was afraid."

Bethany reached across the table, and this time she took the woman's hand. Unpredictable behavior washed over every word, but fear had a way of confusing the mind. "What's going on, Dorian?"

"No one can find Tyler—he's disappeared. He's a good boy, responsible and smart. Not like me or his younger brother, Aiden."

"Where is your younger son? Is he alone?"

"He's in juvie. Supposed to be released next week. Tyler was going to take him in, but now . . ." Dorian burst into sobs. "I used to think the system caused all my problems." She inhaled sharply. "It's not. It's evil people."

"Someone here?"

"Not here. Out there." Her arm swept around them. "It's bigger than you could ever imagine. I made them mad and now Tyler's missing."

"How so?" Of all the things Bethany should be doing, listening to a crazy woman wasn't one of them.

Dorian bent toward Bethany, but when she didn't say anything,

Bethany moved forward. "Evil people must be stopped so the innocent can live in peace. The victims deserve justice."

"You're right, but it's impossible," she said. "If you make it known I gave you information, they'll kill Aiden and me. In that order. If you arrest me, they'll kill Aiden. Either way I lose."

"All right. I'll say you made me furious. Refused to cooperate with HPD or the FBI. But I must have something to go on." She desperately needed the woman's confidence, whatever the state of her mind.

"Find out what happened to Tyler . . . and visit Aiden. Persuade him to stay at the juvenile detention center. He'll get what he needs and an education. And he'll be safe."

"I'll do my best. When they're safe, you'll tell me about this evil that has attacked Elizabeth?"

"Yes. I'll tell you all I know."

Could she really believe Dorian? "How did this evil get inside the shelter?"

Her eyes widened. "Through the walls, like a demon."

Great. What a waste of time. "What can you tell me about your missing son?"

"He's a hard worker. Saving for college. Would do anything for Aiden and me." She hesitated. "He has to be alive."

"So the boys' names are Tyler and Aiden Crawford?"

"Yes."

"I'll do my best to find him. What's his address?" Bethany reached into her purse for a pen and paper, then pushed them toward her.

Dorian wrote the information. "I have a photo of the boys. It's wrinkled 'cause I keep it next to me. Their father was a black man, so they don't look like me. He overdosed when Aiden was born. Stupid man died." She pulled a folded photograph from her jeans pocket and handed it to Bethany.

The older son was the young man who'd saved her life, Zack Adams.

✳ ✳ ✳

2:47 P.M. TUESDAY

Thatcher listened to every word of Bethany's latest report. She'd entered his cubicle wearing stress like a coat of armor. "You agreed to check on Dorian Crawford's sons?"

Her shoulders slumped. "Yes. At the time it made sense. I must find out who hurt Elizabeth. I'm such a softy."

He chuckled. "Not sure *softy* best describes you. When did you plan to investigate the boys?"

"After hours."

"The ones we use to sleep?"

"All I need to do is talk to Aiden, report to Dorian, and see what she can tell me."

"I'll go with you. What are you not telling me?"

She gave him a sideways glance. "Why?"

"We're partners, and I have to keep my eye on you. Might find an object lesson."

She blinked. "I shouldn't have said a word. She showed me a pic of the boys. We know the older one as Zack Adams."

Thatcher focused on the information. "I don't believe in coincidences."

"Neither do I."

"Right. Lucas calls, you nearly get plowed down in a hit-and-run, and the guy who saves you is the son of a crazy woman. There's got to be a connection." He gave her his best unbelieving stare. "Have you run a background on Tyler?"

"Clean. He's been attending night school at the University of Houston. Excellent grades. I have his address, but his cell phone is out of service. His mother's life has been colorful—in addition to the robbery, solicitation, and breaking and entering, Dorian's mental issues are a part of her record."

He'd do a little researching on this one. "How's your friend Elizabeth?"

"She's off the critical list. I'm heading to the hospital at the close of work."

"Count me in."

"Why this time?"

"For us to discuss the Scorpion case. Then follow up on Aiden Crawford. What else?" He simply wanted to be with her—selfish but true. More like tormented. He'd been thinking a relationship between them could work. They could establish guidelines. . . . Who was he fooling? Rules girl would run like the wind at the mention of his growing feelings.

She hesitated. "We might have Lester Willis's interview report. See if his animosity to Eldon Hoveland put our victim in Scorpion's way."

"Right. Agents interviewed Hoveland's landlord and his pastor. The man excelled in reaching out to others. According to his pastor, if he had a dollar in his pocket and someone needed it, he gave it. No enemies."

"Thatcher, what am I doing getting mixed up with Dorian's problems while a serial killer runs loose?"

"I thought you wanted to find out who'd attacked Elizabeth."

"Yes. But I hate being scattered. I'm hoping she recognized her attacker and can file charges. End it."

"An HPD matter. But I learned the doctors refused to let police officers question her."

She sighed. "Another reason for me to see Elizabeth."

CHAPTER 35

Bethany and Thatcher rode the hospital elevator to see Elizabeth, who'd recently regained consciousness. Bethany prayed for her dear friend's healing and for the name of the person who'd attacked her.

In the ICU waiting area Bethany hugged Elizabeth's parents and quietly introduced Thatcher.

"Can we have a few minutes alone with her, to ask what she remembers about the attack?" Bethany said, hoping Mrs. Maddrey's emotional state wouldn't taint her judgment.

"No," her mother said, her face red and blotched from crying. "I won't allow anyone to upset her. The police have already tried, and the doctor and I refused them."

Mr. Maddrey wrapped his arm around his wife's shoulders. "Dear, this is Bethany, one of our daughter's closest friends. She can help find out who did this."

The woman closed her eyes and turned from him.

"Think about the repercussions," he continued. "Elizabeth will recover. If the person who assaulted her isn't apprehended, the next time she might not be so lucky."

"That's why she needs to give up her job at the shelter," Mrs. Maddrey said. "Most of those women are crazy."

"She's no more going to give up her work with those women and children than the moon's going to drip honey."

"She's dedicated to her job, an admirable trait," Thatcher said.

Mrs. Maddrey peered at Bethany with red-rimmed eyes. "If I consent to you interviewing Elizabeth, you have only ten minutes with her."

"Yes, ma'am." Thatcher answered for them. "We'll do our best not to upset your daughter." His kind attention to the grieving couple was one of the many things Bethany admired about him. "We all want her to recover as quickly as possible."

"Promise?" The woman sounded like a child.

"You have my word," he said.

Bethany and Thatcher entered the room where Elizabeth slept amid the steady beep of machines monitoring her vitals. Her head was bandaged, covering the sixteen stitches, and her thick hair had been cut and shaved in areas, but she was alive. Tests would show the depths of her injuries. Praise God for good doctors.

Elizabeth stirred, and her eyes opened to half-mast. "How did you get past my mother?" Her faint voice seemed like music.

"Wasn't easy." Bethany kissed her forehead. "Are you ready to dance?"

"Forgot my shoes," Elizabeth whispered. "Good to see you."

Bethany smiled into her friend's pale face, where a blue-and-purple bruise darkened the right side. "Are they treating you like a queen?"

"You should see my doctor." She closed her eyes. "A hunk." Elizabeth had a way of making the worst of circumstances look better.

"I have a friend for you to meet—my partner."

"The good-looking one?"

Heat burned Bethany's face. "No, that was my other partner. This is Special Agent Thatcher Graves."

Elizabeth opened her eyes. "Drop the last name. It's deadly."

He chuckled. "Good to meet you."

What kind of meds had they given her? Discretion had dropped into a bedpan. "We promised your parents we'd be only a few minutes. Do you remember anything about the attack?"

"Attack? Is that what happened? I thought I fell."

"Very much so."

Elizabeth blinked. "Can I have an ice chip?" She pointed to the bed stand, where a cup sat filled with ice.

Bethany slipped a piece into her mouth and waited. Guilt nibbled at her. Elizabeth needed her rest.

"I remember a little." She swallowed. "I was at the shelter early and set out bacon and eggs. Then decided to check e-mail. Unlocked my office, but the light switch didn't work. Made my way to the desk. That's all I remember."

"Someone was waiting for you, Elizabeth. Have you had a problem with any of the residents?"

She shook her head. "Who found me?"

"The cook. She called 911."

Weariness creased her friend's normally smooth face. Thatcher touched Bethany's shoulder. "We should go."

"Thanks for helping us." Bethany took her friend's hand and gave a gentle squeeze. "Rest and get better."

She closed her eyes, and a smile graced her lips. "Mom said my friend was here earlier. He might be a keeper."

"He'll need my approval."

Elizabeth's smile lingered. "Agent Graves, come back to see me when I'm not so out of it."

"Will do," he said. "Appreciate your talking to us."

In the hallway, Bethany stood for a moment outside Elizabeth's door with Thatcher. "Dorian has no business being at Noah's Loft. She gives *unstable* another line in the dictionary. But she's the only lead I have. Elizabeth is my friend, almost like a sister. I can't leave this to HPD."

CHAPTER 36

Thatcher and Bethany entered the Harris County Juvenile Detention Center on Congress Avenue. There they waited for Aiden Crawford in a bleak visitors' area that reeked of adolescent sweat.

Thatcher took one look at the kid's record and groaned. "Bethany, he will never listen to you. He's already connected to an African American gang that despises Hispanics. I'll talk to him."

"Be my guest. My talks with Lucas only made him madder." She shook her head. "Forget that remark. Whining isn't my style. Anything you can say to curb Aiden's behavior is welcome."

"We can't fix them all, but we can try with this kid."

Bethany's determination matched her features. "I see Lucas in every rebellious face."

He could spend a lifetime getting to know her. Thatcher inwardly startled. Did he just think "lifetime"?

She whirled to face him as though she'd read his thoughts. "This is really beyond the call of duty. An HPD case. I must be losing it to think I can help Elizabeth through Dorian. But thanks."

"No problem." His reasons were selfish.

Aiden entered the room and slumped onto a chair. He wore insolence like gang colors.

Thatcher introduced himself and Bethany. "Aiden, your mother asked us to check on you."

"Why?" His gaze shot lethal arrows.

"Because she cares about you."

"When did this start?"

Thatcher wasn't going to mince words. "Do you know where your brother is?"

A hint of worry swept over his face. "Ain't found 'im yet? 'Cause he might be dead."

"When did you last see Tyler?"

"Don't remember." He swung one leg out in front of him.

"Weren't you supposed to live with him after release?"

He curled his lip. "I can take care of myself."

"Your mother would like to see you stay here where it's safe."

"When I roll outs, I got plans."

"Without a roof over your head and an education, your plans will flush down the toilet. Why is your mother afraid for you?"

"She don't know nuthin'," he said. "Do you know where she put me last time?"

Thatcher had done his homework. "Your grandmother."

"Crazy old lady. All she did was talk to the TV. No food in the house ever but pinto beans and Spam."

"Then Tyler took over."

"Whatever. This ain't about my mama or Granny."

"Right. It's about keeping you safe. Tyler did right by you."

Aiden blew out a sigh that spelled anger. "Maybe. But he done got stupid."

"How?"

The kid humphed. "Ask him if he can talk from the dead."

"What's going on with your brother?"

"As I said, ask him if he can talk from the dead."

Thatcher leaned back in the folding chair. "If he's in trouble, then he needs help."

A muscle twitched.

"Can't help your brother, Aiden? Or won't?"

He glanced at his hands. "A list."

"What kind of list?"

"Don't know. It was in his head. My brother could see something and remember it."

"Photographic memory?"

"That's it."

"What did he tell you about the list?"

"Said he'd probably get killed for it. Wanted to take it to the cops. Then he disappeared."

"And he didn't tell you what was on it?"

Aiden sneered. "My brother didn't want me killed."

"Would he have written it down?"

"I don't know."

"Who are his friends?"

"He was a loner like me. Except for some white girl."

"Do you know her name?"

"It's her fault this all happened."

"We need a name."

"Never met her. Me and Tyler were tight until she came along." The kid clenched his fist. "Look, I done bad stuff. But my brother . . . he was good. He'd do anything for me. Even our no-good mama."

"Have you been threatened?"

"I told the man I know nuthin'. But he wants the list."

"His name?"

The boy hesitated, then focused on Thatcher. "You'll get me out of here and put me in a safe place? 'Cause he got to me before."

"We'll take care of it tonight."

"I don't think my brother's dead. I think he's hiding 'cause a man by the name of Deal wants the list."

"What can you tell us about him?"

"Tyler said Deal had connections."

"How did he contact you?"

"Tyler got me a burner phone. Not supposed to have it here, but I hide stuff good."

"Would you be willing to talk to the police?"

"No. I talked to you. That's 'nough. Are you going to look for Tyler?"

"You have my word." What was Thatcher thinking?

"Deal said he'd call tonight and tell me how to get him the list. I thought you were him. I might know more, but I have to get out of here."

"You've never met him?"

"Didn't ya listen? No idea what he looks like."

"Give me the list, and all this ends."

"I want out of here first."

"This is a safe place."

He glanced around the room. "Sure, I can break out, but what happens when I look for Tyler?"

Thatcher understood a bluff when he heard it. Trust had been dealt a hard blow with his missing brother. "I'll move you to a safe house."

The kid relaxed for a second. "I'll keep my end. I'll do it for Tyler."

CHAPTER 37

12:07 A.M. WEDNESDAY

Thatcher punched his pillow, willing sleep while his mind raced. What would it take for Aiden to surrender the list? What else did the kid know? Did his brother even want it found?

While his thoughts swirled, an image of Bethany refused to let him go. She'd taken on the job to help bring down a serial killer, vowed to find her best friend's attacker, and was plagued by a felon brother and a family who supported him.

He should tell her the case came first.

He should urge her to leave Elizabeth's attack to HPD.

He should have her brother arrested. Between his threatening texts and possibly arranging a hit-and-run—yes, he believed Lucas wouldn't stop until Bethany paid for his last jail stint—the man needed to be locked up. What kind of brother threatened his sister?

Thatcher's mind raced on. . . .

Lester Willis was cleared of anything to do with his ex-father-in-law's death. Thatcher had expected the confirmation—one more item off his list.

One of the things puzzling him was Tyler Crawford. He saved Bethany's life, and now he seemed to be fighting to save his own. With a clean record and positive steps to better himself, did he have a connection to Lucas, or was Tyler's presence at the scene of

Bethany's near hit-and-run coincidence? The FBI had nothing on a man called Deal, which meant Thatcher was wrestling with the claims of a street kid. How bizarre was that? But the possibility kept him awake and concerned about Bethany's safety, a missing young man, and an obnoxious thirteen-year-old who had no future unless he made changes. Aiden now resided with a retired FBI couple on a farm north of Houston.

The need to arrest Scorpion rose with urgency. Couldn't establish motive when all they had to go on was the same gun and plastic scorpions.

Thatcher climbed out of bed and flipped open his laptop. Not sure why the Caswell security video with Mae Kenters bothered him, but he wanted to view it again. After accessing FBI files, he studied the video prior to her leaving for her break, and Ruth Caswell's death.

He slowed the footage and isolated the frame when she glanced at her watch. There . . . a nervous twitch.

He continued as she walked to the window. He isolated the frame again, zoomed in where her right hand rested on the window latch, and slowly observed what was happening. While Mae's attention was supposedly on the left side, her right finger moved slightly. He'd wondered why the window had her attention with cooler temperatures outside.

Now his observations demonstrated an accomplice. Most likely not a willing one.

✳ ✳ ✳

8:30 A.M. WEDNESDAY

After SSA Preston's short briefing on Scorpion, Thatcher made his way to Bethany's cubicle. She appeared glued to her computer screen, so he cleared his throat.

She glanced up, her face troubled. "Hey."

"Are you okay?"

"Sure. Just frowning into the computer."

"I want to talk to Mae Kenters again." He pulled his phone from his jacket. "Take a look at this footage of Mae Kenters prior to leaving Ruth Caswell's bedroom for her break."

"I've seen it," she said.

"I've isolated a zoomed-in segment." He handed her the phone. "Two minutes before leaving the room, she sets aside a magazine and walks to the window."

"The same window where the killer entered?" She watched the video. After thirty seconds, she pressed Pause. "I have no idea what you want me to see."

"Look again." Thatcher watched her narrow in on the window scene.

"Thatcher, her hands are trembling."

"Correct. Although we've put this case on hold while investigating the other two, it does raise questions about her testimony."

"Won't hold water in court."

"But it would make for interesting questioning."

"Figured so with what you discovered." She reached for her notepad. "Will her lawyer be cooperative?"

"This is a house call."

Irritation flashed at him.

Must not be a good day for Special Agent Bethany Sanchez. "What's wrong? Another text from your brother?"

Her lack of expression told him fathoms about what was happening underneath. "Remember when you explained how you handle negative emotions?" she said. "I'm trying to evaluate mine and put them in the right perspective. A long time ago, I chose to confront and stop Lucas's irresponsible actions. Nothing's changed. I stayed awake last night thinking about him and a possible connection to Tyler Crawford. My brother's capable of a hit-and-run, and Tyler's quick reaction on the scene saved my life." She shook her head. "Lucas knows where I volunteer. If I learn he attempted to seek revenge by arranging Elizabeth's attack, I'll be the one out for retribution. Goodness, I rattled off a bunch of stuff that didn't make sense to me." She shrugged. "I'm ready for the lecture about putting my energies into Scorpion."

"You already know the appropriate measures to deal with Lucas." He leaned toward her. "Bethany, how can you work this case when he's constantly taunting you?"

"I'm reconsidering."

"Will you tell me what he said?"

She handed him her phone. "I've kept all of them. They're coming from two burner phones. Here's the latest."

It's over when i say it's over

"That's a threat to a federal agent."

"He threatened you verbally, Thatcher."

"By name?"

She reached out as if to touch him but drew back. "I want a little longer to think about pursuing charges against my brother." She rose from her chair. "Let's see if Mae's ready to change her story."

Thatcher would let it go for now. "Would you lead out? She's fragile."

She slid him a cautious glance. "You're risking a lot with me posing questions."

Mae Kenters lived on the west side of town in a modest town house. They didn't have a warrant and were banking on her cooperation. Mae's surprise etched into her face at the sight of the agents.

"Ms. Kenters, we have a few questions for you," Bethany said. "Can we come in?"

"I suppose. I already told you everything, and I have to work today." She hesitated, then opened the door wide. She gestured down the hall. "I'm about to have coffee. Would you like a cup?"

"No, thank you," Bethany said.

Mae's kitchen had a country feel with splashes of sunflowers and ducks. She moved slowly, finding the exact mug in the cabinet, pouring coffee, adding cream and sugar, and finally lowering herself into a chair. She twisted her watch and repeatedly stared at the time.

Bethany removed a notepad from her purse. "We won't be long. Special Agent Graves has discovered a discrepancy in the security camera video from the night of Mrs. Caswell's murder."

"In what way? I explained everything to the police officers and you people." Her trembling hand reached to her lips. "I loved Ruth."

"Mae," Bethany began, "I know you cared for her. No one disputes your devotion."

"Then what's this about? Should I call my attorney?"

"Contacting your attorney is your choice. All we want is an explanation of a brief moment in the footage."

Thatcher displayed the captured frame and the slight movement of her hand.

Mae swallowed hard while she clenched her fingers into her palms.

"We think you're being blackmailed by Mrs. Caswell's killer. Is this true?"

Mae continued to stare at the pic.

Thatcher cleared his throat. "Mae, you're a good woman and an excellent hospice nurse, and I understand your aging parents live here with you."

"They're still asleep upstairs. Rough night."

"Are you hiding critical information to a murder case?"

Tears seeped from her eyes. "Scorpion doesn't offer empty threats."

"We can keep you and your parents safe. Scorpion's killed four people that we know of. Are there more?" he said.

She trembled. "I hope none."

"Do you want to face murder charges with a serial killer?"

Mae sobbed.

Bethany grasped the woman's hand. "Fear is an ugly enemy. Its venom robs us of our hopes and dreams. Sometimes it takes innocent lives with it. Will you tell us the truth about the night Ruth Caswell was murdered?"

Mae wept as though her very soul wrestled with the facts about the crime. "A man called me about a week before it happened. His voice was distorted, but I distinctly heard him say his name: Deal. I have no idea why he chose me."

No coincidence the same man who phoned Mae threatened Tyler and Aiden Crawford. Thatcher's mind jumped from one supposition to another. How deep were Scorpion's claws and why? One thing seemed certain: Lucas Sanchez had been in jail during three of the homicides and therefore had nothing to do with the serial killer. Bethany's brother had his own agenda.

"It's all right," Bethany said. "Go on."

"He threatened my parents if I didn't give in to his demands. He told me to unlock Mrs. Caswell's bedroom window before leaving for my break. I thought he planned to rob her, not kill her. When I saw the poor woman and all the blood, I . . . I couldn't believe it. Lying is wrong, but murder must come easy to him." She dabbed her nose with a napkin from the kitchen table.

Bethany peered into the woman's face. "Are you ready to swear to your statement?"

"And you'll keep my parents safe?"

"I promise."

Her shoulders slumped. "I'll sign anything to get him off the streets."

Thatcher displayed a photo of Alicia Javon. "You've never seen this woman?"

"No, sir. I'd tell you."

He showed her one of Tyler, and she moistened her lips. "Last spring, I volunteered one night a week at the Lighthouse—you know, the homeless shelter downtown? Forgot to mention that when we spoke before. This young man and I often served dinner. Then my schedule filled with hospice work. I discontinued the volunteering and never saw him again."

"What about this woman?" He pulled out a photo of Dorian Crawford.

"I saw her at the Lighthouse too, not as a volunteer but using the shelter."

"What can you tell us about her?"

"It's been a while. She was eccentric. More like multiple personalities. I remember she always asked Tyler for more food and if he had money." She shook her head. "I told him not to do it, but he never listened. Promise me you'll do everything to protect my parents. I don't care about me. Just them."

"We'll do all within our power," Thatcher said, but he couldn't make her a promise.

CHAPTER 38

Bethany breathed a prayer of thanks. Elizabeth was doing much better, and the doctor targeted Friday for release. HPD hadn't made any arrests in her assault. How could Bethany fault them when her own case lay in the fridge?

Thatcher stood in her cubicle's doorway. "Ever work undercover?"

"Once in a real estate office."

"Late tomorrow afternoon we're going homeless."

"Where?" She held up a finger. "The Lighthouse?"

"Yes. This mysterious Deal might be working there."

"And Deal is Scorpion?" She hoped so because it brought them up another rung on the investigative ladder.

"Looks that way. I'd like a round with Dorian. Her name muddies this mess, and I want clarification. If Aiden is aware of a man called Deal, what are the chances she knows him too?"

"Big-time."

At Noah's Loft, Dorian opened the door. She paled at the sight of Bethany. "Why are you here again? Bad news? My boys—"

"We need to talk to you," Bethany said, evaluating the woman's speech for her mental state.

Dorian let them inside and turned to Thatcher. "Are you FBI?"

"Yes, ma'am."

She raised her fist. "Don't get me or my boys killed. Have you found Tyler? Is Aiden okay?"

Bethany stepped between them, not sure if Dorian would attempt to strike a federal agent. "We haven't found Tyler, but Aiden's safe."

"At juvie?"

"No."

"Where?"

"He asked we keep the information private," Bethany said.

"Then don't be expecting me to tell you about the evil here."

"Dorian, I don't bargain well. If you're withholding evidence in Elizabeth's assault, you'll be prosecuted."

She humphed. "It's a police matter, not yours, Ms. FBI."

Bethany leveled a gaze at her. "So the motherhood thing is an act?"

Dorian's eyes shadowed. "This is one demon trip after another."

The cook appeared. "Excuse me, Ms. Dorian. Did you pick up the chocolate chips? We have the batter all ready for them." She smiled at Bethany. "Some of the kids and I are making cookies. We've talked about it for a couple of days."

"I'll show you where I put them," Dorian said.

"We'll expect you in the director's office," Thatcher said. "We have questions."

The cook disappeared down the hall with Dorian. Bethany led Thatcher to Elizabeth's office and closed the door behind them. The bloodstains had been scrubbed from the floor and her desk was in order, more so than Bethany could ever remember.

"Thanks for defending my honor." Thatcher laughed. "She is a piece of work."

"The woman makes me crazy."

The computer took a few moments to spring to life, and all the while Bethany studied the small room for indications of what happened to Elizabeth.

When the screen brightened, Bethany pulled up a document

titled, "Staff and Volunteers" and scrolled to Dorian's information. Name. Address. Phone number with "landlord" in parentheses. No reference letter. Odd how a volunteer becomes a resident and plays both roles.

Thatcher searched the hard files for volunteer info, including the board of directors. Other than Dorian's missing TB test and reference letter, the information was in order.

Dorian returned, and Thatcher pointed to an empty chair. "Have a seat."

"I'll stand."

"Sit down, Ms. Crawford. Our investigation shows the address given to Noah's Loft on your volunteer application doesn't exist."

"Privacy's my choice. Besides, I'm staying here now."

"I understand Ms. Maddrey contacted you through your landlord." When Dorian affirmed the information, he continued. "Is the number here accurate?"

"Yes, sir."

He turned to Bethany. "Would you call for verification?"

Bethany pressed it in while moments ticked by. "It rang several times. No voice mail."

"He must be out," Dorian said. "Try later."

"Your signature on the volunteer form is supposed to verify your information is true," Thatcher said.

"That's none of your business."

"Another matter comes to our attention," he continued. "As a courtesy, Special Agent Bethany Sanchez attempted to find your son Tyler. At the time, you claimed fear for your sons and a willingness to help law enforcement find Ms. Maddrey's attacker. In doing so, we obtained testimony about a man referred to as Deal, who may be Scorpion, the serial killer. Do you know a man named Deal?"

"Never heard of him. It's evil doings. If you don't leave me alone, Scorpion will believe I talked."

"Give us his name."

"I don't know who he is. A demon told me about him when I was asleep."

Dorian was truly delusional. Talking to her went against everything Bethany believed as logical.

"We're taking you in for questioning," Thatcher said. "You're withholding evidence."

"This makes no sense." Dorian whirled to Bethany. "You lied to me. Said you'd help with my boys, and Tyler's still missing. What do you have to say for yourself, you worthless—?"

Bethany had been called worse. The woman desperately needed medical help. No wonder Aiden held such animosity toward his mother.

"I know my rights and want a lawyer."

"Everyone should have proper legal representation," Bethany said. "We're leaving now. Will this be peaceably or in cuffs?"

"I'm going." She spit a mouthful of curses, and one more time, Bethany was ready to strangle her.

In the hallway, the cook and three of the children met them. One of the children held a small paper plate of cookies slipped into a plastic bag, and the cook carried another.

"One for both of you," the cook said. "Elizabeth and I talked about doing this for you the other day, and the children wanted to help."

"Thanks so much, but remember I'm diabetic," Bethany said.

The cook offered her plate to Bethany. "These are sugar free."

"How very thoughtful."

"If you like them, I'll give you the changes in the recipe."

Bethany didn't want to upset the children with Dorian in custody, so she took the cookies and bent to the children. "Thank you. I can't wait to eat these."

Dorian shook her finger at the cook. "You don't have any business giving away these cookies."

The cook huffed. "You're not in charge, and you knew we planned to give Bethany a few special ones."

The cook handed the second plate to Thatcher. "These are regular, buttery chocolate chip cookies. The kids helped with these too."

Thatcher took the plate.

They did smell good. Bethany wished someone would offer a plate of information to further sweeten their day and end the string of crimes.

CHAPTER 39

Thatcher stole a look at Bethany. This morning she'd chosen oatmeal at Starbucks, and she drank coffee instead of nasty Diet Dr Pepper. He'd make a genuine violent crime agent out of her yet.

They'd worked together for over a week, and he was thinking about her too much of the time.

"What did you eat for dinner last night?" he said.

She startled. "Are you keeping tabs on my food intake?"

"I don't want you crashing on me."

"Just this once, Special Agent Graves. I had scrambled eggs with chilies and cheese. Jasper ate the leftovers and grapes."

Her tone indicated he shouldn't ask about her diet again. "Okay, partner. Dorian's in custody. Any thoughts there?"

"Sometimes I think she's incredibly intelligent, and other times I don't think she could stack blocks."

"Figuring out a person comes with a price." How well he knew that.

"Tyler hasn't been found, and we have a briefing at eight." She stirred three packets of Splenda into her bowl of oatmeal. "Tell me about this evening at the Lighthouse. How do I dress? What am I supposed to do?"

He blinked, snapping himself out of her secret admirer club.

"A long red wig, lots of makeup. Earrings to your shoulders. Short skirt, low-cut—"

She waved her arm. "I get it. A hooker."

"They get hungry too."

"But they have their own place to do business at night."

He laughed. "Okay. Keep the wig. Big clothes, preferably those that haven't been washed for a while. Broken English. Use your imagination. I'm going to ask for Deal, say I was referred to him by Ansel Spree."

Her eyes brightened. "This actually sounds fun."

He pointed to her bowl. "How's the fiber trip?"

"Oatmeal is good for you." She gave him a smile that nearly dislocated his heart. "But a blueberry muffin sounds delish."

"Speaking of delish, did you try your cookies? Mine were great."

"Brought mine for a snack this morning." She pulled the plastic bag from her purse. "I think I'll have one now." She bit off a chocolate chip–filled morsel. "Pretty good."

Their cells alerted them simultaneously. The notification punched fire into his gut.

"Oh no," Bethany said.

"HPD found a body dumped in the Buffalo Bayou. Tyler Crawford. A 9mm bullet to the forehead. Duct tape covered his mouth. A scorpion taped to his chest. Death occurred between one and three this morning."

She buried her face in her hands. "I don't look forward to telling Dorian, but I feel obligated to. And then there's Aiden. We should tell him ourselves."

He nodded, his thoughts on the report. "The duct tape didn't appear on the other victims. A warning to any others to keep quiet."

"Like Mae, Dorian, and Aiden."

"I'm not convinced Aiden doesn't have the list. Deal thinks so."

"Do you ever feel this case is so messy we'll never figure it out?"

"Our job is to clean up messes."

Her cell rang, and she grabbed it. "Hi, Shannon." Bethany caught Thatcher's attention. "I'm so sorry. Yes, we can meet you there." She said good-bye and turned to him. "Shannon Javon is on her way to our office. Says Scorpion murdered her boyfriend—Tyler Crawford."

✳ ✳ ✳

7:45 A.M. THURSDAY

SSA Preston postponed the briefing until Bethany and Thatcher finished with Shannon Javon. Bethany ached for the young woman, the obviously frail daughter of Alicia and Paul Javon.

"I can't believe he's gone," she said, her eyes red. "First Mom and now Tyler. Both killed in the same horrible way. Two people I loved most in the world. I went to sleep last night dreaming about the weekend with Tyler." She paused. "At least Dad was in jail."

Bethany believed Shannon accepted the truth about her dad's temper. "What about Carly?"

She nodded. "I called her first. I'm going to my aunt's after I leave here."

"Good. You shouldn't be alone. When was the last time you saw Tyler?"

"We had lunch yesterday."

"Did he seem upset?"

"No, ma'am. He had this great attitude about life. No matter what happened, he chose to be a better person for it. We talked a lot about Mom and the situation at home."

"You cared for him very much."

"We've dated for about a year. We were going to get married."

"What did your dad think about him?"

She sobbed. "Dad never met Tyler. He'd come unglued about the race thing."

"And hurt both of you?" Bethany handed her a tissue.

Shannon lifted her head. "Tyler wanted me to move in with him. I planned to talk to Mom about it after the concert the night she died." She paused. "He wanted me to convince Mom to kick Dad out."

"Shannon, you'll be okay. You can get through this."

Her lips quivered. "How do I arrange a funeral by myself? His mother's a mental case, and his brother is somewhere on the streets."

"I'm sure Pastor Lee will help you."

She bit her lip. "I forgot about him. Where is my mind? Is this my fault?"

Bethany turned to Thatcher. His psychology background could best respond to this.

His face softened, a tender look she'd come to respect. "The one at fault is the person who killed your mother and Tyler. Not you."

She rubbed her face. "I feel like the killer has stabbed my heart and twisted the knife. I just want it all to go away, for Mom and Tyler to be alive."

"Where are you emotionally, Shannon?"

Her eyes watered. "I'm afraid for me and my sister."

"Let's call your aunt to see if she and Carly can come here to get you. Being alone is not in your best interests."

She nodded, and Thatcher made the arrangements.

Bethany's stomach tightened as though she might shed a few tears. Seeing him with Shannon reminded her of what she wanted someday: a man who truly cared.

CHAPTER 40

Thatcher noted Bethany's pale face when they entered SSA Preston's office. The case was in shambles with pressure from the city on law enforcement taking the brunt of criticism, and the clues leading nowhere. The scowl on Preston's face indicated he had nothing new to offer either. Thatcher's and Bethany's findings, along with the combined task force, hadn't produced a name in the city's database of offenders. Only Deal. A mysterious man. No one had seen his face.

"Tyler Crawford is murder number five. Wake up. What are you missing? No one rests until this is solved. Understand?"

Frustration with the lack of progress pounded him too. He glanced at Bethany. She pressed her fingers against her temples. Twice she'd excused herself from the meeting, irritating Preston. Had her sugar level dropped?

Bethany stood. "Excuse me, sir. I'm not feeling well. Seems—" She wobbled, and Thatcher caught her.

When she revived, she questioned her whereabouts. Weak pulse. Clammy skin. Her eyes fluttered open . . . dull, then drifted shut. He failed to keep her awake. That's when he called 911.

"Sir, I'm following the ambulance," he said when Bethany disappeared with the paramedics.

"You are on a case." SSA Preston seldom raised his voice.

"This is my partner." He hoped Preston was aware of her medical condition. "I haven't noticed any heavy perspiration or shaking. My mother is diabetic, but I'm no doctor."

"You have a responsibility to the people of Houston and the victims of the serial killer."

Thatcher held back his ire. "Sir, I'm not much good without my partner."

Thatcher waited in the emergency examining room at Memorial Hermann Northwest Hospital. He'd given the nursing staff what little he knew about Bethany. At times she was coherent, but then she'd slip back. Moans about head and abdominal pain escaped her lips. Those complaints ventured off the path of diabetic shock.

A doctor stepped into the room, reading her chart. "Is Miss Sanchez pregnant?"

"I have no idea."

The doctor offered a professional smile, the kind photographers hated and FBI agents labeled as fake. "When did these symptoms start?"

"Not sure, but she fainted around ten forty-five."

"Has she ever experienced this before?" The doctor continued to write with about as much bedside manner as a fish.

"Not to my knowledge. I'm her partner. We're FBI agents."

"That means you're together more than eight hours a day." He shone a light into her eyes. "Could she have eaten something? She's not vomiting, but this could be food poisoning."

Instinct washed over him. . . . Elizabeth's attack and Bethany's sudden illness. "She told me scrambled eggs with chilies and cheese for dinner, and I was with her at breakfast. Oatmeal at Starbucks. But what concerns me the most is she was given some sugar-free chocolate-chip cookies last night. She's diabetic."

Bethany moistened her lips. "Please, Doctor, fix whatever it is."

"We'll get an IV going to manage the pain until we know the source."

Thatcher bent over her, his mind heading down a suspicious path. "Bethany, how many of those cookies did you eat?"

"I think . . . two." Her eyes closed, dark lashes resting against her cheeks.

"All this morning?"

"Yes."

"I want to test one of those cookies just in case there's a link," the doctor said.

Thatcher picked up her purse, where she'd placed them earlier. He handed the doctor a small plastic bag with two remaining cookies.

"We'll test these immediately. I'll order blood work. If you think she might have been poisoned, I want to do a tox screen, which will take care of detecting most poisons."

Courtesy of the kids' baking project . . . Could Dorian have added a poison when she left for the kitchen? "Yes, it's highly possible."

"I'll order a twenty-four-hour urine test too."

"Could this be a diabetic reaction?"

"Not at all. We'll have some answers soon. Please call the source of these cookies just in case they're the problem." The doctor gave Thatcher his first eye contact. "Miss Sanchez isn't coherent to respond to critical information. I hope you can help me here. Has she ever had her stomach pumped?"

"Not to my knowledge."

"I should have a test completed within the hour that will confirm food poisoning." He excused himself with a slight nod.

Thatcher grabbed his phone and texted SSA Preston with an update.

When Preston heard about Bethany's possible poisoning and the source, he asked to be kept updated on her condition. Thatcher texted his reply.

Ok. Working from hospital

Thatcher pressed in the number for Noah's Loft and explained the situation to the board member overseeing the shelter's activities.

"Special Agent Sanchez might have been poisoned by one of the cookies given to her last evening. She ate the sugar-free ones."

A few minutes later, he learned Bethany was given all the specially made cookies.

He understood his warning might be premature, but he was furious. "If anyone becomes ill, seek medical attention immediately."

"No one here is sick. Please keep us updated and I'll alert the residents."

✳ ✳ ✳

12:30 P.M. THURSDAY

Bethany's stomach convulsed. What was wrong with her? When would she have test results?

Thatcher sat beside her. He'd made calls and typed nonstop into his phone.

"You don't have to stay here," she said. "Scorpion's running the streets."

"That's the seventeenth time you've said that."

His smile was incredible, and he'd witnessed her vomiting. Not to mention the call for help when diarrhea hit. *Mortified* best described her.

"I want to talk about the case. Keep my mind off my stomach."

"Hush and rest."

How could an order sound, well, endearing?

The doctor walked into the room, his clipboard attached to his hand. "Hello again, Miss Sanchez. Are you comfortable?"

"Not really. What's the verdict?"

"I have the lab results. Traces of arsenic poisoning were found in your stomach and the remaining cookies."

Bethany's head swam, but she hated the thought of the cook poisoning her. "How else could I have contracted it?"

"Well, it *was* in the food you ingested. But other means are drinking from a well contaminated by arsenic or coming into contact with insecticides." He placed his hands and chart behind his back. "Have you been in contact with lumber that could have been treated with preservatives?"

She shivered, refusing to believe the facts. "I'm a city gal and work close to home."

"Also shellfish."

"I don't care for it. Shellfish can contain arsenic?"

"It's not harmful, but it can show up in a test." He turned to Thatcher with rock-hard professionalism. "I'm not one to tell you how to do your job, but if Miss Sanchez had eaten another cookie, someone would be planning her funeral. Foul play might have entered into this."

Confusion hadn't been erased from her mind, and she fought to clear it. "Thatcher, the cook would never poison me, and how do you explain the children?"

"Dorian excused herself for a few minutes when we first arrived. The cook asked for chocolate chips. Add attempted murder to Dorian's list of crimes."

Bethany had to recover in the next few hours. "What's my treatment?"

"After a few more IVs to balance your system, I'll release you around five this afternoon." He held up a finger, almost comical. "You need to feel better. At this point, I want to keep you under close observation. Your best defense against the effects of arsenic are to eat a healthy, well-balanced diet and drink lots of water. Include selenium, antioxidants, and folate. Avoid sun exposure, and follow up with your regular doctor."

Once the doctor left, Bethany fumed. "Thatcher, I'm not happy with Dorian."

"You even tried to help her kid." He typed into his phone. No doubt an update to SSA Preston.

"I want out of here now. All the work we have to do, and I'm stuck in a hospital bed."

"Do you want the flip side of arsenic poisoning?" Lines deepened around his eyes.

She pressed her lips together, fighting tears like a wimp. "Less than two weeks on the job, and I'm poisoned. I want a face-to-face with Dorian." Then she remembered. "We haven't told Aiden about his brother. Will you visit him? Not call him?"

"Yes. I need the kid to open up."

She nodded. "I hope this doesn't make us late to the Lighthouse this afternoon."

"Not sure where that's going, but I'll keep you posted."

Would he work undercover without her? "Thatcher, we're a team."

He took a deep breath. "A serial killer is running loose. I'm not letting the clock run out on another victim. I've talked to Grayson Hall in the bomb squad, and he's going with me tonight. We're old friends from Quantico."

Urgency trickled through her. "Give me a moment to get out of this hospital gown."

"So you can pass out when I need a partner who has her head and body together? No thanks."

She hated it when he was right, but selfishness had a hold on her logic. "All right. I'll take a taxi home." She shooed him with her hands, making the pain in her head intensify to nearly a ten. "Call when you can."

"Will you be all right alone?"

Visions of him earlier running for a nurse to get her to the bathroom tramped across her mind. "My stomach's cramping, and my finger's on the call button."

"I'm concerned about you, okay?"

"If it makes you feel any better, I'll sleep with my Glock beneath the sheets."

He narrowed his eyes, but she saw a hint of a smile. "Promise me you'll text or call when you're released and then when you're safe at home."

"Yes, sir."

He left the room, leaving her empty and alone. Having Thatcher attentive felt so good, and yet she was vulnerable. He'd seen inside her and hadn't run. Mind-boggling. Bethany fought to keep the wall solid between them . . . but with it down, she didn't want to let go.

CHAPTER 41

Thatcher seldom allowed his temper to take over actions. Not only did it go against his commitment to maintain a realist's attitude, but he'd promised himself that he'd quit the bureau before sinking to using his job as justification to be an enforcer. The fury refused to settle, though he'd done the prayer thing. How long until he got this Christian thing down solid? Probably a lifetime. Bethany had nearly been killed, and Dorian denied she'd added arsenic to the sugar-free cookies. They could hold her for twenty-four hours, but then without proof of any wrongdoing, they'd have to let her go. Poisoning a federal agent was low on any decent person's list. Stupid too, but Dorian's record and profile didn't indicate she had many lights on. Or all the lights were on, and she plodded on with some agenda. She had an ID on Scorpion, and Thatcher wanted to be the one who sucked it out of her irrational brains.

His mind raced with one directive—calm down and be professional while explaining to a poor kid his brother was dead.

Thatcher wove in and out of traffic to ensure he hadn't been followed. The road spread out before him where life summoned those who valued a peaceful setting more than the sensory explosion of the city. Although November ruled the calendar, very few trees had turning leaves. The green fields and scattered cattle looked like a slice of heaven. As he left Houston in his rearview mirror, more words to a new song played in his mind. Would Bethany like it?

Pushing aside his feelings for his partner, he concentrated on Aiden. He hoped the boy would thrive with the older couple and find new direction for the future.

At the ranch, the kid's jeans didn't hang at his ankles. He smelled better, but his attitude remained that of the kid in the streets. Thatcher joined him on the porch steps of the farmhouse. He looked ready to bolt, a mix of emotions and tragedy.

"I'm sorry about Tyler," he said after breaking the news as gently as he could.

The kid peered up with red-angry eyes. "I'll get them, you wait and see."

"Look, your brother's dead. You're scared gutless, and your mother's next."

Aiden raised a brow. "Whatcha want from me?"

"The way I see it, Deal isn't giving up, and he'll kill to get that list."

"I think Tyler wrote it down in case there was a problem."

"Like getting killed?" Thatcher said. "Or maybe they didn't find it and were tired of messing with him."

Aiden shrugged.

Thatcher lowered his voice. "Is this Deal character Scorpion? Or who else besides Deal is involved?"

"Don't know. You're the one paid to get answers."

Thatcher pulled his ace. "You have the list, Aiden. Are you willing to die for it?"

He swallowed. "I don't have it."

"You're lying."

Aiden glanced away. His foot danced on the floor. "When you arrest my brother's killer, I'll hand it over."

"Even if your mother's next while you're tucked away here with horses to ride and plenty of food? By the way, Special Agent Bethany Sanchez is in the hospital because someone fed her arsenic. Would you know about that?"

"No, sir. Deal's dangerous." His eye twitched. "I gave you

information before. It's your turn." He stood. "Send me back to juvie. I don't care."

Thatcher jerked him back into the chair. "Because of Scorpion, people are dead. Your brother's on a cold slab, and I take it real personal when someone tries to eliminate my partner. I'm not leaving until I have answers. So where's the list?"

"Do what you want. I ain't giving it to you until Scorpion is dead or in jail. Deal knows him, and I gave you that. Got it, Mr. FBI man?"

So Aiden believed Scorpion and Deal were two different men. Thatcher understood where Aiden came from and where he'd end up unless he changed. He pulled up Shannon's photo on his phone. "Recognize her?"

He peered at it longer than Thatcher expected before returning the phone. "Tyler's girlfriend. Is she dead too?"

"No. But she's very upset."

"Glad she's okay. Tyler loved her, and she was nice to me."

"What about your mom? Do you love her?"

"Not even on a good day."

"Think about what's happened. I'll be back. Count on it."

❈ ❈ ❈

4:20 P.M. THURSDAY

Bethany detested every moment spent in the hospital bed, thanks to Dorian. Naturally, the woman denied her part in poisoning her, and the cook nearly fell apart when agents questioned her, but Dorian had been left alone in the kitchen for a moment.

Bethany wanted to be with Thatcher, but he was working without her. A streak of jealousy rippled at the idea that he'd talk to Aiden and even Dorian. Worse yet, he was working undercover tonight, and from all indications it wouldn't be with her. But how could she argue with his commitment to stopping Scorpion? He'd texted her with new information after talking to Aiden. The elusive Deal and Scorpion were two different people.

A third situation hit her radar, leaving her frustrated and in a foul mood. Her doctor refused to release her until tomorrow morning. Her blood levels didn't suit him. A nurse claimed she'd soon be transported to a private room. Yippee.

Her throbbing head begged for relief, but she refused to let drugs dull her mind. Had Aiden revealed more about what was going on with his brother? The kid knew more than he claimed. Maybe Thatcher could persuade him to cooperate fully.

While she waited for her room, she checked on Elizabeth at Northeast Hospital—but didn't tell her about the poisoning. Reread the latest news on her cell and clicked through the TV stations before turning it off.

God, what am I doing wrong? I thought You wanted me in violent crime. I thought I could make a difference with Your help. Show Lucas and my family Your ways. What am I missing?

Two verses came to mind—rather obscure, but ones she'd memorized during training at Quantico when she'd questioned her decision to enter the FBI. *"Therefore lift your drooping hands and strengthen your weak knees, and make straight paths for your feet, so that what is lame may not be put out of joint but rather be healed."*

God, I've leaned on my own pitiful power too long. I'm sorry. I believe you want me to help make people safe, but it's so hard and I often feel alone.

I never said it would be easy.

Never before had she heard the soft, firm voice of her Lord. Tears filled her eyes, and she whisked them away.

Closing her eyes, she recalled Elizabeth questioning whether her career had taken priority over God. The two had been talking over dinner, shortly after Bethany announced her move to violent crime. Bethany denied it, but her friend's words surfaced again, and she sensed the gentle urging to ask forgiveness.

The sweet rain of love washed over her, and she slept.

CHAPTER 42

Bethany woke from a nap to a text alert on her phone. She'd slept so peacefully, and not responding was tempting. While contemplating how God had given her exactly what she needed, her cell reminded her again of a text.

Do u like ur cookies?

How had Lucas learned this? Could he and Dorian be working together on her demise? What a stretch. A second text interrupted her thoughts.

I really wanted u 2 like me.

Chills seized her. Those weren't Lucas's words. He despised her and repeatedly told her of his hatred. Her family had used his loathing too when she refused to give him money. Her mind crept into places called forbidden, the vile ways her brother treated people he despised. One more sailed into her private world.

U will b stung b4 u find me

She pulled up every text from Lucas since her first day in violent crime. Two numbers had been used, both confirmed as burners. If Lucas's taunts were separate from the ones she just received, then who'd sent them?

She texted Thatcher and SSA Preston with the latest, requesting Lucas be brought in for questioning. Her brother understood the value of intimidation, and his tactics were almost working. In the past, he'd kept his sights on everything in her life. She didn't have time for his junk.

No more.

She attempted to swing her legs over the side of the bed, but weakness and the incessant stomach cramps forced her back onto the pillow. A stronger woman would have jerked out the IV, sucked up the tummy issues, dug deep for courage, and forced herself back into the game.

She remembered how Thatcher handled negative emotions, and his instructions made her feel like a middle school girl on hormone overload. With her fingers wrapped around her phone, she closed her eyes and willed her fuzzy mind to clear. Mind first and strength second. Those would be Thatcher's instructions. And pray.

She watched the steady drip of fluids in the IV tube and pressed the nurse's call button. This stuff had to come in pill form.

※ ※ ※

5:30 P.M. THURSDAY

Thatcher and Grayson looked and smelled like street people. Another agent had driven them to a location where they walked to a bus stop and rode downtown within a few blocks of the Lighthouse. SSA Preston had suggested Grayson accompany Thatcher, dressed as a woman. The likelihood of someone detecting an FBI agent as a cross-dresser was minimal.

Grayson winked at him. "We make a good team, but I'm not as cute as Bethany."

"Very funny. She's a good agent. Any questions about tonight?"

"No, darlin'. I have my script down good." Grayson wore a bleached blond wig to his shoulders. Red glasses, a flowered skirt, and a tight red top.

"You might not make it back to bomb squad," Thatcher laughed.

"I want to see Scorpion stopped. If this is what it takes to find him, then bring on the lipstick." He paused and focused on the front of the bus.

"Trouble?" Thatcher said, feeling for his gun.

"No. Making sure no one can hear us. You're swimming in rough water, bro."

"Because my partner's brother has a BOLO on him?"

Grayson narrowed his gaze. "No, you idiot. You have feelings for her."

"That's crazy. We haven't known each other very long."

"Go figure. I know what I see, and the bureau's regs are there for a reason."

Thatcher wanted his emotions to take a hike. Especially since Grayson had always been able to read him. "I admit she's gorgeous and brilliant. Any guy would be lucky to have her as a partner. Hey, you're the one who fell in love with a potential criminal and married her."

"A whole different scenario."

Thatcher stared into his face. "How do you figure?"

"So you're not denying feelings for Bethany," Grayson said. "Be careful. If she feels the same, better lay out some ground rules. Or is this a—?"

"I'm done with the old life."

Grayson startled. "Whoa. You must have fallen hard."

"This happened before meeting Bethany. I'm mending my ways."

"Since when?"

Thatcher sighed. "I've been spending Saturday mornings with Daniel Hilton . . . doing Bible study. Made a decision to clean up my act."

A rumbling laugh met Thatcher's ears. "Proud of you. So then you meet Bethany Sanchez and your whole faith is challenged?"

Thatcher shook his head. "I'm way out of my norm here. She scares me to death, and I have no idea where she's coming from."

Grayson nodded. "You're in a mess. The issue here is live to make it work."

"Right now I have to put my personal life on hold. This case takes priority."

At the Lighthouse, they stood in line with desperate people. A cold rain splattered their heads and fell onto the sidewalk. The dampness was already soaking through the holes in his shoes, and Grayson's cheap mascara was beginning to run. At least it wasn't summer, escalating temps and elevating the stench of unwashed bodies. He and Grayson picked and argued, irritating those around them. Undercover agents were posted around the perimeter, waiting.

"Keep it up, and I'll black your eye," Thatcher said.

"You've been nuthin' but trouble since you couldn't hook up with Ansel or Deal."

Thatcher stuck his finger into Grayson's face. "Makes me wonder why I stay with you."

"'Cause you love me." Grayson puckered up.

"You're wearin' at it."

He lifted his chin. "When I find what I'm lookin' for, you and I won't need to stand in this line ever again." Grayson kissed him on the cheek.

Way over the top. Decking him entered Thatcher's thoughts. The female impersonation would be a good joke for a long time. But they weren't there for the food or socialization.

Once inside the Lighthouse, they signed the register with fake names and walked through the serving line. A chubby, white-haired woman smiled and nodded at them. Obviously a volunteer or possibly the director, Melanie Bolton.

A hint of bleach met his nostrils, but *dirty* best described the shelter. His mother was Queen Clean, and he habitually looked to corners and woodwork whenever in a new place. Chipped paint, a boarded-up window, and a wall that looked like a fist had gone through it. Not what he expected from a facility supported by generous donations. What about the health department?

They squeezed around a crowded table where they could see the door. Thatcher buried his spoon in a small bowl of watery chicken vegetable stew and corn bread. Definitely not gourmet. Could have used a little more yard bird. Why a skimpy meal when many of these people depended on this as their only source of nourishment each day?

Grayson left his dinner in the bowl. "Could use a little salt," he said.

Around him were the homeless. Some sad. Some pathetic. Some who had long since lost touch with reality. The man beside him had a face that reminded Thatcher of a line from *City Slickers*: "Like a saddlebag with eyes." If a serial killer had a physical distinction, everyone there fit into the category, including the body language. A drug deal went down at the other end of the table, and one man doused his coffee with a bottle of cheap whiskey from inside his torn jacket.

"Time to get this show on the road," he whispered.

"Why are you in such a bad mood?" Grayson said, his shrill voice ringing through the dining hall. "Can't we just eat and chill?"

Thatcher wanted to laugh at his counterpart's disguise. Grayson wore corn bread crumbs on his chin and a milk mustache above pink lipstick.

"I wanted to see Ansel. But he ain't here. Makes me mad."

"That's all you've talked about for weeks: 'Gotta find Ansel Spree.'" Grayson wiggled his shoulders. "Well, look around ya, big man. Do you see him?"

"Hey, he's gone," a toothless man called from an adjacent table. "Bullet to the head."

"What?" Thatcher stood. "Did he get in a fight?"

"Cops said it was one of those serial murders. Scorpion."

He swiped beneath his eyes. "He was a good guy. My friend."

Grayson yanked him down into his chair. "Calm down, hon."

"But Ansel told me he knew of a way to pick up some good money." He covered his face with his hands. "Said he was going to help me. Hook me up with a guy by the name of Deal."

"It's all right." Grayson wrapped his arm around Thatcher's shoulders. "We'll figure this out."

Grayson was enjoying his role far too much. But worth it if

the right person was listening. Playing this charade for very many nights would threaten his masculinity.

"Maybe another guy worked with him." Thatcher focused on the toothless man. "Do you have any idea what Ansel was doing?"

The man dug his spoon into the stew.

"Do you know Deal?"

The man grabbed his bowl and moved to another table.

Five minutes later, a white man in his late fifties bent and tapped him on the shoulder. "Follow me. Leave your cell phone here."

Thatcher turned to Grayson. "Sugar, I'm going to talk to this man for a minute." He slipped his phone onto the tray and left it behind before trailing after the man. They sat at a remote table.

"You know Deal?" Thatcher said, memorizing the man's features.

"Why?" The man had a swastika tattooed on the upper left side of his bald head.

"I heard he could hook me up with a job."

"Why get a job when you can get what you need on the streets?"

Thatcher glanced to his left and right, then leaned toward the man. "I need money, and I'll do whatever it takes."

"If I had connections to money, what would I be doing here?" He narrowed his gaze.

"Because you know how I can get my hands on fast cash."

The man slurped a glass of iced tea.

"Are you going to help me, or do I find someone else?"

"Come back tomorrow night."

"I'd rather get this going now. I can do my own jobs."

"So why the rush?"

"Want to hear what this guy can do for me."

"I'll get a message to him. But it won't happen unless he's interested. What are ya good at?"

"Whatever you got."

"Done time?"

Thatcher grinned. "Three years for armed robbery back in '05. Haven't been caught since."

"Kid stuff. Ever kill anybody?"

Thatcher smirked. "Not that I got caught."

"Have a piece?"

"Yep." Thatcher squared off with the man.

"Anybody looking for you?"

"Not in Texas."

"What about the woman?"

Thatcher humphed. "I'm partial to her. Been with me in the ups and downs. Doesn't ask questions."

The man pushed back his chair. "All right. If I can do business tonight, where can I reach you?"

"Right here with my woman gettin' a square. Who knows? I might decide to move on by morning."

He shoved his fist under Thatcher's chin. "If I find out you've double-crossed me, you're a dead man. No one messes with Groundhog."

He raised his hands. "I'm no fool."

"After the church service. Behind the building by the Dumpster. Alone."

Thatcher joined Grayson, playing the role while watching the clock. By seven, the group was escorted into a chapel area. There, while a young preacher urged the people to find Jesus, Thatcher played bored. When the closing prayer ended, he nudged Grayson.

"I'll meet you outside, sugar."

"Sure, hon. Ain't we stayin' here?"

"Haven't decided."

"Well, if you take too long, I'm leaving for our usual place."

Thatcher exited the building and scanned the darkened area near the meeting place waiting for Groundhog or the man called Deal. When nearly two hours had passed, he made his way to the front. Darkness hid the shadows of those who'd roll him for a dollar. Backup followed him in case the man discovered he'd been set up.

Should he show up tomorrow night at the Lighthouse, or would it be another waste of time? Investigations took time, something the FBI had fallen short of. Bodies were dropping, and the killer still ran loose.

CHAPTER 43

Bethany refused to let yesterday's punch keep her out of the loop. She'd told Thatcher last night to meet her at Starbucks at the same time for breakfast. Except this morning, she sipped on a Sprite, picked up at a convenience store, while her body craved a horizontal position. Although a BOLO had been issued on Lucas, so far he'd managed to evade law enforcement. Nothing new there.

"You look awful," he said.

"Thanks. And for the record, I'm here." She desperately craved a healthy body. "Appreciate your call last night."

He bit into a scone. "Sorry to wake you, but I figured you'd want to hear about it. Tonight can't come fast enough."

"Is Grayson going too?"

He lifted a brow. "Do I see a bit of green?"

"I'm woman enough to admit it. But you can't arrest what you can't see. What about the man who pulled you aside?"

"A thug who's in and out of the system. We're leaving him alone for now."

"Makes sense. Thatcher, last night I was in a groggy state when we talked. What I needed to convey is my texts may be coming from two people—Lucas and a mystery person. Can't be Dorian or Paul Javon when they're in jail."

He laid his half-eaten scone on a napkin. "Who has your work cell number besides the FBI?"

She scrolled through her contacts. "It's the only one I use. Elizabeth, Mom, Lucas, Dorian, and anyone I've given my card. Not sure why I got so bent out of shape when Dorian called me when the number's not that hard to find. Before my mind dissolves into mush, Elizabeth called last night. Saw what happened to me on the news. Apologized for not following up on Dorian." Bethany didn't mention the tears they'd shed over the phone.

"She's out of the hospital?"

"With her parents until the doctor has results from a few tests. Headaches must be excruciating." She paused. "I'm sorry. You were asking me questions, and I raced down a rabbit trail. You're rubbing off, partner."

He grinned. "We're good. Wish you'd stayed home today."

"No way, Special Agent Thatcher." She propped her chin on her palm. Was she flirting? Instantly she resumed an appropriate stance.

"Did Lucas have your number when you received your first text?"

"*Mamá* could have given it to him."

"Can we ask her?"

She leaned her head back, thinking how great the bed had felt this morning. "We have a BOLO out on Lucas. No one in my family will give a straight answer. They've hidden him in the past, and I'm sure he's among them somewhere."

He typed into his phone. "I'll have another agent contact your parents."

"Thatcher, what if whoever texted me in the hospital is Scorpion? From press releases he knows we're assigned to the case. If I'm right, what does it say about his behavior?"

He hesitated as if contemplating her theory. But she'd thought this through.

"Bethany, I've been weighing the same idea ever since you started receiving the texts."

"But why me? You're the dogged investigator. I'm just the limping sidekick. Some of the texts sound like Lucas, but not all. The three yesterday were sent within moments of each other, indicating the sender knew I'd been poisoned from cookies. Who knew about it? Dorian, the cook, and a few six-year-olds?"

"Media reported it within the hour."

She nodded. "Don't concern yourself with the cook being responsible. She's a pastor's wife, highly reputable, and her background's clean. The other two jarring comments were that the sender wanted me to like him, and he insinuated he was Scorpion with the 'You will be stung before you find me' text. Is this bravado on Lucas's part or something else?"

"From the texts you've received, you're looking at a borderline personality disorder. The sender wants you to like him, but he despises you. Can turn emotions on a dime."

"Okay, but Lucas has never cared if I liked him. He cares only for himself."

"He could have a neurochemical problem. The sender knows exactly where you are and hasn't acted. It's more about power and control that makes him tick. This has Dorian written all over it." Thatcher made sense.

"Then you think Lucas is claiming to be Scorpion to frighten me?"

"My observations are without a psychiatric eval in front of me. We have to interview him to answer your questions."

Urgency to see her brother in custody flooded her senses. She picked up her cell to check the latest, more so to see if her brother had been picked up. A derogatory blog post had hit again. She shook her head.

"Bethany, you okay?"

"I wish." She stared into his brown eyes, lost for a moment in what she wanted to deny. "Another anonymous post beating us up again. It's titled, 'Women and Their Chocolate.'"

"Read it to me."

"It's even better than the last one. 'Special Agents Bethany Sanchez and Thatcher Graves are wasting taxpayers' money again. Sanchez is an idiot. She gets herself poisoned by eating chocolate-chip cookies given to her by a suspect. Yes, readers, is she hormonal or what? So dip into your pockets, because she ran up a huge ER bill. How long will it take for her to recuperate? Gorilla SSA Preston needs a brain transplant to keep these two on the case. Wake up, Houston. We have a problem, and I'm tired of this merry-go-round. Aren't you?'"

She rested her phone on the table, depression oozing into the pores of her skin. "I believe there's a reason for everything that happens. I don't understand how Scorpion is evading us, or why my brother is so selfish, or why these posts try to make us look like the bad guys. Seems to me we're fumbling, and I don't know how to gain yardage."

✳ ✳ ✳

10:15 A.M. FRIDAY

Bethany's morning had been routine—boring paperwork and a body working on recovery. She ached as though someone had beaten her with a stick. The FIG reported all her texts had come from burner phones, and SSA Preston had sent them to the behavioral analysts.

Late tomorrow afternoon, she and Thatcher had an interview with Melanie Bolton, the director of the Lighthouse. Bethany took a long drink of Sprite, wishing it were a Diet Dr Pepper. A packet of Goldfish pretzels called her name. The only thing that hadn't upset her tummy.

Her phone buzzed—Lucas had been spotted at the Galleria Mall entering the Apple Store.

"I want him brought in for questioning," she said to Thatcher. "It sounds crazy, but I want to know if he has information that will lead us to our killer."

Thatcher and Bethany rushed inside the second-floor entrance of the Galleria Mall through the parking garage. Her heart hammered and her body threatened to fold.

"You're not up to this," Thatcher said over his shoulder.

"I won't disappoint you," she said breathlessly, her short legs doing their best to keep up with him.

HPD and other agents were on the manhunt too. Security cameras videoed Lucas leaving the Apple Store, then picked him up again entering Saks Fifth Avenue. He wore a baseball cap, torn jeans, and a dirty white T-shirt.

Security cameras hadn't located him inside the store. Lucas held a PhD in avoiding detection.

"Let's take the men's section on the third floor," Thatcher said on a dead run and speaking into his mic. "He could have ducked into a dressing room."

She didn't respond. HPD and other agents were positioned on the street side exit of Saks. Lucas didn't have a chance. She and Thatcher swung through the men's area. She slammed into a display of dress shirts and knocked several of them to the ground. Officers swarmed the floor. A woman screamed.

The dressing rooms were cleared.

No one had seen Lucas.

A thought penetrated her skull. "Thatcher, he'd head for the women's department to throw us off."

"Which floor?"

"The first, contemporary women." She hoped she was right—the area was close to the street exit.

They hurried down the escalator and toward the dressing rooms. Bethany struggled for balance to keep up with Thatcher. She crossed in front of a crowd of teens who seemed more absorbed in their phones than what was going on around them. Didn't they realize they could get hurt? Near a checkout register, she whirled around.

Lucas had been in the crowd of teens, the one wearing a pink fedora and a jean jacket. She raced toward the front door. "Stop. FBI!"

The teens moved through the door, seemingly oblivious to their surroundings.

Bethany pushed by those who failed to adhere to her shouts. She'd made it to the front door when Lucas turned and flipped her an obscene gesture as he swung a leg over the back of a motorcycle. A crowd surrounded him. Lucas and the driver sped off on a Kawasaki with no rear license plate.

You just think you won this round, Lucas. We will have a face-to-face.

CHAPTER 44

For the past hour, Bethany had wrestled with whether to go home or stay at the office. Her stomach tossed and hurt until she could barely focus. Fortunately or unfortunately, however she wanted to call it, she had a twelve thirty lunch scheduled with Carly Javon. She was meeting the young woman at the Red Onion and planned to sip on a Sprite while being a friend—and an agent. At times, her role with Carly bordered on gray, leaving her indecisive about herself. She wanted to be Carly's friend, but even more she wanted the murders solved and stopped. The latter had not been easing off. Every hour that ticked by increased the chances of Scorpion striking again.

Get a grip, Bethany. Do your job.

Lucas had gotten by them earlier, and she blamed herself. Was the crowd an excuse for her not to pull her weapon? She wanted to believe it. Who drove the motorcycle? Thatcher hadn't condemned how she'd reacted, unless he decided she wasn't worth the trouble.

At the restaurant, Carly already had a table for them. Makeup covered any telltale signs of her dad's past abuse. The psychological scars might last a lifetime.

"You were poisoned," Carly said. "I expected you to cancel."

"And let the one who whipped up arsenic in my cookies gloat?"

Carly laughed. "I want to be like you, tough and smart."

"You already are." Bethany's serious side took over. "We've been hurt by our families, and we survived. The best advice I can give is to learn and grow."

"More and more of my mother's advice is sinking in. Do you know this is the first time I've been with you without Special Agent Graves?"

"I have a life outside the FBI."

"You like him, don't you?"

Bethany inwardly cringed. If Carly had picked up on her fragile feelings for Thatcher, who else had?

Carly tilted her head. "From the look on your face, Agent Sanchez, I asked a loaded question."

"It's Bethany." She plastered on her best agent expression and backed it up with a gulp of water. "Agents who find themselves in a relationship with their partner can let emotions override sound judgment. Can't let it happen because one of us could be killed. In short, an impossible scenario."

"I see. But it doesn't stop the heart."

Bethany smiled and picked up the menu and handed it to her. "Maybe I should recruit you for the FBI. Except you're wrong in this instance." Her insides fluttered, and it had nothing to do with stomach issues. "Do you have a boyfriend?"

"No. I want my education first." She moistened her lips. "I hate what happened to Tyler. Shannon really loved him."

"Did you ever meet him?"

"Yes. A great guy. Strange how he turned out good when his mom knew zilch about nurturing her sons." Carly tilted her head. "I introduced them one night at the Lighthouse when Shannon volunteered with Mom and me. The only time she ever went, but for her it was worth it. Shannon and Tyler were inseparable, but Dad never found out. I bet you're wondering how much he told Shannon about his family and the other way around. I think a lot. Shannon and Tyler believed in being open about everything."

"I'm sorry it ended so tragically."

"Me too. I love my sister, and I'm afraid for her. Too many losses."

"How often did you and your mother volunteer at the Lighthouse?"

"About twice a month for probably four months or so until she switched to Noah's Loft." She dabbed beneath her eyes with the napkin. "How much longer will this go on?"

"It will be over soon. I promise."

"Bethany, I'm holding you to the promise. Mom deserved more in this life than she ever received. I'm begging for justice." Carly studied her as though wanting to examine her soul. "I have something to tell you. Should have done so before. It's about Ansel Spree. Happened several months ago at the Lighthouse. I didn't know his name at the time, not until I saw he'd been killed." She nibbled on her lip. "It was late at night, and I'd taken trash to the Dumpster. Heard a man sobbing. I asked if I could help, and he said he'd gotten bad news. I started to go for Mom or the woman who directs the shelter, but he stopped me. Said there was nothing anyone could do and begged me not to tell anyone. He said, 'I won't break the law for nobody, even if I get stung.'"

Bethany's heart pounded. "And you never told anyone?"

"No. I promised him. Mom always told us our word was our integrity. I stayed with him beside the Dumpster for a long time. Then Scorpion kills him."

Carly was in danger, but the young woman had a stubborn streak when it came to taking advice. "Would you—?"

"And I want my dad to stay locked up until I'm old and wrinkled."

"Have you considered forgiveness?"

Carly slid her a half smile. "You sound like Mom."

The server took their drink and Carly's food order. When the young woman ordered the snapper with queso, Bethany hoped she could manage the smell. Before lunch was over, she'd have to find a way to ensure Carly understood the danger she was in.

They chatted about music, Carly's friends, and her plans for the future. Music had been her passion, and she also wanted to explore a singing career in the opera. Bethany purposely avoided asking more about family matters until they were finished. She sensed the young woman needed her as a mentor-type friend, a person to trust.

"How are you managing with your aunt and uncle?" Bethany said.

Carly's face seemed to glow. "They are amazing. We laugh, and we cry. We do things together. Wonderful discussions about everything from musicians to historians. They believe in open communication, like Shannon and Tyler, so if there's a problem, we talk it out. Not at all what I'm used to. Shannon goes to school and that's it. She's afraid to be alone. I suggested counseling, but she says talking about it only makes it worse."

"I'm praying for both of you."

"As I said, you sound like Mom. The choices I made to talk to you and Special Agent Graves, then move out of the house were the hardest and yet the best I've ever made. I haven't given up the idea of finding evidence to prove my dad guilty. I've wondered if he thinks I know what really happened."

"Do you?"

"Not really."

"Your dad won't be in jail forever." Bethany despised the girls' exposure to violence within their home, which should have been a safe haven. Her concerns for Carly sped in all directions. "You know enough for the killer to target you next."

The girl stared at her.

"Would you be agreeable to missing some school?"

"I suppose so. Can't complete my education if I'm dead. Makes me wonder how we'll ever sell the house after a murder has taken place. Oh, that was crude. Not sure where my head is right now."

"First of all, let's get your aunt and uncle aware of possible danger. I'm calling them now."

Bethany spoke to Anita Cooke, scaring the woman, but the fear factor could keep her nieces alive. "Mrs. Cooke, we talked about the danger when Carly was in the ER. If I'd had any idea how much she knew then, I'd have suggested she leave the city. Is there a place the girls could go until this is over? I recommend outside of Houston. If not, I can look into a safe house."

"I'll talk to my husband immediately," Anita said. "Ken and I are having sleepless nights worrying about the girls. I have an idea. We just bought a condo in Tampa. The ink's not even dry, and no one knows about it. The girls could have a little vacation."

"Good. We'll all sleep easier with them safe."

"Is Carly with you?" Anita said.

"Yes, and I'll follow her home. Kindly keep me informed of what you and your husband decide. It's imperative the girls are tucked away quickly until this is over." Bethany ended the call and relayed the conversation to Carly.

"When will this nightmare be over?"

"Soon." Bethany touched the young woman's arm. "Life is filled with challenges, the bitter with the sweet. You *are* a survivor, and you will get past this."

"I'm finished exposing Shannon or myself to a killer."

"As your mother probably would say, pray for guidance and wisdom."

On the way home from the Cookes, Bethany phoned Thatcher and briefed him about lunch with Carly and the information about Ansel Spree. After a nap, she'd either head back to the office or work from her bed. She parked her truck outside her apartment and plodded toward the door.

Inside, she greeted Jasper.

"Probable cause," the bird said.

She laughed despite her body's reaction to life after arsenic. "I'm going to bed."

"Sleep tight."

She stepped into her bedroom. Horror flooded her, and she dropped her purse on the floor. A Bible lay on her bed along with a diamond and sapphire bracelet, two gold and ivory brooches, an emerald ring, and a rifle from WWI.

Her stomach curdled. These belonged to Alicia Javon and Ruth Caswell.

She whirled around expecting to see someone aiming a gun at her. How had Scorpion gotten into her apartment, and how did he even know where she lived?

Her cell sounded with a text.

Wanted 2 leave u with gifts. Soon u & I will play. Luv Scorpion

CHAPTER 45

Thatcher was up to his eyeballs in comparing autopsy reports when Bethany called.

"I need help." Her tone was soft, unsure.

"What's wrong? Are you sick?"

"Thatcher, someone has been in my apartment. Stolen items from Scorpion's victims are on my bed. I'm not sure what to do. I haven't touched a thing, even with my latex gloves."

"Get out of there."

"I have my Glock. I don't think he's here."

"You don't know for sure. Do me a favor and step outside. I'm on my way now." Thatcher grabbed his keys and phoned SSA Preston while rushing to his car.

Scorpion could be inside Bethany's apartment. In her state of mind and with the aftereffects of the poisoning, her brain wasn't firing on all cylinders.

In the short time it took him to drive to her apartment, police cars had swarmed around the building. An officer stood outside her door. This smelled like disaster.

Yanking out his ID, Thatcher exited his car and approached the officer. "This is the home of an FBI special agent," he said. "What's the problem here?"

"We received an anonymous call that the serial killer Scorpion lived here, and the proof was inside."

Thatcher entered and called for Bethany. He expected a pale face, but what he saw when she emerged from the hallway was pure anger. "Calm down," he said. "The officer outside told me what happened. They have a warrant, right?"

She nodded. "Signed by the same judge we use. Thatcher, I feel like a fool. Can't even think straight."

"Security cameras should give us a face." Injustice left a fiery trail through his body. Accusing an FBI agent of a serious crime would spread like a plague through the media.

"What did Preston say?"

"He'll straighten it out, and I'm to bring you in."

She crossed the room and eased onto the sofa. Exhaustion wore at her face. "Am I under arrest?"

"For an obvious plant in the home of an agent assigned to the case? Preston needs to hear your side. The texts you've been receiving are from Scorpion, and this proves it."

"The only thing I can think of is he and I crossed paths somewhere."

Not necessarily so, but he'd not argue it.

"Call the cops. Call the cops," Jasper squawked.

"You're no help." Bethany covered his cage with a thin blanket. "Thatcher, the evidence planted here discredits my role as an agent and sets me up as an accomplice in five murders. I've studied behavior and worked hate crimes. Yet I'm crippled with this." She swung around, but not before he saw watery eyes.

"You're made of stronger stuff than to let him think he's won."

She lifted her head. "Thanks. This is like hand-to-hand combat with the devil."

Thatcher watched the turmoil on her face. "Grayson and I will do our best to make an arrest tonight."

"I'd ask for a promise, but I'm too logical."

He offered a sad smile. "This could be the time Scorpion got sloppy. He'll slip. And with HPD sweeping your apartment, they're bound to find a trace of DNA."

She paced the room until he grew tired of watching her. She stopped and swung to him. "I've figured it out."

"Your brother?"

"No, our victims' link. In chronological order of their deaths— Eldon Hoveland, Ruth Caswell, Alicia Javon, Ansel Spree, and Tyler Crawford. All but Ruth Caswell have used or volunteered at the Lighthouse. Call Nick Caswell. See if his mother ever volunteered there."

He phoned the man and hoped he wasn't with a patient. "Nick, I have a quick question for you. Did your mother have any dealings with the Lighthouse?"

"One of their biggest donors until cancer put everything on hold."

Thatcher thanked him, truth spreading hot and cold. "Bethany, you're right. Every victim has a tie to the Lighthouse."

"You have to find a lead tonight."

His phone rang. SSA Preston.

"Thatcher, you're with Bethany?"

"Yes, sir."

"I expected you here by now. Bring her in immediately."

He looked at her. "Yes, sir. We're on our way."

"Until the case is ended, we can move her to a safe house or assign agents outside her door."

Thatcher doubted she'd comply with either one, but they'd just put together a common thread. "I'll inform her." He dropped his phone into his pocket.

"What did Preston have to say?"

"He's offering protection, either housing you in another location or agents—"

"Forget it. I'm in this fight, and I won't desist."

"Can I sleep on the couch?"

"Nope."

"Outside your door?"

"Nope."

"Bethany, you're shaking hands with two dangerous men. Has your brother ever spent time at the Lighthouse?"

"I doubt it. *Mamá* and *Papá* would be horrified."

"I think this weekend will give us solid answers."

✳ ✳ ✳

9:30 P.M. FRIDAY

Thatcher regretted leaving Bethany in her apartment for the second trip to the Lighthouse. If she were feeling 100 percent, maybe his uneasiness would shrink. But not with arsenic still finding its way out of her system.

SSA Preston had taken one look at Bethany and sent her home until morning, nine o'clock in his office. Thatcher would be there too. He doubted Bethany had ever faced squarely the depravity of her brother.

After the Lighthouse's church service, he had waited by the Dumpster like the previous night.

"What a waste," he whispered to the agents over his mic. "Our killer just thinks he won't get caught. Let's get a BOLO out for the man who goes by Groundhog. He could also be a man known as Deal. Sending Groundhog's description now, and I'll search through photos once I'm at the office."

CHAPTER 46

Bethany tapped her foot on the floor of SSA Preston's office. She'd canceled her volunteer work at Noah's Loft, and the acting director vividly expressed her disappointment since the shelter was short-handed. But Bethany's first priority was ending the serial killings. Lucas hadn't been picked up. Neither had the man who went by Groundhog. Dorian refused to talk, and Bethany was facing the man who wanted Scorpion arrested yesterday.

"The connection at the Lighthouse looks solid. We've taken the artist sketch that Thatcher helped compile last night of the Groundhog character and placed it on billboards." Preston glanced at his computer. "Serial killers usually work alone. But male and female teams aren't uncommon."

"Dorian Crawford has stayed at the Lighthouse," Bethany said. "She has the MO to hook up with a killer, and she was at Noah's Loft when Elizabeth Maddrey was attacked."

Preston turned from his computer to the agents. "How would Groundhog or Deal fit with Scorpion, even if the two are the same man? Motive is the key here, and it has to be money."

"Sir," Thatcher said, "in my opinion, there has to be more on the line than money. How could anyone trust a serial killer when that person could be the next victim? Also, we have a face-to-face with Melanie Bolton this afternoon. We plan to inform her of our suspicions and request permission to go through her files. Her cooperation is in our best interest, especially if we can eliminate the time it takes to obtain a search warrant."

"I want an update when you leave there." SSA Preston's gaze penetrated Bethany's soul. "If Lucas Sanchez is charged with anything leading to Scorpion, you're off the case."

"Yes, sir. Earlier I requested a list of all Lucas's visitors while in jail. Since the murders occurred before and after he was released, if he's involved in this, the killer would have made contact with him then."

"I have the list of text messages presumably he sent. Is that all the correspondence?"

She explained about her grandmother's missing brooch. "It had no monetary value and was the only item taken. Also, I believe he flattened my tire at Noah's Loft. I have the note left on my windshield." From her purse, she pulled the slip of paper fastened around the rusty nail. "I haven't shown this to anyone. I thought about running prints on it, but too many other things took priority."

While SSA Preston slid the rubber band from the nail and read the short note, she glanced at Thatcher. He offered a faint smile and she relaxed.

"Bethany, I understand you believe your brother is a family problem and at the time not relevant to an FBI case, but this is a threat to a federal agent." He frowned. "'You have no idea what I can do.' Has he threatened you since then?"

She inwardly cringed. "Yes, and Thatcher."

"Why haven't you addressed this? A hit-and-run and a poisoning? Hasn't it registered that your brother may have information regarding our killer's ID?" Preston's voice rumbled low, but the irritation surfaced.

"Lucas is like a hungry dog. He feeds on intimidation, an effort to frighten and make me look bad. He's done it all our lives. My only reprieve is when he's locked up. I'm sure he's taken media information to use against all of us."

Preston handed her the items. "We can lock him up, but he has to be apprehended first. Would your family conceal him?"

"Yes." From the look on his face, she imagined what was going through his head. "I gave agents a list of the women he's had relationships with. Doubt it goes anywhere because once he's finished with a woman, he's on to the next one."

"Then we have the self-proclaimed Scorpion sending texts. Two men who are targeting you. What does that say to you?"

She swallowed a baseball-size lump in her throat. "I'm sorry, sir."

"Results, Sanchez. Follow protocol, which was once your procedure in every case. Makes me wonder if you've been around Thatcher too long." The hard look in his eyes didn't show humor.

After the meeting, Bethany and Thatcher met for coffee.

"I want to know everything about your brother," he said. "I've read his files, but I want to know why and your perspective."

Thatcher deserved to have the whole story after all he'd done for her—from carrying food in his car for her diabetes to chasing a nurse down the hall for a bedpan.

"Where do I start? The beginning?"

He gestured, and she crawled inside her soul to tell him what no one comprehended but God. "*Papá*'s first wife died, leaving him with three daughters. He married *Mamá*, and I came along. My stepsisters complained *Mamá* wanted to take their mother's place and she favored me, which was so far from the truth. Lucas was born, *Papá*'s first son, the boy he'd always wanted. My sisters spoiled him horribly.

"Lucas wasn't always cruel. Spoiled but not mean. When we were kids, we were inseparable. Me and my ultra-serious, ultra–rules girl philosophy, and Lucas with his fun-loving, daredevil attitude." She took a sip of coffee and prayed she revealed everything. "When he was ten and being chased by some bullies, he climbed a tree to get away and fell. Hit his head. The doctors said the temporal lobe was damaged. They prescribed medication, but *Papá* refused. He said Lucas was fine. From then on, *Papá* catered to him even more. But I saw a rise of aggression in my brother. He seemed to enjoy inflicting pain on others, animals too. Lies. Ugly accusations." She remembered those days, the constant chaos.

"Bethany?"

She glanced into Thatcher's dark eyes. No malice, only kindness. "Sorry. I got caught up in my own story. Lucas claimed rules were to be broken, and remorse occurred only when he was caught. Teenage years were the worst. He joined a gang. In and out of juvie. My family accepted his every excuse for breaking the law. The scenario repeated: Lucas got caught, gave a ridiculous excuse, went to confession. *Mamá* and *Papá* fought to eliminate or reduce the consequences, and then he broke the law again. My parents rejected teachers, the priest, nuns, and well-meaning friends who tried to tell them he was headed down a dangerous path."

"But you still love him."

She smiled. "Not many understand unconditional love, and nothing's changed. I pray for him to realize God wants so much more for him than another jail sentence, but a purposeful life."

"You told me a friend had been caught in the middle of a drive-by, and you chose law enforcement as a result."

"A few days before my friend died, I witnessed Lucas kill a boy. It cemented everything."

"Erased from his records?"

"Right." She breathed in deeply. His hand crossed over the table as though he planned to take hers. She dropped her hand into her lap and continued. "When he was fourteen, he got into a fight with another boy and killed him. I was there. Saw the frenzied rage in my brother. The boy called Lucas a bully, which was the truth. Lucas had taken whatever he wanted for a long time. My brother got in his face and threatened to kill him. The boy wouldn't cower. I tried pulling Lucas off, but he sliced my arm with a knife. Then used it on the kid." Swiping beneath her eye, she stiffened, praying strength into her words. "He claimed to have taken the knife from the boy, and it was the boy who'd cut my arm. I pleaded with *Papá* to believe me, but Lucas cried like a baby. Said when the boy hurt me, he jumped in to take the knife away and somehow the other kid was killed."

"Manipulation."

"Exactly. My relationship with my family worsened each time I refused to give Lucas money or sided with the police for enforcing laws. Sending him to jail sealed my fate with them." She shook her head. "I'm whining."

"No, you're telling me about Lucas, and it hurts. My belief is that kindness is an asset when the recipient responds positively. Not so with your brother. His records show psychological evaluations that recommend medication."

She hated reliving family drama. "*Papá* always pays for Lucas's attorney fees and fines. One of his stipulations is Lucas can never use temporary insanity or mental illness as a plea. The other is for him to go to confession."

"Why wouldn't he want Lucas to be mentally healthy?"

"*Papá* could never handle his only son being termed as unstable, as though he'd failed as a father."

"Family dynamics can be devastating."

"And we both have fathers who disappointed us." She shrugged. "*Papá*'s father spent the last ten years of his life in a mental hospital. Figure that's why he protects Lucas."

"Here's a reality check. Can you pull the trigger on your brother?"

"God help me, but I'd have to. It's who I am."

Maybe she should have chosen an easier profession. Like a preschool teacher.

※　※　※

11:39 A.M. SATURDAY

Thatcher walked Bethany to her truck. Telling her brother's story coupled with the arsenic lingering in her body had left her visibly exhausted. Tiny lines of stress etched from her pretty brown eyes.

Her phone sounded, and she moaned. "He's on a roll. 'Oscar & Maria r on the short list.'"

"Who are these people?"

"Only close friends call my parents Oscar and Maria. They go by their middle names."

Lucas and his sidekick Scorpion.

Both phones buzzed with an e-mail. "We have another anonymous post," he said.

"'Is the FBI Covering Up Crimes?' Yesterday afternoon, HPD received an anonymous tip that Special Agent Bethany Sanchez had evidence leading to the arrest of Scorpion, the city's serial killer. Better than that, the tip said she *was* Scorpion. Officers took a warrant to her home and discovered items stolen from Scorpion's victims. Agent Sanchez is either the stupidest agent in the bureau or a genius. SSA Preston, our local gorilla, tosses his weight into the mix and she's back at work. Come on, people. Haven't you had enough? If we'd been caught with stolen goods, we'd be in jail. Who are the bad guys? Seriously? Makes me wonder if Scorpion wears a badge."

Bethany closed her eyes. "Let's address both and deal with them before sending to SSA Preston."

That was the agent who had her act together.

She pressed in a number on her phone. "My parents have to be warned." She left a voice message explaining they were in danger and should consider protection. "Please, call me back," she said and dropped the phone into her purse.

"The new post," he said. "I'd like for you to detail where you were during each of the killings."

Pulling out her phone again, she sighed, and he doubted she was even aware of it. "The victims were murdered at different times. Give me a few moments."

Thatcher studied the parking lot. No one suspicious. But serial killers didn't wear T-shirts announcing their occupation across their chests.

"Thatcher, from the estimated time of deaths, I was at home alone. I'm about to be relieved of my role, aren't I?"

"Not if I can help it. If you're removed, it sends a message that the FBI believes there's truth in the post. If you're allowed to remain, it tells the sender that the FBI has no use for lies. My vote is to trash journalism."

"Wish I felt as positive," she said.

"The low-life agenda has been sending investigators searching through web onion sites." When she lifted a quizzical brow, he continued. "It's a system that ensures the information provider and the person accessing the information are difficult to trace. Lucas can't be doing all of this alone."

"Wish we had the list of those who visited him in jail," she said.

"The FIG will send it as soon as it's available. With the weekend, it'll probably be Monday."

"Somebody should tell Lucas and Scorpion to take the weekend off."

"Hey, I have an idea. Let's drop your truck off at the office, have lunch—"

"I'll drive."

He could take over if needed. "Okay, just this once."

"And stop by my parents' before heading to the Lighthouse. I want to ensure they're safe."

"You read my mind. I'll contact the surveillance team."

"This could get ugly."

He gave her an incredulous look. "Bring it on. My partner's honor is at stake."

CHAPTER 47

Bethany drove her truck to the northeast side of town. Thatcher sat on the passenger side. She argued her stomach felt better on the left side and won the debate, or at least she thought so.

She craved some semblance of control, and Thatcher most likely knew it.

She parked at the curb while regret filled her for what she'd never had growing up. The neighborhood hadn't changed much. About half of the residents took care of their property and the rest used trash as yard ornaments. Her parents were wealthy. *Papá* had done well with his business and made sound investments, but they stayed in this community to make a difference, providing a service and jobs. Shaking off the depth of her emotions, she scanned the area. Her purpose was the well-being of her parents. She touched the Glock at her waist and released the seat belt.

"Ready, partner?" she said. "Everything looks normal. *Mamá's* at home. *Papá's* truck isn't in the driveway, which means he's at the shop."

Family matters could be disastrous, and this one could be the worst.

They walked up the sidewalk. The familiar steel bars across the front door brought back memories of attempted break-ins and a drive-by. She rang the doorbell. In the past, she could hear someone inside the house walking across the tile floor. Now silence greeted her.

She rang again.

"Not at home?" Thatcher said.

"My bet is *Mamá* saw us drive up and won't answer." She smiled. "I'm a pretty stubborn Mexican." She counted to ten and pushed the doorbell again.

This time, the clip of her mother's shoes moved toward the door, and it slowly opened.

Mamá looked weary, a tiny, gray-haired woman with a heavy burden, and telltale lines dug across her forehead. "You're not permitted here."

"*Hola, Mamá.*" Bethany wanted to embrace her. "Is Lucas inside?"

"You are FBI now and not my daughter."

"I'm both, *Mamá*. We're looking for Lucas."

Mamá waved her away. "You make sure there's a warrant out for your brother's arrest, then show up with demands? You try to trick us by saying he might hurt us?"

"He's in serious trouble, and I didn't lie to you. I received a text threatening Oscar and Maria. Who knows those names but family? If he gives himself up, I can help him. But if he's hiding and still breaking the law, the outcome will be bad."

Mamá's eyes blazed. "Don't come to see me again. If it's FBI business to see inside my house, send other agents. You've destroyed your relationship with the family. As your father said, you are no longer a Sanchez. I hate this for you, but you make your own choices." She slammed the door.

Bethany drew in a breath. "*Mamá*, I forgive you," she whispered. "I pray God keeps you and *Papá* safe from your son."

CHAPTER 48

Thatcher worried about Bethany, although he'd been told worry meant a lack of trust in God. He'd rephrase his thinking to "concern." She was quiet, preoccupied while she drove to the Lighthouse.

No surprise there after the reception her mother dished out. He and Dad had argued but not with the coldness he'd witnessed at the Sanchez home.

Bethany should have stayed home and let him ask another agent to assist with the interview. Not his girl. "I'm really sorry for what happened back there."

"I'm okay. We'll get the job done and end these senseless killings."

His mind raced with the critical situation surrounding the five deaths. Who had been in Bethany's apartment and planted stolen goods from Scorpion's victims? The security cameras at her complex showed a man of average build who wore a hoodie and avoided the cameras. Online sources hammered the FBI's inept handling of the investigation. The newest post had gone viral within two hours. Results would end the killings, not cheap words. The media coordinator would make a statement before the closing of day.

"I called *Mamá* again," Bethany said. "Went to voice mail. Not sure what I'd have said." She focused on him with a vulnerable gaze. "You've heard more about me than anyone on the planet, even Elizabeth."

"Honesty builds trust." He had no intentions of betraying her like those she loved. Soon he'd label his own feelings in the Bethany arena. Right now this case and her brother's criminal activities took all their energies. Grayson had drenched him in the truth, forcing him to maneuver the ruts in the road of an agent falling in love with his partner.

"Have you found any trust in me?"

He smiled. "We're there. In fact, we're going to make it."

She gave him a look he couldn't read . . . unless she was riding the same four-wheeler over a treacherous path. He needed to get off the metaphors. Made him feel like a weak-kneed schoolboy.

"The Lighthouse interview will take a while," he said. "I want to search their files all the way to the graffiti on the bathroom walls. I'll lead out with the director if you don't mind. But if she's hostile, you go for it. Waiting for a search warrant gives Scorpion time to make another notch on his gun."

"Got it. You know I analyze everything I hear, then twist it dry. Here go my random thoughts. Scorpion's afraid we'll catch him, and he's feeding off the media's response to the derogatory info. Most of the media is generally on our side, but a disgruntled reporter could have his own issues. Negativity spreads like wildfire. In any event, the killer is definitely motivated by discrediting the FBI, namely you, SSA Preston, and me. Makes him look impregnable." She gripped the steering wheel. "My brother used to write letters to the editor for the high school paper. Vicious. I'm rattling and going over the same things repeatedly to see what I'm missing."

"Your thinking is almost out-of-the-box."

"Heaven forbid." She laughed lightly, a sweet sound. "Lucas could not have been involved at the restaurant hit-and-run at the same time we were talking. He's never worked with anyone else in his crimes and has no reason to start now. Not sure I can blame

Scorpion for that incident when he uses a 9mm hollow-tip bullet to the forehead to eliminate his victims. Not running them over." She pounded the steering wheel. "So where do Tyler and Dorian fit in all of this? Tyler died because of a list Scorpion and Deal want. Dorian is nuts, but she may be playing us. And all our victims are linked by the Lighthouse."

Thatcher had picked up on her body language since they'd left her parents' side of town, dark depression. "You're watching the road like it's going to swallow you up, and you're sitting like rigor mortis has set in. We're heading to an interview that has huge potential in identifying our killer."

"You're right. I need to get my professional agent face on. Sorry."

"Do you want to talk about what happened today with your mom?"

A smile didn't quite reach her eyes. "Thatcher, I've always been a private person, and yet I continue to unload on you. Makes me uncomfortable, like what's happening to me? Have I become paranoid in this new role? So, yes, *Mamá* made me feel like week-old enchiladas, but I expected it. Nothing new."

Bethany pulled into the Lighthouse parking lot. The shelter modeled its organization after other facilities in the city that provided rehabilitation and educational opportunities for the homeless. Within a year, the board of directors planned to open a drug and alcohol rehab for men and women. Construction was under way for the housing units. Thatcher admired those who committed their lives to helping others. Assisting the homeless was definitely near the top of gold star careers, right under FBI special agents.

Outside the weathered brick shelter, a line of people clutched plastic bags to their chests stuffed with meager belongings. Others pushed flimsy shopping carts loaded with what most people crammed into garbage bags. When he'd been with Grayson, he zeroed in on playing the role and failed to realize the helplessness of so many. A woman sat on the sidewalk muttering . . . crying.

"Got a few dollars?" a toothless old man said. "I'm hungry now."

"Dinner will be soon, buddy," Thatcher said.

Teens dressed in black huddled together, wearing misery like body piercings and tattoos.

A little girl clothed in a dirty dress stared up at him. Her eyes still sparkled. A look at the young woman holding the child's hand and sitting on the pavement told a different story. She couldn't be much more than seventeen. Her protruding stomach indicated a dismal future unless she grabbed life by the horns.

Bethany bent to the young woman. "Do you need help?"

Red flooded her cheeks. "Lost my waitress job. Hadn't worked long enough for unemployment. No money for anything."

Bethany pulled out her cell and pressed in a number. "This is Bethany Sanchez. I'm at the Lighthouse, and I have a young mother who needs help." She handed the young woman her phone and stood. A few moments later, the phone was returned.

"The lady said she'd arrange for someone to pick me and my little girl up. We're going to a place called Noah's Loft." A tear-filled smile graced the young woman's face.

"They'll provide a home for you and your child until you can get on your feet."

"You're an answer to prayer."

Bethany touched her thin cheek. "Glad I could help."

The more he saw of Bethany, the more he admired, respected. Cared.

After talking to the director, Melanie Bolton, they'd mingle with those looking for a clean bed, a shower, and a hot meal. Some might remember a victim. The director was expecting them, and she'd expressed her desire to cooperate.

Ms. Bolton, a heavily made-up woman of medium stature with long, dark hair, ushered them into a well-organized office. In the corner were three cats but no litter box. The smell was worse than the ammonia permeating the inside of the building. Thatcher introduced himself and Bethany.

Ms. Bolton picked up a tabby cat on her desk that probably weighed as much as she did. "I hope this won't take long." She pointed to a worn love seat. "You can sit there. Earlier in the day would have been more appropriate. We're close to the dinner hour, and that's always hectic. Normally not a problem, but today we're shorthanded."

"We're not the health department." He attempted to cover his annoyance. "This is a murder investigation that points to victims associated with the Lighthouse, either as one who stayed here or as a donor or a volunteer."

She petted the cat while her light-brown eyes shot bullets into his face. "This is a homeless shelter. We cater to the displaced persons of the city and do our best to meet their needs. Some of them would kill for what you dump down your garbage disposal. I'd appreciate it if you'd leave and come back another time."

Thatcher was tired, but the obvious disrespect for the law made his temper flare. To speed things up, he'd swallow his pride. "If you're called away, we'll wait. Your facility helps the homeless to survive, a noble calling."

"The work never ends. This is also my home. I have small quarters in the back." She stiffened. "Special Agent Graves, we'll both need patience this evening. I didn't ask for a search warrant because I want to help. Please excuse my rudeness."

"No problem. If it were possible, we'd change the appointment."

Ms. Bolton didn't wear a wedding ring. According to the website, she'd taken over the facility two years ago after the death of her father, who considered the shelter a ministry. Thatcher couldn't criticize her for dedicating her life to a worthy purpose. They kept records of all the men and women who used their services. What if the woman found a dead body, someone who'd been the target of a killer? Would she be protective of her people then? He nodded at Bethany before he exploded into a stream of sarcasm.

Bethany smiled. "Ms. Bolton, I understand those people outside depend on you, and I applaud your generous heart." The gentle tone appeared to relax the woman. "We'll work around your schedule. We'd like to talk to your guests during supper and speak to them when they're assembled."

She glanced down at her cat. "Before or after the church service?"

"During and after. Special Agent Graves will speak with the pastor to enlist his support."

The woman arched her back like a cat. "Are you using God for your own agenda? This is when someone could make a decision to let Him lead their lives instead of the despair that stalks them like hunger."

Bethany didn't miss a beat. "God's in the business of stopping killers. Wouldn't you agree?"

"You're right. As long as you're sensitive to my priorities, I can encourage my people to speak openly."

"Wonderful." Bethany tilted her head. "Beautiful cat."

"Thank you." She pointed to three more, a tabby and two calicos. "These are my children."

"I can see why," Bethany said. "I had a calico when I was a little girl. She was my friend."

Ms. Bolton kissed her pet. "I love cat people. Okay, where do we begin?"

"If you have a moment, we'd like to show you a couple of photos. Agent Graves, do you mind showing Ms. Bolton what we have?"

Bethany had definitely pulled out her empathy and was doing a mighty fine job. He opened a hard file and displayed photos of all the victims.

"I'm sorry," he said. "Most of these are autopsy photos. All we have."

"I'm used to dirty people, not those covered in blood." She pointed to Ansel. "He stayed here a few times." She touched her heart. "I want to cooperate. The Lighthouse's mission statement is to restore lives, and that means saving people from a serial killer."

"What about the others?"

"Alicia and Tyler volunteered. I don't recognize the other man or the older woman. Their names are unfamiliar too."

She failed to recognize the name or the face of a huge donor?

"Do you work every day?"

"I used to have an assistant, but she neglected my people. I don't trust anyone to take care of those who use the shelter but myself."

"Oh, my," Bethany said. "You don't take any time off?"

"Rarely. I'm happiest here, which is why I live in the back."

"Caring individuals like you are rare. Do you remember anything specific about any of our victims?"

Ms. Bolton's eyes brightened. "Alicia was wonderful. Mostly she served food. Sometimes her daughter joined her. I was sad when she began spending her extra hours at Noah's Loft."

Bethany turned to Thatcher. "Would you show Ms. Bolton a photo of Dorian Crawford?"

Thatcher complied.

"I remember the woman. She stayed here on occasion."

"Thank you. Agent Graves, do you have a pic of Lucas Sanchez and an artist's sketch of the man known as Groundhog?"

Thatcher again complied.

Not a muscle moved on Ms. Bolton's face. "I'm sorry, but I've never seen either of these men."

Thatcher subtracted a few points from her personality portfolio for lying to a federal agent.

"Both are persons of interest in our case. Have you heard of a man called Deal?" Bethany said.

"No, I haven't."

"If you see either of them, please contact us immediately or call 911. Both are dangerous." She handed the woman her business card.

She shuddered. "I will. Sort of frightening. I mean, some of my guests have records and some can become unruly, but murder is unthinkable. Hope I'm not being naive."

"None of us wants to think about others taking innocent lives." Bethany turned to Thatcher, who'd cooled down.

"The building is in need of repairs," he said. "How does the board of directors view this?"

She huffed. "The board is not helpful at all. They want to say they're a part of the Lighthouse, but they never stop by to check on things. Unfortunately donations are down with the economy."

"Do you have anything else to help us?" he said.

"I don't think so." She picked up a ledger on her desk. "This is a log with names of those who use our shelter. Normally this is locked up as soon as the names are recorded."

"May we take a look?" he said.

She handed it to Bethany, obviously her preferred agent. "I need to check on dinner and my workers, so feel free to examine it. If you need me, I'll be in the kitchen or serving in the dining area."

"Do you have these names on a computer file?" Thatcher said. "We could copy them."

She frowned. "I haven't entered data for the past two weeks."

"Then we'll need to take the ledger, but we can image your computer."

Her posture stiffened. "Do you need a court order for this? Maybe I should phone my lawyer because I'm not sure of my legal rights."

Thatcher studied the woman. One moment she cooperated, and in the next she seeped hostility. "Why wouldn't you want to assist in our investigation?"

She lowered herself into her chair. "I apologize. Yes, by all means take what you need. You'll find several files on my computer from vendors to day-to-day operations, even donors. I'm simply concerned about others covering for me."

"Better they cover for you than end up at the morgue," Thatcher said.

She jerked. "Shock value doesn't cut it with me. I deal in reality."

"And I'm a realist. Same thing."

"Okay, so copy my computer files. Understand many of the people don't use the same name from day to day, and we don't have the means to photo ID them. At one time, I had a security camera in the entrance, but it no longer works. Now, if you'll excuse me . . ."

"One more question," Thatcher said. "Do you use the same pastors or are they on a rotation?"

"I never know. Houston Baptist University sends us young men and women for chapel the majority of the time. I suggest you visit with the university. Dinner is served at six and the service follows. I'm glad you're joining us." Nice words, but her tone indicated she didn't mean them.

"We'll examine the ledger, and when we're finished, we'll visit with your guests."

She walked to the door.

"Final question," he said. "Do you mind unlocking the file cabinets before you leave?"

Her face flushed. "You have my ledger and my computer. Isn't that enough?"

"We need to find the killer. We're on the same team. Are the names of the board members in your computer files?"

"Yes. All yours." She pulled a set of keys from her pocket and unlocked the four-drawer file cabinet behind her desk. "These files will not lead to a serial killer. You're wasting your time and mine while a killer walks our streets. Oh, the cats stay inside my office." Grabbing an oversize man's watch on her desk, she slipped it on.

"I'm Mama Lighthouse for a reason, and although I want your investigation to be successful, my guests come first."

His patience wore thin with uncooperative people, and Melanie Bolton rode the racehorse on this one.

CHAPTER 49

Bethany searched through the ledger while Thatcher imaged the Lighthouse's computer and sorted through hard copy files. The cats remained with them, brushing against her legs and causing her to squirm.

"Obviously you don't care for cats," Thatcher said.

"Not my favorite, especially when I'm working." She chuckled. "I did have a calico when I was a kid, but I stretched the fondness. Lucas is the cat lover. I have Jasper."

He opened a file drawer. "I've done a little research on African grays. They have an extensive vocabulary capacity."

"Some of his phrases aren't worth repeating."

"Does he sing?"

She slid him a look. "Remember I'm not his first owner."

"I was thinking of a duet."

"I'm sure he'd sing harmony." She liked Thatcher. Very much. "I'll have to talk you up to Jasper. He gets jealous." She blew out her exasperation at the mess before her. "The handwriting is atrocious."

"The people who use the Lighthouse or the director's?"

"Ms. Bolton's. She prints, but it's shaky, and I have two weeks that you don't. Glad the ledger's going with us, but I wish we had tonight's group in it. Wonder why she neglected registration, unless she was nervous about our visit."

"She's obviously wrapped up in the facility and caring for others." He glanced at his watch. "Time for us to do the mingle thing. I'll take the men."

She laughed. "Are you afraid one of the women might come on to you?"

"You saw the women at the club. Imagine this group."

They left the box of files in Ms. Bolton's office until the evening was finished and walked into the dining area. The homeless ignored her and Thatcher as though the two were in charge of busing them out of town. Bethany's heart softened at the sight of their need. Although some of them claimed they preferred living on the streets, the majority suffered as society's discards, runaways, or victims of current economic conditions or mental health problems. All of them were hungry, and not necessarily physically. A few antagonistic people complained of others having gotten more food dished onto their plates. She'd seen the same behavior at Noah's Loft, but the Lighthouse had more instances of temper flare-ups.

The sight of a familiar man in the hallway caught her attention. She wove her way around the people to check, but he was gone. Her imagination? Lucas? Didn't she admit earlier to being paranoid? Still . . .

"What snatched your attention?" Thatcher said.

"Crazy as it sounds, I thought I saw Lucas."

The two searched the hallway that led to the men's quarters, but no one surfaced.

"I'm sorry," she said. "Weird, though."

After dinner, Ms. Bolton shepherded the group into a meeting area for chapel. There, a young pastor played a saxophone and encouraged them to sing a few hymns. He preached a short message on love, using the example of Jesus reaching out to all those around Him. After talking about allowing God to take over their lives, he urged them to cooperate with the FBI. Thatcher and Bethany joined him at the front of the room with Melanie Bolton.

"These two agents are here to help you," Ms. Bolton said. "A horrible tragedy has claimed the lives of good people who have visited and volunteered here at the Lighthouse. Any information you can give is greatly appreciated." She smiled at Bethany, an obvious invitation to take over.

"Thank you, Ms. Bolton." A fresh supply of adrenaline poured through her, and she craved it. She explained the reason for their visit again, naming the victims. "All comments are welcome, no matter how insignificant. We'll be at the back of the room, and we have their photos. Please, take caution. The killer could be someone you see every day. We want all of you to be safe."

Ms. Bolton's face flared red. No doubt she didn't value Bethany's warning.

The pastor ended the service in prayer and encouraged the homeless to talk to Thatcher and Bethany. Most of them were in a hurry to leave for a clean bed and shower. Considering how some of them looked and smelled, it wasn't a bad idea.

A toothless man waited until the room had almost cleared. He remembered Eldon. They'd talked a few times. All he could remember was Eldon had a daughter. Wanted to make things right with her. A woman claimed she and Ansel had been close, but he'd been nervous about something. Never told her why, then he broke off their relationship. The woman's breath reeked of alcohol. That could have been a deciding factor for Ansel, considering the cost of keeping up an addiction.

An hour later, Thatcher collected the box of hard files, and they left Ms. Bolton in the kitchen clanging pans and cleaning up. She dismissed them with a condescending frown. A hard woman to read. Bethany filed her observations away. As they made their way to the rear door, the woman raced after them.

"Please, call me if you need anything. I want this killer stopped. It breaks my heart to think anyone would target my people. Try to hurt them."

Strange. "We appreciate your assistance," Bethany said. A canned response, but what else could she say?

"My people are a product of our government fixing the economy. I can catch them before they hit the sidewalk permanently. A precious few of the younger ones claw their way up and make something of themselves. But not many."

Melanie Bolton and Elizabeth had much in common.

Thatcher and Bethany walked to the chain-link fenced parking area behind the Lighthouse, where she'd parked her truck. A gate swung wide enough to allow a service vehicle to pass, but it didn't have a lock or a security guard. One electrical pole near the exit offered a dim light.

She stared at the frame of the building. "A little dark back here. More light might reduce the crime in this part of town."

Bethany unlocked the passenger door, and Thatcher set the box of hard copy files on the floor before climbing in. "Considering the shelter is supported by donations, we shouldn't be surprised. But remind me to talk to the director about lighting her parking area," he said.

"I'm sure she'd welcome your comments."

"She likes you better than me. I must scare her."

"Uh, did you see some of tonight's guests? Don't think you scared her at all. The problem is she refused to fall for your charms." Bethany laughed.

"You got me there," he said. "Did you see her texting while the pastor gave the message?"

"I was studying the crowd. Rather sad-looking group."

"At least the shelter offers assistance, and the plans for the future will benefit all of them."

She slid into the driver's seat and pressed the engine into action. A bullet slammed into the rear of the driver's door.

She grabbed her Glock and hit the accelerator, speeding to the gate while lowering her window. She whipped her attention to where the shot had originated. The figure of a man near an electrical pole gripped her attention. Then he disappeared around the left side of the building. Couldn't be.

"Bethany, step on it."

She floored the gas pedal.

"Do you see anyone?"

"Yes." Lucas. So she *had* seen him in the hallway before the church service.

A second bullet sank into her upper left arm, as though a lit match had entered her flesh. A third hit the front driver's side tire.

She gripped the steering wheel and guided the truck through the gate. Another pop sounded from the opposite side of the truck. Thatcher moaned and slumped down in the seat.

Bethany continued to drive while her gaze darted for a view of the shooters. "You okay? Can you call for backup?"

The gunfire stopped.

"Thatcher, answer me." She reached to check his pulse. Thick slime covered her hands.

CHAPTER 50

Agent down. Not the call Bethany wanted to make. The world needed fine men like Thatcher Graves, and she'd let him down. One more time.

In the ER, a doctor examined her left arm, and disappointment at God grew septic. Her belligerent attitude was wrong, but she couldn't ask for forgiveness while she ranted against the unfairness. Thatcher battled for his life because of some crazed idiot. He'd taken a bullet to the base of the neck. Nicked the jugular vein. His right lung collapsed. How was that remotely for the good of anyone?

Thatcher had lost so much blood before the ambulance arrived, and all she could do was keep her firearm ready in one hand and apply pressure to the gaping hole with the other. No one from the Lighthouse responded until the sirens blared. Insane.

Bethany stared at the wall of the ER room. A perky nurse had printed her name and a flower complete with a stem on a whiteboard in case she needed assistance. What she wanted, a nurse couldn't supply. She recalled how close she felt to God when she'd been poisoned, but she was too angry to be humble.

SSA Preston had phoned her in the ER. His first words were "This has gotten way too personal. I'm on my way."

Nobody—nobody—tried to take out her partner without

paying for it. Not a godly thought, but honest. Thatcher's chances of survival were slim, and the knowledge haunted her. The shooting fed into her ongoing problem with God allowing corrupt people to exist and carry out their own agenda. Like Scorpion and her brother.

What was faith about if the One in charge refused to intervene in critical situations?

What did being sovereign mean except to make sure the bad guys were handled?

So why, God? You're not doing Your job.

She wanted answers now, beginning with reassurance that Thatcher would pull through surgery. How had she grown so close to him in less than two weeks? She'd worked with two other partners in her FBI career, but she'd kept her distance—doing her job and that's it. No wonder she had the ice-queen title going.

As she glanced at her own blood-soaked shirt, a thought pressed her. How much had Thatcher lost?

Reaching into her purse, she gripped the flash drive with the contents of the Lighthouse's computer. She'd pulled it from his jacket pocket in the ambulance, believing it stored missing puzzle pieces. Someone didn't like them snooping around the Lighthouse, and that someone was her brother. And possibly Scorpion or Deal.

She demanded the hard copy files be brought in with her, as though Thatcher had been shot for them. The paperwork might contain a lead to the shooters, and she wouldn't rest until she'd searched through every one.

Tonight would be a long wait.

The alternative was unthinkable.

"I'm going to do a little digging," said the doctor, an orthopedic specialist who happened to be in the hospital when she and Thatcher were brought in. "You'll feel a pinch even with the numbing."

The man prodded like he was digging for gold. Bethany clenched her fists, willing the pain to dissipate so she could think logically. She stared into the face of the doctor, a muscular man with silver hair and a car-wash tan. "I want the bullet."

"I figured so. Then I'll set your arm. You are one lucky woman. The bullet did just enough damage to break the bone. Surgery won't be needed, only time for it to heal."

"Can't you speed this up?"

"Got a date?" The doctor chuckled, raising her irritation meter.

"I wish. My partner's in critical condition. Shot in the back of the neck."

The doctor frowned. "Hey, I'm sorry. But you can't do a thing about his condition."

"I'm an FBI agent."

"You still have to be stitched up."

"My point."

"You're tough for a little lady."

She glowered at him. Her arm stung and throbbed at the same time. Why didn't the numbing meds work better?

A moment later, the doctor dropped the bullet into a metal dish.

"Can I have a glove?" she said.

When he handed her one, she grabbed the bloody demon. It came from a 9mm. Hollow-tip. That's what he meant by the bullet not doing more damage. God was looking out for her after all. Spiritual remorse and a myriad of other emotions pelted against her heart.

"Taking off after whoever did this to you and your partner isn't smart," the doctor said. "You're in bad shape. Fatigued. From your charts, you were recently poisoned. Rest up and heal."

"Would you?"

He stepped back as though to evaluate her. "I'd hope a doctor would persuade me to take it easy first. Half an agent means another bullet."

She hated it when people were right.

"Do you have someone to drive you home?" His tone was gentler.

"When I'm ready."

"Miss Sanchez, don't drive in your condition. The pain pills I'll prescribe when we're finished will knock you out."

She had no intention of taking drugs to stupefy her senses. Right now the man she'd seen outside the dining hall and possibly later near the electrical pole fired at her logic. She couldn't be right.

Papá stepped into the room, his face pale. His slight frame and slumped shoulders made him look older. Regret for the problems between them heightened. But why was he here? How had he found out? He swallowed. No doubt the blood on her shirt alarmed him.

"I'm fine. This isn't my blood."

"Some of it is." He stepped closer and turned to the doctor. "How is she? I'm her father."

"I just tried telling her about the importance of rest. In the past few days, she's been poisoned and shot."

Papá inhaled sharply. "My daughter's stubborn."

He called her daughter.

"I earned stubborn honestly. But I think the doctor's over-dramatizing my condition. How did you know I was here?"

"News tells us much. We got your message, but we believe God will protect us." She'd missed the way he spoke, his Mexican heritage blended with English.

"I can't leave until I'm convinced my partner is okay. Right now he's in surgery and in bad shape."

"I'll stay with you."

Why? "Thank you."

He watched the doctor prepare to set the bone. She didn't want to look or anticipate the pain.

"Does your partner have family?" *Papá* said.

"Only his mother, and she lives in Tulsa."

"Then I'll be his family."

Tears pooled in her eyes. Why *Papá*'s turnaround?

"No need to cry, Bethany. We don't agree on many things, but I don't want you hurting alone . . . or worse."

She wrapped her uninjured arm around his neck and blinked

back the tears. His sobs clawed at her heart. *I'm sorry, God. I'll take a bullet any day to feel my* papá*'s love. Please, oh, please heal Thatcher.*

"You and your partner were at the Lighthouse when this happened?"

"Yes, investigating a serial murder case." She feared he'd bring up her earlier visit at the house. "We were leaving the parking lot when bullets came from two directions." She paused. "I was afraid he'd bleed out before the ambulance arrived."

She jerked at the pinch of a needle mingled with excruciating pain.

"This is a local anesthetic," the doctor said. "Won't take away all the discomfort. I'll manipulate your arm into place, check the alignment with an X-ray, then apply a cast."

Papá's attention was on the doctor and his procedures.

"Don't look at it." She spoke tenderly, wishing she were a little girl again, and he'd make it better.

"Does it hurt much?"

"Not now." The lump in her throat thickened.

If the doctor weren't listening to every word, Bethany would say more. She didn't need anything repeated for the media or on Facebook and Twitter, and she didn't trust anyone. How was *Mamá*? She stared at the metal pan of bloody instruments and touched her stomach. The doctor yanked the bone into place. She cried out.

"Bethany?"

"I'm okay." Her words weren't convincing even to herself. "Talk to me. About anything."

"*Mamá* and your sisters are making tamales this Saturday."

She smiled, remembering.

"Your oldest sister will make me an *abuelo* in the spring."

"Number six," she said.

"Maybe a *nieto* this time."

A boy who'd be different from Lucas. Her thoughts drifted to Thatcher, prayers and pleas for a man she truly cared for.

The doctor cleared his throat. "A nurse will take you to X-ray, then bring you back. Shouldn't take long."

"Can I go with my daughter?"

"Sounds like a good idea. Wouldn't want her taking off."

The doctor might have considered it a joke, but the thought had crossed her mind. "I can walk," she said.

"Not this time," the doctor said. "We have wheelchairs for transportation."

A nurse helped her from the examination table into a wheelchair. Her mind seemed dull and on alert at the same time.

"Bethany, are you going to be okay?" *Papá* said. "I broke my leg once. Wanted to die."

"I was thinking about Thatcher and all the blood at the scene."

Papá kissed her cheek. Affection she hadn't received in years. "I was afraid you were gone, and nothing is worth that price."

Her chest burned in wanting to find out what changed his mind. Lucas must have committed something horrible.

They chatted about small things, safe topics while they waited for the doctor to return with the X-ray results.

Within twenty minutes, the doctor reported her arm was in place. Once again, she lay on the examination table while he cast it. "Sir, do your daughter a favor. She's hurt and I hear the need to make sure her partner pulls through surgery. But she has no business leaving the hospital in search of whoever opened fire on them. Doctor's orders."

Papá's shoulders stiffened. "I'm just as determined to keep her from doing a foolish thing."

Bethany wanted to sleep, but Thatcher was more important.

The doctor stepped back. "Stay put until the nurse brings your treatment plan." He bid them good luck.

"Thank you for taking care of my daughter." A tear trickled over *Papá*'s cheek, and he quickly whisked it away. "Is your truck outside?"

"No. It endured a few battle scars. I rode in the ambulance

here. The FBI will pick it up, do a sweep for evidence, and then have it towed to their repair shop." Right now she needed to put some lightness into their conversation. "All it'll need is a little body work, like me."

"Do you like working for the FBI? It's very dangerous."

"I believe it's my purpose. I care about people and want to see them safe." She opened the palm of her gloved hand to view the bloody bullet. Did *Papá* know a 9mm was a common handgun? "I'll have this tested to see if it's the same gun that Scorpion used to eliminate his victims."

"You'll help find him."

She stared into his brown eyes. Most people thought her eye shape and lashes came from her mother, not *Papá*. She breathed in deeply. When the pain in her arm lessened, she could think more clearly.

When Thatcher was out of danger, she could relax.

Right now, a nagging realization persisted, and she had to talk to SSA Preston privately. Something worse than she'd ever imagined. She hoped not, prayed not.

Lucas had been at the Lighthouse tonight. The shadowy figure in the parking lot held a gun in his left hand. The horror of it all made her ill. She could be mistaken. But had her brother sunk to the lowest level of mankind? All these years she'd tried to show him a better way. And failed, just like she'd failed Thatcher.

One of Lucas's threats . . . he'd suggested she write Thatcher's obituary.

Her gaze flew to *Papá*. Why had he come tonight? Did he suspect the same thing, or had he experienced an epiphany confirming Bethany was still his daughter? He'd keep his thoughts private, just like she did.

"*Papá*, you don't really have to stay with me. I have a box of files to go through."

"I want to be with you." He lifted her chin. "Let me do this. Not argue or accuse each other of the past, but being father and daughter."

Tears flowed no matter how much she tried to stop them. "Thank you."

"Good. There's nothing we can do for Agent Graves but pray . . . So once the nurse brings your papers, let's go to the cafeteria, get some coffee." He picked up her box as SSA Preston walked in.

Bethany introduced him to her father. "I'm waiting on the nurse to bring me follow-up instructions. Any word from surgery?"

His drawn features bore evidence of Thatcher's critical condition. "Not yet. His mother's catching the next flight from Tulsa."

"He has to pull through this," she said.

"Too many of us are after him," Preston said. "Quite a few agents are upstairs. Anything I can do before you head home?"

"I'm not leaving the hospital until Thatcher's okay. My bullet came from a 9mm, hollow tip. What about Thatcher's?"

"A .38."

"Do you have your laptop? He copied the files from the Lighthouse, and I want to check out what we learned tonight."

"It's in the trunk of my car. I'll have it upstairs in the OR waiting room."

"Sir, I have a couple of things to discuss about tonight." How could she convey the information was about her brother, not something she could state in front of *Papá*?

"Other than in the initial report?"

"Yes, sir."

"We can do so in the waiting room." He handed her keys to a loaner. "Here's your ride until you get your truck back. Before I leave, I'll show you where it's parked."

"Thanks. We'll be up once we get some coffee and pray."

Preston nodded. "I imagine lots of the latter will be happening. He's not good, Bethany. Lost too much blood. I'm afraid he's not going to make it."

CHAPTER 51

Bethany's arm throbbed no matter how many times she told herself otherwise. She was sandwiched between *Papá* and SSA Preston, two men she respected. Two men who shared her concern for Thatcher. Men from two different worlds. They all waited for news about Thatcher, who remained in surgery. Critical.

Thatcher, you have to make it.

How had she, Bethany Sanchez, grown so attached to a man who had the reputation of an outstanding agent, out-of-the-box thinker, lady charmer, and whatever else she'd heard about him? Yet he confessed to being Christian. Every prayer and thought were about him, more than as a work partner or a friend—genuine caring.

Before accepting the position in violent crime, she'd mentally reviewed her training at Quantico, exercising her mind in anticipation of her new assignment. Her body, mind, and spirit were ready to accept the challenge of being a special agent. The FBI was her home and security, and she'd found that aspect easier to handle than her dysfunctional family. Which brought her thoughts back to *Papá*. She never expected him to show up at the hospital . . . to sit beside her. Call her daughter. Maybe *Mamá*, but *Papá* had disowned her, excommunicated her. What was going on?

Not now. Her concentration and prayers were for Thatcher. Falling in love with him had endangered their partnership.

What had she been thinking? She should have gunned down at least one of the shooters without hesitation. Had she allowed her feelings for Thatcher to cloud her judgment? Had her concern for him gotten him shot? Was that why he lay near death? Personal matters seldom made sense, which was why she preferred logic. Act on reason with a sprinkling of faith. Work alone. No point analyzing the confusion until she had facts.

Her thoughts drifted back to the dining hall, and queasiness assaulted her stomach.

Dear God, help me to separate my brother from a ruthless killer.

"Sir, can we talk privately?" she whispered to SSA Preston.

"Of course." He gestured to *Papá*. "Mr. Sanchez, I'm going to talk to your daughter in the hallway. We'll be right back. Then I'd like a word with you."

Papá nodded with narrowed eyes.

She followed Preston to the empty area and made eye contact. "My brother was one of the shooters tonight. I saw him at the Lighthouse. Makes me sick to say this. We now have evidence he's involved. He threatened Thatcher and me, but I never imagined he'd follow through." She swallowed hard. "He shot either Thatcher or me, since we're looking at two different guns. Hard to wrap my brain around that depravity. However, I firmly believe he's the key to finding Scorpion. He is no longer a coincidence linked to the investigation." She closed her eyes to control a surge of pain. "I simply want him and Scorpion found before anyone else is killed."

Preston yanked his phone from his pocket. "Has your father mentioned Lucas?"

"No." She glanced back at him. "His behavior, showing up here, staying with me, it's highly unlike him."

"I thought you were estranged. We'd better talk to him."

"Please, let me first."

He moistened his lips. "All right. I'll be listening."

They returned to the waiting area. When she eased onto the chair, *Papá* patted her knee.

"We'll get through this," he said.

Did *Papá* know the truth?

Around the waiting room, vigilant agents spoke in hushed tones. Their jobs were laced with danger, but was anyone ever really prepared for the ultimate sacrifice? She searched the faces: a few drank coffee while others held quiet conversations. Grayson Hall sat with his wife, and Laurel Evertson held the hand of a man who must be her fiancé, Daniel Hilton. They prayed, and she should join them. Instead she stayed glued to the chair, trying to get past all the pain and produce something worthwhile that would end this.

She was so performance oriented.

Her watch slipped to after 3 a.m. The need to determine her brother's whereabouts pressed against her pain. Would *Papá* know? Dare she ask? Did he know about her earlier conversation with *Mamá*? She nudged him.

"How's Lucas?" she said.

"He's fine." His two words clung to the air, and he removed his hand from her knee.

"Is he living with you?"

"Don't you think it's better we don't speak of him since the police and FBI are looking for him?" Hostility laced every syllable.

"He's my brother just like he's your son. I love him."

He kept his attention straight ahead. "But you never show family support for him."

This was heading south. "I believe in right and wrong. Not gray."

His face flamed. Still no eye contact. "I came here tonight because I feared you were dead."

She blinked. "I'm glad you're here with me. Nothing's changed regarding how I feel about you or him."

"Then let's not speak of family disputes. Lucas is fine. The rest of the family is helping him get on his feet."

By hiding him from the police? Pity swept through her. *Papá* was doing his best to quiet her, but ignoring problems never made them disappear. Lucas had shot Thatcher or her. Victimized others. He had to be stopped so justice could take over.

Focus, Bethany. "Do you know where he was tonight?"

He whipped his attention to her. His eyes flared. "Why? Is this what your boss wants to talk to me about?"

"I was curious."

"Bethany, you're never curious." He clenched his fist. "You're always looking for a way to condemn Lucas. It's time I leave." He stood, his body rigid. "If you would help your brother, you could be family again."

That was *Papá*—shut down logical communication and blow up. "Will I hear from you?"

He simply stared at her.

She breathed in and slowly out. "Thank you for coming. It meant more than you will ever know."

"One day you'll see family is all you have. But it will be too late. What does a person have but family and the church?"

"What about you?" Her question brought out the little girl inside.

Papá walked away. She shouldn't be upset, but for a short while, she'd hoped for more.

She sensed SSA Preston's gaze on her. "You okay?"

"It's normal." She watched *Papá* step into an elevator. *God, help me get past this. Only You can restore my family.* How many times had she shed tears over this wasteland? Didn't help then and wouldn't now.

"Bethany, how much more can you handle?"

She wanted to paste on a smile. Tell him what she presumed he wanted to hear. "Thatcher is the one in serious shape. I'm sure you heard every word, and I can't help but believe my father knows where Lucas is hiding."

"We're watching your father. Tell me, what happened tonight?"

"We interviewed Melanie Bolton. Thatcher imaged her computer files, and I have the flash drive." She pointed to her feet. "We took the hard copy files."

"I've noticed you're wearing the box like an appendage."

"Maybe so. We talked to the homeless and stayed for the chapel service. Nothing substantial. We were fired on when we left the facility."

"How many shooters?"

"Two. I'm certain. Whoever they were made Thatcher and I look like blundering idiots. Degrading details for the next anonymous post." She measured her words.

"Our killers made a serious mistake. There are at least two people involved. Like you said, Lucas is playing a role in the crimes somehow, although he was in jail during some of the murders. Additional information will move the investigation ahead."

"Even when it means following my *papá*." She caught her words before emotion took over. "My family has a blind spot when it comes to Lucas. You've seen his record. Reads like a grocery list."

"You have my sympathy. You understand this means you're off—"

"Please, my partner's been shot. My best friend attacked. I have to complete the investigation."

"Impropriety. You are emotionally connected on all fronts."

The memory of Thatcher bleeding . . . the helplessness . . . the white-hot fury . . . "I'm an agent. My partner may not survive. I have personal stakes in finding the shooters. My brother's a part of this in some way I can't figure out. He's spent his life bullying and hurting other people. No more. I ask for the opportunity to filter through the evidence and find out where the killers are and make an arrest."

"My role is to inform you that you're off the case. So is Thatcher."

She tamped down her disappointment. "You weren't there." Had she hesitated when she saw Lucas? She didn't think so. Doubts pricked her judgment.

"I've always heard we don't pick our family," he said. "We're attached to those who can despise us. Love and hate are two sides of the same coin. Blaming ourselves for their actions is a ludicrous attempt at playing God. And I'm not a religious man."

Did he fault her for Thatcher's injuries? An intense shot of pain stole her breath. "I grew up with Lucas's habits. He's cruel and has a way of manipulating others. He uses people, then spits them out. How did someone convince him, fresh out of jail, to be a part of these murders?"

"End of conversation. The FIG is working on those who visited your brother in jail. He obviously didn't have many friends, because at this point, the list is predominantly family members. If you want to help while here, you have potential evidence at your feet." He lifted his laptop onto her lap. "We go through the hard files together while we wait."

Would he change his mind? "Sir, I'd like to check a few things on the computer first. Do you mind?"

"No. Are you on pain medication?"

"I have Tylenol in my purse. Just haven't taken it."

"You can't save the world."

"But I can help find out who shot Thatcher."

"Bethany, the FBI isn't a one-man show."

"Right. That's why I didn't audition for a juggling act." Regret washed over her attitude. She stared at the bloodstains on her shirt, Thatcher's blood mixed with hers. "Sir, I was way out of line. I apologize."

"None of us will be able to think straight until an arrest is made." He peered down his nose. "But you won't be the one making the arrest."

She turned her attention to the software programs available to the FBI. It didn't offer suspects for a Houston killer who frequented a homeless shelter, but the psychological workup provided the killer's traits. All those who had criminal records similar to Scorpion's profile had been questioned. A thread was all she needed to run with, something more that connected the victims and ultimately Scorpion and Lucas.

The computer files looked in order, everything from food and medical suppliers to financial. She saw a file listed as "Lighthouse Miscellaneous" and opened it. She inwardly groaned. Pages of scanned information had been entered: names of those who'd used the facility, names of pastors who'd preached at various services, a recipe to prepare spaghetti for one hundred people, an electric bill, a plumber's estimate, and the pages trailed on.

Bethany lingered on a page that she finally deduced as "donors," poorly written and scanned. Ruth Caswell's and Alicia Javon's names were there. Both had stopped giving in the past year. She continued to scan the list. Jafar Siddiqui had also contributed to the Lighthouse, but his donations ended years ago.

"Sir, I've found something to connect the Lighthouse victims." Bethany turned the computer his way, and he pulled it into his massive hands.

"Some of these people are longtime friends. Others are influential in our city. Tough economic times and priorities determine what organizations receive funding," he said, studying the screen. "Special Agent Laurel Evertson's future in-laws are on this list."

Bethany didn't know her personally, but the blonde-haired woman had always been pleasant. "Sir, do you think a member of the Lighthouse's board could be responsible?"

Preston rubbed his face. "Send the information to the FIG for backgrounds. We're issuing a press release in a few hours about the shooting and the victims' commonality, encouraging listeners to contact us."

"With the public aware of who's a possible victim, Scorpion might go dark."

"Or the public will aid us in finding the killer."

She didn't agree, but he did have insight and experience. "I recommend an interview with Melanie Bolton, the director of the Lighthouse. She lives at the shelter. I'm concerned she might be in danger."

"I'll arrange for a couple of agents to bring her in. Send her an e-mail and place a call. The critical situation dictates a warning. I'll phone Jafar Siddiqui and inform him of the same."

Bethany pressed in Melanie's number. It rang four times and went to voice mail. Bethany left a message warning her about possible repercussions from tonight's shooting and the agents' mission to pick her up. Images of the victims inched into her mind, the blood, the evil.

She refused to acknowledge Preston had taken her and Thatcher off the case. While she often had the mind-set the investigation weighed only on her and Thatcher's shoulders, the battle spread to every law enforcement official in the city.

She reached for the Lighthouse's ledger. She searched through the list of men and women who'd registered during the past two weeks. The poor handwriting took time, but after noting the curve of specific letters, she was able to make out names. No mention of Lucas Sanchez. No surprise.

A doctor stepped into the waiting area a few feet from where she and Preston sat, an older man with thinning hair. His emotionless face showed what the crowd feared. "Is a family member present for Thatcher Graves?"

Preston walked to the doctor's side and introduced himself. "His mother lives in Tulsa. She'll be here tomorrow."

He stared into Preston's face. "I have vital information."

"What are his chances?" Preston said.

"I don't give stats for life and death. But Mr. Graves continues to be in critical condition."

"Can you discuss this with me and his partner?" When the doctor nodded, Preston motioned for Bethany to join them. "I'll phone Mr. Graves's mother immediately upon completion of our conversation."

The doctor gave a thin-lipped smile. "As I said, Mr. Graves is in critical condition. He lost a lot of blood before he was transported to the hospital. We stopped the bleeding, repaired the jugular vein, and inserted a chest tube to re-expand his lung."

"Are machines keeping him alive?" Bethany said, anticipating his response.

"Yes," the doctor said. "It's necessary right now."

"For how long?" At the moment, the idea of living without Thatcher was unthinkable, even if her thoughts were selfish. *Please, God, keep him alive.*

"We can resume this discussion once he's through recovery." His gaze swept to Preston. "Are either of you aware of a living will?"

"Yes. I checked his files before coming here," Preston said. "He specifically states not to keep him alive via life support."

Bethany's chest hurt far more than her wounded arm.

"I'm not asking for permission. Right now, he's holding on. Let's anchor our thoughts there. Once he stabilizes, we'll move him to ICU. We'll need a copy of the living will."

"I'll make the request," Preston said.

She forced strength into her voice. "How long before we have more news?"

"Every minute he's alive increases his chances of survival. Every hour moves him closer to recovery. He's a fighter."

He's my wounded lion.

Preston pulled out his phone. "Special Agent Graves's mother is waiting for a call. I'll give her the update, but I won't mention the life support unless she asks. Once he's out of ICU, how long is the recuperation period?"

"Difficult to say at this point," the doctor said. "We found further complications. The bullet hit the clavicle and shattered it, lodging a bone fragment in the soft tissue. When his chest expands and the vein is fully healed, we'll need to remove the fragment and pin the collarbone. The vein needs to be reinforced by fibrous healing around the area before we can stress it. If all goes well, we can perform the surgery in about a week. He'll need a day or two afterward in the hospital to watch for fever."

"How long before I can see him?" She trembled, so uncommon for her.

"At least two and a half hours. I'll let you know when he regains consciousness."

CHAPTER 52

Thatcher heard his name through a cloud of whispers. He couldn't move. But it didn't matter. Sleep, peaceful sleep, beckoned him.

"Open your eyes, Mr. Graves," a female voice repeated.

He struggled, wanting to ignore her, but the woman's persistence interrupted his comfortable world. He cracked one eye open a slit.

"How are you feeling?"

He focused on a woman with a round face and a kind smile. "Where am I?"

"Recovery. You had surgery."

"For what?"

Then he remembered . . . The Lighthouse parking lot. Caught in a firefight. He attempted to lift his head. "Bethany. Is she okay?"

The nurse gently held his shoulders. "Sir, you were badly wounded. You must stay calm."

"What about Bethany Sanchez, my partner?" The effort to speak brought insurmountable agony. He'd been shot. "Is . . . is she okay?"

"I presume so. There's a young woman and a gentleman waiting to see you."

Must be SSA Preston. Bethany, she wouldn't leave him unless she'd been hurt too. "Can I see them?"

305

She spoke to another nurse behind her, one he'd not noticed, asking her to escort the couple back to him. "Sir, the visitors can stay for five minutes. You need rest." She placed an object in his hand. "This is for morphine. Use it as needed. Don't be a hero."

He closed his eyes. "I'll probably see snakes."

She chuckled. "Or spiders. Use the button."

After he'd made sure Bethany was all right. "What's my condition?" He sucked in a jolt of pain.

"Upgraded to serious."

Thank You. One of the prayers he'd uttered often since Daniel helped him see his need for God. He drifted off to sleep.

"Thatcher." Bethany's soft voice tugged him back to the present.

He forced his eyelids open and met those fantastic brown eyes. "Tell me you weren't shot." His words croaked out like a sick puppy. His attention rested on her cast. "Your arm?"

"I'm fine. The doctor pulled out a 9mm bullet and cast it." Her eyes were filled with concern. "The waiting room is humming with prayers for you."

Every cell in his body screamed in torment. He wanted to push the morphine into his veins, but not yet. "People are here?"

"Oh yes."

His mind turned to what brought him there. "Did you bring down the shooters?"

"No." She glanced away. "SSA Preston is with me."

He stepped from behind her. Why hadn't Thatcher seen him?

"Sir, I appreciate your being here." Speaking sapped his strength.

"There's a waiting room full of agents and friends. Daniel Hilton said you were to get better fast because you're supposed to be his best man."

"All sounds good." He dragged his tongue over his lips. The nurse spooned ice chips into his mouth.

"Your mother will be here before noon," Preston said. "Look, I'm heading back out there to tell her about your progress and let the others know you're going to make it."

"Was there a doubt?" Thatcher said.

He nodded. "Touch and go. Plenty of room for improvement. I'll check on you later. You'll have round-the-clock protection." He turned to Bethany. "You have two minutes left."

"Yes, sir."

Thatcher closed his eyes. "Did you plan my funeral?"

"Impossible. Too many bad guys wanted to be pallbearers." She rested her hand near his.

He wished she'd take his hand. "And here I thought you'd miss me." He gasped as a burst of pain stole his breath. "After two weeks, you realized we were the best team since Frodo and Sam."

"I'm going now, Thatcher. You need time to rest and heal."

"Who did you see in the parking lot?"

She hesitated. "Lucas. He was one of the shooters."

"Bethany," he whispered through a ragged breath. His fingers inched toward hers until he touched the tips. "I care—"

She jerked back her hand. "I have to go." She hurried from the room.

CHAPTER 53

Bethany received a text from Elizabeth to call. Her dear friend was worried about her and Thatcher.

"You should have called," Elizabeth said. "I'm chained to this bed, but I could have sent Mom to be with you. Don't lie to me, Bethany. Were you hurt?"

"I took a bullet to the arm. I'm okay, a few stitches and a cast. No surgeries in the future. I'll be fine." She glossed over the pain. "Just realized it's Sunday. Your parents at church?"

"Yes. I'm sure everyone's praying for you and Thatcher."

"Tell them thanks. You'll never guess who showed up in the ER." She explained *Papá*'s visit. "Seeing him made me feel like a little girl who'd just scraped her knee."

"You had a glimpse of what could be."

"He'd probably still be here if I hadn't asked about Lucas." She went on to tell Elizabeth about recognizing her brother at the Lighthouse. "Not so sure I should have told you, but I'm existing on fumes and coffee."

"Have you eaten? Of course not. I know you, and you need to eat regularly. A big plate of bacon and eggs should be on your menu. You need nourishment to fuel your body and mind."

Bethany laughed. "Okay, I'll get something in the cafeteria. I want to see Thatcher on the hour and be available when his mother arrives."

"Your heart's showing."

"I made a decision to distance myself. It's against everything I believe in."

"Keep telling yourself that."

"I have to, for his sake and mine."

"Bethany, I want so much for you." She sighed. "I owe you a huge apology for not listening when you urged me to run a background on Dorian. I realize we already spoke about it, but I do feel like I betrayed our friendship. With Dorian, she sent her résumé, a copy of her Social Security card, a copy of her driver's license, her recent TB test, and chest X-ray results via e-mail. I was so grateful, I didn't do my part."

"Was there ever a time you doubted her sincerity?"

"Now that I think about it, she claimed I was overworked. Continuously offered to take over some of my duties. At times, she invaded my personal space, but when I confronted her, she apologized profusely."

"Was she ever alone in your office?"

"A couple of times I had her file papers. They weren't confidential things. I can see how she obtained your contact information. Do you think she made an office key and attacked me?"

"Possibly."

"Why?"

"I can't say for sure, Elizabeth, but it makes sense. Maybe when you entered your office, you surprised her. Dorian's not mentally stable."

"I love you, my friend. Now go get breakfast and let me know about Thatcher."

Bethany thanked her and slipped her phone into her pocket.

Her thoughts swept over the case and on to the shooting. She forced herself into professionalism and focused on each detail from the moment she and Thatcher left the Lighthouse.

Odd, Melanie Bolton hadn't been located. When the shooting occurred, no one rushed from the facility until after the firefight ended. Then Melanie was at Bethany's side, offering assistance. Lucas could have killed her too. Dread started at Bethany's toes and heated her weary body. How could she stop the killing?

Thatcher's friends had left after eight, some for breakfast and others to head home for a few hours' rest. They spoke briefly with SSA Preston and Bethany and planned to return later on in the afternoon when Thatcher might be up for visitors. Preston had taken the box of files, his laptop, and the flash drive. He'd check back after dealing with matters related to the investigation. She had her phone to keep abreast of what was happening.

"Remember, you're no longer working the case," Preston had said. "This is an order."

She forced her aching body to the nurses' station and learned Thatcher was sleeping peacefully. *Good. Thank You.* Slowly she made her way to the elevator and the cafeteria for breakfast.

Everything about Lucas pummeled her thoughts. He'd always been a narcissist, from self-absorbed to manipulative to his brutal nature. Lucas did nothing unless it benefited himself.

Why couldn't *Mamá* and *Papá* see him for who he really was? What could she have done after his head injury to persuade them to follow the doctor's recommendations? Her mind swept back to Lucas's many fights. Always had to be pulled off the other person, and he didn't care if the victim was a man or woman.

One time he chased her with a butcher knife. *Papá* overpowered him and took the knife from him. Even then, Lucas claimed she'd upset him.

While eating scrambled eggs, bacon, and wheat toast, she drifted toward sleep before refilling her coffee. Special Agents Hall and Evertson had invited her to join their group, but being a loner had its advantages, and stepping out of her comfort zone was more than she could handle at the moment.

She closed her eyes, and when she opened them, Daniel Hilton stood before her, his brown eyes warm.

"Mind if I sit down?"

She forced a smile. "Be my guest. I've heard good things about you."

He seated himself across from her. "I'm on a mission. You're wearing guilt like a uniform. This wasn't your fault. You and Thatcher were ambushed. If it hadn't been for you, he'd have died."

Heat flooded her face, and she blinked back the tears. "I want to believe that."

"Bethany, only God has perfect timing and knows what others are thinking. The rest of us do our best and rely on Him."

"Okay," she whispered. "Thanks."

"Are you sure you should be alone?"

She nodded. "I'll be okay once Thatcher improves."

He smiled and rejoined his friends, leaving her with words she needed to ponder. Yes, she blamed herself . . . and God for not interfering with the shooters.

Her phone alerted her, a call from SSA Preston. He asked about Thatcher, then gave her an update on the investigation. "I'll officially notify Thatcher he's also off the case. The two of you need time to recuperate. In two weeks, you can report to work, and we'll discuss your duties then."

"Sir, if anyone can find Lucas, it's me."

"Conflict of interest. Should have removed you before now. I don't doubt your relationship with your brother provides an advantage, but the decision has been made. The new lead agent will be in contact with you since your connection is a valuable asset."

"Who's the lead investigator?"

"The announcement will be made Monday."

Why the secrecy? A dose of reality hit her. "You don't trust me."

"The agent needs to be notified first."

Suspicion sailed into her mind. "Have you been following me?"

"What do you think? Lucas is a person of interest."

"How long has a surveillance team kept me in their sights?"

"A few days. It has nothing to do with your ability to handle your job, but everything to do with your brother making contact."

"As if I wouldn't report him?"

"What about the texts and notes you believed he sent but failed to confirm?"

"That's ridiculous." If she didn't shut up, she'd lose all credibility as a responsible agent. "Yes, sir. I understand." She drew in a breath to calm her rising temper. "I respectfully request to sit in on Melanie Bolton's interview. She trusts me." She counted the seconds until he responded.

"The interview will be your last function until further notice. If you insist upon continuing your investigation afterward, you will be disciplined."

"Yes, sir." She wanted to scream, shout he couldn't stop her. But she understood. Lucas, the poisoning, the stolen property in her apartment, the shooting. FBI policies and procedures. No explanation needed.

She still had her badge and her dignity.

She had insight into her brother's behavior.

Preston's ultimatum meant nothing when she was motivated to work the Scorpion case. Inside information could be obtained other ways. Thatcher would have resources too. Shaking off the setback, she focused on a serial killer who thought his or her cleverness with her brother had yanked her and Thatcher off the case. They'd simply be more creative.

Her thoughts rested on a scorpion's characteristics and how much the venomous insect translated into the serial killer. Always a chance a drop of sweat or a hair could find its way to the crime scene, but Scorpion was a pro. Her stomach soured. What if he purchased clothes, boots, undergarments, thick gloves, and a hat outside of Houston and used new clothes for each kill, reducing the likelihood of investigators discovering his chemical makeup? Had he bought what he needed weeks in advance at different locations?

Thinking wore her out, and her body pleaded for sleep. She wanted Lucas arrested. She wanted to question him. She wanted Scorpion found. But what would it take to end it all?

CHAPTER 54

Bethany maneuvered the FBI's loaner car through the busy streets of Houston and considered the idiocy of driving with sleep deprivation, a gunshot and broken arm, and the aftereffects of arsenic. But agents had picked up Melanie Bolton, and Bethany intended to be there for the interview. A question needled her: where had the woman been during the night? It was none of Bethany's business, but it bothered her when she expressed so much dedication to the homeless. She'd have a conversation with Ms. Bolton in less than thirty minutes and hopefully put together a few pieces about the previous night's shooting. How ironic, the shooters could have heard the gospel last night.

Thatcher's mother had arrived at the hospital shortly before noon. A tall woman with light-brown, shoulder-length hair and features similar to her son's, especially the brown eyes. No tears. Stoic. Over the years, Bethany had observed people handle tragedy in a variety of ways. She put on her agent-logic face, and Mrs. Graves obviously kept her emotions bottled up. The woman had passed the nurses' station and disappeared before Bethany could greet her. But she had things to do, and Thatcher was in far more capable hands with his mother.

Who was she fooling? Any attraction to Thatcher had to be deposited in a place never to be visited again. Her phone alerted

315

her to a text. Some days she wanted to toss the device into the street and run over it. Several times. At a traffic light, she took a look.

Heard Graves pulled thru. How sad. What a pity if another FBI special agent was wiped off the taxpayers' payroll.

Lucas or Scorpion? She'd send a mouthful of responses into a text, but why bother? She grasped her Diet Dr Pepper and took out her fury on a giant gulp. Once the word was out about her and Thatcher being off the case, maybe things would ease off. Maybe.

At the next light, she texted SSA Preston with the text's contents. Let him do with it what he wanted.

Get through the day. Find answers. Visit Thatcher. Sleep. And fill the pain medication prescription in her purse.

At the FBI office, Special Agent Grayson Hall joined Bethany outside an interview room where Melanie Bolton awaited them. According to Preston, Grayson had requested being a part of this interview. But he worked bomb squad, so she doubted he'd be the agent assigned to Scorpion. She finished her drink and dropped the container into a trash receptacle. Caffeine jarred her body and mind into action. Unfortunately Diet Dr Pepper didn't lessen the agony in her arm like a painkiller or three extra-strength Tylenol, her new best friend.

"Good to see you," she said to Grayson. "I imagine both of us would have preferred better circumstances in the last several hours."

"We all took this personally." Sincerity emanated from his ice-blue eyes, and his square jaw tightened.

"Thatcher and I have only been partners for a short while, but considering what has happened, it seems longer."

"He's tough. My guess, he'll be back before we have time to miss him."

They stared at Ms. Bolton through the one-way window. The woman sat straight, sipping coffee. Face free of stress. No shaking.

"What's the word on bringing her in?" Bethany said.

"Agents waited at the Lighthouse for hours until she returned and dressed for the interview. It would take dynamite to remove her makeup. Juxtapose the cement on her face with a skinned-back ponytail, black jeans, and a black T-shirt, and I expect her to expose fangs." He paused. "Sorry. In a bad mood. She conducts a valuable service for the city and deserves my commendation. Looks like she's worked with strange people for so long that she now resembles one."

"She likes cats and is protective of those who use her facility. A strange personality who responds well to kindness when she believes she's in charge. Flatter her. Dive into her sympathies for the poor and needy. I picked up a bag of Hershey's Kisses. Saw some on her desk."

He shot her a look of admiration. "You take the lead on this."

"I'm on pure adrenaline, but I'll do my best." They stepped into the interview room, and the woman stood to greet them. "We appreciate your agreeing to this interview." Bethany introduced Special Agent Hall.

Melanie shook their hands before Bethany and Grayson seated themselves across from her. "I'm sorry it took a while to find me. Around eleven thirty last night, I received a call that one of our regular guests was threatening suicide. I had a difficult time locating her and not only talking her down but sobering her up. When I returned to the Lighthouse, agents were there." She sipped on a Styrofoam cup of coffee, and the lipstick stain looked like blood. She was much more congenial than the previous night. "They were kind to wait while I showered. You cannot imagine the smell—the poor woman vomited on me."

"We're glad you're here. Looks like we all had a rough night."

"How's Agent Graves?" She shuddered.

"He's stable. Resting. The doctor says he'll pull through."

"Please give him my sympathies. Does he have family?"

"Just his mother, who's with him now."

"Tell him several of us are praying for him and you too. We'll start a fund-raising campaign to install proper lighting for the parking lot. I told the agents I didn't see anyone. Heard the shots. But by the time I found you and the other agent, the firing had ended."

Bethany had relived the incident over a dozen times in an effort to remember any detail. "Was there anyone unfamiliar at your facility last night?"

"No." She touched her heart. "Do you think the serial killer waited for you agents?"

"Ms. Bolton, we don't have the killer's identity, but your safety is important to us."

"Call me Melanie. Makes me feel more comfortable." She wrapped her fingers around the coffee cup. "I'm guilty of negligence. This is my fault for not paying attention."

"Not at all, Melanie. We're all working for the same end. Everyone who walks through your door is now a possible suspect or victim."

"Even me? It's ridiculous I'd be in danger." Hysteria mounted in Melanie's voice.

"Even you. Have you been threatened in any way?"

"No, ma'am."

"I'm assuming you have means of protecting yourself?"

"I have a handgun locked in my desk drawer and my office has a keyed entry. I can't risk anyone stealing what little I have, and I need a place to keep my kitties."

Great. Her cats. "I understand. How do you access your residence?"

"Through my office. Under normal circumstances, I seldom leave the shelter."

"Are the shelter's doors secured at a certain time?"

"No access without a key. If not, people would pour in all hours of the day for a meal and bed. I only have room for so many."

Bethany observed her grasping her right wrist under a bulky sweater. "What about fights or arguments among those using your shelter?"

She closed her eyes. "Many disagreements. Most of these people have mental issues. They live in their own world, and when someone steps into their space, they explode. Irrational is the norm. I told you some of them would kill for what others toss in the garbage, but no, I don't believe they'd commit violence for the sake of drawing blood."

"For your own safety, you need to keep your eyes and ears open."

"Yes, ma'am."

Bethany turned to Grayson. "Special Agent Hall, do you have questions or comments for Melanie?"

He folded his hands on the table. "Considering the dire situation surrounding the Lighthouse, would you be willing to close the doors until this is resolved?"

Melanie stood. "If I close the doors, who will take care of my people? They'll be hungry. Subject to the elements while you're sleeping in a comfortable bed in a safe home." She paced the room, stomping the floor like a four-year-old. "You know Houston has these crazy regulations in place about feeding the homeless. We're one of the few facilities who're licensed to help."

"I have total admiration for what you do, Ms. Bolton," he said. "We—"

"I simply can't close. My people wouldn't have showers or a means to seek medical attention. How could I make a decision that would devastate so many?"

"Please sit down."

She narrowed her eyes, then slid into the chair. After the past several hours, Bethany wasn't in the mood for tirades either.

They waited while Melanie appeared to gain control of her emotions.

"The FBI is working through sensitive information," Grayson said. "We all want the serial killer found. From Scorpion's history, socioeconomic conditions don't play into his kill list."

"Yes, sir. I apologize for my outburst."

Grayson nodded. "Melanie, we must be able to contact you at any time. Is that a problem?"

"No, sir. I'll give you my cell number before I leave. Please understand the Lighthouse is my ministry. My purpose."

"A fine one too. We don't want your sense of duty to get you killed."

Melanie's face reddened. "Aren't you supposed to provide me protection? Keep me safe from some wild killer? Part of the FBI's mission statement is to protect and defend."

She'd read their mission statement, probably online. "A specific threat has to be made before we can place you in protective detail."

"Oh, so if you find me with a bullet in my head and a scorpion on my chest, you can arrange for agents to escort me to the morgue?" She closed her eyes. "Doesn't matter. I'll cooperate, beginning with having security cameras installed. They're expensive, but I can approach a generous donor."

Bethany analyzed Melanie's body language. One minute she was rational, and the next drowning in the deep end. The one good aspect was she'd agreed to help. Too many of her actions reminded Bethany of Dorian. At least Melanie was more rational.

"Anything else, Agent Sanchez?" Grayson said.

"Not at this time." Bethany smiled. "We'll be in touch, and please be careful."

"I will, and I'll contact you immediately if I see any of the men you're looking for."

Bethany escorted her to the parking lot, being diligent to ask about her cats and thank her for her help and obtain her cell phone number. Back inside, she talked with Grayson. "What are your thoughts about the interview?"

"Melanie Bolton is highly intelligent. On a mission. A bit eccentric. My guess is she knows more than she's revealed. Have to look at the situation from her viewpoint. If she admits to knowing more, the welfare of the homeless is at stake. Easier to deny it and keep herself and them alive."

"Can't blame her for being frightened."

"Or protecting him unknowingly like she does the others."

Processing in fuzzy-brain mode frustrated her method of operation. Bolton's agreement to help had been the first real perk.

And to think SSA Preston believed she was finished with Scorpion.

CHAPTER 55

Thatcher sensed Mom's hand firmly holding his own. He inhaled her upscale perfume while forming the words to ease her fears. Just when he was ready to speak, he dozed off without voicing his appreciation for her presence. Easier to manage the pain when he pressed morphine into his veins and allowed medically induced sleep to spare him from thinking about what happened at the Lighthouse. But not until the agony became unbearable. The thought of Bethany's brother opening fire on them filled him with anger and confusion. He had no siblings, and his family's relationship had been far from ideal. Their battles had been verbal, not with bullets.

Tomorrow he'd think through what happened last night. Put together what he'd been missing.

Tomorrow he'd not use morphine.

Tomorrow he'd have a long talk with Bethany about Lucas.

Tomorrow he'd fight sleep.

Tomorrow he'd get out of bed and walk.

And Tuesday he was heading back into the investigation.

"Mom," he whispered.

"I'm right here, Son." Her voice was strong as he expected. "What can I do?"

"Order a steak, medium rare, baked potato, loaded, Caesar salad, and banana pudding."

"Take a nap, and I'll have it ready when you wake up."

323

He smiled but couldn't bring his eyes to focus on her. "Thanks for coming."

"I'm staying until you run me off."

"My apartment's a mess."

"When isn't it?"

"True. Should have hired a maid to clean up."

"Thatcher, give in to sleep. I'll cook and bake whatever you want."

"I'll get fat and slow on the job."

"Son, you nearly died."

"That's why I have to get out of here. Pray for me."

"What?" She drew her hand away from his. "Not sure I know how. You've never asked for such nonsense."

"I changed." He blinked and forced a glimpse at her.

"Last night?"

"A few weeks ago. I'm a Christian now."

She startled. "You've never been one to use a crutch. This job has muddied your thinking. Is your job so stressful that you had to find religion?"

He chose not to reply. Too much conflict. Daniel told him to tell someone, but he should have stuck with Grayson and Bethany.

If God was a crutch, then bring him two. From what he'd heard from the doctor, it was a miracle he was alive.

✳ ✳ ✳

3:30 P.M. SUNDAY

The prescription pain meds and antibiotic sat on Bethany's kitchen counter. She'd played hero agent long enough. Her mind and body needed sleep to heal and focus. First she'd phone the hospital to make sure Thatcher was recovering, then eat a bowl of soup and take her meds, and last shower and crawl into bed.

By habit, she double-bolted the lock and turned on the lamp that shone through the living room window to the parking area. She walked to Jasper's cage.

"Hey, buddy," she said.

"Call the cops," Jasper said.

"Not a bad idea."

"You're looking good."

"Then you're blind." She almost laughed, but that took too much energy.

"Lucas wins," Jasper said in a male voice.

Bethany froze, her senses paralyzed. Jasper learned phrases when they were repeated . . . which meant Lucas had been in her apartment more than once.

Sinking onto her sofa, she felt horror rush through her. She glanced around as though Lucas were in the room. For several minutes, she curled up on the sofa, hugging a pillow and weeping. It started with Lucas and her family, moved to the victims' families and their sorrow, and on to Thatcher's injuries. When her eyes finally dried, she got down on her knees.

God, I can't do this anymore. I'm sorry I blamed You for the shooting. Please help me to do my job. Not to be afraid. Not to cower. Show me how to help end these killings.

With a deep breath, she reached for her phone and contacted the nurses' station about Thatcher.

"Mr. Graves is sleeping and remains in stable condition."

"Is there anyone in the waiting room from the FBI?"

"Hold on. I believe so."

A moment later, SSA Preston responded. "Bethany, he's doing better. The doctor claims it's a miracle. I'm not into those things, but this is good. You're at home?"

"Yes, sir. Moving toward the bed. But I've found evidence that Lucas has been in my apartment."

"Nothing was revealed in the sweep. What do you have?"

"My parrot said—"

"Your parrot? Like that would stand up in court." He paused. "Look, you need rest. You're not thinking clearly. Please, let us handle this."

She agreed verbally, but not in her heart.

Scrutiny of every situation helped her survive as a child, and although a psych eval might use it against her, the trait played into her logic. The only person Lucas would ever trust came in the form of a woman. In the past, he came to trust a couple of women who nurtured and loved him while fulfilling his physical and emotional needs. He'd never trust a man because that man could become more of a bad guy, diminishing Lucas's ego.

A girlfriend? One smart enough to equal his intelligence? Feed into his selfishness? Knowing Lucas, he'd escort her like an arm ornament. Show her off to the world because it would be more about him than her.

She texted the FIG. They didn't know she was no longer on the case.

Have we received the list and camera footage that shows who visited Lucas Sanchez in jail?

Monday

Not the time for a nap. She had an idea.

She could volunteer to serve at the Lighthouse tonight—single-handedly. Make friends with the homeless, the other workers, and Melanie Bolton. This would be like helping Elizabeth at Noah's Loft, not working an investigation but helping others. Nothing for SSA Preston to file a complaint about.

She gathered up her volunteer paperwork and drove downtown. Near the shelter, she parked the loaner, a black Mustang sure to impress Thatcher. A public parking garage had availability, but it meant a four-block walk to the Lighthouse. Once at the facility, she noted the door was locked. But she had Melanie's number. A moment later the woman answered.

"This is Special Agent Bethany Sanchez. I'm at your front door. Do you have a minute?"

"I'm rather busy, but I did give my word to help the FBI. I'll be right there."

The door opened. Melanie still had purple and black going on. "I had a couple of free hours and wanted to see if I could volunteer." Bethany lifted her casted arm. "Maybe something in the kitchen."

Melanie gestured her inside, and they walked to the dining area. "We have health department regulations."

The room could use a good cleaning. "No problem, an easy fix. I volunteer at Noah's Loft, so my TB test and chest X-ray are up to date." She handed Melanie her paperwork. "My background check is clean."

Melanie smiled. "Surprised to see you with so much happening, but please don't mention your investigation to the staff. The knowledge could frighten them."

Which was exactly why she wanted to volunteer, but she'd find a way around it. "Of course. What can I do?"

"You're a bit handicapped, and I'd get frustrated watching you make beds or clean."

"Anything in your office for me to do?" The cat smell would be horrible.

"Not really. The FBI has my hard files. I have a few things to do before dinner, so I guess I'll send you to the kitchen."

In a huge industrial-type area, two Hispanic women busied themselves over simmering pots. The chatter and enticing smells reminded her of being with family.

"We have a volunteer. She'll do whatever you need," Melanie said, then turned to Bethany. "Thanks for helping out today. Who knows? You might find Scorpion tonight."

While Bethany clumsily cleaned and swept, she noted the two women rarely spoke. "Excuse me. Do you have a moment?" she said.

When the elderly woman smiled, Bethany showed her a pic of Lucas. "I'm looking for my brother, and I wonder if he's been here."

The woman looked at the picture and stepped back. She returned to cutting carrots.

"Por favor." Please.

The woman pointed to the door. "Leave now. I don't know this man. We have work to do. Your arm is no use."

"Back to work." Melanie scowled from the doorway. "You heard me." She twisted an oversize watch and pushed it up her arm, as Bethany had noted before.

"This is my fault," Bethany said. "I posed a question if these ladies had ever seen—"

"I fully understand what you're doing, upsetting my staff. This was not a good idea. I suggest you leave." Her eyes cast a cold stare. "These women are busy. They don't have the luxury of running about town on taxpayers' money. I'll show you out." She lifted her chin. "Investigating a crime in this part of town could get you shot again. A smart agent like you should realize the danger."

Bethany wove through evening traffic on the way home, her mind weighing Melanie's volatile personality. In the middle of a jam, she scrolled through her cell for the latest news. Her attention went to an e-mail directed at her. She wanted to scream. Couldn't this guy find another topic? The e-mail pointed to yet another post about Houston's FBI. The title made her want to crawl back into bed—"When FBI Agents Kill."

SSA Preston is covering his rear big-time. Makes me question his relationship to Special Agent Bethany Sanchez, but I have no proof. She is cute. Does it surprise you that Special Agent Thatcher Graves was the one nearly killed in Saturday night's firefight? Sanchez escaped with a few stitches and a broken arm. I bet Preston removes Sanchez and Graves from the case. What does DC think about the unsolved killings and the information on Sanchez? Here's my question for you citizens: Where was Sanchez during the killings? Unless Preston and Graves can provide an alibi, you'll learn she doesn't have one for any of Scorpion's murders.

Who was the source of info here? Had the media announced her and Thatcher's status?

CHAPTER 56

The moment Thatcher's doctor entered the hospital room, yesterday's vows rolled across his mind. He should have informed his mother to bring clothes, but if push came to shove, he'd double the gown and call a taxi.

"How are you feeling, Mr. Graves?" The doctor's too-cheerful bedside manner agitated him.

"I want to be up and walking this morning."

The doctor leaned over the bed. "Mr. Graves, that won't happen until late this afternoon. I value your fight, but we must be sensible."

"Who's we? I want to be released today. I know you have this procedure to do in a week on my shoulder, but I'm not doing the convalescent thing."

"We'll see."

"There's no 'seeing' about it. Release me today or I check myself out."

The doctor gave him a bug-eyed stare. "You nearly died Saturday night."

"But I'm alive today."

"Is there someone at home to take care of you?"

Thank goodness his mom had gone to the cafeteria to grab him a cinnamon roll and decent coffee, or she'd be on the doctor's side. "Yes."

"If you make substantial progress today, I'll talk about it in the morning. Early release also depends on who your caretaker will be."

That made him sound like a candidate for a nursing home. "I'm getting out of here either way." He gave the doctor his best agent glare.

The doctor turned heel like a general and left without a word.

Every time Thatcher thought about SSA Preston's announcement that he was off the case, he saw red. But as long as he stayed in the hospital, his chances of convincing Preston he was fit for work were lessened.

Mom returned with a cinnamon roll, cold and stale. The coffee shared the same characteristics. Bethany walked in, and he instantly felt better. Dressed in jeans and a button-down shirt. Her hair hung long, straight, and she looked, well, good. Even with her arm in a cast.

"Good morning." Her smile would light up his worst day.

Mom reached for Bethany's hand. "You're Bethany Sanchez, right? Thatcher's partner? I saw you when I arrived yesterday, but I was too upset to be friendly."

"It's my pleasure. Excuse me for intruding on your time with him."

Mom grabbed her purse. "I need to make a few calls, so he's all yours." She winked at him. "Your partner is gorgeous."

Great. Mom had ideas. "Thanks. She has ears too."

Mom left the room, and silence assaulted them. The firefight had crushed their egos and mousetrapped their tongues. The thought of being stuck at home for at least a week made him want to fight. Monitors beeped and reported vitals, and an IV dripped three bags of life fluids into his veins.

This was ridiculous. "How's the arm?"

She eased onto the chair his mother had occupied. "Feels like someone shot me. What about you?"

"The same."

She laughed. "But I don't have the hospital gown and IV."

He frowned. "You had those things earlier in the week. We're pathetic. I'm getting out of here today."

"Bad idea, Thatcher. You're not leaving the hospital. And you're the color of the sheets. It's not the height of fashion."

"I told the doctor I was leaving whether he released me or not. Besides, I'm not staying here until my lung expands and the vein heals so I can have my shoulder pinned."

"You're delusional enough to make it happen."

"Watch me."

"Okay, so who's been to see you?"

"Daniel and Laurel, and Grayson and Taryn. Thanked them for their prayers and for waiting to see if I didn't make it. They're bringing my Mustang to the hospital for Mom to drive me home."

She grinned. "And if you leave, what will you do with all your free time?"

"Find Scorpion."

Her eyes hardened. "What about being off the case? And we look like a couple of warhorses."

Not a good picture. "Has Lucas or Groundhog been picked up?"

"Neither. Lucas won't crawl out until it's dark." She told him about Jasper.

"Are you absolutely sure it was Lucas at the Lighthouse?"

"Yes."

Had her brother fired at her or him? "Thanks for not giving up on me Saturday night. I dreamed you were telling me to hang on."

"That was no dream, partner. I shouted it when I thought you'd bleed out."

"I listened." Enough of this. "Early this morning, I saw ants the size of my fist crawl up my arm." When she laughed again, he realized she was more addicting than the drugs.

"Maybe you need to cut back on the morphine."

"Cut myself off. Got to toughen up. What have you been up to?"

"Thinking and sleeping." She relayed the latest post.

"He doesn't let up. We'll see who writes the final chapter." Her eyes told him she had new information. "Spill your guts, Special Agent Sanchez. You have the look of someone who just confronted a few gangbangers, pedophiles, thieves, and murderers."

"Nothing concrete. Grayson Hall partnered with me during Melanie Bolton's interview."

"Anything there?"

"She offered her help. Frankly I'm afraid for her safety, but she believes the homeless come first. Do you feel up to brainstorming?"

"I'm your man."

She blushed, and he loved it. "When I consider Lucas's traits, he's self-absorbed in every respect. If you can't give him what he wants, then he despises you."

"Have you considered the family that provides for him is also the family he hates? He's never had any boundaries, so how could he respect any of them? Only those who have committed crimes measure up to his standards."

Her gaze flew to his. "True, and what you're saying feeds into my thoughts. Lucas has never trusted anyone. But if a woman who was also in the habit of breaking the law said and did all the right things, persuaded him to believe he was the most intelligent and the best-looking guy out there, she might have him in the palm of her hand."

A burst of pain exploded in his body, and he closed his eyes. "A narcissist only sees how he can use another person. The woman would understand this and give him what he couldn't get at home—sex. She'd draw him into her world by making him think he's in control. That way he thinks he's using her. She'd know what motivates him." He looked at her. "Bethany, you represent the opposition, what he hates."

"Me?" Her eyes widened.

"Think about how close you were as kids, his head injury, and how the rest of the family caters to his every need. But you refused. You're the sister who was kicked out of the family and joined the FBI."

She tapped her chin. "Scorpion kills because of a link to the Lighthouse. Scorpion, who let's say is a woman, uses Lucas to assist her in the killings. In turn, she promises to help him eliminate me."

"The smaller boot print could be a female," he said. "When I think about Alicia Javon, and the higher probability of her opening her door to a woman instead of a man or how a woman can appear less of a threat, even manipulative, you could be onto something."

She paused. "One problem: Lucas was in jail during two of the murders."

"Hold on to our theory until we see the list and view the footage from jail. Not sure how fast SSA Preston can pull our clearance, but I'm betting he's preoccupied with all of this. I don't take someone opening fire on me and my partner without retaliation. One more reason why I'm walking out of here." They'd been to hell and back and survived, and it wasn't over. "We're done cleaning up after Scorpion's killings."

"No matter who he or she is. I'm heading home. Call me if you're paroled."

"Very funny."

Thatcher seized the opportunity to gaze into those eyes that held him captive. Heat zipped through his veins and it had nothing to do with the IVs. He should have put a guard on his heart, because he'd lost it to Special Agent Bethany Sanchez.

CHAPTER 57

Thatcher held his breath while Mom pulled into his garage. He'd rather ride with a blind woman or entrust his Mustang to an eight-year-old, but he had no choice, and being home was worth risking a fresh dent in his newly repaired car. After nearly dying on Saturday night, what else could go wrong? Not a smart idea to go there.

He took in the familiar sights of his garage and looked forward to the scent of home. He hurt like someone had dropped him into a vat of boiling grease. Yet here he could think without the smell of sanitation, the steady beep of monitors, and the vampires drawing blood. As long as Mom didn't drive him nuts. Usually she got into organization mode and rearranged his kitchen and cooked. He could work while she played the doting mother.

He ripped off the self-righteous badge. His thoughts were selfish, and he appreciated her willingness to stay a few days when she had a busy life in Tulsa.

Couldn't believe he was able to persuade the hospital crew to let him leave.

"I meant to get you a wheelchair." Mom turned off the car engine. "My back isn't what it used to be. Being mobile is important."

"I'm just glad you didn't drive through my garage."

"Very funny. I see you've repaired the wall from the last time I was here."

He chuckled. "Yep. Note I have nothing in front of the car but wall, in case you get a heavy foot."

She frowned. "You're pale."

"I imagine so. What are you going to whip up in the kitchen?"

"Changing the subject doesn't make you well again, but I'll attempt to fatten you up."

He grabbed the door handle of the car. "First, let me get inside." He pulled his keys from his pocket. "Take these. At least the elevator's not far."

"Okay." Mom scooted out of the driver's seat and hurried around the rear of the car to open the passenger door. "Lean on me. I can take it."

"No thanks. I'm a big boy." Thatcher had already figured out how he'd get inside. Slow but steady. As he turned to give himself a boost out of the car, a stab of pain zipped through him, and he moaned.

Mom gasped like he'd fallen. "Not so fast. You'll start bleeding."

His eyes watered, then stung. "Give me room, and I'll manage fine."

She stepped back a bit warily, and he used the next several moments to ease himself toward the door leading to the elevator. Mom clung to him like he was an invalid.

When his feet finally hit the tile floor of his condo, he wanted to shout. Instead he slumped into a chair and drew in several ragged breaths.

"I'm resting a minute, then back to my bedroom."

"I'll bring water and your pain pills."

"Not so fast. I have to make a few phone calls first and do a little research online. The last time I took one of those things, it became a truth serum."

"That's how I learned about Bethany." She gave him the narrow-brow, know-all mom look. "But if you're not careful, you'll end up dead. And I heard your boss state you were off the case and not to report to work for two weeks."

He focused on Mom's watery eyes. Dad hadn't been gone but a year, and the shooting must have scared her. "Mom, I'm all right. I'll take the meds in a couple of hours. How about a pot of your special tortilla soup?"

She blinked. "All right. Will you be okay while I run to the store?"

"Yes, ma'am." He eased up from the chair. Blinding pain accompanied him, but he'd keep it to himself.

Mom wrapped an arm around his waist, and he didn't protest. His room seemed a mile away. "Tell me more about your partner," she said.

"She's an incredible agent. Analytical. We're a good combo."

"Combo as in a relationship?"

"We haven't known each other very long."

"I saw the way you two looked at each other. Definitely more than professional."

He paused to gather his strength. "It would be dangerous for us to date. When emotions are involved, decisions are no longer based on training but on the welfare of the other person. One of us could get hurt." He should practice what he spouted.

"Hadn't considered that aspect. Sounds like you've spent time thinking it through."

Thatcher could almost touch his bed. He leaned on the footboard while Mom smoothed the sheets and fluffed the pillows. For once she didn't mention his lack of bed-making skills. She helped him ease down onto it. Felt so good.

"Would you mind bringing me my cell phone and laptop?"

"Don't suppose it would do me any good to argue," she said and disappeared through the door. "All superheroes have their kryptonite, Son, and yours just happens to be a bullet."

Thatcher laughed. "Good one. I'll remember your sage advice, right along with how to sort dirty clothes."

With his investigation tools and his mother busy taking

inventory of the fridge, he made a few inquiries and online searches, then phoned Bethany. "Are you resting?" he said.

"Are you?"

"Of course. I'm in bed at home."

"Thatcher, did the doctor spring you?"

"Sorta. Wanted to check in with my partner."

"Today's been uneventful. Yesterday afternoon I drove to the Lighthouse on a hunch—"

"Since when do you have hunches?" he said.

"Since I started hanging around with you, and it doesn't work. Melanie Bolton appeared friendly enough. I asked to help and she was willing until she overheard me asking one of the cooks if they'd ever seen Lucas there." Bethany went on about the sudden twist of Melanie's behavior. "She's worked with those people for so long that she's becoming like some of them. I'm sorry, Thatcher. I'm being facetious."

"You're easier than I am. Don't sweat it."

"Thatcher, you sound like every word hurts."

She had no idea.

"Or you have a mouthful of nails," she said. "Or you need to hang up and rest. Please, take care of yourself. I'd never seen that much blood from a person who survived."

"Sure." And he meant it for no one but her.

"Now take your meds and kiss your mother good night."

"Not yet. The FIG told me we'd have the footage of Lucas's jail visitors today, but the day is dwindling. All we have is a list of names."

"I saw the list, and it's all family except for three women. I asked the FIG to run a trace on them. If Preston doesn't stop it."

"Doubt if he's made it official about us, and we're still agents and on the payroll," he said. "The FIG's not fast enough."

"You're whining."

"What do you suggest?"

"I can be there at eight in the morning," Bethany said. "We can go to work with clear heads and lots of Tylenol."

"That's way too logical."

"Your point?"

Had he met his stubborn match? The throbbing in the back of his neck had made him nauseous. Glancing at the glass of water and bottle of pills on his nightstand, he realized this agent needed to sleep. "Okay. But make it seven thirty."

CHAPTER 58

Bethany drove to see Thatcher—to work on a case they'd been booted off of and instructed to leave alone. Protocol she understood, but her life's convictions rode the priority roller coaster. The FIG's security video footage of who'd visited Lucas in jail arrived as she drove through Starbucks to bring Thatcher his Pike Place coffee. They'd view it together. SSA Preston and whoever was assigned to this case would analyze it too.

She despised not being at the office.

She touched her cast, and what it symbolized deepened her resolve. Her arm merely ached, an improvement over the past few days, thanks to Tylenol. She looked forward to seeing Thatcher, yet suspicions of a surveillance team kicked in when she approached his condo. Opposing the forces of those who attempted to control her life was not a foreign concept. As a teen, she'd followed Lucas and eavesdropped on his friends' conversations. Her parents would have grounded her for a month at the thought of her invading his privacy. But she'd always confirmed her distrust for Lucas, and it looked like her path was there again. The commitment to stop her brother from any more crimes overrode the fear of forfeiting her career to find him and learn the identity of Scorpion. She'd deal with the backlash when the time came.

She drove to the exclusive loft condos where Thatcher lived.

Very nice. His fashionable, high-rise condo suited him. Austin stone blended with brick four stories high within a gated community. She spotted what looked like familiar FBI agents. Waving crossed her mind, and she did. When had she become so rebellious?

The security guard phoned Thatcher, and moments later she stood at his door. She rang the doorbell. Slowly it opened, and her pulse blew past the speed limit. Hadn't she chosen to ignore the attraction? Ever since he was shot, she'd tried to squelch her feelings. But her efforts were proving futile.

"Hey, partner, I brought you something." She handed him a bag of red licorice.

He looked inside and grinned. "You remembered." He looked incredibly pale and weak, and his attempt at a smile would have been better painted on. "Good morning. Come on in."

She stepped inside his home. "Thatcher, you have no business working. You're going to fall on your face and end up back in the hospital."

"And miss all the fun?" His half grin did little to mask his injuries.

"I tried to convince him of his foolishness." Mrs. Graves's voice sounded behind him. She handed Bethany a small plastic bag filled with meds. "Make sure he takes all of these according to the directions."

"Yes, ma'am. The wounded lion needs to heal."

"Sounds better than crip," he said.

"You two have fun. I have to catch up on my reading." Mrs. Graves disappeared down the hall.

Thatcher hobbled to a chair in a living area to the left of them, and she set his coffee beside him. He nodded his thanks.

A white stone fireplace with bookcases on both sides took up an entire wall. An adjacent wall displayed floor-to-ceiling windows looking out over the bayou. Guitars were mounted on another wall, collector's instruments. Each one had a small metal plate with information about the original owner. His own guitar rested against a stool in the corner. To the right was a pristine kitchen with contemporary white cabinets, black granite countertops, and high barstools. Very much the Thatcher she'd come to know.

"This is so you," she said. "My *papá* collects Spanish guitars." Unfortunately Thatcher would never see them, between the estranged relations with her parents and her vow to force him out of her heart.

"Thanks. I'm ready to work. So you got the FIG's report too?"

"I'm praying for a revelation, since the women who visited Lucas used aliases." She slipped onto a chair across from him in the living room. "It feeds into my theory about a woman manipulating him. When I take what you've explained to me about behavior and juxtapose that with Lucas, a woman has to be a part of Scorpion. But questions keep pelting my brain. I know a foursome goes against historical serial murder cases, but I can't let it go. But if Lucas, Deal, Groundhog, and Scorpion are working together, why?" She clicked on her phone for the videos while Thatcher did the same with his laptop. "We need a break here. We're walking a tightrope."

"Watch this with me. Bigger screen."

Carly's observations about Bethany's feelings for him streamed across her mind. Had his mother picked up on it too? "Sure." She dragged a chair beside him. Even wounded, he smelled fresh and . . . *Stop going there.*

For the next hour, they viewed Bethany's parents' and sisters' visits to Lucas and a monthly visit from a priest whom she recognized. Three separate times women were in the video. Each time the woman hid her face, but none appeared to resemble the others.

Bethany pointed to the screen. "Freeze that section. Look, here one of the women is wearing heels. Another has tennis shoes, and this one is in four-inch spikes. If all were without shoes, they'd be the same height."

He handed her his laptop, and she configured the height of the women without shoes.

"The same woman," he said. "She walks differently in each one according to the persona, but her build is the same."

"Unfortunately, she's been successful in avoiding the camera." She stood and paced the room. "Let me see one more time." She took his laptop and viewed the three separate images, then watched the woman in action. "Why didn't I see this before?"

"What?"

"In each visit, the woman periodically holds on to her right wrist. Sometimes she holds it, and other times she pushes something up her arm. Melanie Bolton has the same habit."

"The director of the Lighthouse?" He studied the screen. "You're right. She had access to each victim, though she denied knowing Ruth Caswell."

Bethany eased back in the chair with his computer resting on her lap. She recalled Melanie's proclamation of how much she cared for the homeless, her protectiveness. If she'd been a part of the killing, then why?

"Do you have the photos taken at the crime scene of each victim?" she said. "I have a hunch."

"Another one?"

She smirked. "I stuck with you about scorpion traits, so give me a little slack. I'm assuming HPD's and our reports are there too."

"Right. What's your idea?"

"Crazy, I know. But I want to see if watches or timepieces play into the killings. We already know Ansel Spree was homeless and wearing a broken watch." She studied the details in his report. "We assumed it was the actions of an eccentric man." She lifted her gaze. "It was set at 11:17."

"Most people use cell phones these days."

"I know, Thatcher, but the thought won't let me go."

He gave her the file name of Scorpion.

She clicked on a subfolder for Eldon Hoveland. "He wasn't wearing a watch." She continued to read the report. What else?

She zoomed in on the body found in the kitchen. "How did I miss this? The clock on the stove was stopped at 11:17."

Thatcher straightened. "You have my attention."

She pulled up Ruth Caswell's folder and read for the next several minutes. "Here it is," she said. "Ms. Caswell's watch was on her dresser, set at 11:17. The investigator thought the battery had run down."

Shaking, Bethany clicked on Alicia Javon's file and looked for specifics on her death. Reading every detail, she almost gave up. Then, "I found it. Remember Alicia was heating water to cook lasagna? The digital timer beside the burner was set at 11:17." Blowing out a pent up breath, she turned to Thatcher. "Do you want to make a bet about Tyler Crawford?"

"Check his file. I believe he was wearing a watch."

Bethany opened Tyler's report. "You're right, and it stopped at 11:17."

Her stomach fluttered as a critical piece of the case hovered over her. "Each victim had a timepiece on or near them when they were found. Thatcher, the killer intended for the victims to appear as though they all died at the same time, but what does it refer to?"

"Melanie Bolton . . . 11:17." He picked up his cell and typed. "I'm informing Preston. They'll pick her up. This whole thing could be ended today."

Bethany typed into the FIG requesting anything to do with eleven or seventeen: a time or a date or even an address.

"I can see how stumbling onto Paul Javon's abuse and affair shoved aside any evidence pointing to her." She closed her eyes. Finally. She breathed in a taste of satisfaction. "I want to talk to Aiden about the numbers. See if eleven or seventeen means anything to him."

"I'm ready."

She frowned. "You aren't in any shape to travel or conduct an interview."

He struggled to stand. "I'm still the senior partner here."

She didn't deliberate her feelings because they were all over the place. "I vowed after you were shot—"

"*We* were shot." He punctuated each word. "If you're going to wear the jersey, then you have be active in the field."

A few moments later, she linked arms with him to walk to the door and onto the elevator. "By the way, my rental is a black Mustang. Thought I'd warn you."

He chuckled. "Go figure."

"You're moving much better than I expected."

"I'm in excellent physical condition. Been practicing my stride." He pushed the button to the first floor, although she flinched with his difficulty. How quickly they took simple movements for granted. "Just say it," he said. "I know you're enjoying this far too much."

Honestly? She peered into his face. "I think you're one courageous and determined agent."

His eyes flashed surprise. "Thanks. Mutual admiration here. Before this is over, we might be cell mates."

Reality had a way of sobering the most honorable of intentions.

If Thatcher were discharged from the FBI, he could get his doctorate in counseling or step back into the music world. But what would she do?

"I don't want you hurt," he said, once they were in the car. "In case you haven't figured it out, my potential as a defender is almost zero."

"Imagine your potential when you're not a wounded lion."

"As in a pain-crazed animal?"

"You're in a witty mood."

"Could be a good thing. I could scare Aiden into a confession."

"Should I give you a mirror?"

"Spare me. My lady-killer status might go south."

"Trust me, it would." She aimed a smile at him. "Can't sing or dance in your condition."

"With you either? Because I'd sure like to try."

She kept her attention on the road. "What do you mean?"

"The elephant plopping its big rear in the car between us."

She gripped the steering wheel. "Do you want to feed it peanuts? Take it for a walk?"

"I want us to talk about it."

"I'd rather deposit it at the zoo, where it belongs." Her pulse sped.

"It won't go away because you ignore it."

Stop before it's too late. You can be a professional. "We can't." Her voice softened when she wanted to sound resolute. "Impossible."

"So we live in denial?"

"If we don't, one of us could be killed. We're already off the case, unable to work for two weeks."

"What's new?"

"Thatcher." Her gaze flew to his. That's when she saw in his eyes what she felt. "Look at what has happened since we started working together. The odds would be more against us if we . . . acted on your feelings."

"Mine? I'm not blind, Bethany."

"Maybe I should ask for a transfer."

"And what would that accomplish? Unless you're thinking we can explore our relationship if we're not partners."

She pressed on the gas. "We've already broken enough rules for Preston to end our careers."

"Answer my question first."

"Have you forgotten I have diabetes?"

"And that means what? Oh, I have ingrown toenails."

She frowned. "If we survive the bullets, ugly accusations, being removed from the investigation, and whatever else Scorpion tosses our way, we can talk about you and me."

He reached across the car and touched her arm. "In the meantime, I have no control over myself while under meds."

She forced a laugh into a situation that wasn't funny. "From the office chatter, you've always had a problem ignoring women."

"Maybe so, but this time I'm in quicksand."

"A moment ago you wanted the zoo. I really need to turn around and take you home."

"After we talk to Aiden."

She sighed, wanting to discuss the case and not their trivial attraction.

"Bethany, you didn't deny feelings for me."

She whipped to him. "You're in no mood to be rational."

He chuckled and closed his eyes. "Oh, the sting of truth."

CHAPTER 59

Thatcher fell asleep while Bethany drove to the safe house. She had no plans to wake him. The last time they spoke with Aiden, Thatcher had said all the right words. Now it was her turn. She had years of experience in handling Lucas, the mistakes and the victories. The farther she ventured into the rural area outside of northwest Houston, the more she relaxed. Here some of the trees were trimmed in vibrant oranges and golds. Holidays approached. Where would she spend them? In the past, she'd accompanied Elizabeth to her parents'. She dreamed about where she wanted to be, then pushed the thought away as quickly as it took root.

If they lived through this, if their careers weren't destroyed, they still had no future.

She swung a look at her wounded lion. Mouth agape. Nothing romantic about his pose. But his heart had captured hers.

She neared the horse farm where Aiden was living. The wife had begun schooling him, and according to her, he was exceptionally bright. No surprise to Bethany. His intelligence had kept him alive.

Leaving Thatcher in the car, she found Aiden in the horse barn brushing down a quarter horse.

"I hear you enjoy riding," she said.

His face revealed a calm young man. "I do. When she runs, it's like flying. Best high I ever had."

She patted the sleek mare. "Makes coming down easier. You look good, Aiden."

"Thanks." He continued to brush the horse. "I like it here. Not like other foster parents. These people are honest, blunt." He shrugged. "Seem to care."

"Tyler would have been pleased."

"I think so too. Where's your partner?"

"Asleep in the car. We got ambushed on Saturday night." She held up her cast. "I'm the lucky one."

"Deal?"

"Maybe. Maybe Scorpion. Look, Aiden, I need your help. I have video of a woman who could lead us to your brother's killer. These were taken when she visited my brother in jail, and we think both of them are connected to Scorpion."

He stared at the brush. "Okay."

She showed him the three captured pics of the unknown woman. He shook his head and returned her phone.

"Looks like my crazy aunt," he said.

"Dorian has a sister?"

"Half sister. They're both crazy."

"What's her name?"

"She goes by Melanie Bolton, but it's not her real name." He shrugged. "Don't think I've ever heard it."

"Any other siblings?"

"I have no idea."

"Can you tell me anything about your aunt?"

"Not really. Tyler said she was bad news and not to trust her. She's in charge of the Lighthouse."

"Have you any information about my brother, Lucas Sanchez?"

He shook his head. "Never met him."

"Will you help me finish this so you can go on with your life?"

He looked at the brush in his hand. "These people asked me if I wanted to stay with them. Permanent."

"Good."

"I don't want them hurt because of my mistakes. What do you want?"

"Confirmation on what Thatcher and I believe is true. Tyler found out about the hit-and-run aimed at me and stopped it."

"Yes. But I don't have names."

She blew out her response. "Did your mom and Tyler argue?"

"Big-time. Tyler didn't want to be mixed up with any crimes. The next thing I learn, he's missing."

"But there's more, right? The list Tyler saw."

He slowly nodded.

"It's why Scorpion is after you. I need the list, Aiden, before anyone else is killed."

"I've been thinking about it. Whoever killed my brother has to be stopped."

"Do you have the list here?"

"Shredded."

"The FBI has software to put the pieces together. Digitize them and run them through a computer program."

"Why?"

"Because it's the right thing. It's what Tyler would want you to do."

Aiden stared at her for a long moment, then finally removed his left tennis shoe, ripped at a worn side, and pulled out a small plastic bag filled with shredded paper.

Bethany walked to her rental car. An SUV was parked behind her. She made her way to the driver's side, and Grayson opened the door.

"Are you expecting a bomb here?"

He shrugged. "Not my favorite assignment. Looks like Thatcher's asleep."

"He should be in the hospital."

"Before he kills himself. What part of 'off the case' did Preston not make clear?" Although his words were gruff, his eyes held compassion.

"This is personal business and not short-term." She handed him the plastic bag. "Scorpion's hit list."

✳ ✳ ✳

1:00 P.M. TUESDAY

The moment Bethany headed toward Houston, Thatcher woke. She quickly explained Aiden's confession and Grayson's appearance. "He promised to text or call with the latest updates."

"And I slept through it all." He moaned. "I talked a good talk back at my condo."

"We made a huge dent, partner. For certain, Tyler did his best to shelter Aiden."

"I have unanswered questions, like how your brother fits in. How about something to eat?"

"Your mother's making tortilla soup."

"I can't have her hearing details about the case, and I feel even worse chasing her to her room."

"I'm sure she understands confidentiality," Bethany said. "We can't go to my apartment because I'm concerned Lucas hid a bug in a place where I haven't looked."

"Okay." He closed his eyes.

She should take him back to the hospital, but he'd probably unload his Glock on her. "Preston will hear about our ventures and won't be happy."

"We're not off the grid, and besides, we've given him an ace. Have you always been such a rules girl?"

"Go back to sleep."

Home sounded good, but not practical. First on her list this week was a new lock with a sophisticated alarm system. Too bad Jasper couldn't alert her, but he'd done well in repeating the Lucas phrase. Oh, the irony.

She remembered their meds. A task when they reached his condo.

Once inside his garage, he opened his eyes. "I'm ready to climb

Mount Kilimanjaro." He looked pale, but she thought twice about mentioning it.

In his condo, the aroma of tortilla soup made her stomach growl. Mrs. Graves's face blanched. "Do I need to call an ambulance for both of you?"

"I'm fine," Bethany said. "Thatcher needs to sleep."

He protested the whole way as Bethany helped him to his room. "Men are such horrible patients," his mother said, then softened. "What can I get you?"

"Nothing. Wake me in about thirty minutes for the soup."

The doorbell rang and his mother left to answer it.

SSA Preston stood in the doorway of Thatcher's bedroom. "Hello, you two."

CHAPTER 60

Thatcher stared at SSA Preston. A house call signaled a problem, a real rear chewing, if they were even allowed to keep their badges and firearms.

Bethany motioned to a chair in the bedroom. "Would you like to sit down?"

"From the looks of both of you, I think you need a chair worse than I do." SSA Preston didn't budge from the doorway, where he towered.

"Did you receive the list?"

"Yes, ma'am."

"Plan on arresting us?"

"Tried removing you from the case. Threatened discipline and discharging you." His stony face told her nothing. "The one thing going for you is you haven't concealed information. We work as a team. No solos. No self-proclaimed heroes. No Captain Americas. I gave you both an order, and neither of you deferred to my instructions or the bureau's policies. Do you have any idea the danger you've put yourselves in?"

"Our choice," Thatcher said. If only his voice held forcefulness. Bethany remained stoic.

"Such heroics," Preston said. "In a way, I wish I had more agents like you, and in another I don't want to see either of you again."

Thatcher refused to look at Bethany. He'd figured out on day two that her self-worth was wrapped up in her identity as an FBI agent. "Which is it?" he said.

"Haven't decided yet. Thatcher, stay right where you are. Bethany, agents will escort you to your apartment and wait while you pack a few things. Not safe for you there. You might be physically in better shape than Thatcher, but our killers are out for blood."

"What are the latest findings?" he said.

Preston maintained his position in the doorway. "I'll fill you in since agents will be within close proximity of you both until arrests are made." He paused, his usual expression of displeasure and control. "You received information about Melanie Bolton. Since the shooting Saturday night, the FBI and HPD have been working with the Lighthouse's board of directors, specifically examining bookkeeping discrepancies."

Thatcher blinked to listen to every detail, read every aspect of Preston's body language.

"Melanie Bolton is missing."

Bethany startled and eased onto a chair in his bedroom. "You haven't picked her up?"

"We're on it as well as HPD. The FIG has just given us critical information. Her real name is Margo Immerman, a fugitive who's been on the FBI wanted list for fifteen years."

Thatcher vaguely recalled seeing the name on a list.

"Margo Immerman grew up on a Mexican family compound called Scorpion. There were nineteen siblings fathered by Lecket Immerman. They ran drugs and sold weaponry to anyone who paid the right price, often eliminating the competition and anyone who opposed them. They raided small communities for whatever they needed. Those who worked for Lecket Immerman were in for life. Authorities say no one escaped his control except in a coffin. He ruled his family with an iron fist and was to be revered and obeyed. Margo was trained to kill and follow orders just like her brothers. Her mother died mysteriously. When Lecket's brother and family, including two small children, fled the compound to start over in Arizona, he murdered them. Mutilated their bodies. Took photos and left a note for others to see as an example if they betrayed him. Margo participated in those killings at the age of fourteen. The authorities traced several robberies and murders to Immerman and those within the compound. When law enforcement attempted to close in, she and her father disappeared, while the rest of the siblings escaped into South America. Some have been found and prosecuted for their crimes while others, like Margo, are still at large. FBI offered a $20,000 reward for any information leading to Lecket or her."

"Then they settle in Houston as do-gooders for the Lighthouse?" Thatcher said, his mind a bit fuzzy.

"We have a theory. Essentially, ten years ago the Immermans, posing as the Boltons, took advantage of the Lighthouse directorship vacancy. They made their credentials look credible and advocated community development. We've learned their recommendations for the position contained falsified information. Research done in the last several hours has proved they skimmed from the donations."

"Which explains the building's need of repairs and the poor quality of food," Thatcher said.

"Are you thinking she killed her father instead of a heart attack?" Bethany said.

"Not really. With her unstable past, we believe she's carrying out his legacy and punishing those who offend her."

"The name of the compound could have given her the serial killer's scorpion theme," she said. "Eldon Hoveland was the only one who didn't fit the pattern. Unless the scorpions became an afterthought."

"We're looking at revenge as motive, but we don't have it all yet."

Thatcher saw more. "She's blaming others for her father's heart attack. The oversize watch is probably his too." He thought back over Margo's infatuation with the man's watch. "What was the time of her father's death?"

Preston typed into his phone. "Shouldn't be difficult to find out." He lifted a brow. "Eleven seventeen."

"The same time on the watches and clocks of each victim," she said. "We have revenge as a motive."

"I believe you're on point," Preston said. "How she fits with Lucas Sanchez hasn't been fully determined. Speculation is she must have established a relationship with him before his last jail term."

Those findings made sense with everything he and Bethany had learned.

Bethany typed into her phone. "Sir, Lucas must be her errand boy, which would be a difficult task. Unless she calls the shots and lets him think he's the brains."

Thatcher added more. "Ruth Caswell and Alicia Javon stopped donating, certainly motive if she was filling her pockets."

"No matter where Margo and your brother, Lucas, are hiding or plan to go, we'll find them," Preston said.

Thatcher wanted more answers. "Where does Dorian Crawford fit?"

"From our intel, Margo searched out her sister when she and her father moved to Houston. Could be why our city was chosen. Intel shows the Immermans were planning to connect here and bring in their business efforts—drugs, prostitution, and gunrunning—like they've been doing in Mexico and South America. The explanation of how Dorian escaped her father is dubious. She's being interrogated as we speak to find out how much she knows. We believe her mother died, and Lecket remarried. From all indications, his new wife gave birth to Margo and several sons and encouraged Lecket to expand his illegal business. The man known as Groundhog is Margo's full brother. We were able to arrest him, but he's refusing to talk."

"Would you call when you have an update?" Thatcher said. "I don't care what time."

"Whatever you learn," Bethany said.

Preston stared at them. "I need your word you will leave the investigation to those who are in good physical condition."

Thatcher glared into Preston's face. "I'll agree as long as there are no agents posted outside my door."

Mrs. Graves, who'd said nothing, walked to Thatcher's bed. "Sir, I'll call you if either of them attempt to disregard your instructions."

✳ ✳ ✳

11:24 P.M. TUESDAY

Thatcher stirred at the sound of a phone. Distant. His eyes fluttered. Mom had moved his phone from his dresser. Irritation yanked at him, but Bethany answered it.

"Yes, sir. I grabbed his phone. What have you found?"

Thatcher switched on the lamp and cringed. For a moment he'd forgotten about his gunshot. Bethany appeared in sweatpants and a baggy T-shirt, staring at him while continuing the conversation.

"Have you picked up either of them?" She shook her head at Thatcher and said nothing for several minutes. "Thank you."

She returned the phone to his nightstand. "They reassembled the list and received a bonus. Aiden's now my hero."

"Pull up a chair." He smiled. "Like your pj's."

"Thanks. Perfect for sleeping on the sofa at your partner's condo." She dragged a chair closer to the bed. "Along with a list of victims is a timetable of when they'd be eliminated and why. Dorian got scared and gave the FBI a statement. She attacked Elizabeth and thought she'd killed her, a mandate from Margo. Elizabeth once donated to the Lighthouse before taking over Noah's Loft. The Immermans were blackmailing the homeless into committing crimes and handing over the proceeds. But the biggest motive for the serial killings is revenge. Margo blamed all those who refused to commit any more crimes and those who no longer donated to the Lighthouse for her father's death. Thus the kill list." She held up a finger. "The watch is their father's, like we thought. Dorian claims Margo talks to it, and their dad gives her instructions."

His psychological background kicked in. "Fits her disorder. The attachment is a source of comfort, a connection to her past that she must keep close to her. If she lost it, the psychological disruption would be bizarre. She'd become enraged, causing her to do whatever it takes to regain peace again."

"Is this a part of borderline personality disorder?"

"Yes. It's self-soothing, much like a child has a favorite blanket, viewing the object as sacred."

"Thatcher, how did she function as a professional, attending city functions and interacting with the board?"

"Driven by madness to play the role. She believes her father is with her, counseling her, guiding her. Years ago, while in private practice, I had a client who'd kiss and cry into a stuffed dog during our sessions. He confessed to spending hours, even days, on the Internet trying to find a replacement for a previous one that he'd lost, obsessing, going without food. The one he brought to sessions was the replacement." Thatcher dug his fingers into his palm. "In severe cases, the person believes the object talks to them. Add OCD to the mix, and we're dealing with a dangerous and violent woman."

"She can't be found soon enough."

"Any mention of your brother?" he said.

"Lucas was used. Which tells me he's about to lose his worth."

He wasn't going to add that Lucas might be the next victim. "Remember when we discussed her borderline personality disorder? Couple the instability with narcissism and the combination is combustible, deadly. She didn't receive from her father the nurturing every child needs, and she has his DNA. She's ruled by power and dominance, which means her mind is messy enough to be uncontrollably angry. That anger goes inward and outward."

"As in the taunting texts and what we've seen in her relationships."

"Ordinarily being around people would make her uncomfortable, so her agenda takes precedence." Thatcher closed his eyes, while sleep clouded his mind.

"Dorian slides in behind her with mental instability too," she said. "Margo obviously persuaded Lucas to help her by playing into his desire for revenge against me, to destroy my credibility."

"I want out there on the investigation."

"Preston reminded me of his ultimatum." She touched his bed but not him. "Thatcher, what else can we do? We're no match for either of them."

"I have Diet Dr Pepper in the fridge just for you. We could keep up with what the office is doing online."

She sighed. "Pain meds make me do crazy things too. I'll brew a pot of coffee for you."

"Bethany." Should he shut down his emotions? Or blame his meds for what he wanted to do? "The elephant's here too."

Her gaze rested on his. "Send it back to the zoo."

CHAPTER 61

After SSA Preston's call, Thatcher had made a futile attempt to research where Lucas and Margo might be hiding out. But sleep consumed him.

The aroma of bacon and eggs woke him, along with a rumbling stomach and a jolt of Saturday night's reminder. Would it ever end? He despised this so-called recuperation period. He stared at his bedroom window, where morning light crept beneath the blinds. No excuse but to roll out of bed and follow his nose to the kitchen. He'd slept with his clothes on except for his shoes.

Fumbling for his phone, he stumbled to the door, absorbing the steady throb to his upper shoulders. Would his body respond like this in fifty years? Not a pleasant thought. He stepped through the door and to the kitchen, craving a caffeine fix and good news.

Mom and Bethany sat on the kitchen barstools. What could they be discussing? Did he really want to find out?

"Are you conspiring against a decrepit old man?"

Bethany peered into his face. How quickly he got lost in those eyes, dimples . . . He had a bad case of Bethany Sanchez. "We're arranging for around-the-clock nursing care. Ordered a supply of bedpans and hospital gowns."

He feigned irritation. "I already have all the special care I need from my mother."

"My son, the perfect patient," Mom said, perky and put together. Her lipstick even glistened. "We've been chatting about our diabetes and gardening."

"Gardening?"

"I grow herbs on my patio," Bethany said. "So does your mother. We both like to cook, and I asked what herbs she preferred. And she gave me a Thatcher Graves CD. Anything else?"

He slumped onto a kitchen chair. "I'm sure you don't want to hear my complaints or listen to me sing."

"How are you feeling?" Mom said.

"Like playing football." He closed his eyes. "Forget about me. What's going on with the case? Then I want a plate of scrambled eggs and bacon." His nose detected something else. "Fresh biscuits too."

Mom slid from the stool. "I'll see if I can accommodate you." She filled a plate and set it before him. "Now you two can chat alone."

"Mom, it's not necessary."

She gave him her best mom look. "Yes, it is, if I want the animals who shot you two to be found. I'll be in my room watching a recorded TV crime show in which the bad guys are arrested or shot. Frankly I prefer ending the lives of killers." She started toward the door of her bedroom, then turned around. "I've learned Bethany has the religion thing going too. I've never stepped inside a church or picked up religious literature, but I see a difference in both of you."

"My Bible's on the nightstand."

She grinned. "I'll think about it. Your father viewed it as a crutch."

He waited until she left the room and focused on Bethany. "Mom's blunt."

"I like her. She was horrified with your faith statement, but we did talk. Anyway, she's incredibly worried about you." Bethany looked rested.

He pointed to her cast. "How long do you have to wear it?"

"Don't know until I have a follow-up with a specialist. I'm doing my best to ignore it."

They had so much in common. "I'm ready to party, Agent Sanchez. What else have you been up to?"

Bethany poured him another cup of coffee. "Every law enforcement official in the city is looking for Margo and Lucas. Billboards are in place, and crime watch has offered a $20,000 reward on each. They will be found." She pulled a Diet Dr Pepper from the fridge.

"I'm sorry."

She raised a brow. "Why?"

"Your role in violent crime has left you alienated from your family."

"The relationship was destroyed before the case. My beliefs have to take precedence over enabling a criminal. I'll make it."

"This partner doesn't plan on going anywhere."

Her dark eyes shadowed with confusion. "But we must."

✳ ✳ ✳

9:00 A.M. WEDNESDAY

Bethany's cell phone rang, and she recognized the number as one Lucas had used. She glanced at Thatcher. "This is my brother. We might have hit pay dirt." She answered on the second ring.

"Hey, Sis." Lucas sniffed. "I need help."

When he came down from a high, he was like a baby. Pitiful. "What kind of help?"

"I've made a mess of things. Can't go on this way."

How many times had she heard this? How many times had she swallowed it only to have him prove her a fool? "Are you alone?"

"Yes. Melanie left me. Told me I didn't have what it took to make her happy. I've done plenty for her," he scoffed.

He hadn't called her Margo. "You need to turn yourself in." She spoke calmly as though he were a child.

"I know, but I'm scared. What if the cops or FBI shoot me?"

"Not if you surrender." His sobs, the ones she'd heard so many times when he was broken, clawed at her heart. "Lucas, why did you call?"

"Help me with this thing. Make the arrangements with the FBI, walk out with me. Then they won't kill me."

"Did you help Scorpion kill people after you were released from jail?"

He broke down even more. She had her answer. "Will you cooperate with the FBI and tell them who else is involved?"

"Yes, Bethany. I'll do whatever you want. I can't live like this anymore. Her brothers are worse. They talk about the people they've killed. The nightmares . . . all of it."

"You mean Groundhog and Deal?" Why would he implicate them unless he was ready to live straight? "Where are you?"

"The other side of town near the ship channel. Are you alone at your apartment?"

She wrestled with her answer. "Why?"

"So many things I want to tell you before I turn myself in. I'll bring *Abuela*'s brooch. You're the only one who's ever cared for me, who ever understood me. Promise me, Sis. I beg of you. Can I come to your apartment and talk before turning myself in?"

He'd killed innocent people, and he had to be stopped.

"Sis?"

She must help him before he was shot. "Yes. I'll meet you. When can you come?"

"As soon as I can. But if I see any sign of the law, I'm running. Believe me, I don't want to."

"Don't worry. I'll listen to your story, and then we'll contact the FBI together. Bye, Lucas."

She whirled to Thatcher. "We have him."

CHAPTER 62

Thatcher burned with Bethany's announcement. "You're in no shape for a takedown. Have you forgotten you're off the case?"

She frowned and pressed in a number on her cell phone. "SSA Preston, Lucas called me. Says he wants to meet me at my apartment right away, talk, and then have me bring him in."

Thatcher attempted to put together the one-way conversation.

"I'm leaving now. Thanks."

"What's going down?" he said.

"They're forming a SWAT Operations Unit. Will pick him up when he arrives. It's over."

"I don't like any of this. Anything could go wrong."

She bit her lip. "If you were going, you wouldn't be upset."

His face grew hotter. But she had a point—if he was seen with her, Lucas could kill her or run. Or both. "This is too risky, Bethany. I should have agreed to agents posted outside my door. They would have stopped this ludicrous idea."

"I have no plans to go down as another victim." She turned to his mother, who'd entered the kitchen when he'd raised his voice. "Take care of our wounded lion." Without another word, she left.

No way was he sitting there while she had a face-to-face with a killer. He'd seen her crumble when a bullet sped through his car window.

✳ ✳ ✳

9:51 A.M. WEDNESDAY

Bethany drove to her apartment and phoned SSA Preston.

"Stand down until the SWAT team is in position."

"Sir, this is my brother. Family. I have to try to stop him." She'd talk to Lucas first, then accompany him to surrender. Her insides churned. She'd have to watch the parking lot and get to him before the SWAT team. Lucas would fight before facing arrest.

"You go through with this, and your career is in jeopardy. Do I need to mention he could kill you? We have a team to pick him up."

"My conscience would be in worse shape. This has to stop, and I can get Lucas to surrender."

His response was a little colorful. "The operation takes priority."

"I'm leaving my cell on in case anything goes wrong."

She pulled through the security gate to her building. She scanned her complex for agents and her brother. No one appeared, except for the SUV following her from Thatcher's condo. Might be Grayson Hall. The concession eased some of her nerves.

She'd left Thatcher without saying the things faintly etched on her heart. Better this way in case she found the wrong end of a bullet. If he'd been in full performance, she'd have begged him to be her partner. She forced acid back down into her stomach. Years ago, she'd vowed to stop Lucas no matter what it took. Reckoning had come.

Margo was still at large, but Lucas could be dead in less than two hours. Bethany would be blamed . . . failed her brother and her family because she'd taken on the role of the great crusader. Love scaled higher mountains than rejection could ever accomplish. Pushing aside fragile emotions, she dropped her cell into her purse.

She climbed the steps to her apartment, wishing her left arm wasn't bound by a cast. A cripple . . .

She pulled her Glock from her purse. A tingling soared from

her belly to her fingertips while her senses breathed in everything around her. *Please, God, help me not to need my weapon. Not my brother, God.*

The door to her home showed no signs of forced entry or new scratches. No wires. Bethany used her key and stepped inside.

The folded piece of paper left inside the doorway lay on the floor intact. In the shadows of closed drapes, nothing looked out of the ordinary. Jasper chirped a greeting when she removed his blanket and snapped on a light.

"Pretty Jasper," she said.

"Pretty Jasper," he mimicked.

She thought better of unlocking his cage. Her apartment needed to be cleared first. Quiet. Was this uneasiness or her instincts? She'd set the trap for Lucas, not the other way around.

Jasper squawked. "Jasper wants grapes."

"In just a moment," she said. "I left you plenty of food yester-day, but I know you're hungry."

Lucas stepped into the hallway, her nightmare in flesh. "I'm hungry, too, Sis."

"Not this time." She raised her firearm. "You're coming with me."

He grinned. "Don't think so. Melanie, would you bring our trophy."

Papá emerged from her bedroom with his hands raised. Margo Immerman had a gun to his head.

CHAPTER 63

Thatcher wrestled into a button-down shirt. Hurt like fire. His jeans were zipped, though the effort had brought tears to his eyes.

"What are you doing?" His mother's voice rose toward hysteria.

"I can't leave Bethany to fight Lucas on her own," he said, catching his breath.

"Look at you. You'll be shot again. You care about her, and I'm glad. But let others fight this battle." Her lips quivered, but her pleading couldn't deter him.

"Impossible." He kissed her cheek and left, realizing part of what she'd said was true.

He drove to the FBI staging area, where SSA Preston and other agents were positioned adjacent to Bethany's building.

"You follow orders like a pro," Preston said, peering at Bethany's apartment through binoculars. Her windows were covered.

"What would you do?" Thatcher said, watching the closed door. All he could do was listen to the conversation inside through her phone connected to Preston's. Before Thatcher had arrived, Preston said, Bethany had given up her weapon when Margo threatened to pull the trigger on the elder Sanchez. Since then, Lucas had thrown around accusations, mixing them with how he planned to kill her. Margo reminded him of how many times Bethany had belittled him.

The SOU had moved in with a negotiator. Snipers were taking positions in the apartment building beside them. Thermal imaging revealed four, possibly five people inside Bethany's apartment.

Thatcher pointed to the computer screen set up inside Preston's car. "She has a parrot. We're looking at four people. Did a surveillance team follow Oscar Sanchez here?"

"A lot of good it did. Her apartment door was unlocked when the elder arrived."

"Which means Lucas let himself in before Bethany left my condo." Thatcher wanted to make a few accusations of his own, especially when Preston failed to reply.

Lucas's voice bellowed. "You thought you had me. Really?"

"Why bring *Papá* into this?" Her soft voice indicated her control. "Let him go, Lucas. Your problem is with me."

"Both of you. He dies first. I want you to watch."

Thatcher dropped his head.

"You're not up to this," Preston said.

"I'm fine. Praying."

"When did this happen?"

"When I stopped believing in—"

A crash sounded.

✳   ✳   ✳

10:22 A.M. WEDNESDAY

Nightmares were easier to accept than reality.

Bethany struggled for focus. Lucas had grabbed a lamp and thrown it at her, but she'd dodged him. *Papá* was unharmed but shaken. Lucas meant every threat—he'd pull the trigger on *Papá*. How hard this must be for their father . . . watching his son self-destruct.

"Hey, Sis, how do you like the way we destroyed your credibility as an agent? What about Melanie's texts and my posts? Media has you tried and convicted. Payback for eleven months in jail." He nodded like a bobblehead, a mannerism of his manic times. "Your epitaph will be the pits."

"Lucas, did you hurt *Mamá*?"

He laughed, a crazed sound she'd learned to dread. "Haven't seen her. The old man came here. Since when are you two on speaking terms?" He swung his attention to where Margo held a Ruger LC9 to *Papá*'s temple—9mm bullets, Scorpion's choice.

"I followed you," *Papá* said, his face a road map of distress. "I'm not a *loco* Mexican. When I met with you Monday afternoon, I planted a GPS under the rear chrome of your Harley."

No, Papá. *He'll blow.*

Jasper screeched a deafening, high-pitched sound.

Lucas grinned as though the bird's confusion fueled his rage.

"Son, let your sister go. It's my fault you're running from the FBI, that you killed and robbed people."

"Don't even think about it," Margo said. "Or I'll blow his head off."

Lucas punched *Papá* in the face, shoving him backward.

"Lucas, leave him out of this," Bethany said. "Let me help you. I've loved you since we were small. We were more than brother and sister—we were friends. Things haven't changed."

"You changed. You got educated. Made money while I had to get cash my way." He whipped a .38 at her. "Big superachiever sister always made me look bad. Should have killed both of you at the Lighthouse."

"Kill her now!" Margo screamed and gripped the man's watch on her wrist. "She's ruined your life. Father said they must be punished."

"When I'm ready."

She shoved *Papá* toward the closed drapes and held a gun to his head while looking outside. "No one's out there. We're good. Just get rid of them."

Bethany needed to calm him. "We can walk out of here together."

"You made me feel like leftover garbage."

Bethany kept her focus on Lucas. "How?"

"Finding me jobs that made me sweat while you slapped on makeup and drove to an air-conditioned office?"

She shook her head. "I worked hard too. I'm sorry if I made you feel badly. But you can't go on like this. You've got to turn yourself in."

"For what? To lock me up? Death row?" He sucked in a breath. "Money and power belong to those who can figure out how to get it. Right, Melanie?"

He called her Melanie for the third time.

"Right, babe," Margo said. "You're smarter than any of her FBI friends. Just like I promised. You help me punish those who killed my father, and I help you take down your sister and whoever gets in our way. Look at the ways I played cat and mouse with her, taunting her, making her look like a crazy fool."

"You weren't raised to steal and kill," Bethany said, ignoring Margo. "Yes, you're a genius. But you made one small mistake."

"I don't think so."

"Your girlfriend hasn't been honest with you."

"She's the only one who has ever seen me like a man." He stepped forward, but Bethany didn't budge.

"You call her Melanie. She lied to you." Bethany ushered tenderness into her words. "Her name is Margo Immerman."

"Kill her." Margo seethed, wielding her weapon. "Babe, she's filling you with lies."

Bethany was ready to take a risk, but Margo had nothing to lose. "Ask her, Lucas. What's her real name?"

Lucas's face reddened. "Melanie, answer her."

Papá inched back from the scene, foreseeing the violence coming.

Margo rubbed her arm holding her father's watch. "Father says she must die. She has no idea what she's talking about."

"So I'm right. You lied to Lucas about your identity."

Lucas trembled. "You said Bethany lied."

"She's confusing me." Her voice rose to a grating squeal while Jasper's incessant shrills hammered against Bethany's brain. "Nobody gets in my way. Don't forget what I did to Dorian's kid. Killing is easy, so what's wrong with you? Why can't you pull the trigger like a man?"

"Lucas," *Papá* said. "Listen to your sister. Your girlfriend is using you. Not sure why she's killed innocent people, but she hasn't given you her right name."

"It's true," Bethany continued, taking what she knew about the case into her own hypothesis. "Did she pull you into her plan to murder because the homeless refused to steal? Some donors were no longer giving to the Lighthouse? Offended her daddy? Did she tell you about her childhood on a compound where she learned how to steal, torture, and kill?"

"Lucas, get rid of her or I will. I gave you this one thing to do, and you can't pull the trigger?"

Bethany bored into his face. "What about the watch she won't let out of her sight, the one she keeps touching? I have documented proof of everything I've said."

"No, it's a trick." Margo shouted obscenities. "You're stupid. Father would never approve." Her words rang like shattering glass.

"Your name," Lucas said, keeping his attention fixed on Bethany.

Margo lifted her chin. "None of your business, loser."

He whirled and fired into her chest. She glared at him wide-eyed as she slumped against the wall and to the floor.

Lucas turned to Bethany.

"It's over, Brother," she said. "You can put the gun down and not have one more killing on your record. *Papá* and I are here to support you. You're a smart man."

"I have a right to more."

"Of course, and I'll always be here for you." She saw a softening in his brown eyes. The ones that used to glisten when they were kids. "Please, Lucas."

He hesitated for a moment, but in an instant he aimed the gun at her. "No, you won't talk me out of this."

"Son, soon law enforcement will be surrounding this place. You won't be able to get away."

"I don't care, old man. I have a new plan. You can watch what I do to your daughter before I blow out your brains. It's all gone. Nothing left."

He aimed at Bethany's face.

Papá grabbed at Lucas from behind, knocking him off-balance. The gun fired, leaving *Papá* bleeding in its wake.

CHAPTER 64

Bethany scrambled for her purse and gun, but Lucas grabbed her in a neck hold.

"One more time, you've made my life miserable."

"No, Lucas." She pried at his arm blocking her air. Her words refused to come.

The door burst open to SWAT.

"Release her now." A special agent aimed his HK.

"Back off," Lucas said. "The only way I'm coming through is with her dead body."

The barrel of his weapon dug into her skull. She collapsed her legs and dropped, forcing him to release her with the weight. She reached across him with her right hand and grabbed his gun, twisting his left wrist back against its natural bend.

Lucas screamed in pain and dropped the .38.

Agents overpowered him.

"I'll kill all of you." Lucas cursed like she'd heard so many times before. "You won't lock me up again. I have friends."

Bethany ignored him.

The killings were over.

Finally. Scorpion lay dead with a bullet in her chest, and Lucas wore cuffs. He wouldn't hurt one more person.

Bethany rushed to *Papá's* side. Blood flowed from his outer right thigh, while he lay still and ashen. One of the team members radioed that Lucas was in custody, and requested an ambulance.

"*Papá*, help is on the way." She took his hand, squeezing it lightly.

He nodded and barely opened his eyes. "We meet like this too often."

"I'm sorry. Better it were me."

Papá held tightly to her hand. "How does a blind man say he's been wrong? I thought you were lost, but you were never lost to God."

Tears filled her eyes. "I love you."

"I love you too, *mi hija dulce*."

"We'll see Lucas through this," she said and kissed his cheek. "We're family."

A hand touched her shoulder, and she sensed Thatcher behind her. "Does my wounded lion have my back?"

"Always."

She heard more than a partner's commitment. Maybe now they could talk. Really talk. If God could bring her back to her father, then He could work out her and Thatcher's feelings. "Thanks. *Papá*, this is Special Agent Thatcher Graves, my partner."

Papá attempted a smile. "My daughter's bird is noisy."

Her mind had tuned out Jasper. "I can hush him, but I'll have to leave you for a moment."

Thatcher patted her shoulder. "Go ahead."

She opened Jasper's cage, soothing him with gentle words. He perched on her shoulder and she hurried back to *Papá*. How much of a little girl lived inside her. "I want you to meet someone else."

He chuckled. "Better than a watchdog."

The diversion would help until the ambulance arrived. Jasper rubbed against her neck with soft coos. He moved to her cheek.

"It's okay, little man," she whispered. "We're okay."

"I'm jealous," Thatcher said.

"No need to be." She wanted more with him. So much more.

Sirens grew closer. "When I get fixed up, you bring my daughter to dinner."

"I will," Thatcher said. "I promise. I hear you have a collection of Spanish guitars."

"*Sí*. I play too."

"Can I bring mine?"

"My daughter chose a good partner."

She swallowed the tears threatening to expose her facade. Maybe it was okay. Maybe it was okay to accept that life wasn't happily ever after but love was unconditional.

EPILOGUE

Bethany joined Thatcher outside of the physical therapy room. "What's the verdict?" she said.

"Done. I'm good as new, except for a few PT exercises to do at home."

"You were good as new when you were cleared psychologically for active duty."

"And now you're cleared too." He took her hand, and they walked to the door and outside into the crisp air.

She'd passed her psychological eval last month. Waiting on the disciplinary action from the Office of Professional Responsibility for her insubordination had taken over six weeks. But due to the mitigating circumstances, she'd been cleared. The OPR insisted upon a review in six months and then in a year, but she'd passed the debriefing. "We've come a long way, partner."

He squeezed her hand. "I'm a better man because of you."

His words brought a lump to her throat. "I don't know what to say, except I feel the same way about you."

"We agree. I need to record those words."

"It's not the first time."

"You're right. Do you mind sitting on the bench in the park across the street?"

"Sure. It's a beautiful day."

They hurried across the street and to a bench beside a huge fountain. The sun shimmered off the water, and the trickling sound offered a sense of tranquility.

"I've been thinking about the last few months," he said. "The things we learned while working Scorpion. Your logic reined in my out-of-the-box methods of investigation, and then the other way around. I suspected Eldon Hoveland and Ansel Spree were forced into crime by Margo until they refused and she killed them, but it helped to have Lucas confirm it."

Her brother would spend the rest of his life in prison, but there he might be open to God. It was a miracle Lucas agreed to medication. But once he did, he became more rational and confessed to everything, even in locating Deal, allowing the FBI to press additional charges against Margo's brothers Groundhog and Deal. The things Lucas had revealed to their family and law enforcement shoved the Scorpion puzzle pieces into place.

Margo'd had no idea Bethany was in the FBI. She'd met Lucas at a bar and told him of her desire to avenge her father's death and how her brothers would help. When he told of his hatred for his FBI sister, she offered to handle it for him. While he was in prison, they put the crimes together, although Margo carried out all the executions. Lucas and Margo scheduled the killings when they believed Bethany was at home. Somehow Margo persuaded Dorian to get involved. Even killed Tyler to keep her sister in line. Margo texted Bethany, wrote the derogatory posts, at first pretending to sound like Lucas. So he later took the credit. She had driven the car that nearly hit Bethany. Then her own mental disorder took over. Lucas didn't know why Margo enlisted her brothers' help, perhaps to set up a family business again or possibly to pin the murders on them.

"Although Dorian's in prison, I hope someone sees that she needs medication," Bethany said.

"What ranks at the top is we helped stop a serial killer and brought you closer to your family."

"And not in a way I would have ever imagined. I'm still

amazed." She sighed, a bittersweet reminder of God's provision. "When I consider how long I'd prayed for him and our family, I shouldn't be surprised."

"Bethany, God was with you the whole time."

"If only my parents could have seen Lucas's need to be on the medication long before his crimes escalated. It's like my diabetes. I need to watch my diet, and if the doctor recommends a pill, then I'll take it so I can survive and function."

"Speaking of functioning, I'm having problems this morning keeping my head in line with conversation."

"What's wrong?"

He pulled a rectangular gold box from his jacket pocket. "This is for you."

"How sweet. Are we celebrating our agent status?"

He frowned. "Not exactly."

She lifted the lid and revealed a solid gold bracelet. A half-inch band gave it a rich feel. "This is beautiful." She set it in her lap and hugged him. "You were extravagant, but I don't care because I love it."

"There's an inscription."

She curiously looked inside the band. *Partners for Life.*

She glanced at him while countless emotions soared around her heart.

"What do you think?" he said. "I was going to bring my guitar and sing for you, but that seemed more about me than you."

Her heart leaped like a frightened deer. "SSA Preston said we could continue together as long as we followed protocol."

"I don't mean for the FBI. I mean you and me for a lifetime. I love you, Bethany."

She trembled. "Thatcher, what are you saying?"

He pulled another gold box from his jacket, a square one. "I wanted to do this over dinner, but I can't wait." He grinned like a schoolboy. "I have your father's permission to marry his daughter. I just need your yes."

Her eyes widened. "Uh . . . when did this happen?"

"Us or your dad?" His eyes sparkled.

She breathed in deeply, her attention first on him and then on the diamond glittering in the morning sun. "I know us. Felt it within a week of working with you. But *Papá*? Was it when you two were playing guitars last weekend?"

"Nope. Remember when he and I went to see Lucas? I asked him then."

"What did he say?"

Thatcher laughed. "Said I was his favorite gringo, his *león herido*."

"Wounded lion. But now you're my *león rugiente*—" she kissed his cheek—"my roaring lion."

"Bethany Marie Sanchez, will you marry me? I need you in my life for as long as I walk this earth. You're my strength. You make me complete."

Her mind swept back to the moment they met, her misgivings about the relationship, her mistakes, their victories, how he helped her through the trauma with Lucas, and how the two of them now visited Lucas together. Most importantly the love that filled her with joy, a gift from God. "All those things you just said are how I feel about you. I love you, Thatcher, and yes, I'll marry you."

He took the box and slipped the ring over her finger. "My promise to love you. We'll work through the problems of life together. Thank you for showing me Jesus in action."

She hadn't viewed herself in such a light. In fact quite the opposite. She raised her head to kiss him, a kiss of longing and hope for tomorrow.

"Where to from here?" he said after their kiss. "I want to tell the world, but maybe we should wait until after Laurel and Daniel's wedding tomorrow night. I don't want to interfere in their special day."

"We could make our official announcement after they leave for their honeymoon. Are you sure I'm the woman for you? We clash far too often."

"Makes life interesting." He put his arm around her shoulder, and she laid her head against him.

"I never told you something," she said.

"What?"

"Best day of your life? Other than my faith, meeting you. Favorite vacation place? Anywhere with you. What matters to me most? My faith and you."

"I'll hold you to those answers." He squeezed her.

"What are you not telling me?" she said. "I can read you."

He chuckled. "Preston would like for us to consider working as a team undercover."

She covered her mouth and giggled. "In what way?"

"Let's get married and then figure out what he means."

A NOTE FROM THE AUTHOR

Dear Reader,

Story takes me into my characters' lives. Their desires, goals, problems, strengths, and flaws direct their actions. Some of their problems are difficult, especially those involving the dynamics of family. The characters of *Deadlock* are no exception.

Thatcher experienced a rough relationship with his father, and the man died before they were reconciled. Hard reality, and many of us wish we'd said and done things to those gone from this world.

Bethany grew up with doubts about her family's views regarding her brother. She disagreed with his lawbreaking, and the result was devastating. Standing up for truth and justice can ostracize us from our families, but do we have a choice with God as our judge? Bethany loved her family, but she loved God more.

If the past haunts you with unforgiveness and lack of restitution, I suggest you face those challenges. You'll find peace in the journey.

Blessings,

DiAnn

Expect an Adventure
DiAnn Mills
www.diannmills.com
www.facebook.com/diannmills

PROLOGUE

Special Agent Laurel Evertson had done everything required of her and more to gain Morton Wilmington's affections. The gaudy diamond on her left hand proved it. She was prepared to end her undercover work tonight and walk away from this despicable role. All she had to do was find the flash drive that would send her fiancé to prison for life.

Morton reached into his closet and pulled out designer pants, a shirt, and a sports jacket. "Babe, I'm taking a shower. Thought we'd grab dinner downtown before the play."

"Perfect. I'm ready. So looking forward to tonight." She despised the lies and the counterfeit love.

"What are you going to do? Read here?"

"I am. A new romance novel." She pointed to a window seat that offered a scenic view of his condo's pool bathed in late-summer afternoon sun.

He chuckled, his deep-blue eyes smoldering. "As long as I'm your main man."

"None other." She kissed him lightly. "I'm turning on a little Andrea Bocelli to put me in the mood."

"For what?"

"The book, the play, dinner, and us."

"Another reason why I love you. Even if you did beat me last night in Monopoly." He disappeared into the shower.

The moment the sound of water met her ears, she confirmed his location. Four times she'd found herself alone in his condo and attempted to access his safe, but each time she'd failed to hack into his computer, where he stored the safe combination that changed daily. Today she knew his password, and she quickly located the code on his laptop.

She placed the novel on the bed and removed a framed picture of a tank at Fort Knox from the wall to reveal the safe. Odd for a bedroom, but Morton had served four years in the Army. Probably the only thing he could be proud of. She rested the picture against the nightstand while the digital combination bannered across her mind. Squeezing her fingers into her palm to steady herself, she pressed in the code, hoping Andrea Bocelli's tenor voice drowned out the low click. If she was wrong, the alarm would blare throughout the condo, bringing Morton out of the shower along with his bodyguard from the kitchen.

Big business had made him one of the most powerful men in the country, and certainly in Texas. Murder, money laundering, and organized crime were his best friends—legitimacy his enemy. But he'd made one mistake, exposing it all on a flash drive. He'd bragged about where it was hidden one night after drinking too much. It had taken her months to locate the safe and figure out how to gain access.

Was she any better than he, using another person for her own agenda? She shook off the thought and concentrated on her commitment to stop Wilmington from breaking the law.

She secured the flash drive and replaced the picture. Stealing her way to the bathroom door, she confirmed Morton was still showering. His laptop sat on his desk as though beckoning her to prove the FBI's suspicions. She inserted the drive. Her heart pounded, ached.

"Babe, had an idea for our honeymoon," he called from the bathroom.

"Great." She breathed deeply to calm her scattered nerves. "Are you going to tell me?"

"Maybe."

"You know I love surprises." The details on the computer rose like rich cream: names, places, bank accounts. She ejected the device and slipped it into her shoe.

"I sent a check to MD Anderson this morning," he said.

"For the kids or in general?"

"The kids. The fund-raiser we attended hit me hard."

But you'd killed men who got in your way. "They stole my heart too." She texted the FBI and Jesse, her partner, providing the code to the condo's alarm system and telling them where the armed bodyguard was located. "Do you need anything?"

"That's a loaded offer, but I'm good."

He wouldn't be so good once the FBI arrived for the takedown. "What time are we leaving?" She moved back to the window seat and opened her novel.

He stepped from the bathroom, a towel wrapped around his waist. "Is six okay?"

She smiled. "Sure." Finally this charade would be over.

While discussing what Wilmington wanted to do for the children at MD Anderson, he dressed and she touched up her makeup. Her hands trembled.

"Are you okay?" he said. "You're shaking."

"Just hungry." She hated this game, made her feel as dirty as Morton.

"Want a glass of orange juice?"

"You're so sweet. Thanks, I'd love it."

He left the room and went down the hall to the kitchen. She checked her phone.

W r n place. Now

With a confident breath, she pulled her Glock from her purse and trailed after Wilmington. Only moments remained.

A crash sounded from the kitchen and seized her attention.

Morton swore. "Laurel, stay back. Call the bodyguards."

She rushed from the bedroom, her hand fused to her Glock.

Gunfire exploded. One. Two. Three shots.

A bodyguard sprawled facedown on the floor, blood seeping from beneath him.

Jesse hid in the back of the kitchen by the utility room, trapped but able to fire.

"Morton, drop the gun." She inched closer.

"You're part of this?" His eyes and gun stayed fixed on Jesse. "You set me up?"

"It was my job."

He called her vile names that would echo forever.

"FBI. Lower your weapon." She moved closer. "Morton Wilmington, you're under arrest. Agents are waiting."

"You know how I operate. No one gets the best of me."

"You can give orders to the prison guards."

"You have a choice," Morton said. "Put down your gun, or I'll blow a hole right through this guy."

"That works both ways."

Morton swung a seething look at Laurel, allowing just enough time for Jesse to move into position.

Morton whirled and fired, sending Jesse backward to the floor, a bullet in his neck. Blood seeped across his upper body. His eyes wide-open . . . The cost of her undercover work.

Agents poured through the door. Morton dropped the gun and glared at her. "I have people everywhere. You can't hide, Laurel. No matter how long it takes. You'll pay in blood."

CHAPTER 1

FIVE YEARS LATER
9:30 A.M. WEDNESDAY, SEPTEMBER 23
HOUSTON FBI

Special Agent Su-Min Phang stood in the doorway of Laurel's cubicle. "How's the progress on the elderly fraud?"

Laurel spun her chair to face her. "I don't see much in common with the crimes, but I'm not saying someone hasn't covered his tracks. If it's the same bad guys, they're smart to lay low, then strike again in a different way."

"What do you have? We need this handled."

Laurel hadn't worked in the field since the day her partner died. She'd paid the price of bringing a criminal to justice. The guilt refused to release its tentacles, and maybe it shouldn't.

Now she was investigating white-collar crime and its surplus of lying, stealing, and cheating. Made a few bad guys exchange their suits and offices for jumpsuits and six-by-eight cells. The responsibility filled part of the hole in her heart.

This morning she concentrated on a series of Houston scams targeting the elderly, specifically wealthy senior citizens who bore the weight of dementia. The latest operation used fraudulent life insurance to steal thousands of dollars from their victims. The case revved up anger and fueled her determination to stop the crimes. Abusing those who could no longer make good choices? That was low.

A dear woman who'd raised Laurel had suffered from Alzheimer's, and she'd been treated like an animal. For her, and for all the reported cases, Laurel would help stop those who preyed upon the elderly.

She mentally reviewed the initial reports. Eight years ago, an outbreak of counterfeit prescription drugs swept across Florida, north to Georgia, and along the Gulf states to Texas. An estimated two million dollars was reported lost by the elderly. Investigators suspected a money-laundering source in Miami. No doubt more money had been made, but victims were often embarrassed when they realized the truth and chose not to report the crime. No leads, and the bad guys went dark.

Six years ago, another deception hit the innocent. Funeral plans and caskets were sold to unsuspecting elderly. Again the crimes began in Miami and spread through the Gulf states, but this time Arkansas and Oklahoma were involved. More money than before vanished. An agent in Miami received a tip that a dozen elderly were gathered at a hotel to learn how to make economical funeral arrangements. When the agents arrived, the scammer had disappeared. The results were a paper trail that led to a computer housed in an empty office. The hard drive had been removed. A dead end with the criminals again going dark.

Four and a half years ago, wheelchairs and remodeling projects geared toward the elderly hit the scene, infiltrating Florida and the Gulf states. Five months into the scam, the team shut down. Investigators saw the pattern, but the bad guys were smart enough not to leave a paper trail and to stop when things got too hot.

Two years later, a real estate fraud sold condos for luxury retirement high-rises in Florida, Alabama, and both Carolinas. Four months and they closed up shop. An estimated $50 million was made on that scheme.

This latest scam against the elderly might be the biggest moneymaker yet. Although the operation worked the same range of states, different cities were targeted. How soon before greed caused them to make a mistake or the FBI exposed their methods?

Su-Min stepped into Laurel's cubicle. "I have info. A gentleman in River Oaks stumbled onto an e-mail that his elderly father received regarding the purchase of a life insurance policy. It contained part of another e-mail in it and we found encryptions. Looks like the bad guys might have gotten a little sloppy. Since you worked cryptology, I wanted you to take a look."

"Did you locate the sender?"

"Bogus. I just forwarded it to you."

Laurel clicked on the e-mail attachment, read the message, and studied the text. A sickening fear twisted her stomach.

"What's wrong?" Su-Min said. "You're ghastly white."

If only she could mask her turmoil. "I recognize part of this code." Laurel faced her partner and friend. "Morton Wilmington used a similar encryption to text his men."

"The exact?"

"No, but similar enough for me to see a connection and decipher most of what's written."

"No wonder you're a mess. What does it say?"

Laurel moistened her lips. "'Same instructions. Contact me after. New leads.' That's all I can make out without spending time on it. But whoever wrote it didn't give specifics."

"Do you think Wilmington's operating from prison?"

"Why not? He doesn't fit the mold for rehabilitation." Memories rapid-fired through her mind, burning thoughts that stoked the flames of regret.

Su-Min crossed her arms over her small Korean frame as though holding back a tiger.

"What are you not telling me?" Laurel said.

"Two things." Her voice softened. "We need boots on the ground to question him."

"I agree. Needs to happen immediately."

"There's more," Su-Min said. "Word is Wilmington's found religion. Christianity. Lawyers are working on an appeal."

No matter how long it takes. You'll pay in blood.

Laurel gazed into Su-Min's coffee-colored eyes. Admitting her deep, bloodcurdling fear of this man would make her look weak. "An appeal will take years, so I'm not the least bit concerned. Let's sort this out. I see a link between a fraud targeting the elderly and Wilmington's method of encoding messages."

"He's in the thick of Bible studies and donating money—"

Laurel waved away her concern. "He's always given to charities. Helps ease his miserable conscience."

"While advocating faith?"

"Su-Min, my findings cement the unlikelihood of him ever reaching parole. I'll get the truth out of him. After all, I put him there, and he's not getting out. He can spout Bible verses all day long, but crimes are to be paid for. No one has more of a stake in him staying put than I do."

"He's already gaining notoriety for his religious stand."

"Remember, Robin Hood loves the limelight. Our focus is the elderly fraud."

Su-Min shrugged. "Another agent can question him."

Laurel drew in courage. The only way she'd end the nightmares would be to face him. "I have to do this. And I'll nail him for the scam. Arrange the interview."

"Hope you're right. You know he hasn't forgotten the past. I'm surprised one of his men hasn't taken care of you." She tapped her foot. "Are you careful when riding Phantom?"

"Always." She refused to fall prey to her friend's caution. "Wilmington's too busy running his business to care about me. I'm not worth it."

"Or maybe one of the reasons he has a new platform is to walk out of prison free and kill you himself."

DISCUSSION QUESTIONS

1. Bethany has more than one reason to be nervous on her first day working with Thatcher. Have you ever started something new with negative thoughts dogging you? How do you put aside those emotions? What could Bethany have done to dispel some of those negative feelings?

2. As new partners, Bethany and Thatcher struggle with trusting each other. How do they overcome this obstacle? How do you establish trust with others?

3. The first victim, Alicia, had an abusive husband, yet she wanted to remain in her marriage until her elder daughter finished college. What did you think of her decision? What counsel would you have given Alicia?

4. As much as we want perfect families, we are all imperfect. In what ways do you relate with any of the issues in the "nightmare families" from *Deadlock*?

5. Before the FBI, Thatcher wanted to spend his life performing music, but his father didn't approve. Why does Thatcher say the FBI is where he belongs? Has someone in your life steered you in a certain direction? How would your life have been different if you'd taken another path?

6. Bethany's self-worth is largely wrapped up in her identity as a good FBI agent. How does this play out in her life? With

Lucas? What good and bad qualities does she display because of this?

7. As a new Christian, Thatcher has a hard time telling his mother about his faith, and when he does, she isn't very supportive. Have you ever encountered a similar situation? How did you handle it?

8. When Thatcher realizes he's worrying about Bethany, he remembers hearing that "worry meant a lack of trust in God." Do you agree with that idea? Why or why not?

9. In chapter 50, Bethany wonders why it seems God refuses to intervene in critical situations. How would you answer that question?

10. A few years ago, Houston (and other major US cities) began regulating who could feed the homeless on public property. Some pastors in Florida have even been arrested for passing out food. Do rules like this make sense? Why or why not? How do you respond when you hear about laws like these? How do you feel about people who break those laws?

ABOUT THE AUTHOR

DiAnn Mills is a bestselling author who believes her readers should expect an adventure. She currently has more than fifty-five books published.

Her titles have appeared on the CBA and ECPA bestseller lists; won two Christy Awards; and been finalists for the RITA, Daphne Du Maurier, Inspirational Readers' Choice, and Carol Award contests.

DiAnn is a founding board member of the American Christian Fiction Writers; the 2014 president of the Romance Writers of America's Faith, Hope, & Love chapter; and a member of Inspirational Writers Alive, Advanced Writers and Speakers Association, and International Thriller Writers. She speaks to various groups and teaches writing workshops around the country.

She and her husband live in sunny Houston, Texas. Visit her website at www.diannmills.com and connect with her on Facebook (www.facebook.com/DiAnnMills), Twitter (@DiAnnMills), Pinterest (www.pinterest.com/DiAnnMills), and Goodreads (www.goodreads.com/DiAnnMills).